Priest to Mafia Don

Father
Patrick Bascio

Branden Books
Boston

Library of Congress Cataloging-in-Publication Data

Bascio, Patrick, 1927-
  Priest to Mafia Don / Patrick Bascio.
      p. cm.
  ISBN-13: 978-0-8283-2157-0 (pbk. : alk. paper)
  ISBN-10: 0-8283-2157-4 (pbk. : alk. paper)
  1. Mafia--Fiction.
  2. Priests--Fiction.
  3. Italian Americans--Fiction.
  4. Catholics--Fiction.
I. Title.

  PS3602.A845P75 2007
  813'.6--dc22

                                            2007019370

Branden Books
www.brandenbooks.com
(Division of Branden Publishing Company)
PO Box 812094
Wellesley MA 02482

ACKNOWLEDGMENTS

I wish to thank the following kind people who in one way or another were involved in this project.

- Bunny Bissionette, of Palm Beach, Florida, who did a lot of early editing.
- Sue and Dexter Hurst of Aurora, Indiana who housed and fed me for two summer vacations as I wrote the book.
- Denese Denman, of Aurora, Indiana who did the final editing and formatting of the manuscript.
- The priest, member of a Mafia family, who inspired the writing of the book. He shall remain anonymous.
- Adolph Caso, my publisher, who in less than one year risked taking me on as one of his authors twice.
- The Holy Ghost Fathers, Trinidad & Tobago Province, men of exceptional character who have walked many miles with me over the years.

DEDICATION

To Archbishop Anthony Pantin, C.S.Sp., deceased, the greatest member of the hierarchy I have ever had the privilege of knowing. I admired the courage he had of inviting me to work and live with him in Trinidad when other ecclesiastics were concerned about my association with the Caribbean Black Power movement.

CONTENTS

FOREWORD

Much ink has been spilt, midnight oil burned and many volumes penned on the subject of the Mafia, almost all of it focused on violence. What further words could be written, what new light shed on the topic? I believe Father Bascio's novel does bring some unique perspectives— "takes," if you will, in modern parlance, on the history, workings and inner "Family life" of this famous and infamous organization. He has resisted the temptation of focusing on gratuitous violence by drawing a complete picture, a picture that formed in his mind as he spent many hours discussing the inner life of a Mafia family with a priest member of that family.

His fifty-plus years in the priesthood and extensive background in psychology, sociology and theology have given him insights into human motivation, human faults and failings and the pain many undergo in making moral decisions amid conflicting religious and personal beliefs and loyalties. Father Bascio's novel reflects also his in-depth knowledge of the inner workings of the institutional Catholic Church that enables his characters to move, act and interact realistically. Through the tapestry of the Father Don's life run the many-colored threads of the author's core beliefs in the pursuit of truth and the primacy of conscience.

Mary S. Hurst
Aurora, Indiana
February

INTRODUCTION

This is a work of fiction based on reality. It is the story of a priest, Carlo Albanese, nephew of the famous Godfather, Julio Albanese, who must deal with his ethnicity, his Mafia family relationships, his sexuality, and his desire to be the best priest he can be within that context. This was no ordinary family. It was the most powerful and most respected of the twenty-four Mafia Families that stretched across America from coast to coast. The Albanese Family can only be understood if one understands the real-life story of two young men who committed the crime of brutally raping and disfiguring a nun in Harlem. The author was pastor of St. Mark the Evangelist at 138th Street and Lennox Avenue in Harlem at the time of this horrifying violation. The entire city, indeed the nation, was outraged. The October 14, 1981 edition of *The New York Times* described the crime:

A 30-year-old nun was raped in a South Bronx convent on Saturday by a man who scratched a series of crosses on her body with a sharp instrument. The nun, who was not identified, was listed in serious condition in St. Vincent's Hospital yesterday, three days after two men slipped in through an unlocked roof door on the three-story Sisters of Charity Convent at 456 East 116th Street, adjacent to Our Lady of Mount Carmel Church.

A week after they fled the scene of the crime, it was revealed that the rapists suddenly and voluntarily surrendered to New York City detectives. The October 24th edition of The New York Times explained this amazing development:

The first suspect arrested, Harold Welles of 62 East 125th Street, was met at 6 A.M. at a bus terminal by a Chicago police sergeant as he got off a bus that had just arrived from New York City. According to an Associated Press report, Sergeant Kelley said that Mr. Welles had confessed to raping the nun on Oct. 10 and had told him that he had fled to Chicago because of a $25,000 organized crime 'contract' on his life.

Thus, a most heinous crime had been solved and justice had been rendered because of the long arm of the Mafia, which selectively resolves issues of justice that regular law enforcement agencies fail to uphold and administer.

Neither can the exploits of Carlo Albanese be understood unless one understands why the Friars of Mazzarino, in Sicily, acted as messengers for the delivery of Mafia ultimatums. These monks were not naïve holy men who gullibly bought the Mafia line, or men who were seduced by generous donations. They were, rather, men who had the courage to choose between the lesser of two evils: foreign domination or local control. The Mafia gave Sicilians a measure of local control, thereby enhancing their reputation and popularity throughout a nation that continuously experienced foreign domination for centuries.

Julio Albanese was quick to remind his family members of the close relationship between the Church and the Mafia. "Many Mafia members in Sicily studied for the priesthood, and formed close relationships with seminary colleagues who later became archbishops, bishops, and priests. These friendships remain important in our Family."

We should also be acquainted with Julio's personal devotion to the Catholic Church. The blessing of the Church and the smile of the Madonna were of such significance that Julio, who was often seen fingering rosary beads, insisted, "A man who doesn't go to church is not really and truly a member of the Albanese Family." This complex symbiosis of Mafiosi, Catholicism, and the Sicilian people, including churchmen of every rank and persuasion, did not develop overnight. It was a seed watered in the blood of an oppressed Sicilian citizenry who looked to the Mafia for safety, salvation and justice.

Julio, a self-educated man and history buff, clearly enjoyed his role as family historian. He never missed an opportunity to explain the Mafia organizations from an historical perspective. "For over two thousand years, Sicily was under foreign domination. The Arabs alone remained there for over three hundred years. "The cries of the oppressed were carried across the length and breadth of Sicily by the hot and dusty sirocco winds that blew across the sea from the Libyan Desert," Julio would cry out.

His research was meticulous. "In the 1920s and 30's the Mafia dominated every detail of Sicilian life. The Family Don became the judge, the jury, and the dispenser of favors." Julio pointed out that the people revered Mafia Dons. "Old and young alike bowed their heads in prayer at the mere mention of their names." His favorite Don was Don Carlo Vizzini. "Two of his relatives were bishops and two were priests. Another was the founder of the monastic order, Maria Santissima del Carmelo. Vizzini's funeral attracted the largest gathering of Italian clergy ever seen outside of Rome. The sign mounted outside the main entrance to the Church at the funeral reflected the feelings of Sicilians everywhere, including the clergy, 'He was a man of honor.'"

Julio's favorite story was that of the origin of the word, "Mafia." At Family gatherings, with dramatic gestures and a piercingly poignant voice, he told the tale of the Sicilian Vespers. "The tragedy took place during Easter week, in the year 1282, a time of French occupation. As parishioners of a parish church in Palermo were gathering to attend Vespers, a French soldier named Droetto forced a young girl into an alleyway behind the church and raped her. The mother of the girl, beside herself in horror and outrage, ran throughout the city screaming, `Ma fia, ma fia!' (My daughter, my daughter!) Sicilians used this rape as a call for further resistance to foreign occupation, adopting the battle cry, 'Morte alla Francia, Italia anela,' (Death to France, Italy cries out), the first letters of each word becoming the acronym, `Mafia'."

Julio admitted to Mafia imperfections but encouraged the Family members to join him in his crusade. "My task, and yours, is to bring back the pride and integrity of our Mafia ancestors. We have responsibilities. We are bound by the sacred fetters of land and blood" This was his life's dream, and he knew that among the Family members only his nephew, Carlo, destined for the priesthood, had the qualifications, personality and strength of character to bring that dream to reality. He knew not how this would come about. Carlo's destiny was, as yet, an invisible penmanship that would become legible only as events unfolded. Julio left all of that in the hands of God. But, of one thing he was sure, Carlo was destined to be the Father Don.

Chapter One
MARIA AND TONY

Our chronicle of the life of Carlo Albanese begins with his mother, Maria Amaretto, a native of the small Sicilian town of Trapani. Maria's mother, at the age of forty-eight, suffered from a brain tumor that Dr. Umberto Carolla, the family physician, said "will almost certainly end her life unless she gets the very best medical treatment."

"What can we do to help her?" Maria pleaded, tears sprinkling her face.

Dr. Carolla leaned over the desk in front of him and presented the facts very succinctly. "Philomena will not survive unless we find the funds to send her for surgery either to the United States or England."

Maria appealed to the local Mayor, Giuliano Santini, who in turn appealed to the social welfare agencies in Palermo. They turned him down. "Too expensive," was the general tenor of their replies. The Mayor sent for Maria, meeting her in the flower garden that circled his office. He awkwardly handed her a freshly-picked rose. He was frustrated. He knew, from the inside, how intransigent and vapor-like is the heart of the political animal. "I'm deeply sorry, Maria, but all the agencies I've contacted said they are unable to help in this case. If you need food and medicine they're ready to help, but a trip to America or England; that's out of the question."

"Oh, my God! Jesus, Mary and Joseph help me."

Mayor Santini sat wiping his sweaty brow and frowning at his knuckles. The mute appeal of Maria's face, awash with tears, deeply moved him, so he reached out to political expediency. "There is one possibility. Perhaps you could beg a favor of Don Luigi. Right now, as we speak, he's at home. I know because we had a conversation only fifteen minutes ago. Try."

Maria's father, Sergeant Mento Amaretto, was a member of the town's carabinieri. Would Don Luigi Navarro, the local Mafia chief, help the daughter of a local policeman? Could the sun shine at midnight? She ran to find out.

For many townsfolk, a visit to Don Luigi's home revived memories of Roman Emperors reclining in splendor and sucking on freshly plucked grapes. He invariably greeted his visitors from a reclining position, his hands on the shapely legs of one or more of his paramours. As Maria walked along the large verandah that led to his ground floor reception room, accompanied by an elderly servant, the late August afternoon bore the scent of cut grass and ripening fruit. "He's in the office with a young lady."

Maria tapped her forefinger against her lips. "I can wait."

The servant waved her head. "Oh no, it won't be necessary. He is always occupied like this. Come."

Don Luigi sat on a large sofa in his grand villa; an empty wine goblet swinging upside down between his fingers and thumbs, one arm draped over a young woman with long black hair, slender legs and the exquisite, finely chiseled face of the Ethiopian. Since he was not embarrassed, Maria saw no reason to be. "Thank you for seeing me, Don Luigi," was her greeting. She pretended not to notice as, with a firm slap on her buttocks, he dismissed the scantily clad teenage girl. "Wait in the kitchen," he called out as the girl, with a determined walk and her eyes focused on the parquet floor, hastily left the room.

He looked up at Maria, his lips moist with wine. "Have a seat, my dear, and tell me what's on your mind."

"Don Luigi, my mother is gravely ill. The doctors say that her life can be saved if we can get her to an English or American hospital. I've come to you for help. I've tried everywhere else."

He listened to Maria with an air of respect and gentleness, but the vacant look in his deeply set black eyes was not encouraging. "My sweet girl, you know that I'd like nothing more than to help your dear mother, believe me." His practiced words flowed with the richness of the fruits of his vineyard.

Maria felt his deviousness like a sharp pain, but still held out hope. "Then you will help me?"

Don Luigi's fat fingers twitched, as he fingered the luxuriant mat of hair flowing onto his brow, and along the curve of his nose. He observed her with a wry smile and arched eyebrows. "You're talking about a very expensive trip and a very expensive operation. I must tell you honestly my dear girl that I cannot find that kind of money. My charitable contributions have drained my modest savings."

Maria shrugged to hide her discomfort. Her lips moved and her eyelids fluttered as she internalized a hum of protest. *He's a liar, such a big, fat, ugly liar.* She paused for a moment, chewing on her lower lip, then, "If you don't help us what can we do? My mother is dying."

Rising, he placed his right arm around her shoulder he said, "I will pray for your mother. We'll all pray for your mother. May God bless her and help her."

She tensed involuntarily. What a hypocrite. She was frightened and disoriented. To the startled Don she cried out, "You're a liar! You walk arm-in-arm with my father in the village streets. Now my mother is dying and you won't help her. It's not fair!" He noted with alarm the flushed cheeks and piercing flash in her eyes that conveyed the deepest contempt. The thrust of her chin and her body language conveyed her feelings, but he was unmoved. Staring out at the sea that lapped the edge of the estate's extensive lawn, he said, "I understand how you feel, my dear." With an audible sigh he almost whispered, "It's impossible to help everyone." He spoke as if in a void, like a faint echo at the end of a long tunnel.

Maria's reaction gelled in her facial expression, as she felt a sharp pang of distress in her churning stomach. He knew she did not believe him, and he did not care. He took a long drink of wine and wiped his mouth of glistening drops with the back of his hand. Then staring vacantly into space he paused for a moment and said: "I know what you're thinking, my dear, but people don't understand how great my financial responsibilities are."

Maria had run into an impenetrable wall. It was well known that Don Luigi either said Yes or No or never changed his mind. She was frustrated. "I will turn to God. Perhaps it was evil of me to come to you, a man without honor."

Don Luigi stared in shocked disbelief. Her tone brought a wrinkled frown to his brow, for no one in Trapani had ever spoken to him in this manner. "I'll pretend I did not hear such disrespect." He turned away from her and called to the old servant woman. "Show her out."

Maria tented her hands, folding them over her forehead, and moved away from his presence. As she left the verandah, the young Negroid girl was returning, her eyes glued to the floor. Maria anguished at her foolishness. *Why did I come to Don Luigi for help? Whatever was I thinking about? He's a murderer. I betrayed God by depending on a bad man. I have humiliated myself. Lord, forgive me a sinner.* Her words of pleading with a known murderer now collapsed back into her throat.

"He would not help," Maria informed her brother, Stefano, that evening. She was dispirited as she shrugged her shoulders and tossed her head in his direction, "It was a big waste of time."

He was unsympathetic. "You silly little girl," he chided. "Don't you know they're friendly with daddy only because it makes them look more respectable? Don't you know they invite Father Trevino to their homes every Sunday afternoon for the same reason? Father Trevino takes great pride in the fact that he is `converting' Don Luigi. The priest is so foolish. He is simply being used by the devil, that's all," as he tossed a napkin into the air.

Realizing he was being a bit harsh, he lowered his voice and spoke softly. "Listen, Maria, the Mafia only helps Family members, strong supporters and corrupt officials. True, in the old days Mafia meant community help, but that day is long passed. Now they live on their old reputation and suck our blood. That's the way it is."

Maria turned to prayer. In the harshness of her situation, she found a space of succor in her faith, spending the next fourteen days in Novena prayers imploring the Blessed Mother at the shrine, Our Lady of the Pines. Each passing day she became increasingly confident of a cure. On the morning of the fourteenth day, the doctors called the local press to the hospital and announced: "Against the greatest odds and possibly miraculously, Philomena Amaretto is responding favorably to the medical procedures."

Father Trevino preached from the pulpit, "A miracle has been performed among us. Blessed be the power of God, the Father Almighty."

The entire village rejoiced. Even Don Luigi sent his favorite mistress, Carla Germana, to the Church service. She presented Maria with a bouquet of flowers and a basket of fruit. The basket contained an envelope with the message: "It is clear that our prayers have produced a miracle. Praise be to the Blessed Virgin Mary."

Maria wanted to toss the basket and bouquet into the garbage and burn the letter, but decided that would not be a Christian thing to do.

At her parish church that Sunday morning Maria, draped in milk-white veil and rosary beads wrapped around her right wrist, declared publicly, "I know what I must do now that the Blessed Virgin has answered my prayers at the shrine of Madonna del Pindaro."

Maria followed the religious tradition of making The Promise to offer her first-born son to the Church for extraordinary favors received through the intercession of the Virgin Mary. The village women accompanied her to the Virgin's shrine in a long procession. Father Trevino, dressed in a heavy black cassock, his face covered with rivulets of sweat glistening in the noon-day sun, held the Sacred Host in a gold Monstrance close to his chest and chanted, "Behold the Lamb of God who has sent his Mother to deliver us." The procession was led by ten altar boys in red cassocks carrying a large crucifix, and smoking vessels of incense that always annoyed Father

Trevino's nostrils and throat. Four of the women sang "Ave Maria, Mater Dei," while the rest prayed the Joyful Mysteries of the Rosary.

At the Shrine, amidst all her friends and well-wishers, Maria vowed The Promise with deep emotion, "If Almighty God grants me a male child I will consecrate him to the Madonna in the priesthood." She knelt. "This promise I make on my knees before my family, my friends, and all of God's people."

The crowd made the sign of the cross and shouted, "Amen, Amen, Alleluia." The women wept at the solemnity of the occasion. The men watched with interest, wiping the sweat from their brows and eyeing the younger women. Don Luigi moved among the men, whispering his conviction that the Virgin "has come to stay in our village." He regretted having denied Maria assistance, for he sensed that the townspeople were no longer as deferential as before. He made a tactical decision to take the lead in thanking the Virgin, but few were impressed with his performance.

To her mother, Maria confided, "I must speak to Tony right away. I must tell him that I cannot marry a man who would object to my vow to the Virgin Mary." Tony Albanese, a neighbor, was her boyfriend, the man she hoped to marry. He was both handsome and unfailingly courteous, a virtue not commonly found among his village peers.

Her mother, unaccustomed to hearing a young woman decide what her man must agree to, was cautious. "I would be very careful about that, Maria. You could lose him, you know, if you are insistent."

Maria was confident. "I believe him to be a man of God, and a man of God will understand."

The following day Maria visited the Albanese home. Tony Albanese was pruning in the vineyard. "Were you at Our Lady of the Pines yesterday when I made my promise to the Virgin Mary?"

He nodded affirmatively, "Yes, of course, but I stayed a bit behind, with the men, not wanting to disturb you."

Her words tumbled out, "You understand that any man I marry must agree that our first-born male become a priest?"

His response was immediate and comforting: "I would be honored to be betrothed to a devoted woman who, God willing, shall one day provide His church with a priest."

Tony Albanese had loved Maria since their days in Secondary School. He was the soccer team captain; she disliked sports. "One day you'll be my wife," he insisted after he led his team to the regional championship.

"I'm not a prize you get when you win a soccer game," she teased. She became so accustomed to his company that she told him. "I could never be comfortable with any other man."

Tony's parents and brothers, Victor and Julio, had migrated to America, but a kidney infection caused him to be left behind in the care of his aunt, Albena. "You'll join us as soon as you feel better," his mother said the day of the family's departure. She kissed and embraced him. "We don't know what kind of difficulties we'll face along the way, and you're too weak to travel."

Tony's slow progress in his condition resulted in a delay of several years. Then, love, in the person of Maria Amaretto, further delayed his departure. He wrote to his mother: "Please forgive me, dearest Mama, for not coming to America, but I'm dating the most wonderful girl. I need time to see what will happen. You know her. Remember our neighbors the Amaretto family? It is Maria, and she has become as beautiful and as sweet as the Virgin herself is. Perhaps you remember her. I'm sure she must have played in our yard when we were kids. She sometimes works as a nurse in the hospital, and as soon as she appears in the geriatric ward the sad eyes of the patients turn to joy. They feel so good because the head nurse, who is thin as a stick and sour as vinegar, makes life miserable for them."

The intense courtship lasted for less than six months. Philomena, fearing an unplanned pregnancy and the scandal that would result from such an event, advised Tony, "Both families should agree that you two get married soon. I don't want Maria's dress bulging at the wedding. It would be a disgrace." She had seen evidence of such a possibility many times after dates Maria had with Tony. Her disheveled hair and torn buttons on the front of her dress, and lipstick marks on Tony's shirts indicated what was developing. She needed to preempt a scandal.

Tony was more than eager. He wanted the marriage as quickly as possible. "Just tell me what to do and I'll do it."

Philomena explained: "Tony, you understand that Maria's father is the only one who can give permission. You must approach him when he's in a good mood. Right now is not the time. He lost a bit of money on a batch of wine that went bad. Wait a few weeks."

Tony rushed to see Maria. "Your mother believes we should marry. She has confidence in us. I must talk with your father."

Maria had no intention of being part of a deal made between Tony and her father. She scanned him with her probing dark eyes. "Tony, do you really love me? Are you certain?" Her voice was sharp.

"With all my heart." He quoted an ancient Italian proverb: "If truth is with fools and children, then believe this fool when he tells you he loves you."

She pressed on. "Do you love me more today than you did yesterday and the day before?"

He answered with vigor. "I've already given you all my love, and yet it continues to grow. And what of you? You know I'll never be a rich man. Do you worry how I'll support you?"

Maria replied with a proverb of her own, "Loss and gain are brothers twain."

Three weeks later Tony met Philomena in the marketplace. "Is this a good time?"

She responded. "Only this morning he was talking so nice about you, and the abundant vegetable garden more than made up for the money he lost on the wine, so go quickly."

He kissed her on the cheeks. "Gratias, Philomena, I love you," and ran off to her home with great anticipation. He found Mento Amaretto swinging in a hammock in the grape arbor behind the house, singing a Sicilian love song. The old man showed signs of aging as fleshy lines bracketed his mouth and fell away from his eyes like eddies.

"Tony, welcome." His speech was thick. It was clear he had drunk more than his usual portion of wine for that time of day.

I'll warm him up with a description of last night's soccer game against Progono. He hates Progono.

"Good day to you, Mr. Amaretto. You'll be happy to hear that we beat Progono last night, a great victory. It makes us the division champs."

Mento was elated. "Tony, you bring good news. You are captain, manager and treasurer, so it's you whom we must thank for this championship. The whole town loves you." He planted wet kisses on Tony's cheeks and neck.

"Thank you, Mr. Amaretto, but you know the boys practice so hard, even on Saturday. They even wanted to practice on Sundays after Mass, but Father Trevino said it would not be appropriate."

Mento swished his head left, then right, looking for the correct response. "Yes, well, the priest needs to set limits you know. If he didn't, all sorts of things would happen in our village." Waving Tony to the table, he said, "Come, have a drink with me and sample one of my newest oranges. They are special, crossed with a variety from Greece, like an Italian princess mating with a Greek god. Beautiful combination."

Tony patiently waited for an opening as the old man rambled on. It came as Mento stood up to stretch. "I've come to speak to you about your daughter, Maria."

Mento quickly sobered. "What about my daughter?"

"Well, I love her very much and I have reason to believe that she loves me. I'm asking your permission to take her as my wife."

"What do you mean you have reason to believe she loves you? You haven't."

"Oh no, no, not that. It's just that I'm proud to say she hasn't refused my offer of marriage. She is, I'm sure, awaiting your decision. Nothing can happen without your permission and blessing."

Mento assessed Tony out of his dark brown eyes. *The young man is an excellent athlete, a good Catholic, and earns a decent salary as manager and treasurer of the soccer team. If she loves him, why not?*

Mento put on his elder face. "This is not something I can easily answer, Tony. After all, it's a serious matter requiring some reflection. I must, of course, discuss the matter with my daughter. She's a strong-headed girl and doesn't believe in arranged marriages."

Tony put on his obeisance face. "I understand. I will await your decision."

The following month, Father Trevino was advised by the Amarettos that their daughter was engaged to Tony Albanese and would be married in the parish church. The priest promptly began the first of the required three publicly announced banns of marriage from the pulpit, and the village rejoiced that their favorite daughter and the town's sports star would approach the altar and give themselves to each other in marriage.

The heavily attended wedding ceremony took place at the village church. It hadn't rained for almost two weeks and the town was covered with a blanket of heat, causing odors of every kind to float over the streets and alleyways. Tailors, vendors, and cabaret patrons moved their tables, wares and chairs out onto the sidewalks, hoping to catch the slight puffs of breeze coming from the ever-present sea. The Mayor said to his wife, "I hope the smells won't be noticed in the church. The poor girl has had enough troubles in her life as it is."

Arriving at the church before Maria were the bridesmaids, her two younger sisters, Angela, and Elena. Dressed in smooth pink dresses, with flowers in their hands and hair, they giggled, not knowing why. It was contagious. The youngest, Elena, commented, "We'd better stop this before Maria gets here. She'll kill us."

Tony walked from the barbershop to the church with Mr. Guerilli, the sacristan. He was dressed in a black broadcloth suit, the trousers sporting knife-sharp creases straight down the legs. His patent leather boots were a gift of the local soccer club. Six feet tall, with an intelligent face, a shock of jet black hair that swayed attractively during soccer games, and a muscular body, Tony presented a handsome presence. "Mr. Guerilli, do I look OK? I'm really not a dresser you know."

"You look fine, Tony. Anyhow, don't worry. They'll all be looking at the bride."

That was reassuring. Brimming with emotion, Tony walked down the center aisle to the front of the altar and joined the best man, Felix Andante, the town's Don Juan. Slim to the point of thinness, Felix chose his favorite summer gray suit for the occasion. "I hate black, period." His hair flowed down to his shoulders, his earlobes shone with gold rings, framing a lean and narrow face. His natural charm and good looks kept him busy in the town's social scene. "Don't be nervous, Tony."

But Tony was. The palms of his hand dripped with nervous sweat. He stood silently, staring at the altar and thinking of the night to come. Maria's trim, lithe body, considered by his friends as plain and unattractive, conjured-up for him erotic images. His imagination painted moving color images of himself lying with his naked wife as he explored her beauty and received from her the comforts of her sensuality. Momentarily, he wondered if it were sinful to have such thoughts right there in the sacred precincts. Her effect on him had been intoxicating from the first day he met her.

Felix, broke the silence with a mocked-serious, "ciao friend, Arrivederci."

"You make it sound like you're attending my funeral."

Felix folded his arms as in a lecture. "Well, for me it would be a funeral. I like to play the field. They're all so different. Why be confined to one personality? Or one body? Not me."

Tony tossed Felix a wryly-amused glance. "That's a hell of a thing to tell a groom at the altar," as he playfully buried his fist in the Best Man's shoulder. "Besides, when the right woman comes along, you'll be putty in her hands. I know you, you rascal."

"Listen to me. I'm serious. I'd rather be in Spain, at the *encierro*, early in the morning when they run the bulls to the corrals before the fights. The bulls can't wait to be getting loose. When they are, they go crazy. Some of those damn things weigh over fifteen hundred pounds, but it's a question of manhood to run with them along those narrow streets. I run with the best of them, without fear. Competing with men is what makes me feel like a man. Women? I love them, but they tame me. I hate it!"

The pews were adorned with bows of pink and blue ribbons with attached miniature bouquets of lilies of the valley. The church bells called the wedding party to the newly dusted and waxed mahogany pews. As Maria entered the church, all faces turned to her; eager faces with noses pressed forward like racing dogs.

"Where is daddy?" she whispered to the usher, her voice lighter than usual, drifting and expressionless. He ran outside and spotted Mr. Amaretto nervously smoking a cigarette. "Mento, get your ass inside. For God's sake

man, your daughter's getting married. You have to walk her down the aisle."
Nothing ever goes smooth with these peasants, the usher thought.

Mento fanned his mouth in a vain attempt to rid himself of the smoking odor, and then rushed to seize his daughter's arm. They answered the organist's processional music by slowly walking down the aisle. At the foot of the altar he kissed his daughter's cheeks and handed her over to Tony.

She whispered a tiny "I thank you, Papa, for everything. I love you."

Father Trevino intoned: "Tony and Maria have you come here freely and without reservation to give yourselves to each other in marriage?"

Each answered, "Yes."

Father Trevino adjusted his glasses. "Will you love and honor each other as man and wife for the rest of your lives."

"Yes."

Tony added, "Of course."

Father Trevino made another adjustment to the loosely fitting glasses, then, "Will you accept children lovingly from God, and bring them up according to the laws of Christ and his Church?"

"Yes."

Maria's thoughts focused on her promise. *I must have a male child. I must be able to fulfill my promise to the Virgin. What if I have a girl child? Will I be disappointed? Will I love her? Oh, God, please help me. I want to give you a priest, just for yourself.* Try as she may, Maria could not contain the beads of sweat that trickled down her cheeks as she exchanged vows.

Father Trevino continued. "Since it is your intention to enter into marriage, join your right hands and declare your consent before God and his Church."

Shivers of doubt still plagued her. *I so want to be with Tony, but my mother and father–how do I leave them? What if we have to move to join the rest of his family in America? How will all of that be?*

"I, Tony, take you, Maria, for my lawful wife, to have and to hold, from this day forward, for better, for worse, for richer, for poorer, in sickness and in health, until death do us part."

Tony pinched himself. *I can't believe this is happening. I can't believe she's mine, Forever! She'll never betray me, never leave me. She's so good. Marriage is so important to her. Thank you, God, for this great, undeserving gift.*

"I, Maria, take you, Tony, for my lawful husband, to have and to hold, from this day forward, for better, for worse, for richer, for poorer, in sickness and in health, until death do us part." *I belong to Tony. It's all so final, so scary.*

Father Trevino blessed the couple saying; "I predict a long and happy marriage for Tony and Maria." To Tony, "You may now kiss the bride, but don't take too long; it's hot in here." The townspeople laughed and clapped dutifully, and the organist played a love song that brought tears to the eyes of the nuptial guests.

After the wedding ceremony Tony embraced his mother-in-law. "Philomena, I believe that God put your family right next to mine, so that I could grow up knowing what a wonderful person Maria is. And, did you not take the place of my mother when she moved to America?" His words brought tears to her eyes.

That night, Maria, who had been anxious about sexual contact, surprised herself by feeling totally relaxed. Without conversation, standing near their nuptial bed, Tony unbuttoned her dress, slipped it off her shoulders, and let it drop in sensuous folds to the floor. He unfastened the brassiere, cupping her bountiful breasts, and put his lips between them. She was just as he had imagined. Maria shuddered as he gently lay her down. The new and exquisite feeling of being a wife compensated for the pain. *Perhaps this very night I will conceive a priest for God's Church.*

Within a fortnight of his marriage, Tony received a phone call from his brother, Julio. "Tony, I need you here to take care of some of my most personal affairs. Come with your new bride. I'll prepare a nice apartment for you. You'll be well taken care of." He knew how hard things were in Sicily and wanted to provide Tony with a job.

Tony explained to Maria, "Julio wants me to work with him in America. You know he's Mr. Massaro's right hand man now. He's got Victor there, but they don't seem to be getting along too good." He paused because he knew how Maria felt about the Mafia. She remained silent. He nervously pinched his nose and pressed the point. "Well, Maria, what do you think?"

"I'll go wherever your work takes us. A wife's place is at her husband's side."

He wanted to be reassuring. "I'm not going to be involved in anything you have to worry about, darling. Julio just wants me to help keep the books for Massaro's legitimate businesses. You understand?"

"I understand," she said with a feigned firmness. Her sweetness and loyalty gave him contentment.

When asked by Philomena, "What kind of work is Tony going to be doing in New York?" she answered, "Bookkeeping."

Chapter Two
CARLO'S EARLY YEARS

Two months after receiving Julio's request, Tony and his wife were settled in an apartment overlooking the East River, in Manhattan's "Little Italy." Julio saw to it that the apartment was nice enough to welcome his brother. Long, uncurtained windows fitted with wooden blinds looked out at the United Nations just two blocks away and over the East River curving alongside glittering street lights. A large bedroom was the center piece of the apartment, cleverly configured to accommodate a three-piece-furniture nook facing a bay window angled to ensure a panoramic view of the sky. On clear nights stars, clusters of blinking lights, accompanied the moon on its cyclical journey. It was here that Carlo Albanese was conceived.

The following September he was born. The entire family came bearing gifts. The parish priest, Father Adolfo, apprised of Maria's vow, announced, "This male child is a gift of God, a blessed omen, an eternal guarantee of God's favor, and a remembrance of the Madonna's intercession with her Divine son." In response to this joyful news, the Ave Marias were uttered with pious gusto and inexpressible joy. The family knew that Carlo was destined to be a priest, and they were glad. Father Adolfo assured Maria that her vow had been divinely inspired. "God has chosen you to bring forth for service to the Church another Melchizedek. The suffering your mother endured was the test required of the family before God would give you such a gift."

There were tears in Father Adolfo's eyes. His whole being trembled with a sudden premonition, the nature of which he did not understand. *This child is a sign of contradiction for the family. Such children suffer.* He was uneasy.

Years later, as a priest himself, each time Carlo baptized a child in the dark recesses of St. Anthony's baptistery, he wondered what unspoken intentions might be floating in the baptismal air. *Have these parents already consecrated this child for the priesthood, or the convent?* As he made the sign of the cross on tender breasts and foreheads with the sacred oils he instinctively searched out meanings in faces and gestures. Although he was happy in the priesthood, he wondered about the wisdom of "promising" newly born children to the Church. He had already begun to feel the burdens of it.

Carlo's childhood centered on his future as priest. At an early age he became aware of his destiny and rejoiced at the thought. He dreamt of angels, and saints in priestly robes. *I'm going to bless everybody when I grow up. I'm going to say Mass in St. Patrick's Cathedral.* On the occasion of his First Communion, his parents bought a Missal that opened in the middle, releasing a thin cardboard replica of an altar prepared for Mass. Candlestick and Chalice cutouts were attached in the proper locations. In addition, Maria supplied the table with candles blessed at St. Anthony's. The smell of incense and melting wax was ever present both to his nostrils and, more importantly, to his consciousness. Before leaving for school, Carlo would say a "Mass".

Tony had reservations. "Perhaps you're going too far, Maria." Self-doubt began to bother her. She called on Father Adolfo. "Do you approve of this? I thought it would be a good idea for Carlo to become familiar with the Mass. It'll be the center of his life. Tony thinks it's a bit extreme. What do you think?"

Father Adolfo rarely discouraged anyone from doing what he or she wanted to do. His theory was, if it doesn't work out, it can always be changed. "Well, so long as Carlo understands this is just practice, I see no harm in it. Keep your eye on him so he doesn't start having illusions. OK?"

"You are so understanding," Maria gushed, and planted a kiss on the surprised cleric's cheek. From that day onward, she set aside her doubts. During Lent, Maria placed a Holy Childhood collection box on the "altar" and the family deposited their spare pennies "to help baptize the pagan children of Africa." So versed in the Mass was her son that on Sundays he would recite with the priest the opening prayers. "In nomine Patris, et Filii, et Spiritus Sancti. Amen"

On Carlo's seventh birthday, Father Adolfo announced from the pulpit that a new name had been added to the altar boy roll, "Carlo Albanese, son of our beloved parishioners, Tony and Maria Albanese."

His family saw the assignment as altar boy as an initial "vesting," a first step toward the altar. "This is his pre-seminary training," Maria would say. In Carlo's case, the altar boy gowns provided by the parish were set aside. Father Adolfo approved the use of a fine linen cassock and surplice sewn by Carlo's aunt, Grace. The day she delivered them to the parish she said,

"There is a difference between a simple altar boy, and an altar boy who is destined for the altar."

Father Adolfo, as usual, agreed.

For Tony and Maria, their life was one of marital bliss, piety, and joy.

Tony Albanese made sure that his son understood the relationship between Mafia and Church. He told him the story of Salvatore Bonanno, uncle of the young Mafia Don, Joc Bonanno, popularly called Joe Bananas. "Your uncle Julio knows more about this history than I do, but Peppe Bonanno, grand uncle of Joe Bonanno, was the Don of the most powerful Family in Sicily. In the early 1900s, his enemies, the Bucellato Family, murdered him. The question then became: who will take over the Family?"

"Who?" was Carlo's excited question.

"Everybody wanted Peppe's brother, Salvatore, but there was a problem. Salvatore was in the Seminary, studying for the priesthood. What was he to do? He loved the seminary life and just wanted to be a priest, leading a quiet life reading, and enjoying classical music; but the death of his brother put him right in line to become the Don, to take on the responsibility of leading the Family."

Carlo's voice trembled with excitement. "Did he do it, dad?"

Tony was happy to report that, "Yes, son, he did, and it was very difficult for him, but it was his duty to help the family."

"So, he left the priesthood?"

"Yes, Carlo, he did, but he always remained close to the Church. In fact, he and his wife went to communion every morning.

Carlo wanted to know, "Did he live in New York?"

"No, he was the head of the Las Vegas Family. That's in Nevada, out West. He was a good friend of the bishop there. So you see, Carlo, the life of the priest and the life of the Family both demand self-sacrifice, loyalty and discipline."

Carlo vowed that if he were ever called upon he would do the same. To those who argued that the Mafia should be abolished, Tony responded, "We don't need to get rid of the Mafia. We need to bring it back to its roots." His brother, Julio, had convinced him of the correctness of this position.

Father Adolfo, their parish priest, supported Tony Albanese's view of the relationship between Church and Family. On one occasion he was invited to address the New York Athletic Club. He said, "Every society has gone through stages of development. The kind of organizations and institutions that exist reflect the needs of that society. We Sicilians needed the Mafia, just like the Irish need the IRA. It's true that the Families have gone astray, but new leadership promises to get the Families back on track. Now's not the time to abandon them or hypocritically criticize them."

Father Adolfo believed in evolution, not revolution. "We don't need to get rid of the Mafia. We need to bring it back to its roots."

The President of the Athletic Club spoke when Father Adolfo finished. "I know I express the sentiments of my fellow-members when I say that this was the most unusual talk we've ever had."

Maria gave birth to her second son, Nicky, in the early hours of a wintry January morning. The drive to New York Hospital was perilous, as Tony negotiated the wind-driven snowy streets of lower Manhattan. Carlo thrilled at the thought that he would have a sibling to play with, to help him build the world of the young. He told God that he would accept a sister and would love her forever, but could God please give him a brother so that they could be altar boys together? Of course, he would be too small to "say Mass" with him at his cardboard altar, but he could be a "parishioner."

Carlo verbalized his feelings. "He's going to be great. We're going to have fun, go fishing. I'll show him how to fight, how to turn on the radio, how to pick up the cat without getting scratched, how to hide stuff in the back yard." He waited for news from the hospital. He was angry when told that small children could not be at the hospital when their siblings are born. Why? They allow strangers!

As with other children, Carlo drew no limits between himself and the external world. He lived in the magical world of wonder; the stars being part of his arms and face, the moon his reflection. He lay in bed that night with the most wonderful imaginings, waiting to get the news. He was ready to forgive God if it was not a brother, but he might possibly scold Him. His heart leapt when he heard his father's car pull into the driveway just as dawn broke. Tony rushed up the stairs and into his bedroom to announce the good news. "You have a brother, a very healthy brother."

God had heard his plea! Nice God. The entire world was his and he belonged to the entire world. He had to know immediately what name his brother would bear. Tony said, "Since it is so close to Christmas, your mother and I have decided to call him Nicholas."

"When do I see him?"

"Don't worry. Nicholas will be with us in a few days."

When Nicky did arrive, Carlo smothered him with love and affection. There was no room for jealousy since he assumed that, as the big brother, it was his responsibility to guide the "kid brother" as he grew older. And, just as Carlo wanted, when Nicky was old enough, he became Carlo's "altar boy" at the daily home ritual. This consisted in sitting near the "altar" in a white shirt, white tie and black knickers. He was taught to say "Amen" at the end of every prayer Carlo recited. He had no idea of what was transpiring but it was fun. At "Communion" time he was allowed to run to the table and gobble down the Kellogg's Corn Flakes he loved so much. On Holy Days and Major Feast Days, the cereal would be topped off with strawberries or blueberries. Nicky got to love the "Mass".

Carlo overshadowed his young brother from the beginning. Maria seemed unable to control that special feeling she had for the son who was destined for the priesthood, for the son who was promised to the Blessed Virgin. The brothers were very different personalities and did a fair amount of arguing, but she taught them to shake hands and hug immediately after every argument. This, she thought, would create a non-competitive atmosphere; but day after day and year after year, Carlo's natural energy and lightness of spirit swept over the household. For Nicky, it would prove impossible to compete with the exceptional Carlo. He began to develop opposite tendencies. He brooded, was quick to cry, and became hyper sensitive. Maria wondered how it was that her second born was darker in spirit. No amount of solace from her seemed to make a difference. It was almost as if he insisted on being unhappy. At some point in time she gave up trying.

Nicky absorbed these subtle changes in his mother's attitude into his consciousness. Inequity in familial love became his reality. He thought it unfair. *I'm kinder than Carlo. He always wants to win everything. He's really kind of mean. I should be the priest.* He recalled one incident in particular that demonstrated he was a better person than Carlo. It took place when he was four years old and Carlo was eleven. He and Carlo were kicking stones down an alley one afternoon when they spotted a filthy, emaciated kitten half hidden by a garbage can, whimpering and unable to move. The tiny ball of fluff was hardly anything but skin and bones. In one swift movement Carlo picked up a large stone and thrust it on the kitten, extinguishing what little life was left. Nicky was horrified. He shouted, "You are cruel; you are no good. How could you do this to a poor kitten?" He then attacked Carlo, kicking and punching him.

Carlo held him off at arm's length and tried to calm him. "Don't you see I had to do it. The poor kitten was suffering." Carlo was certain he had acted with the highest moral sense. For him, it was the logical thing to do since the kitten was in agony. The "right" thing to do, for him, was always the logical thing.

When they attended the same District School, Nicky in Primary and Carlo in Junior High, they shared the same playground. What began, one day, as a playful tug-of-war over a football jersey got serious. Carlo was determined to retrieve his shirt from Nicky, who had playfully seized it. A crowd of boys gathered to watch the struggle. They divided into two cheering and boisterous groups, one for Nicky and one for Carlo, while the shirt was being shredded apart.

Nicky described the fight that evening to his mother. "I was embarrassed because Carlo got mad. We were just having fun, and then he got real mean and serious. I kept telling him to take it easy, that this was just a game, but he slapped me. He always wants to win at everything. This time I decided to fight back. We looked terrible fighting with each other. He doesn't care. He's real mean. He made us look like we're not brothers."

Maria's response, "Well, it is his shirt" further deepened his depression. That night he tossed and turned in bed, exhausted and discouraged. As they grew together into their teenage years, Nicky assumed that second place was his place. He admired, but at times feared, Carlo's forceful presence. The situation worsened as they reached each plateau of maturity. What was growing in his psychological underbrush was an inferiority complex that would haunt him for the rest of his life. Shortly before his premature death, Nicky speculated: *Maybe with a different brother or a different birth order things might have been different.*

Nicky had to find a way to be his own man. While Carlo academically and socially surpassed all his peers, Nicky sought refuge from peer indifference in Don Juan escapades encouraged by his nubile girlfriend, Teresa Maneti, a volatile, sexually propelled young girl his own age. Teresa was only the beginning of Nicky's conquests. He went through girls like water and at last he was able to say, "I've got something Carlo doesn't have. He's not man enough." This area of superiority was the straw he clung to as he moved closer and closer to life's jagged edge.

Carlo was as interested and as hormonal as any teen but, being promised to the Church, he resisted jumping into the dating world, even though many pretty classmates appealed to him. *I'm going to become a priest. That is it.* Nicky's teasing was daunting at times, but Carlo made light of it, defusing a possible superiority based on sexual prowess. An incident further dampened whatever sensuality Carlo did feel. One day, while his parents were at a wedding reception, Carlo inadvertently walked in on a naked Nicky wrapped around an equally naked Teresa Maneti. It all looked so crude that Carlo became even more convinced that it was not for him.

Nicky employed feigned indifference as a way of coping with his alienation. He also developed a great fear of being put down, of not having the right answers, of not being witty enough. His isolation increased. Maria and Tony worried about what appeared to them to be a self-imposed alienation. They sought help from the school Counselor. No progress was made. They resigned themselves to the perception that he was a slow learner whom the family would have to nurture and support well into the future. It never occurred to them that the attention lavished on Carlo was a contributory cause to Nicky's problems. Their reaction was expressed in frustration. What in the name of heaven is wrong with him! How could he be so different from Carlo? Why doesn't he learn from him?

Nicky resigned himself to abandoning any attempt to compete with his brother. "Whatever you say, Carlo," became a fixture in his vocabulary.

Carlo, by the time he entered the seminary was convinced that his brother was frivolous and weak, a family burden. Just as Tony and Maria failed to recognize that their own actions had contributed to the problem, so Carlo also failed in any such understanding. Nicky's relationship to his own immediate family eventually extended to the larger Family, the members of the Organization.

Julio's upstate New York estate was the gathering place where the extended Family inter-mingled, adjusted to each other's personalities, assisted each other in their private problems and shared their joys. The estate's center was the large main lodge; built of rough-sawn cedar, with steeply cantered roofing, surrounded by tall pines and forest-carpeting ferns. The master bedroom was kitty-cornered between the gables, with guestrooms, equidistant, lining the circular walkway that ran along the length of them. A ten-foot wide porch at the second-story level wrapped around the house's exterior. In the spring and summer the constant refrain of song birds delighted all who stayed there. In the fall and winter, corn husks were scattered among the ferns to attract deer for photographing from a secure bedroom overlooking the spot.

Baptisms and confirmations were held in Manhattan at the parish church, but weddings, thanks to Father Adolfo, were performed at the estate; elaborate ceremonies celebrated new beginnings, healthy sexuality, and future children to carry on the Family tradition and business. Summer cookouts were a regular weekend feature. Julio scolded those who did not attend, insisting that Family solidarity was the key to Family success. It was in this atmosphere that Nicky fulfilled his own growing misperception of himself, acting the fool he was fictionally created to be. What he had to say was not taken seriously, so he seriously avoided saying anything serious. He became a clown because that's what he was told he was. He fulfilled everyone's expectations. He was the Family fool, but the Family was unaware that they had created him. And now, his brother was about to be ordained a priest and his own position could only spiral further downward. Carlo, already a god in the family, would overshadow everyone and everything. Nicky wanted to die.

Father Adolfo was to become a major influence in Carlo's life. He guided the young man in coming to grips with the tension between his consecrated calling and the need to support his family's role in the American-Sicilian community. Adolfo's intuition told him that Carlo's life would be a critical mass in the explosive potential of the Albanese Organization.

Chapter Three
FATHER ADOLFO

Father Adolfo was one of a tiny minority of Sicilian priests in the vast Archdiocese of New York and the only one to reach out to and fully serve the Sicilian underworld. "Mine is a lonely and often misunderstood ministry," he confided to his sister, Dora. She loved her brother but, privately, had doubts about his ministry. *Why does he stick his neck out the way he does? Why can't he just be an ordinary priest and enjoy his nice parish? Being Sicilian doesn't mean you have to support the Mafia.* These private thoughts she never shared with her brother but she did try to caution him. "The authorities' just need someone to pick on, and you stick out like a sore thumb," was as far as she would go.

Adolfo Cabrini was born five blocks south of St. Anthony's in the apartment above his father's Italian Imports shop. The sign really should have read Sicilian Imports, but his father, a shrewd businessman, knew that such a sign, evoking Mafia connections, would result in cutting his customers by two-thirds. Italians thronged his shop, especially on Saturday mornings after attending Mass, for wine, cheese and salami products. "Every Mafia chieftain in the Tri-State area buys my products," his father would boast.

Adolfo knew them by their first names. They applauded his decision to enter the seminary. "We need a Sicilian priest in this city who'll serve our needs. The ones we have are too Americanized."

Adolfo wanted to be that priest. "I will do it," he assured them. He kept this desire secret during his seminary years for fear he would be dismissed if it were known. The seminary director was a strict Irish disciplinarian who would never countenance such bizarre thoughts. But, at his ordination, the archbishop observed to the clergy as they were about to process to the altar, "Every bloody Mafia chief and underling from New York and New Jersey must be out there in the pews."

Early in his priesthood it became widely known in Manhattan that Father Adolfo was a close friend of Mafia Don Vito Massaro and his chief lieutenant, Julio Albanese, Tony's brother. It was also known that other Mafia Dons from the Tri-State area considered him "Chaplain of the Families." It was in his church that they held their baptisms, confirmations, marriages and funerals. Father Andrew Malkowski, Dean of the Lower Manhattan Deanery, at a Clergy Conference, protested. "It's against the spirit and the letter of Church law to encourage people to receive the sacraments outside their own parishes. It violates the territorial rights of the pastors of those parishioners."

His fellow-clergymen joined him in his protestations. Adolfo responded by claiming, "They are interested in the money they would receive from Mafia church functions. This pious front is bullshit."

The clergy indignantly countered that money had nothing to do with their position. "It's the principle of the thing," said Father Malkowski, who directed the first question to Father Adolfo at the Deanery's monthly meeting. "Do you deny that you regularly baptize, confirm, marry and bury persons who are parishioners of other parishes?"

"When requested, yes."

"Are you aware that you're obliged to inform such persons that they must receive the sacraments in their own parishes?"

"Not when there are mitigating circumstances."

Malkowski was adamant. "There are no mitigating circumstances. Church law is clear."

Adolfo countered, "It's not really a law, Father; it's more like a strong recommendation."

"That's your interpretation."

Referring to the Cardinal, who quietly sat in attendance, Father Adolfo bowed his head and said simply, "Whatever the Cardinal wishes in this matter, I'm prepared to faithfully obey."

The beaded clerical eyes focused like laser beams on the Cardinal, fully expecting their righteous anger would be reflected in his response. The Canon Law was clear. A nervous tension took hold of the room as the Cardinal thoughtfully, slowly, prepared his reply. Father Malkowski was not amused. Why the hell is the Cardinal hesitating? Not only is Adolfo breaking all the rules but, for God's sake, he's breaking the rules to accommodate the mob. It's ridiculous. It's obscene.

The Cardinal rose slowly, composed himself, and gave his reply. "This is a matter which requires consultation with my auxiliary bishops. I shall get back to you with my reply in due course."

Tension turned to shock. Everyone in the room was aware that "This is a matter which requires consultation with my auxiliary bishops" meant the issue was dead, would never be heard from again. Adolfo had won. "The goddam Mafia rides again," was Father Malkowski's parting remark, but he found another way to get at Father Adolfo. "I'll work through the ecumenical clerical conference."

"Good idea," said his secretary.

"I'll embarrass the Cardinal into taking action," he proclaimed. "I'll get all the guys, including the Protestant ministers and the Jewish Rabbis to vote unanimously at the conference. The Cardinal is big on ecumenism."

"Great," his secretary affirmed. "The strategy will receive instant support. All the clergy, Protestant, Catholic, Jewish and Muslim are scandalized by Adolfo's friendships."

At the very next ecumenical clergy meeting, Father Malkowsi put his plan before the members present. He received strong support from the Reverend Samuel Stanislaus of the Methodist Church in Crown Heights, Brooklyn, chairperson of The Concerned Clergy for the City of New York and Its Environs. Stanislaus expressed himself unequivocally. "How the hell does he get away with it, openly cavorting with mob figures? Why doesn't the Cardinal zap him, or at least remove him as pastor?"

Father Adolfo, who had declined to attend the Group's meetings on the grounds that they never dealt with substantive issues, was not present.

The Daily News, after some of those present at the meeting asking for anonymity disclosed the results, reported:

The many attempts on the part of clergy and laypeople alike to influence the Cardinal's attitude toward the young Sicilian priest, Adolfo Cabrini have been met with complete silence. Repeated phone calls to the Manhattan and Brooklyn Chanceries have drawn "No comment."

Cynics claimed to have information that Vito Massaro personally supported the Cardinal's favorite charity, a school for the blind in the South Bronx. When asked by the press if he would care to comment on the rumor, Vito Massaro responded, "I never comment on controversial statements." The statement itself caused a great deal of controversy in the South Bronx. Even the New York Times noted: Mr. Massaro's cryptic reply to a question from the New York Post reporter appears to lend credibility to the widespread rumors.

Several days after the Times' comments, Father Ed Flanagan received information from a parishioner who worked at the school for the blind that Father Adolfo had urged the Cardinal to accept Mafia money. This was the last straw. He called the Reverend Stanislaus and asked for an urgent meeting of the Concerned Clergy for the City of New York and its Environs. Stanislaus was cooperative. "Of course, Ed, even better, you are

Adolfo's best clergy friend, so call him and ask him to come to the meeting. If we meet without him it will be a total waste of time."

Father Flanagan did just that. "Sorry, Dolphi, hate to be the one chosen to do this but the group has asked me if they could meet with you. They'd like to ask you to explain the reason for your close association with the mob. They are demanding that you break that relationship forthwith."

Adolfo was pleasant. "I'm always open to listening to others. All you guys are free to visit me in the rectory anytime you wish."

"OK, let's tie it down. What about this Friday afternoon? Five PM?"

"You got it."

Adolfo put Flanagan on the spot. "By the way, Ed, do you share their concerns?"

After a pause, "Yes, I guess I do, Dolphi, but nothing personal."

"Sure, I understand." *Ed Flanagan's a nice guy, but he's not Sicilian. He'd never understand.*

The members of the clerical group arrived in a mini van promptly at five. The tree-lined street was wrapped in gold filters, as wide fans of sunlight slipped through the dark green limbs that hung over it like a massive umbrella. It had been a halcyon day, the air soft and silky. The Japanese Maples brightened up the neighborhood. Father Adolfo greeted his peers in the rectory parlor. "Welcome to my humble home," he said. "There's plenty of ice and drinks; help yourselves."

The group helped themselves to refreshments, and then quickly got down to business, launching into a collective tirade. "We have a lot to say," said the Reverend Stanislaus. Adolfo listened attentively and with great patience, in spite of the many innuendos and outright insults heaped on him. Rabbi Herskovits, whose full-time profession was that of a Brooklyn prosecuting attorney, did most of the questioning.

"Father, we come here as your brother, not as antagonists."

Here's where the hypocrisy goes into high gear, thought Father Adolfo.

"There are all sorts of rumors about your relationship with mob figures, so I..."

Father Adolfo interrupted. "All God's children are my sisters and brothers. I seek relationships with all of them....Don't you?"

"Of course, Father, I agree; spiritually we are all one family."

Adolfo affirmed, "Correct."

The Rabbi was flustered for a moment, then regained his composure. "Is it true, Father, that you're a friend of Vito Massaro, and his chief lieutenant, Julio Albanese? ...."

"One is a member of my parish and the other attends Mass from time to time, yes"

"Uh, you didn't quite answer my question, Father. I asked if you are a friend of these men."

Adolfo spoke distinctly. "I'm friendly with all my parishioners and any outsiders who choose to attend services in my church, yes."

The Rabbi looked for solid ground. "Let me phrase the question in another way."

Adolfo was polite. "Please do." But, before Rabbi Herskovits could launch his salvo, Adolfo stood up and said "Just a moment please. The Cardinal is crooked and I can prove it." There was an audible collective gasp. After all, the Cardinal was his protector. They watched as Adolfo moved deliberately across the room to the mantelpiece and adjusted a slightly askew photo of the Cardinal. "There, I've straightened him out." Turning to Rabbi Herskovits, "Sorry, Rabbi, please continue."

The Rabbi flushed with frustration but regained his composure. "I hope, Adolfo, you are taking this meeting seriously."

"I am, certainly."

The Rabbi slumped into his chair with a resigned grimace, his eyebrows nervously dancing. "Would it be accurate, Adolfo, to say that many members of organized crime consider you a priest in whom they can confide and with whom they can socialize?"

"I hope so."

"You hope so?" The Rabbi was startled.

"Yes, of course."

"And why is that?"

Adolfo tented his hands and twiddled his thumbs. "Well, I hope that all sinners consider me a priest in whom they can confide and with whom they can socialize. That's my main function as a priest."

A momentary confusion reigned as the clergy looked to each other for a better way to get at the subject. Father Banister, of the Episcopalian Church, took the initiative. "Surely, Father, you're evading the question. You know very well that the point we're making is that you're aiding and abetting criminal activity by blessing it with your friendship. Is that not so? Are you a Mafia-fixated ecclesiastic?"

Adolfo screwed up his face. "A, what?"

"A Mafia-fixated cleric."

Adolfo belly-laughed. "What the hell is that? I've never heard such an expression."

Father Banister was stern. "Don't play games with me, Adolfo."

"Games? I don't play games. I'm too old for that. I've answered the question that was asked. The Rabbi asked me if I were a friend of certain people. I answered in the affirmative, saying that I'm friendly with and accessible to all the faithful who visit my church." Adolfo pointed the forefinger of his massive hand directly at Father Banister's forehead. "Now listen carefully." His presence suddenly became intimidating.

"I'm listening."

Adolfo was blessed with a lanky and muscular frame, towering at six-foot-three. Most people considered him a nice guy, but the occasional antagonist did not. His massive square jaw and hulking shoulders could generate a sense of unease if projected with hostility. "Your question is a different one, Banister. It's very provocative, but I'll be Christian with you and try to answer."

The rebuke caused Father Banister to shift in his seat and nervously flicker his eyebrow with his left forefinger. Adolfo leaned in his direction. "One of Mary's titles is Refuge of Sinners. Now, I'm not saying that Mr. Massaro and Mr. Albanese are sinners, but your questions imply that. If they are sinners, then, yes, I am in imitation of the Blessed Mother, their refuge. Are you suggesting that the Blessed Virgin is somehow engaging in criminal or offensive activity by loving all of us sinners? Are you?"

Banister was enraged. "This comparison, Father, is quite odious. You're twisting the meaning and intent of my questions. You're clever, but perhaps not honest."

The tone now became very personal, with clergyman after clergyman attacking Father Adolfo, accusing him of minimizing the seriousness of their questions and concerns, and of giving scandal by his persistent friendship with murderers.

When Father Adolfo decided that the clergy had said enough, he asked, "You have all had your say. May I now make a statement of my own?"

All looked to the Rabbi, who nodded affirmatively. "Yes, Father, of course. We're here to listen to what you have to say."

The room fell into an uneasy silence, as Father Adolfo spoke. "I also have a question of you men. Would you be willing to change the name of your organization to Concerned Clergy for the Immigrant Families of the Archdiocese of New York? There are many serious socio-economic problems in this great city that need our attention and, quite honestly, I've never seen a reflection of that in our agendas. I think you fellows are fighting ghosts instead of real problems. You really should think about your priorities."

A collective gasp followed. Adolfo's words produced a fiery reaction from Rabbi Herskovits. "You're a man who will not listen to reason, who stubbornly follows his own conscience instead of listening to the voice of the Church, even your own Church."

Adolfo responded calmly. "You're not the first cleric to make such an accusation, Rabbi. In Joan of Arc's trial the assembled bishops roared out at her, 'You are not listening to our voice. You are following your own conscience.' Her answer, my brothers, is my answer. 'What conscience can I follow except my own conscience?'"

The outpouring of righteousness following that remark brought all possibility of further dialogue between Father Adolfo and the Concerned Clergy for the City of New York and Its Environs to an abrupt and unceremonious end. The Rabbi rose from his seat and pointed a quivering finger at Adolfo. "No one will ever be able to accuse us of not having tried to reconcile with our brother who has gone astray. We came with good intentions. We tried to bring you back to reason, to clerical propriety. Obviously we've failed, so we shall now say good day."

Adolfo's last invitation, "Please, you haven't had much to eat and drink. There are plenty of hors d'oeuvres left over. Eat up," went unheeded. The righteousness of the Concerned Clergy for the City of New York and Its Environs was splashed all across their serried brows and stern faces as they trooped out the front door and into the mini van. One priest present at that meeting, Father Mike Malone, called the Daily News and reported that Father Adolfo had actually said to his colleagues as they departed, "Screw you guys." The reporter, whose night editor was a close friend of Vito Massaro, declined to print the information. Sean Kerrigan, writing for the Village Voice, had no such qualms.

It is reported that popular Little Italy priest, Father Adolfo Cabrini, confronted his fellow-clergy at a recent meeting of the Concerned Clergy for the City of New York, convened to discipline him for associating with Mafia figures. A reliable source has informed the Voice that at the conclusion of the meeting, Father Adolfo shouted 'F...you guys.' When contacted by the *Voice* to confirm or deny the report, Father Adolfo said, 'I don't remember the exact words, but your report does convey my feelings'.

In a later edition, not wanting to be outdone by the *Village Voice*, the *Daily News* reported:

If recent reports of a clergy meeting held in Manhattan to discuss the rumored Mafia connections of Little Italy priest, Father Adolfo Cabrini, are true, one is prompted to ask the question, Why is the Archdiocese silent on this matter? One Westchester County pastor, who prefers to remain anonymous, told this reporter, "Well, after all, the Pope is Italian."

Chapter Four
JULIO

The day that Vito Massaro died of a heart stroke while on a flight to Miami, Julio Albanese was chosen, unanimously, as the godfather. There was no meeting, no conference, no arguments between the various factions, just a rush of people, led by his brother, Tony, to Julio's simple, white clapboard house. They found him in the dank-smelling basement, among stacked wrought iron lawn furniture, fixing a dripping water faucet. He had not heard the news of Vito Massaro's death.

"Lift him up," they shouted, lifting him to their shoulders. "Long live Julio, long live Julio. We want you and you alone," they chanted.

Overcoming his feigned resistance, the noisy, jubilant group carried Julio, flush-faced, up to the living room. His mother had lived with Julio and Tina before she died, so, after her death, they kept intact the devotional alcove that reflected her Catholicism. In a corner, catching light reflected from a large bay window stood a small statue of the Virgin and a red votive candle that filled the air with the odor of mutton fat. Directly across from the niche, a large portrait of the Sacred Heart of Jesus set in an ornate Florentine frame looked down approvingly.

The *Daily News* noted:

Julio Albanese, a rising star among Mafia Families, appears to have been appointed, without fanfare, as the new Don of the Massaro organization. A confidential source has informed us that his accession to power took place without an election or even a discussion. He is a man respected by his peers. Preliminary research on his background suggests that he will bring a new and more progressive style to the Organization.

Vito Massaro had been a member of St. Thomas Aquinas Parish, in Flatbush, so Julio went to visit the pastor, Monsignor Carney. "I'm here to arrange for the Mass and burial of Mr. Massaro."

The Monsignor was cool to the idea of a public funeral for Vito, explaining to Julio, "You understand, Mr. Albanese, it's nothing personal, but Vito Massaro was a public sinner. The Church does not wish to dignify such a life with a public funeral of a religious nature."

Julio was not pleased. *The hypocritical sonofabitch; everybody knows he drinks like a fish.* He held anger and responded mildly, "With respect, Monsignor, I understand your position, so perhaps I can approach the Cardinal myself. That would relieve you of having to make the decision."

The Monsignor stiffened. "That won't be necessary, Mr. Albanese. It would be official if I approached the Chancery on your behalf."

Julio parried, "That's fine, Monsignor. I shall do nothing unless I do not hear from you by noon tomorrow. I know you're a busy man so I'll not take up any more of your time."

Monsignor Carney's eyes widened. He liked neither the tone nor the content of Julio Albanese's remarks. He fully grasped the implied challenge and he displayed a hard smile. *This guy actually thinks he can go over my head. Let him try. This is one time a Mafia hood won't get what he wants.*

As he accompanied Julio to the door, the Monsignor took a stab of his own. "I can assure you, Mr. Albanese, that if I don't receive permission for the funeral, no one else will be able to do so. I am the pastor here."

Julio was polite. "Well, Monsignor, you certainly know more about church matters than I do. I leave the matter in your hands. Good day and thank you for your time." *The bastard won't do a damn thing.*

The Monsignor had thoughts. *He's mocking me, the son-of-a-bitch.*

"I'll contact you tomorrow before noontime, Mr. Albanese, as you've requested."

Julio cleared his throat. "Uh, huh."

The Monsignor was not happy. *This Mafia guy is trying to out-psyche me. He also thinks he's an intellectual. I hate intellectuals.*

Julio stepped out into a Brooklyn street opalescent in the hot summer heat. Two blocks south of St. Thomas', on Flatbush Avenue, he instructed his driver to pull over to a public phone. He called the family priest, Father Adolfo, at St. Anthony Padua. "Oh, Julio, it is good to hear your voice. I'm so sorry about the death of Mr. Massaro, so very sorry. I've prayed both for him and for you since I heard the news over the radio."

"Thank you, Father. I'm going to come right to the point. I need a favor. I want Vito to have a Catholic funeral and burial, like any other Catholic."

Father Adolfo, as usual, was sympathetic. "I understand how you feel, Julio. Is there a problem?"

Julio's voice had a sharp edge. "Well, we want it to be at St. Thomas Aquinas, where he's been a member and a contributor for many years. You know that before Monsignor Carney became pastor, Vito contributed the money to paint the entire Church and refurbish the statues and pews - about sixty thousand dollars."

"Yes Julio, I'm aware of Vito's generosity to St. Thomas's. The whole diocese is."

Julio's voice retained its sharp edge, tinged with sarcasm. "I just spoke with Monsignor Carney, Father, and he gave me the runaround. I don't believe he has any intention of having the funeral. He said he'll contact the Archdiocese, but I think he's just stalling for time. Can you help?"

Father Adolfo put down his coffee mug and responded. "Ah yes, Julio, the Monsignor is from the old school. Besides, he can't handle controversy. He even refused to bury an IRA sympathizer who was suspected of running guns to Belfast, so you know he's not going to go to the wall for a Sicilian!"

"Julio, I'll call the Cardinal tonight. He's in Mount Vernon today, but will be home about eight this evening. No promises, but I'll try. The Cardinal is a reasonable man."

Julio was satisfied. "Good enough for me, Father. You know where to reach me?"

"Yes, Julio, I've got your number right here on my desk."

"I'll wait for your call."

Julio was confident that something would be done. "Adolfo's our man," he muttered to himself.

Julio never did get a call from Father Adolfo but he did get his response. It was contained in the following morning's edition of the New York Daily News. His eager eyes scanned the large headlines that filled the entire page:

VITO MASSARO DIES OF A MASSIVE STROKE ON MIAMI FLIGHT. FUNERAL TO BE HELD AT ST. THOMAS AQUINAS PARISH IN FLATBUSH FOR WELL-KNOWN MAFIA FIGURE

Just below the headlines, encased in a thick rectangular black border, was printed the notice from the Chancery Office:

The following statement was released by Monsignor Harold Minter, Chancellor of the Archdiocese of New York, following the death of Mr. Vito Massaro of a massive stroke during a flight to Miami, Florida aboard Eastern Air Lines Flight 348. The right to Christian burial, even in doubtful cases, cannot be denied to any Catholic, except under circumstances specifically mentioned in the Code of Canon Law. In spite of allegations of criminal activity, Vito Massaro has never been convicted of a felony. On the basis of these facts, and in accord with the principles of both Civil and

Church Law, Vito Massaro cannot be denied the right to Christian burial. May he rest in peace.

Julio threw his paper at the ceiling, embraced his brother, Tony, and said, "Old Monsignor Carney is going to have kittens! Woweeee, is he ever! Old stiff bones are going to be rattling around his rectory tonight!" The joyously triumphant brothers danced an old Sicilian dance, shouting "Salute, salute, salute," as they raised glasses of Italian red.

In somber contrast, Monsignor Carney entered his study, collapsed into his favorite overstuffed chair and chatted with a close friend, Father Guthrie. They heard the shouts of their housekeeper coming down the corridor. She appeared in the doorway, her face flushed, the strings of her loosely-tied apron fluttering, and her eyes blazing erratically under her horn-rimmed glasses. Moving swiftly into the room, she flung the morning paper onto the startled Monsignor's lap. "Read this!" she commanded.

Monsignor Carney trembled, shaking the paper as he read the headlines, his eyes lost in squinting furrows, his lips thinned.

Guthrie wondered, "What's wrong, Steve?"

"What's wrong!" He pointed out the headlines. "Why, that no good Mafia, he went over my head! Who the hell does he think he is, anyway? And what the hell is wrong with the Chancery! Why do they keep giving in to these punks?"

Guthrie wanted to see for himself. "Let me see the paper."

Shaking his head, Carney snapped the paper shut and tossed it to Guthrie, who drew up a chair beneath his heavy body and read. He ventured, "Holy cow, Steve. Somebody got to the Cardinal last night, but who?"

Carney had no doubt. "Adolfo, for Pete's sake, who else? He should be defrocked for being part of the Mob."

Guthrie tried to help. "You've got to be philosophical about these things, Steve. It's just the way the ball bounces. You can't win them all."

Stephen Carney found it hard to accept the idea that he could not win them all. "I need a drink. Pour me a stiff one."

Guthrie poured two scotch-and-sodas as a nervous hush suffocated the room. "Here, it'll do you good, and cheer you up."

Cardinal Spellman's faded portrait, slightly atilt, looked down on the sad-eyed, sipping clerics. "Let's face it Steve, Massaro put out over sixty grand into fixing up this parish. It's pay back time. Besides, I hear these guys made big donations when the Catholic Conference of Bishops was building the Cathedral in Washington. That's the real world."

It was precisely the real world that Carney thought he had a handle on. He slumped into the leather couch that dissected the northeast corner of the spacious study. "I don't know, Guthrie, I just don't know. I think it stinks." Carney glanced, vacantly, through the study's open window, feeling the humid air suspended beneath the low slung sky. It would take time to adjust. Late that afternoon his humiliation was complete. A call from the Chancery Office informed him that Julio Albanese's request that his nephew, Carlo, be altar boy at the funeral had been honored, and he was advised not to place any obstacle to the boy's presence.

The sun's rays had barely flashed above the horizon when police lines were being set up in the Flatbush section of Brooklyn, in preparation for what was certain to be a very large mob of titillated onlookers. Channel 7 News began its morning report: "Today is a big day in Brooklyn. There are cops all over the place. Flatbush looks like an armed camp, and it's not the bad guys who are carrying the guns for a change; it's the cops." Brooklynites of all races and nationalities lined the streets.

The proprietor of the liquor store at the corner of Flatbush and Bedford Avenues stuck his head out the door and asked, "Is Jane Fonda in town? What the hell's going on?" An off-duty bus driver shouted, "Benny you must be the only guy in town who hasn't listened to the news this week. Whataya doing? Hibernating?"

Vito Massaro's funeral was well attended and well organized. It reflected less the popularity of the deceased (though he certainly was popular) than the new style of Julio Albanese, a style both elaborate and disciplined.

Mary Cortese, special-reports editor for NBC, spoke from a platform set up at the beginning of the funeral route: "Representatives from every Mafia Family in the United States have formed a funeral cortege a half mile in length. Stretch Cadillacs, symbol of the mob's hierarchy, are winding their way from Avenue Y and Flatbush Avenue, to the entrance of St. Thomas Aquinas Church. Fifteen open limousines trailing the sweet scent of jasmine, are carrying expensive flowers; some of them, according to one of our reports, were flown in from as far away as the West Coast."

Above Mary's stand, Channel 7's News helicopter pilot, Arthur Goodwin, called in. "Mary, I think I got something for you."

"What?"

"There's a fleet of black limousines, led by two motorcycle cops, moving very rapidly across the Verrazzano Bridge. Check it out. Bet it's for the funeral procession."

"Thanks Art."

Mary turned to police captain, Rolf Rothmere. "Captain, our helicopter reporter has spotted a line of cars escorted by two motorcycle cops coming over the Verrazzano Bridge. Can you confirm that this group is heading here to join the procession?"

"Yes, I can."

"From..?"

"Newark, New Jersey."

Mary ventured, "Friends of the slain godfather?"

The Captain was hesitant. "Uh…Could be."

Mary sensed she should back off. She couldn't expect a captain of the NYPD to admit that police were providing escort service for New Jersey's leading crime families.

"Thanks Captain. You've been very helpful." Over the air she said. "Our Channel 7 helicopter reports a long line of black limousines now crossing the Verrazzano Bridge. Speculation has it that the autos contain the leaders of New Jersey's top crime families. We will update you if we can confirm that report."

Ms. Cortese's hobby of flower-gardening gave her the expertise for reporting the scene. "The flowers have been formed into wreaths, crosses, and gargantuan bouquets made up of pristine white Calla lilies, multi colored Dutch tulips, French golden mimosa, all mingled with arm-loads of long-stemmed American-beauty roses. It's an incredible sight!"

Walking along the funeral cortege as it moved along Mulberry Street (the heart of Little Italy) Ms. Cortese's partner, Jack Ingram, cut in with his report. "Mary, immediately behind the flower limos is the Massaro family Cadillac, carrying Vito's wife."

Mrs. Massaro's string of pearls reflected off the car's windows. A specially equipped van with photographers from *The Daily News* kept breaking into the funeral line to get close-ups of Julio, relaxed in the back seat with Tony and his nephew, Carlo. Ms. Cortese reported: "Tony Albanese's presence, together with his young son, Carlo, beside his brother is an early indication of who will be his closest advisor and confidant."

As his limo pulled up in front of the church, Julio saw Monsignor Carney standing on the front steps of the church, enveloped in luxuriously embroidered white vestments imported from Italy. The material was used to attire Rome's most important ecclesiastics. *Pompous jackass.* To Tony he said, "Father Adolfo doesn't dress like this jerk. This guy hides behind his priest robes. He's got nothing else going for him. If he wasn't a priest he couldn't get a job in a soda fountain."

"Don't talk like that, Julio; that's a terrible thing to say about a priest."

"Uh, huh!"

In one hand the Monsignor held the Holy Water sprayer; in the other he gripped a large red ritual book, the pages of which fluttered from slight but persistent puffs of wind. His "Let us recite the prayers for the dead," got lost in the sound of traffic. As Julio's limo slid up next to the curb, the Monsignor's face grew taut; his body stiffened as he squinted his eyes. He shuddered as Sergeant O'Shea, a parishioner in full uniform, saluted the newly appointed godfather. He was scandalized and appalled. The sight of an Irish policeman paying respects to an Italian Mafia Don disgusted him. *What has happened to the faith? The whole world is falling apart.*

The casket was carried up the steps to the Church entrance. Carlo rushed to the startled Monsignor's side dressed in his altar boy's cassock, looked into Carney's eyes and said, "I know all about funerals."

Carney was annoyed. *This kid's an arrogant Mafia bastard already. They start them young.*

Julio and Tony waited until Vito's family had entered the church before emerging from their car onto the flint colored pavement. Julio did not want to upstage the Massaro clan in their moment of sadness. He instructed his personal bodyguard, "Gambi, keep photographers away from me as we approach the church door." Gambi (known in the organization as "the Enforcer") had the face of Sitting Bull, and his big-boned, lean physique was enough to intimidate even the foolhardy. His hair was long and pulled back into a ponytail. A diamond earring in his left ear twinkled. His large, knuckled hands hinted at a powerful body hidden beneath a loose-fitting blazer. The Monsignor caught a glimpse of him and was disgusted. *It's a black day for this parish.*

The Monsignor began the ritual:

"I bless the body of Vito Massaro with Holy Water that recalls his baptism of which St. Paul writes. `All of us who were baptized into Christ Jesus were baptized into his death. For if we have been united with him by likeness to his death, so shall we be united with him by likeness to his resurrection.' May the angels, Vito Massaro, lead you into Paradise and welcome you to the new and eternal Jerusalem."

Tears moistened Julio's face. He remembered all the good Vito Massaro had accomplished in his lifetime: the kids he sent to school, the suits he bought for all the guys in the Clancey Street poolroom, the wood stoves he placed on Bowery streets for the shivering homeless. He had broken with the other Dons and did his best to become, as he said with a grin, "a modern gangster." He set aside what he called the "emergency fund," short-term investments in CDs, and others in Money Market Funds. He was feeling his way. He meant well. Julio prayed, "Oh God, please take Vito into your house and into your bosom. Oh Lord, be kind to him. May his generous soul rest in peace, forever and ever."

Tony proudly watched young Carlo as he went about his altar duties without hesitation. Even at this early age, Carlo's determination and ability to handle every event and every problem calmly and effectively manifested itself. Tony fingered the papal rosary Vito had brought him from Rome. Mother of Sorrows, pray for us. Maria, as was the tradition, sat with the Family women. She was now pregnant again and felt some guilt in continuing to focus on Carlo, her wonder child, the child of the Promise.

Victor relished the spotlight suddenly focused on him and his brothers. The liturgy served as a vehicle for introducing him to the general public. *Is this the beginning of a more prosperous time for me?* Julio had never offered him an important post in the organization. The reason? "You see, Victor, I can't be bringing the whole family into top positions; it's Vito's show." But now things were different. As Don, Julio had to pay attention to him andmust include him in the organization. It was a tradition, and Victor sensed that Julio would keep everybody happy, would do the "right" thing.

Julio and Tony stood alongside the Monsignor at the graveside without invitation. As mourners murmured condolences, Julio took a handful of dirt, held it for a moment, and then let it fall in a tight spray on the casket of his benefactor. *I was supposed to do that,* thought the Monsignor, as he intoned, "Thou art dust and unto dust thou shall return."

The grass was spiced with the scent of newly-exposed soil. Its aroma, distilled through the sweat of the mingling crowd and abundant shrubbery, was distinct. Cathedral-height billowing clouds hung low and immobile, adding to the somber mood. As the priest continued, Julio turned to his brother and whispered, "What is death, Tony? Is it a friend or an enemy? What does the gospel say?"

Tony was the Family scripture expert. "Unless we fall into the ground and die, we cannot bear fruit. That's what it says. I'm not sure what that means exactly, but it's a positive statement anyway."

"We'll talk about that sometime, because I want to know about death. It haunts all of us in our business."

Tony, distractedly, "Yeah, we'll talk about it."

Julio's gaze swept in the scene, as the soft-spoken conversations of the mourners merged, indistinguishably, in a stream that flowed past his ears like a muted Requiem. His eyes narrowed into slits as he took in the scene. For a moment he felt transfigured, a phantom observing the scene from afar, detached. His new responsibilities momentarily overwhelmed him. In an effort to come back to reality he clenched his fists and set his jaw, turning away from the grave without glancing at Monsignor Carney or taking his proffered hand. *The bastard. He didn't even want this funeral, but he doesn't have the gutss to say so publicly.*

He strode deliberately to his car, saying to Tony, "We've buried Vito with dignity and respect. Now it's time to move on. He would want us to take care of business. There are things that need to be done right away." Then he motioned Carlo to leave the Monsignor's side and join them.

Victor observed this easy exchange between his two brothers in uneasy silence, noting that he was not included. *Why does Julio ignore me?*

From that day, Julio became the most powerful Don in the New York, Tri-State area. He was a master at the art of give-and-take in his dealings with the other Families. He enjoyed their confidences and strategically ceded to each a corner of some lucrative market in order to keep the peace. His particular genius was his ability to sort out practical solutions to complicated problems. He made friends of Massaro's long-time enemies. He made clear his goal. "There are enough goodies out there for all of us. For God's sake, we've got to stop killing each other. There are no arguments that can't be settled with a bit of patience and some common sense."

His influence stretched from the Atlantic to the Pacific, spanning the sea to Sicily and Naples, like an overarching rainbow. Through an international network, his tentacles reached into the bazaars of Pakistan and Iran, where dope was purchased for eventual shipment to America. Julio denied to the day of his death that he ever dealt in "dope and coke," but history does not verify his claims. His keen sense of timing enabled him to outwit and outpace his competitors in the American La Cosa Nostra. He deferred to the Sicilian Mafia, allowing them to operate without opposition in Chicago, St. Louis and San Francisco. To the objections of his American Mafia peers he said, "There's plenty to go around."

One of their numbers, Vincent D'Ostilio, Seattle boss, interpreted Julio's spirit of compromise as weakness. He made the mistake of declaring this publicly at a bar in suburban Seattle. "Julio Albanese is new in the game. He's a softy. He won't last."

Speculation ran wild within and outside the Mafia community when, fourteen days after he made that statement, he was found dead floating in his pool, his decapitated mistress tied to his waist. An enterprising neighbor photographed the bloody scene and sold it to a local newspaper for $1000. In an editorial in *The Gay Press,* under the banner, Vincent D'Ostilio Sucks, questions were asked. "Was it the Sicilian Mafia? Was it Julio Albanese?" The question became academic as the brotherhood got the message.

Chapter Five
FATHERS O'REILLEY AND CALLAHAN

Father Francis O'Reilly sat at his desk in his seminary office staring out at the seminary grounds. The Blessed Virgin Grotto, sitting in a torrent of bright, May sunlight, was a milky-white spot in the middle of the wide expanse of green lawn. His mind was on the seminarians he was about to approve for ordination. *I wonder how many of these guys will remain in the priesthood?* He believed this to be the finest ordination class he had directed for many years. The previous year's ordination class has already lost two priests. Why the leakage? What happens when they leave here? The seeds of defection must have been planted right here.

O'Reilly worked to enlighten the minds of his young charges, determined to open up the world to them before they ventured out into it. He once recommended to the Cardinal that courses in economic and social problems be included in the seminary curriculum, but the conservatism of his staff caused that suggestion to be aborted.

Father Rhinelander, the scripture professor, observed "Are you feeling well, Francis?" The tone of sarcasm was evident. "That's economics and sociology, not theology. We seem to be mixing them these days. We must be careful you know."

Another suggestion: A married couple be hired as part-time teachers to provide a better understanding of married life and problems to young seminarians; this suggestion brought immediate negative reaction. Father Collins, professor of Moral Theology reflected the thinking of the seminary staff. "If we do this, we're going to give the impression that priests cannot deal adequately with marriage problems. It would be sending the wrong message."

Father O'Reilly had rejoined, "Perhaps we'll discover that we're not adequate, that perhaps we have been sending the wrong message. Ever think of that?"

Collins discounted the idea. "Too far-fetched to waste time thinking about. That's like saying you'll never understand sin unless you commit sin."

Francis waved the air with his hands. "Maybe that's so also? It does make sense."

"Jesus knew all about sin and he didn't commit any."

Francis responded with ease and quick grace for an answer. "That's true, but I'm not Jesus and neither are you, Collins."

Father Collins changed the subject. Because Francis was a friend of the Cardinal, not one of the conservative professors ever made a formal complaint against him, but as one of them remarked, "We'd sure love to."

A milk truck driving through the courtyard focused Father O'Reilly's attention on the Grotto below. It was only then that he noticed Carlo Albanese kneeling at the foot of the Virgin. That's a real man, he mused. Delicate in form and appearance, Carlo, nonetheless, radiated virility and his speech, although gentle, had a determined firmness about it. Father O'Reilly had already remarked to the seminary faculty. "There's steel in that young man, steel I tell you."

The red phone rang. It was intended to insure privacy between the Cardinal McManus and Francis. The Cardinal's secretary was on the line. "Hi, Francis, John here." Father John Newstetter was unpopular with the auxiliary bishops. He was perceived as too young, too arrogant, and too ambitious. He was, as one of the auxiliary bishops once remarked, "a pain in the ass." Newstetter had the habit of responding to the news that an auxiliary bishop had undertaken some pastoral initiative with, "Who the hell gave him permission to do that?" Collectively the bishops waited for him to be separated from the Cardinal by a new assignment. They would then take their revenge. But, for the time being, they had no choice but to allow *Newstetter* to continue his arrogant ways.

Newstetter controlled a yawn, "Hold on a second, Francis, the Cardinal would like to speak to you."

Father O'Reilly both liked and felt sorry for Cardinal McManus. Before his consecration he had been a great mixer with his fellow clergy, a man to whom young, troubled priests had often turned in time of stress. Father O'Reilly remembered his reassuring sentiments delivered at the post-consecration dinner. "I shall continue to remain close to my fellow-priests. The door of the Archbishop's house will always be open to a priest. That's a promise." How idealistic it all sounded, in retrospect. The position of Cardinal Archbishop of New York City made it literally impossible for this promise to be kept. The Archdiocese had over one thousand priests and, even if the Cardinal were able to meet one priest a day, it would take about three years to meet them all. Thus, he had become increasingly isolated. The four walls of his office became "this bloody cage in which I live." In his loneliness, he consoled himself with the fact that he had become a prince of the Church, a sacrificial lamb dressed in rich man's robes. To Francis he complained: "I feel like a machine that spews out confirmations, ordinations and boring dinners." But there was no way out. He was the Cardinal Archbishop of New York. Francis O'Reilly, his classmate and counselor, was his window to the real world.

The Cardinal spoke with firmness. "Now, Francis, I don't want this ordination to become a damn circus. I know you can't control the media, but don't give them any more ammunition than necessary. Do you understand that, Francis?"

Father O'Reilly said he understood.

The Cardinal continued. "Another thing, I don't want our clergy and seminarians getting near the Godfather. Keep them a mile away. I think it would be a good idea for you to start calling the pastors around town, instructing them to pass on that message to their assistants."

"I will do that, Your Eminence"

The Cardinal was annoyed by "Your Eminence."

"For God's sake, Francis, why do you insist on this formality."

Francis pinched his nose. "I'm sorry, Mick"

The Cardinal collected his thoughts. "Where was I? Oh yes, all we need is a photograph on the front page of The Daily News of one of our priests shaking hands with the Mafiosi. I'll bet you their editorial board is already plotting something like this. Some of my own men would like to see me embarrassed. Don't let them get away with it, Francis."

O'Reilly had no intention of allowing his friend to be humiliated by "the guys." "I'll do my best, Mick, but, as you know, news people are very difficult to control."

This satisfied the Cardinal. He continued in a warm but serious tone. "Francis, you're the only man I can trust to take care of this job for me." And then, with a chuckle, "There are a lot of bishops out there in hick dioceses that gnash their teeth at night watching the TV coverage I get, while they're out blessing corn stalks on some foul-smelling farm. How they would love to see me squirm! We don't want to give them any ammo, Francis. I leave everything in your capable hands. I'll be in Boston if you need me."

"Don't worry about anything, Mick." The Cardinal packed for a trip every time a difficult situation arose. Par for the course, Francis mused.

Father O'Reilly thought it prudent not to mention that he was expecting a visit from Carlo's father and his uncle, Julio. They were due to arrive within the hour. Julio Albanese had called the previous evening to suggest that he and Carlo's father visit to discuss the ordination and the reception that would follow. Julio Albanese, to Father O'Reilly's profound relief, was well aware that the Archdiocese would want the presence of the Family to be as low-key as possible. Over the phone he said, "You can be assured, Father, that I'm aware of the delicate nature of our presence at the ordination. We can work out everything."

This politeness did not surprise Father O'Reilly. It was well known among the clergy that there was an "understanding" between the Church and the Families in Manhattan and in the other Boroughs. It was also well known that the Bishop of Brooklyn was a frequent guest in the homes of mob-connected politicians and businessmen. Some said it was because of his Italian heritage. Others said that Mafia coffers funded many charities of the Brooklyn Diocese. In the intimacy of clerical gatherings it had been rumored for years that at a secret meeting in Rome the Cardinal had protested to the Pope about the Brooklyn Bishop's "indiscreet attendance at Mafiosi dinner parties." Much to his distress, the Cardinal had been rebuffed. For some it explained, according to reports filtering out of those gatherings of clergy, why Father Adolfo, the pastor of St. Anthony of Padua, was never disciplined for being openly sympathetic to the Mafia. A few even went so far as to remark, "His Eminence got a cold reception in Italy. The Cardinals there know on which side their bread is buttered."

Father O'Reilly knew he had to talk with Charlie Callahan, NBC Program Director, who was breakfasting with his wife when O'Reilly called. Sharon answered. As with many other executive wives, her task was to filter out the calls. "Oh, you just missed Charlie," she would say when an enthusiastic young producer at NBC could not wait to explode his creativity on the boss. This time she called to her husband, "It's Father Francis, dear."

Charlie Callahan and Father Francis had been buddies from grade school. They made St. Hyacinth's basketball team the same day; two hot shot hoopsters who complemented each other on the court. Three basketball championships in a four-year period were credited to the teamwork of Charlie Callahan and Francis O'Reilly. The Yearbook predicted, "They will be law partners." As grown men with different careers they faithfully helped each other with one problem or another, as when Father Francis baptized the child of a Callahan associate. The parish priest had refused because the couple was not in regular Mass attendance. Father Francis discreetly arranged for the baptism at the Seminary. Only recently, Father Francis had helped get an annulment. It was issued three days before Christmas, a fine Christmas present for a married couple working at NBC who mutually agreed that their marriage had been a mistake from day one. Now it was Father Francis's turn to ask the favor. "Charlie, I need your help, but it's a toughie. It's about Carlo Albanese. As you know, he's going to be ordained next Wednesday at St. Patrick's Cathedral."

"Of course, Francis, It's all the networks are talking about right now. It's a winner. Lots of advertisers lined up already." It promised to be the media event of the year. "Yes, Francis, we're preparing to cover the ordination with a large crew. All three major networks will be there. Next to a Papal visit, this has got to be the biggest religious news story in years. It's a TV station's dream. Big bucks here, guy."

Francis spoke slowly. "The Cardinal is concerned, Charlie."

"Concerned about what? Why, this is great publicity for the Church. Statewide television coverage." Incredulously, "That's something to worry about?"

Father O'Reilly spoke forthrightly. "Charlie, the Cardinal wants you to talk with those guys over at CBS and ABC to see if the three of you can tone-down the media coverage of the ordination. Anything you can do will be very much appreciated. He does not want this to turn out to be free media coverage for the Mafia, especially in the Cathedral!"

Charlie's reply was expected. "Francis, I would have a hell of a time trying to downsize the story right here at NBC, to say nothing of a rival network. Performing miracles is your business, not mine. It would take a ton of holy water and the patience of Job, both of which are sadly lacking among folks in my trade."

Francis knew that, with a little persistence, his friend's first "no" could be transformed into a cautious "maybe." "Charlie, you fellows in the media know what is appropriate. You also know that you have a responsibility to play fair. The ordination of a priest is a very sacred ceremony and, if not covered delicately, a lot of Catholics out there are going to be offended. Remember, you guys have to work in this town."

A long "Mmm" was the signal that Charlie Callahan was getting the message and was ready to make a deal. For his part, Callahan had always marveled at Father Francis's sharp political sense, and complimented him. "You're a people's priest, in spite of the stuffy jobs the Cardinal gives you."

Father Francis responded simply, "My business is people. The priest who takes care of his business will be a good politician. It goes with the territory, Charlie."

Charlie listened attentively. "No argument there, Francis."

Father Francis continued, "I'm sure that if you sit down with your people you can make them see the practical side of it, and they will go along with you. What do you say, Charlie?

Callahan capitulated. "OK, Francis, I'll give it my best shot, but remember that the ordination of a priest, with all the color, the ceremony, the shots of the Cathedral, is a very big visual event. What you're asking me to do is to cover the coronation of the Queen of England and leave out the pageantry. Not easy, Francis. To add to our problems, the top figures of the Cosa Nostra from the Tri-State area will be there and that, my friend, is really big news. We've got sponsors on their knees begging for time. Money is no object. We're talking lots of money here, Francis."

As the conversation ended, Callahan turned to his wife, put his hands on her shoulders and said, "I guess you got the drift of the conversation. What do you think?"

She stroked the nape of her neck with her long fingers and expressed a reservation. "Charlie, remember that this is the twentieth century. We're not back in the Middle Ages. A priest's ordination is a public ceremony. The fact that one of the nephews of the godfather is being ordained is not a reason to muzzle the media. After all, the Cardinal agreed to have the boy ordained, so let him act as though he's not ashamed of his own decision. Anyway, Cardinals don't have the clout now that they used to have in this town."

Charlie was not so sure of that. "Don't kid yourself, Sharon. The Catholic Cardinal is still a big force in this city. I think Francis is right. If we don't tone it down, we may get a backlash from the Catholic community. Nothing is more sensitive an issue than religion, even in the twentieth century."

Charlie's driver, Carlton, a former FBI agent who packed a .44 caliber, was a tall, muscular and discreet man. Sharon was pleased when NBC tightened their security and hired former lawmen to protect their top people. Each morning Carlton pulled into the driveway oval, opened the limousine rear door, come to attention, stared straight-ahead and said, "Good morning sir."

Charlie kissed his wife goodbye as she flung her arms out to embrace him. Carlton folded his burly frame behind the wheel of the limousine, draping his stubby fingers over the wheel.

Sliding into the back seat, Charlie waved him on. "Ready, Carlton." Barely out of the driveway, he used the limousine phone to call his executive secretary, Betty Weaver. "Betty, I want you to set up a meeting between Bill McIntosh and myself as soon as possible - today if you can manage it. Tell him it's very important. If he can come, cancel all my other appointments."

Bill McIntosh was Callahan's counterpart at CBS, also an Irish Catholic. If he got Bill to go along, Karl Levin at ABC was likely to follow. Karl, a liberal Jew, was not very reverent about things ecclesiastical. In fact, he let it be known more than once that he thought the Catholic Church had too much influence in New York politics. "Not that I've got anything against Catholics, Charlie," he would say in jest, "Some of my best friends are Catholic."

Karl was, however, in Charlie's debt. Charlie had helped him raise much-needed money for the Israeli government at a bash in New Rochelle. "I see you Gentiles also have a little money stashed away for good causes," he said to Charlie after the party. The Israeli Ambassador was so pleased with Karl's efforts that he invited him and his family to a private dinner at the Waldorf, on the occasion of the Israeli Prime Minister's visit to the United States. It was payback time.

As the limousine passed over the toll bridge from Riverdale into Manhattan, the car phone emitted the gentle, soft beep that Charlie often wished could be used on his telephones at home. It was Betty. "The appointment you requested with Bill McIntosh is all set; he'll be here in about half an hour." The traffic was heavy along the West Side Highway and Charlie took some long looks at his city. He was depressed at the thought that a great nation would think so little of itself as to allow its major cities to fall into such a state of disrepair. "Why can't we be as proud of our city, like the Parisians?" he would often complain.

Charlie strode briskly through the long rectangular hallway lined on both sides with his staff's offices. Betty greeted him as he entered, handing him mail and a few inter-office memos. "One of the girls wants a few days off; another has asked for pregnancy leave. I presumed your permission to OK the requests. What the hell, we'd probably lose them if you said no."

Charlie nodded in agreement. The movement of staff in and out of the office was so rapid that he scarcely got to know them.

The intercom buzzed. "Bill McIntosh is here to see you. Shall I send him in?"

"Right, Betty."

Charlie sat at his desk, clearing a space. He looked out at St. Patrick's Cathedral, two blocks away. Beyond that inspiring view stood tall, faceless buildings, masses of glass reflecting the changing colors of the daytime sky. In contrast to the classical architectural lines of the Cathedral, they appeared anonymous. *Are we the anonymous generation? We should do a show about that.*

The office sported a very masculine look, with large leather chairs and an expensive oak desk given him by a retiring executive vice-president of the company. Brushed aluminum window blinds and soft lighting cascaded from hidden ceiling niches. A large Monet print, a pastoral scene in Provence, added to the room's sumptuousness.

"Good morning, Charlie." Bill McIntosh walked with a wide stride, even in the small space of an office. "He still thinks he's running the quarter mile at Harvard," his secretary would say to curious onlookers.

"Good morning to you, Bill. You look great."

MacIntosh floated his long-boned body across the room effortlessly. "Exercise, Charlie, exercise, that's the name of the game. What in the name of heaven is so important that you had to see me today?" He removed his glasses and joined Charlie Callahan on a dark maroon leather sofa that afforded a view of St. Patrick's Cathedral and a bustling Fifth Avenue.

Both men represented important news organizations based in New York, manned by interesting and talented people, whose genius spread out into fingers of inquiry that tentacled the globe. Each felt the responsibility of accurately reflecting the cultures, political turmoil and social progress of the world's people. The world watched them as they watched the world. Such responsibility had to be exercised in a manner that also assured the revenues needed to finance the vast army of reporters, newsmen, technicians, and support staff. It was not an easy balancing act.

"Something to drink, Bill?"

Bill shook his head. "Not whiskey, not this early in the day, but I'll have some of that coffee Betty's got out there. What's up?"

Charlie got down to business. "Listen, Bill, the reason I asked you to come over here today is to discuss a very delicate situation. You know that Father O'Reilly, over at the Dunwoodie Seminary, is a good friend of mine, school buddies."

"The whole town knows."

Betty served coffee as Charlie scratched his forehead. "You also know that he's the Cardinal's right-hand man. Well, he's been given the job of coordinating the ordination coverage with the media. What they really want - he and the Cardinal - is to keep the lid on this as much as possible. They don't want to have a circus just because the top Don is there."

Bill McIntosh shuddered, "Whew! Charlie, how the hell can we keep the lid on the ordination of Carlo Albanese? It would be like trying to ignore the installation of the President of the United States. It just can't be done.

Did you tell him he's asking for a miracle? That's Father Francis' vocation, not ours."

Charlie raised his arms and shoulders, as if reaching for an unseen object, "My exact words, Bill, my goddam exact and precise words! Father O'Reilly understands this. He knows he's asking for the moon. But, he does have a point, Bill, he really does. If the coverage does become a circus, then we'll have our butts nailed to the wall, not by the Cardinal, but by the public."

Bill was languid. "You think so?"

"This is a Catholic town, Bill, you know that. The people won't stand for any real or imagined nonsense when it comes to the Catholic Church. You know that as well as I. Breslin would crucify us in the News. Remember when Clyde made that joke about the Cardinal - those effeminate hand movements? He didn't last long on that Talk Show. And he's not been employed since."

"You're right. I'd forgotten about that. So, how do you see the picture? How do you think we should handle this?"

Charlie explained. "All he's asking us to do is to come to some sort of agreement among ourselves, the three networks, not to make a farce out of the ceremony."

"Yeah, Charlie, I hear you, specifics?"

Charlie Callahan leaned forward and placed his right hand on Bill McIntosh's left shoulder. "No interview with the godfather or any of the others in his entourage, not even members of Carlo's immediate family - just a concentration on the religious aspect of the ceremony. He's asking that references to the Albanese clan be brief and without any hype. Reasonable requests, Bill?" He then answered his own question. "I think so."

"What about Karl? Do you have him on board?"

Charlie paused to sip on his coffee. "No, but I'll remind him that he owes me for all the money I raised for Israel. I'll have to push him along. He'll resist. Dislikes the Catholic Church, but he's a realist. We've all got a stake in being careful on this one; people-backlash, brother, people-backlash. That's the dragon we got to be careful about. Karl reads the ratings as well as we do."

Bill offered, "I'm with you. Makes sense and keeps us safe from the Roman masses."

The two men shook hands on the agreement as Charlie accompanied Bill McIntosh to the elevator, satisfied that he had done all he could do. "From here on in we keep our fingers crossed."

Shortly before lunch Charlie called Karl Levin. Referencing the Israeli money, he said, "You owe me one," and explained Francis' request.

Levin saw the practical side of things. "You know what, Charlie?" with a chuckle, "I was thinking the same thing, so you didn't even have to stiff me with the Israeli money thing."

His spirits buoyed, Charlie turned to his daily ritual, beginning with a cursory reading of two Long Island newspapers, then the Daily News, the New York Times and the Washington Post. Correspondence and telephone calls to be returned were next on his agenda. This took him to noontime. Then he suited up for a grueling half-hour of exercise in the company fitness room, followed by a quick lunch of salad and yogurt. Then a telephone call. "Francis, I've got good news for you. The deal has been made with CBS. Karl Levin at ABC will also go along."

It was at times like this that Charlie, a devout Catholic, was happy in the belief that the Catholic Church remained an important force in what appeared to be a very cold and calculating city.

Chapter Six
THE ORDINATION

According to the Today Show weatherman, June 2nd was to be a cool, cloudless day, with moderate winds coming in from the East River. He predicted that the unseasonably hot, humid days of late May drenching the faces and necks of subway commuters would evaporate during the early hours of the morning. He also advised that air conditioners could be turned off. "Cool it with your air conditioners. We don't need another brownout, to say nothing of a blackout."

Carlo and his fellow ordinandi were on their way by bus from the seminary in Dunwoodie, in Yonkers, to Manhattan. The previous three days had been jammed with discussions about celibacy, homosexuality, power in the Church, good and bad pastors, and assignments. Now, there was quiet and reflection, each shrouded in his own thoughts as the moment of truth arrived. Each understood that in a few short hours they would no longer be masters of their own destiny. Carlo, once again, envied his classmates. For them, the already complicated psychological and social aspects of ordination were not further complicated by being a member of a Mafia family. Carlo was concerned about tomorrow's headlines. Would the Daily News have a headline such as, Mafia Member Ordained to Priesthood? The imminent prospect of his ordination being associated with mobsters and mayhem disturbed him. *Am I really doing a service to the Church by my ordination?* These last minute doubts rankled him, clouding the occasion.

Michael Kelly, custodian for St. Patrick's Cathedral, looked up at the shifting sky with squinty-eyed focus, then lowered his gaze to take in the faces of worshipers filing into the Cathedral. The good Lord has ordered a nice day for the ordination. Pigeons filtered through the wafer thin clouds that drifted over the enormous granite blocks shaped into America's most famous Cathedral. One of the birds wheeled around in a large curve, and swooped down in a determined plunge. A knot of passersbys gathered to watch, as the pigeon pulled itself up in a sweeping U, just short of a passing taxi. There was spontaneous applause.

Every morning, rain or shine, winter or summer, Kelly opened the Cathedral doors. The Cathedral was his life. He had worked through the reigns of four Cardinals and loved each of them, believing them to be the embodiment of priesthood and shepherd. He would get especially angry when he heard criticism of the Cardinals by Cathedral priests and parishioners. Where is the loyalty?

Michael entered St. Patrick's through the 51st Street entrance and made his way to the main entrance on Fifth Avenue. As he flung open the doors, he greeted TV technicians from the three major networks sitting on the Cathedral steps waiting for him. "Good morning, gentlemen. Top of the morning to you."

Several large television-satellite vans, marked CBS, NBC, ABC, were strung along Fifth Avenue, with a police car at either end of the line flashing red and white lights. Camera crews were busy setting up for remote telecasts. Behind police lines set up along the Avenue's sidewalk, hundreds had already gathered to observe what one newscaster that morning had called "the soap opera of the year." The TV crew manager approached Michael. A nameplate on his breast pocket identified him as "Crews Manager."

"Hi, I'm Jack Carpenter. I've got a letter from Monsignor Lamar, authorizing our people to set up equipment in the Cathedral. My job is to coordinate all of this activity. The Monsignor says he'll be here about nine. In the meantime, OK if we get started? Here's his letter,"

Michael glanced at the letter and recognized the Monsignor's stationary and smudged signature. "All right, Mr. Carpenter. Just make sure these men respect the fact that this is a church."

Carpenter agreed to keep an eye on the crew. They had exactly an hour and a half to complete preparations for the telecast. He began to issue orders at a fast clip, moving men and equipment to the right places, testing equipment and keeping in constant communication with Charlie Callahan who, in turn, was keeping in touch with Bill MacIntosh and Karl Levin. By 9:15 a.m. all was in place. He had done a professional job. The considerable amount of equipment had been skillfully placed, causing little visual disturbance. The spectacular color and pageantry of the ordination rite would, he thought, more than compensate for the hard work

Nuns in blue habits prepared the main altar, which was decorated with clusters of red, white, and pink roses standing in Tiffany glass vases. In the sanctuary, Italian marble tables were being placed around the altar to hold wine, water cruets, and towels. The ordination texts lay on ornate wooden stands. The glory and ethereal beauty of the liturgical function began to take shape as flowers, candles, lights, nuns, priest vestments and clerics merged and harmonized in glorious splendor with the majestic walls and ceilings of St. Patrick's Cathedral.

"Test the lights on the upper left corner," shouted a technician. "They need to be moved forward a bit." Huge strobe lights bounced their brightness off the Cathedral's walls and ceilings. Twelve heavily armed soldiers of the Godfather manned every door and took their places in the choir loft. Usher's tags rested on the bulges that betrayed their armaments.

TV cameras recorded every movement; commentators explained every nuance and subtlety of the day's feature event. Anchorman Richard Savory reported. "The scene in St. Patrick's Cathedral is unreal. Believe it or not, there are armed security men here awaiting the arrival of Julio Albanese, the nation's most prominent Mafia leader. We don't know if they were provided by the Cathedral staff or by the Albanese organization, but we can catch glimpses of shoulder holsters underneath their jackets. We are told here that the Cardinal is in Boston and the Chancery has no knowledge of the arrangements. The Cathedral Rector said that, for security reasons, 'we never discuss Cathedral security procedures'."

Janet Webster, an NBC newsperson, then reported directly. "The church has begun to fill with laity, seminarians, and the families of the ordained. The young men to be ordained assembled earlier in the vesting room below the main altar to await this important event in their lives. After years of preparation for the priesthood, they are now vested for the first time in priestly garments. The white albs, cinctures, golden stoles and chasubles have absorbed their personal uniqueness."

"Over here." Father Milton Sharp, Father O'Reilly's young assistant at the Seminary, began to line up the *ordinandi* and priests for the procession. "Priests first, followed by the *ordinandi*, with Bishop Kramer and his assistants taking up the rear."

From a door in the vesting room, auxiliary Bishop Richard Kramer would emerge as soon as he received a signal from the Diocesan staff. Advised by a TV technician that tape footage often portrayed persons as ashen-faced, Kramer agreed to have his face covered with a thin coat of powder and blush. *I can't afford to come across badly on TV. It would be just another nail in my already-leaded coffin.* "Milton, keep an eye open. This is my first ordination, and I don't want to screw it up."

The Cardinal already thought very little of him. One evening, while they were returning from a lawn party in Westchester County, the Cardinal leaned back in his seat and said, "Well, Dick, I hope you'll be a trusted aide of mine for many years to come." This statement was the kiss of death as far as his career in the Church was concerned. The Cardinal had sent him several times, incognito, (he used the name Alberto Winslow) to a drying-out place in the Berkshires. His priesthood was in total shambles. He was the butt of clerical jokes, a pariah among his own. "I wouldn't mind dying," he said in a moment of discouragement. One possibility for saving face with the local clergy would be an assignment in the Vatican, but a tentative inquiry elicited a discouraging comment from a high Vatican official, "There are a lot of alcoholic bishops seeking a limited number of posts."

When first ordained as an auxiliary bishop, Kramer resided in the Cardinal's residence, where he was privy to all that transpired in the archdiocese and enjoyed the glittering dinners and soirees attended by political, Hollywood and social superstars. Abruptly, one evening, as he and the Cardinal were watching a basketball game on television, he received a shock. Without taking his eyes off the TV screen, the Cardinal said, "Dick, the nuns at the Children's Hospital would like a resident priest for their daily 6 a.m. Mass. I checked around and could not find a priest available, so I told them you would move in there by the end of the week. They were thrilled. Sister Marietta, the Superior, will be calling you sometime tomorrow to arrange to move your things to the Hospital." The Cardinal then declared, "This game is boring. I'm going off to bed." There was no dialogue on the subject then, or at any other time. Within two days, Bishop Kramer was sleeping in a small loft above the nuns' quarters.

Bishop Kramer had just downed his scotch when the buzzer rang, signaling that all was in readiness for the ordination. He stood with Crozier in hand and miter firmly placed on his head. He and his aide passed through the door to the Cathedral proper, where he exchanged greetings with the clergy and the *ordinandi* before taking his place at the end of the line. With a clap of the Master of Ceremony's hands the procession began. Choir voices bounced off the Cathedral walls in polyphonic unity. "Christus vincit, Christus regnat."

The stirring music lifted Kramer's spirits and brought to respectful attention the long line of clergy dressed in amice, alb, cincture, stole, maniple and chasuble. The scene provided just that visual excitement that never failed to draw large crowds of the faithful. For this one moment, isolated among a thousand hurtful moments, he felt himself the priest, the shepherd, the successor of Peter, of Christ himself. He was transported to another dimension of time and place.

The reverie, however, was short-lived. His thoughts were sharply interrupted by a din of noise coming from the main entrance to the Cathedral. The Godfather had arrived. From where the Bishop stood, halfway along the side aisle, he could see the bright flashes of popping flashbulbs. In his peripheral vision he was aware of a surge of people in both aisles attempting to catch a glimpse of the Godfather. The shouting and confusion lasted for at least five minutes. To the Bishop, it seemed a lifetime. His eyes blinked in pain as the bulbs exploded continuously. Network crews captured the scene live.

The Bishop could see Julio striding down the center isle, as a phalanx of city policemen, aided by several strong-arm men of the Albanese entourage, cleared a path. He watched in horrified wonder as the Godfather's guards in the choir loft took up positions, ready to draw their firearms. "I don't believe my eyes!" He also shuddered at the thought that at this very moment the Cardinal was watching the chaotic scene from a comfortable seat in the Boston Cardinal's living room. He would now, right now, be the butt of the Cardinal's jokes.

Kramer glanced at Carlo Albanese, standing very still, wrapped in brocaded gold, his head bent, his arms folded in front of him. He marveled at the young man's silence and serenity. For his part, Carlo observed the scene with the full realization that the sudden insertion of chaotic movement into this sacred ambiance would characterize the juxtaposition of his priestly work and Family ties. He was fully aware that this could be repeated, in one form or another, many times. His own nature cried out for order and a quiet priestly life, but he was prepared for inevitable intrusions marked by violence and death. His love for his family would require him to suffer what he despised. He would divide the canvas of his life into two different landscapes.

Jack Carpenter was on the phone hookup with Callahan. "All hell has broken loose here. The Godfather just came to the entrance of the Cathedral and there must have been a hundred photographers waiting around the corner. They sprang out of the woodwork."

Jack could hear Charlie's disgusted, "Oh my God".

Jack was sympathetic "Now listen, Charlie, I know how you feel, but we've got a real problem here. We simply can't allow the newspapers to get all the action, so we've moved our cameras right up the main aisle. The whole containment plan has to be abandoned. Sorry, Charlie, I did what I could."

The police, shoulder to shoulder, created a formidable line of attack. With locked arms they pushed the isolated photographers to the side doors.

"Clear the aisles," shouted Captain Donovan. "Stay in tight formation."

"Yes sir," responded Sergeant Mantico.

The police moved forcefully and, with renewed confidence, got the upper hand. Three cameras fell to the floor, where they were stomped on by the crowd, spreading crushed plastic and glass in every direction. In the choir loft, three invited paparazzi from Sicily, feeling quite at home in the melee, cheered. A tourist standing on the front steps of the Cathedral pointed at the scene and said to his wife. "Honey, they're making a movie in there."

The Albanese family appeared quite unaffected by all the commotion as they filed into pews at the left front section. Julio waved to no one in particular. "It's a great and sacred day for all of us." Nicky and his wife, Lisa, joined Julio, Tina, Tony, Maria, Victor and Grace in the front pew. Nicky saw the ordination as another Carlo adoration event in his life. *I have spent my life lighting candles on his altar. It never ends. Here he is, nephew of the most powerful Mafia Don in the US and no one questions his being ordained to the priesthood. Not a word of criticism from anyone. My own wife glows at the mention of his name. Hell, maybe she is falling for him. I think she's in love with him!* He shifted his legs abruptly in nervous tension. He had grown into manhood confident that Carlo's entry into the seminary would signal the beginning of his own rise in importance in the inner circles of the Family. It did not. In fact, Carlo the priest, it was clear, was going to be the family superstar, the power behind the throne. He tried mightily not to blame Carlo for his good fortune. That, he reasoned, would be unfair. Nevertheless, he needed some stability, some sense of Family security, Family respect, but he did not know if that were possible.

Finally, the aisles were cleared and the procession cautiously began to move along the side aisle toward the main entrance. The clerical gold line now appeared much less majestic. Bishop Kramer was despondent. *I've got to remain dignified throughout all of this.* He was fully aware that the cameras had recorded every nuance of the chaos.

Father Francis offered words of consolation. "Sorry for all of this, Bishop."

"Not your fault, Frank."

The procession had now reached the main entrance and was poised to sweep majestically along the aisle in the direction of the main altar. Father Milton Sharp gave the signal. "We may now proceed."

St. Patrick's Cathedral had finally settled into solemn silence. The police succeeded in moving all of the photographers away from the immediate area of the Albanese family. The organist, inspired by the glittering procession below, created a crash of sound, accompanied by the forceful, floating voices of the best choir the city could muster. As the *ordinandi* approached the altar, the entire congregation rose and clapped in polite, muted tones, perhaps fearful that a louder applause would set off another eruption. The clergy formed a large semi-circle around the main altar. The Bishop, assisted by Father Francis and Father Milton Sharp, moved directly to the altar, and the three of them kissed it simultaneously.

The *ordinandi* prostrated themselves on the floor, their heads buried in their arms. The marbled floor of St. Pat's became the site of their triumph. All was now ready for the ordination. The Bishop invited the *ordinandi* to rise and step forward. He laid both his hands on the heads of each, in silence. They had, at that moment, made the transition from layperson to priest. Then he took each of their hands in his and prayed "whatever they bless may be blessed and whatever they sanctify may remain sanctified."

All now continued to celebrate the Mass together. Finally, Bishop Kramer knelt to receive the First Blessing from the newly ordained, the other priests doing likewise. Julio waited until the Bishop stood aside, then, tear-eyed, knelt to receive his nephew's blessing. Julio gave a blessing of his own. "May God bless you always, Carlo, and all of us through you." Those tears were to appear on every television news show in the Tri-Boro area that very evening, and the next morning on the front page of New York's major newspapers.

Nicky's wall of concern crumbled as he was swept up in the emotions of the moment. Seizing Carlo's hands, he once again gave in and paid homage. "I can't believe all this. I'm so proud of you." Following the family in seeking Carlo's blessing were the heads of the major crime Families in the United States, who had flown into New York for the ordination. "Out of respect" for the religious nature of the occasion, there was to be no post-ordination gathering of Mafiosi members. They were not invited to the Westchester Country Club for the afternoon celebrations. All would return to their respective areas of the country immediately after the ordination. None would make statements to the press.

In wave after emotional wave, relatives and friends knelt before their brothers, sons and friends. It was a moment of magic and signaled the end of the ceremony. The new priests then donned their black clerical garb and filtered out through the several entrances with their families, disappearing in family automobiles into the busy traffic of Fifth Avenue. The ritual had been performed; the priesthood lived on in yet another coterie of men.

Immediately after receiving his nephew's blessing, the Godfather made the sign of the Cross and, flanked by four heavily armed men, left the Cathedral.

Bishop Kramer had been completely ignored by the *ordinandi*, their relatives, and now by the curious tourists who were allowed to wander through the emptying Cathedral. Several visitors from Japan elbowed the Bishop as they rushed to photograph the flower-bedecked altar before the ushers closed the main doors. Father Milton Sharp accompanied the Bishop back to the Cardinal's residence. "Bishop, thank you for the wonderful job you did today, especially considering all the commotion. The Cardinal will be proud of you."

The poor guy is trying to make me feel good. Bless him. The Bishop's stomach rumbled hungrily as he entered the dining room of the Cathedral rectory, where an already departed housekeeper had left a note on the dining room table: "You will find a lunch of bologna, potato salad and potato chips in the fridge." A bottle of the Bishop's favorite whiskey stood on a side-table, the final, humiliating reminder of his low position and his debilitating weakness. It occurred to Bishop Kramer, with both resentment and resignation, that had the Cardinal officiated, the Cathedral dining room would have been very much alive. He would have presided over a dining room table ablaze with majestic candles, laden with fillet mignon, and crowded with luminaries from the political and entertainment world. For him, there was nothing to do but drive home, watch the three o'clock movie on HBO, then take a nap before driving to his cramped quarters at Children's Hospital. That evening he would join the community of nuns for a miserable supper of onion soup and stale crackers.

Chapter Seven
THE RECEPTION

Julio Albanese straightened his back as his driver approached the Hudson Parkway toll bridge, on their way to the Westchester Country Club. He stared blankly into the red-streaked horizon of the warm June afternoon. The color red. How it frightened him, haunting his dreams and interrupting his daytime reveries. At times pools of blood and mangled limbs lay across the landscape of his tortured imagination. They alternately enticed him to lie beside them, and pointed accusing fingers at him. On a tree branch overlooking the Hudson sat a heron, mangling and swallowing a catch in his mouth. He stared studiedly, his beady eyes fixed directly on Julio.

Julio feared death. His Maker would confront him and hold him accountable for his stewardship of an Organization that employed force and assassination as tools of compliance, and dealt in dope and prostitution. He tossed the disquieting images as far away from his consciousness as he could. He prayed that the good he tried to accomplish would, in balance, outweigh the evil. Sister Anacita, his 4th grade teacher in Sicily, taught the class what to say when they were in trouble. It was from Psalm 120, "In my distress I cried to the Lord and He heard me."

A wisp of fog rolled in across the bridge as Julio gathered his inner thoughts. The leafy reflections of the wooded roadside crisscrossed his face as he called out from the rear seat of his limousine to the coin collector, an old neighborhood friend. "Hey, Roger, how are the horses doing these days?" God would put everything in balance. After all, he had moved the Family toward legitimate enterprises, and Carlo's ordination marked a breakthrough in that process. He made the sign of the cross. Today is for celebration. Tiny whispers of consolation filled his heart, as hope for redemption clung like a limpet to his troubled soul.

As an ordination gift to his nephew, Julio had rented the Westchester Country Club for the reception. To the Club's manager he said, "I want the best of everything. My nephew is being ordained a priest." The manager assured him that the reception would be "first class."

Julio's driver, Gambi, turned into the Country Club's long driveway and stopped at the Club's entrance. He noticed that most of the family had already arrived. Someone spotted Julio's car and, from the Club's hedges and lawns, the Family members poured out to welcome him. Carlo's younger cousin, Tracey, her face flushed from running across the lawn, was the first to reach the car. Her diamond studs twinkled at her earlobes and her dress was still billowing as she pulled open the rear door, guiding Julio out of the car. She wrapped her arms around his neck and kissed him on his cheek. "I love you, Uncle. I don't see you often enough."

"Let's talk about that sometime and do something about it. Eh?"

Tracey was delighted. "Oh, yes!"

"I like your dress," Julio said, as he returned her kisses and fingered her long, black hair. Julio was never completely successful in hiding the fact that this girl, not quite eighteen, was his favorite niece. What others did not know was that she reminded him of the girl he did not marry, a girl he dated before he met Tina. Tracey was, like the person from his past, a pretty wisp of a girl with cloudy brown eyes that hinted at sensuality. Her life was enmeshed with the arts – music lessons, art lessons, and ballet lessons. She was preparing herself to be a significant partner, a mother who would lavish her children with the luxury of the finer things of life. Her hands all aflutter, she called, "Uncle Julio, you are so beautiful."

"You are a tease!" He peered over the crowd looking for his nephew. "Tracey, where's our priest? I want to congratulate him."

She flipped a strand of hair away from her eyes. "He's talking with Uncle Tony inside. He'll be right out."

Julio was accustomed, in his fatherly if somewhat autocratic manner, to getting instant responses to his wishes. He wanted to say, "Well, tell him to get out here right away," but held his tongue. Even a godfather had to be careful how he handled a priest. He reflected that he would need to adjust his paternalism to this new situation. Then, as he glanced toward the Club entrance, he saw Carlo coming out to greet him.

"Uncle Julio, how wonderful to see you at the Cathedral this morning!" Carlo pointed to the crowd and table settings, "This great celebration; I....well... thank you, Uncle. You are so kind."

By now, everyone was grabbing at Julio and hugging him. He waved to his brother, Tony. "Hey, Tony, my blessings and congratulations on this wonderful day," he said with open and uplifted arms. "You have given our family a priest! You have given us a great gift, a gift we never dreamed we would receive. In the name of the family, I thank you." Everyone cheered.

Tony received the compliment in his usual modest way, bowing his head in the direction of the godfather and raising his arms in acknowledgment.

His feet shuffled nervously in the dry spring grass. "I thank you my brother and our godfather for your love and care of us."

This exchange marked the opening of the festivities. The Family responded with their feet and hips to the music. A large platform, decorated with bright green laurel boughs and banked with pots of salmon-pink geraniums, held the six-piece orchestra. A swirl of pretty gowns and well-tailored suits moved rhythmically to the strains of the Westchester Six, a popular musical ensemble. Between the dance floor and the West entrance to the clubhouse stretched a red carpet, flanked on either side by round tables covered in white starched damask, adorned with centerpieces of pink camellias. Each table held bottles of red and white Italian wine of excellent vintage, set amidst glistening silver chafing dishes licked by blue flames. White linen dinner napkins were strategically placed for use by the guests. There was a faint smell of pollen in the air.

Food attendants stood quietly waiting to serve and looking very professional in well-tailored black and white uniforms. The women drifted slowly in groups of twos and threes, as their husbands moved towards the outdoor bar. The crowd sipped champagne from glasses offered by circulating waitresses. The ladies animatedly exchanged compliments on their outfits, discussing both designers and prices. They admired each other's jewelry, describing the great occasions upon which they were received. At one point, a ripple of giggles spread among them like grass fire.

Carlo, his mother on his arm, moved from group to group, accepting embraces and giving his priestly blessing. Maria was elegant in her soft beige lace gown. A choker of Majorca pearls adorned her neck, and a matching bracelet covered her wrist. Father Adolfo approached Carlo and knelt to receive his blessing. As if this were the prearranged signal, the ladies brought their children to Carlo for his blessing. Julio watched the scene with great pleasure. He knew that Carlo would play an ever-increasing role in the affairs of the Family. He would fill the vacuum soon to be created by Julio's illness. Carlo's ordination to the priesthood was a setback, but Julio was a man who knew how to wait. He would bide his time for Carlo's "manifest destiny" to manifest itself.

Carlo's mother took him by the hand. "Let's have a dance. I want to make your father jealous!" Carlo valued her sense of humor, a contrast to the quiet seriousness of his father. They were, he thought, well matched. He guided her to the platform, and placed his arms around his mother's waist as they entered the whirlwind of a lively tarantella. The rest of the family stopped dancing and, holding hands, formed a large circle around the priest and his mother, shouting, "*Bene - fantastico - bene*".

Father Adolfo, sitting at table with a starched linen napkin carefully spread over his knees, shouted, "Yes, Carlo, yes!"

To everyone's delight Carlo danced like a pro, turning his mother left and right, back and forth in decidedly confident steps. "See what they're teaching in the seminary these days," observed Father Adolfo, smiling.

Aunt May shouted at Carlo, "What about me?"

Carlo shouted back. "If I had two pair of arms I would dance with both of you at one time."

Everyone laughed and clapped. The Family resumed dancing. The tempo speeded up. Round and round they went, until some of the dancers sank, exhausted, to the polished floor. Those standing on the lawn beside the dance floor cheered. Some of the young men shouted, "Nice, Carlo! Show us your stuff! You should have a girlfriend!"

Even the Godfather joined in. "Let all the girls eat their hearts out!"

Waiters weaved in and out with large stainless steel trays bearing steaming platters of *aragosta* and *scampi, risotto* and *scaloppini*. Other trays were loaded with Italian pepper sausage, *lasagna, ravioli* and stuffed *manicotti*. The tossed Italian salads smelled of fennel and fresh garlic. Desserts were arrayed on separate tables - trays of cassata, fedora, gelato, and torta. Some of the dancers drifted over and sampled the tempting assortment. Nearby, a third table held an enormous basket of early summer flowers that added to the visual beauty of the setting.

Julio shouted out in a shrill voice, "*Mangiamo, mangiamo*," leading the way to the heavily laden tables.

As the Family began to eat, the orchestra struck up, "O Solo Mio," Julio's favorite. Between mouthfuls of food, everyone began to sing the verses, shouting for the Godfather to dance with his wife. "Julio and Tina, Julio and Tina, Julio and Tina!" they cried, clapping their hands in rhythm.

Julio and Tina obliged. As he whirled past the circling Family, he shouted out to the children. "Come boys and girls, learn the words of our national anthem. You can't call yourselves Italian unless you can sing this song." He continued chatting in an animated exchange with Family members, raising both hands, setting his weight first on one foot then on the other. The dancing and eating continued for several hours, as the earthy smell of newly-mowed lawns gave sensuous fragrance to the warm June evening. The "small party" his uncle Julio had promised turned out to be a very big party indeed, but Carlo was happy. He loved nothing more than a family celebration - no artificial conversations or body language, no pretensions. He needed the love and security that only the family can give.

He stood alone for a few minutes. It was now late afternoon and the crowd thinned. Those who remained were completing their last round of dances. The servers were beginning to clear the tables. The sun was just above the horizon, and the air had a touch of coolness. The tree-lined borders of the expansive lawn began to meld into the early twilight. Shadows stretched across the lawn and several blue jays winged in and out of the weeping willows that occasionally broke the open expanse of lawn. The air was perfumed with young poplar leaves, roses and lilacs. A soft rustling behind Carlo was followed with a lilting, "Hi."

Carlo suddenly became aware of his sister-in-law standing in front of him. "Oh, my God, I didn't see you coming," as he gave her a familial hug and kiss on the proffered cheeks. Lisa wore a neatly pleated challis skirt splashed with summer hues of peach. Her blouse was softly tailored and trimmed with elaborate but delicate embroidery. In the softening light her skin was milky white. Her shiny black hair rolled down along and around her shoulders. Her dark, penetrating eyes, sprouting a thicket of lashes, were set far apart. Even in the dimming light Carlo saw a hint of sorrow in eyes that did not sparkle. Something about the contour of her lips conveyed sensuality. Her composure conveyed vibrations of suffering borne alone. She released a breath quickly in forced relaxation and said, "Please, Carlo, may I see you tomorrow? I need to talk to you."

Carlo stared and drank in her presence. It was not the first time she had transfixed his gaze. The roving searchlight of his eyes swept gently across her frame as the warm scented air reflected the muted hum of insects in flight. *What happens to me when I see her? What the hell is going on in my psyche? This is my brother's wife. I've just been ordained a priest! Yet I want her.* Try as he may, it seemed impossible to disobey the aching and the yearning, as Nicky's words came back to haunt him. In the open expanse of lawn the evening shadows danced on her hair and lovely face. In the distance a small, short-tailed doe loped on the edge of the woods, alone. "Yes Lisa, of course. I'm free until I receive my assignment. I'll expect you tomorrow."

Lisa was grateful. "Oh, thank you Carlo. What about ten o'clock at your house? Is that OK with you?" She took his hand in hers and her warmth seeped into his palms, relaxing him.

She spoke so softly that Carlo leaned his shoulder and head toward her, catching the scent of her perfume. "Fine," he said, placing one hand on her neck, but avoiding eye contact.

Lisa continued to stare at him, unable to look away. Her silence was as soft as down. She reached out and laid her hands on his folded arms. Then, absorbed in her own thoughts, she turned and walked across the lawn, softly, yet rhythmically as if in a minuet. Looking back, she said, "Love you."

A startled Carlo continued to watch her sensuous walk, and inhaled the lingering scent of her gardenia perfume trapped in his nostrils. Her departure was a vacuum he filled with longing. Desire ran through his body, causing him to recall the old saying, "Sicilians have so few brakes." It had always been a source of uneasiness and irritation to him that his brother did not seem to appreciate this beautiful and warm woman. At the same time he was aware, deep within his subconscious, of a willingness, an eagerness, to be Lisa's comforter, should the marriage dissolve.

From across the lawn, Nicky observed, with increasing alarm, the interactions between his wife and his brother, but reserved judgment on its meaning. He had determined to put his emotions aside and embrace Carlo. As Lisa joined Julio and Tina, Nicky approached his brother. "*Fratello mio.* Carlo, you are the only celibate in this crowd and you have more women running after you than anyone else. I think I'll get into this celibate thing myself!" He playfully jabbed his fist into Carlo's waist. "Your ordination was just great, brother of mine, just great. You know I put off my trip so I wouldn't miss it. We're all proud of you."

For a moment they wrestled with each other as they had done so many times growing up in the small house near St. Anthony's. Carlo changed the mood. "Listen, Nicky, there are things you and I have to talk about when you get back from California. Let me know when you get in, OK?"

"Ooh, sounds serious. Important?"

Carlo was evasive. "Well, kinda private stuff, you know."

Nicky jabbed again. "No preaching?"

Carlo spoke firmly. "No preaching."

"Deal."

Carlo felt pangs of guilt as he embraced his brother. He was unable to subdue the feelings he had for Lisa. Nicky had warned him about the overpowering sexuality of the Sicilian genetic. How ironic that it was his wife that had brought that out in him.

The orchestra started up again for the last time. The children began pairing off on the dance floor, and Carlo noticed that they moved nimbly when Italian music was being played. A professor of anthropology at the Seminary had said, "We're a lot more than what we eat, but sometimes what we eat says a lot about who we are."

Carlo recalled responding, "There's a lot of food for thought in that statement!"

The tired voices of the Family were muted now. Small groups were beginning to gather together and move out to their automobiles. Carlo approached each group, kissing and embracing all. "I will notify all of you as soon as I get word of my appointment." He knew that they were hoping he would be assigned to St. Anthony's.

"I will bring you all the Italian food you want if you get stuck in an American' parish," his Aunt May shouted, as her car slowly moved past him. The June evening pressed in on Carlo, increasing the sensuality of his attraction to his brother's wife. *How vulnerable I am to her.*

Tina joined her husband in the back of their limousine as a bodyguard occupied a front seat. Turning to her husband she said, "What a beautiful day this has been, darling. We've got a priest in the family now. Isn't that marvelous?"

Julio went through the motions of agreeing, while staring out across the lawn, his eyes squinting into the lowering sun. Why didn't God choose one of the other children instead? This `mistake', he was convinced, would lead to much heartache in the life of Carlo Albanese. He took one last look at Carlo as he stared into the dwindling daylight. Julio could only guess what was going through his nephew's mind. Carlo's life will be very hard, but that is the sacrifice he must make for the Family. It is his destiny and none of us can do anything about it. It is God's will.

Chapter Eight
LISA AND NICKY

Lisa arrived for her appointment with Carlo the morning after the ordination. Dressed in a tight bodice and swirling skirt, Lisa embraced Carlo, imprinting his cheeks with a dab of lipstick. She squeezed her curves between the cupboard and a kitchen chair, joining him at the breakfast table. She looked out at him from long eyelashes, her eyes deep brown, flecked with gold, her face framed in soft, curling hair. "I love these bran muffins your mother makes." Lisa felt the heat of Carlo's eyes falling on her. She returned his glances, admiring his plain white T-shirt covering a lean torso framed by brown and sinewy arms.

"Coffee with your muffin?" he asked.

"Is it fresh?"

"Almost."

"OK, but plenty of cream."

Carlo's pressed blue jeans and simple white socks highlighted the length of his slender legs as he stood in a wedge of light slanting in from the east. He was, for her, a real man, his head a Greek sculpture, his eyes beguiling charmers. As she sipped her coffee, she explained the reason for her visit. "Carlo, it's about, Nicky. I'm going to leave him. I hate to tell you this the day after your ordination, but it just turned out that way." With downcast eyes and soft lips, she propped her forehead against the open palm of her hand, her long black hair cascading along her bared arms. Her sadness was somewhat relieved by her conviction that she had found a reservoir of strength and self-awareness to make a very difficult decision and stick to it.

Carlo reacted with genuine surprise. "Lisa, I knew you didn't have an ideal marriage, but I had no idea things had gotten as bad as this." He glanced at his shoes. "A separation in our family is very rare. I really don't recall that we've ever had a wife leave her husband." He experienced a certain amorphous advantage in her distress, a seeping selfishness tinged with sensuality, which he moved quickly to contain. "Lisa, when did all this trouble begin?"

She stared vacantly at her palms, her head drooping to one side as she fought back tears. Her face was solemn and withdrawn, almost rigid, and her lips trembled. "Carlo, we've had problems for about three years, and I keep forgiving him and we keep making up, but I can't take it any longer." In a flood, she spilled her emotions, pouring out her hurt and disillusionment. "Nicky is on cocaine; Nicky likes to slap me around when he has been drinking; Nicky calls other women, sometimes, even from our bedroom if he thinks I'm asleep. It has just been horrible." The pain in her face was even more expressive than her words.

Carlo was moved. "I'm so sorry. I didn't know."

"Carlo, you have to understand I'm a person on my own. I have my own rights."

He let his eyes travel from the top of her head, along her frame, down to her toes, drifting back and forth, with a comforting smile on his lips. "Of course." He placed both hands gently on her shoulders, his admiring gaze now blanketing her face. Then, gently, he released her.

She flung her palms up to head height and spoke with frustration, "I'm not a trophy on Nicky's mantelpiece. I don't intend to be kept under glass, a toy he comes and plays with when he's in the mood, or when another girl lets him down."

Carlo fought his own emotions as he cautioned, "Lisa, why don't you wait until Nicky gets home and talk it out with him? Then move out, if you can't settle your differences."

Lisa shook her head and continued to wipe away tears. "If I wait until Nicky gets home and then tell him, he wouldn't let me out of the house. You don't know your brother. You live in a different world. Your brother thinks he owns me - a piece of property. The Albanese men treat their women like crap. Only your father and Uncle Julio show their wives any real respect. The others think they are living in seventeenth century Sicily. I refuse to take it any longer."

Genuinely, "I strongly support you on that."

She folded her hands and glanced upward. "Thank God we don't have children. I wanted a child, Carlo, you can understand that, but Nicky didn't, and now I'm glad." Her brown eyes magnified in the wash of tears that trickled down her cheeks. "I want to live, not just be someone's woman. I need to find out who I really am. The image of me as Nicky's wife is dead now and it'll never return." She stopped to wipe her eyes with tissue, fixing her gaze on his shoe tips. "My marriage is a cage I need to break out of."

"I'm so sorry." Silence draped them as they stood close to each other. She nodded her head, then lowered it to her chest. He put his hands in hers. "I wish I could wave away all of your pain."

She stepped back and fanned an open hand. "I'm so fed up with everything. I went into this marriage with such high hopes and now everything has fallen apart."

As Carlo listened, concentrating on her presence, there occurred at the level of his imagination, a transparent sensuousness that until recently had remained obligingly opaque. Doubting his own sincerity he said: "I'm really sorry, Lisa," his dark eyes reflecting the restraint he imposed upon himself. As the conversation continued, he wanted to touch her body. The sensation brought him a greater awareness of his own masculinity than he had ever experienced. As a distraction, he stretched his arm above his head, his powerful shoulders straining against the fabric of his shirt.

He tried to focus as she continued. "Nicky has never been an attentive husband. I guess a wife can learn to live with that, and recently he admitted what I had suspected for a long time. He's seeing other women." Lisa lit a cigarette and fingered the belt buckle at her waist as she crossed her shapely legs. It tugged at her heart to disclose her problems with Nicky, but she had had enough of his philandering. "About two months ago, I went to meet Nicky at LaGuardia. He was returning from California. He wasn't expecting me to meet him. I knew the flight number so I just drove out to the airport. Well, Carlo, Nicky came strolling into the terminal with his arms around a young girl who was falling out of her dress - maybe eighteen, maybe nineteen. He had a hand on one of her tits, and they were laughing and joking together."

Carlo slapped his right hand against his forehead "Damn, what a fool; he's acting like an ass."

Lisa palmed her waistline and tilted her face to look straight at Carlo. "My stomach went sick. I just ran out of there before he could see me, and I drove home. Nicky got in after midnight and when I asked him where he had been, he said Uncle Julio had met him at the airport and they had gone directly to a meeting. Carlo, I've accepted lies like this a hundred times. This time I simply told him straight out not to lie to me anymore, that I'd been at the airport and had seen him with this young girl."

Her plaintive eyes pulled at his heartstrings. "What did he say?"

"It was none of my business. He was a grown man and didn't want me spying on him. You know, Carlo, sometimes I wonder if he tries to dominate me and feels free to womanize so much because he doesn't have any power in the Family. Maybe he needs to feel he can be someone's boss. But, I'm no psychiatrist, and I sure don't want to stay with him just to figure him out."

Carlo placed his hands on hers as she talked. Then for a moment he put one arm around her shoulders, letting his right hand sweep along the length

of her black hair. He angled his body as if shielding her from harm.
"Sounds like Nicky lives in a dream world. That's what happens to some
guys when they go on ego trips." Carlo reached for her and held her tightly.
"I'm so sorry."

His embrace comforted her like the first soft breeze of spring. Tears filled
her eyes as she struggled to speak calmly, pressing her fingers into her
palms. "After that, I began to think about what I should do. I know it's a
disgrace in this family for a husband and wife to separate, but I also know
it's a disgrace for a woman to live this way. I'm taking another apartment
before Nicky gets back and I don't want him to know where I am."

"Lisa, it's hard to believe Nicky would behave like this, but it does
remind me that violence is part of our lives, the way to solve all our
problems, including family problems. That's where we are at this point."

Carlo looked at his sister-in-law with profound sympathy, as their
physical closeness began to dissipate shyness. She was so sad, so lost, so
vulnerable. He felt a love for her that was not entirely familial. "Lisa, once
you are safely in your new apartment, Uncle Julio will take some action on
this. I'll talk with him tonight. You may need protection. The family owes
you this. Call me if you need anything, or if you're just afraid."

As she prepared to leave, they faced each other and embraced. This time
he pressed the palm of his right hand firmly against her lower back, her
limbs lightly touching his. She blushed but looked into his eyes with
obvious affection. "You're so nice," she said, as she cupped his face in her
hands. She could feel his heat and it stirred her. Her eyes were as warm as
soft light in a darkened room.

Carlo accompanied Lisa to her car and followed the outline of her body
as she drove off.

She could feel his eyes like heat patches. *There is another person hiding
inside him, a more humane person, one who can love a woman, any
woman?... just me?* It was at least another hour before the hot blood slowed
in her veins.

Carlo felt caught up in the winds of a personal history, floating toward an
eventual destination decided by the gods. He could see Lisa, like a
mountain, looming over the valley of his needs. He was certain of one
thing. He was about to become immersed in the real life of the Albanese
family. It was, for him, inevitable and, in some sensuous way, desirable.
Being an Albanese was, for him, a narcotic.

That night Lisa fell into bed, her body weary and aching from the
emotional strain of recent events. But, there was one consolation. *I feel
someone understands me, and cares about my feelings and what happens to
me.*

Carlo called Julio and asked to see him. "Come right out. It'll be good to see you. Come." Carlo felt a tinge of excitement each time he visited Julio. Julio's strong and decisive personality energized him. Tina greeted him as she answered the door. "Why, Carlo, this is such a nice surprise. Your uncle will be so pleased to see you. Did he know you were coming?"

"Yes, he did."

Tina feigned a pout. "Imagine, after all these years there are still things that your Uncle Julio does not confide to his wife. Isn't that awful?"

Tina not only loved her husband; she also respected and admired him. If Julio had not been the head of the Organization he would, in her opinion, have been an excellent lawyer, doctor or priest. In the course of their life together she had met, in their home and in Julio's Plaza Hotel suite, senators, judges, union bosses - even the Secretary of Labor. But none of the learned men she had met had the unique combination of intelligence and wisdom, graced with the compassion that Julio possessed. He was also a lover of Italian opera, spending hours listening to his valuable collection of Caruso recordings. He told Tina: "Salvatore Maranzano, who organized the first Mafia family in New York, sang operatic arias every time he had a problem to solve. It calmed his nerves." Salvatore was one of Julio's heroes. "After all, he divided the city into various districts so we wouldn't be shooting each other up. Sicilian, Italian, Sicilian, Italian, killing each other. *Stupido!*"

Julio's voice bellowed from the second floor. "I will be right down. Give me a minute."

Tina whispered, "He's had a sleepless night and I'm a bit concerned about him."

Julio was admiring the sea from the large bay window in his bedroom. The day wore a light blue sky. He stared at the sea-grass swaying in the breeze to the right and left, and an airborne gull's fluttering wings. He could hear Carlo downstairs and did not mind pulling himself away. He listened as his wife pleaded with his nephew. "Ask him to slow down. He's not well and he's running the Organization as if he's twenty years younger and in excellent health." She was about to say more, when Julio appeared at the landing.

"Well, here we are."

The two men embraced and Julio suggested, pointing the way, "Let's go into my den. Don't listen to your aunt. She worries too much. Come."

Carlo loved the sight of that den, walled with books of literature, politics and science. He knew his uncle to be an insatiable reader and a first

class intellect. The room somehow defined him. It was a decidedly masculine room, with four large black leather chairs, the kind found in men's
clubs all across America. A large stone fireplace, the room's centerpiece,
rose to meet the wooden beamed ceiling. It was here that Julio retreated
from the many demands of his office, sipping what he called "peasant"
wines, as distinguished from the expensive brands. Julio sat and invited
Carlo to do likewise. "Now, Carlo, tell me what's on your mind."

Carlo breathed deeply and exhaled noisily. "Nicky's acting like a damn
fool, messing-up his marriage with Lisa. She said she's going to move into
an apartment before he gets back from California, and I OK'd it. After all,
Uncle, there is no excuse for abusing a woman, and it's not in our family
tradition. Respect for the mothers of our children and the consolers of our
men has always been part of the statement we make about ourselves."

Julio noted that Carlo took the initiative to OK her leaving her husband, a
rare occurrence. No one ever took an action concerning another member of
the family without prior reference to the Julio's wishes. Ordinarily, that
would be a reason for punishment but, in this case, it was exactly what Julio
wanted. "What the hell has he been up to?"

Carlo explained. "For starters, he is whoring around; he beats her; he
smokes pot; he sometimes wants to have kinky sex with her "for fun," stuff
a decent man should not ask a woman to grant. The list is long. Now is the
time to act, to put a stop to this nonsense. Lisa, in her mind, is a liberated
woman; now she needs to translate that into physical liberation. We need
you to speak out on the subject. I'm asking you, dear Uncle, to take action
right away, before Nicky returns."

They discussed Julio's options as equals. Carlo suggested, "What about
an apartment, uptown? The seventies, on the East Side, is a good location."

Julio nodded. "Yes, that is a good area. I'll get on this right away. In the
meantime, my dear nephew, get yourself back to the parish and take care of
your work. I'm sure Father Adolfo could use a couple of days off! I keep
you informed. OK?"

Carlo was pleased that Julio understood the gravity of the situation, and
that they worked together in harmony. That's how it's going to be from now
on.

Shortly after Carlo's departure, Julio spent some time talking to realtors,
and decided on a location on 72nd Street. Then, he phoned Victor. After explaining the circumstances, he instructed him. "Look, Lisa is going to separate from him, at least for a while. Send somebody to keep a watch on her.
I'm going to put her in an apartment at 346 East 72nd Street. Put one of
your men out there, let's say, Giorgio, to watch her. Tell him to keep his

mouth shut about this. We want to make sure Nicky doesn't know where she is, at least not until I put the fear of God into him. Lisa was born and brought up in this country. She doesn't want to live like our Sicilian women, and I don't blame her."

Victor was not convinced that one bad marriage should lead to actions that would begin to loosen family ties, but he had no intention of arguing. "All right, Julio. Will do."

Nicky Albanese was enjoying his flight to California. He was proud of his accomplishments. There were very few men of his age, or any age, that flew First Class when they traveled. The isolation and quiet of the flight afforded him an opportunity to think about the problems with his wife. For him, the heart of the problem was sex. She did not understand the difference between sex and love. She did not understand men. He had tried to explain his occasional infidelity. "It has nothing to do with love, I tell you!" he would insist. "I do love you, but you don't try to satisfy me. You're too cold. If I ask you for oral sex you look at me like I'm something dirty. So, I take care of those needs elsewhere. Try to understand."

"Never," was her uncompromising response.

On another occasion he said, "Why do you wear such drab dresses around the house. When we go out you dress sexy, but I can't have sex with you in restaurants. In the house you wear those old faded dresses? It's in the house I want to get aroused."

But Lisa did not understand. "Did you marry me for love or for hot sex?"

"Both."

He remembered Lisa slamming the palms of her hands on the kitchen table. "That's bullshit."

He had his own question. "What did you marry me for? Security and boredom?"

Lisa shook her head in annoyance. "I won't waste time answering such a stupid question."

Their problems intensified and he found it increasingly difficult to hold everything together. Another irritant for Nicky was the growing homage paid by the family to his brother Carlo. He tried not to be jealous of him; in fact, he loved him. But the rumors that Carlo was destined to play a much larger role in Family activities could not help but further damage Nicky's already wounded ego. He did not believe in astrology, but he was convinced that some heavenly influence was causing the long string of bad luck that plagued him. But, at the moment, he was flying First Class over the Rockies, while flirting with a pretty airhostess. He shook his worries loose from his mind, putting unpleasant thoughts aside and ordering bourbon on the rocks.

"Yes sir." The airhostess looked at him with cat-like, almond-shaped eyes, admiring his handsome frame and self-assurance.

He wished aside his problems. Why should I be worried about a non-cooperative wife. The world is full of beautiful women. He felt a sudden surge of exhilaration, as he opened two more buttons on his shirt, exposing his hairy chest dotted with two gold chains. This is the life. His family had insured him a plateau of success which men his age could only dream about.

As he exited the cab at the hotel entrance, Nicky felt the strength of belonging to a wealthy and powerful Family. He not only belonged to the Family but, by virtue of birth, ranked in its highest echelon. Staying at the Hilton was just one of its benefits. Nicky paused in admiration of the large stone entrance lined with stately palm trees shipped in from Cuba. The hotel consisted of twin towers, each ten stories high, built around an open courtyard and connected by a gracefully arched arcade. A hotel brochure claimed that its popularity was due to the fact that both the architecture and interior design reflected local themes and scenes. He could not help but compare it with New York hotels; the Big Apple can be just plain ugly. After settling in his room and showering, he dressed in his blue blazer and summery white slacks, then headed for the restaurant, an elegant and cool atmosphere highlighted by pastel colors. The subdued lighting brought out the subtle pale floral that covered the walls.

A waiter appeared out of nowhere, dressed crisp and starchy. "Your table, sir."

Nicky had not called for a reservation. *They've gotten the word I'm here. I love it.*

The *maitre'd* had been given his photograph by management and instructed to "take special care of this guest." The attention was just one more reason why he was happy to be an Albanese.

At dinner he noticed a lovely woman in a white blouse and pink ruffled skirt sitting at a nearby table. His eyes quickly encompassed her, assessing her beauty. She stole a glance at him and he met it, pursing his lips as he moved his eyes up and down along her frame. She lifted a water goblet and paused, holding it in mid-air as she chatted with a waiter. Her breasts appeared as tight fists pushing against the white blouse. After sipping from the goblet, she leaned forward to place a tissue in her over-sized shoulder bag resting on the floor, exposing her cleavage. A high hemline accentuated slender legs curved beneath laced hose, her hair a mass of loosely falling curls. Her carefully applied makeup gave the illusion of not being there. A bit of shadow was all she had applied to her eyelids. It did not interfere with the blush color of her high cheekbones. In contrast, her long, honey blonde hair lay loosely on her shoulders, excitingly unkempt. *I love girls who don't give a damn about their hair. They've learned it's not what a man looks at.* He asked for the wine steward, who promptly arrived wearing his chain and tastevin. Pointing to the pretty girl, Nicky gave instructions. "Please bring a bottle of your best white zinfandel to that young lady, with my compliments."

The girl nodded her head in acknowledgment, flattered by his unabashed interest in her. His tanned skin was pulled tightly over his cheekbones, giving him the aura of a handsome athlete. She was very conscious of his masculinity but tried to hide her noticing. After several more exchanges of glances, Nicky approached her table. "No one drinks wine alone. May I join you?"

"It looks like you already have."

Bibi Cash had saved for a month to treat herself to dinner at the Hilton, a dining spot for many of Los Angeles' political and social elite. *Perhaps somebody important will notice me.*

Nicky sat across from her and said, "Thanks. It's tough to be alone when away from home."

He liked her eyes, the eyelids shaded modestly, having just the right effect. Her lips were colored a light pink and outlined with a slightly darker shade. *Here's a girl who takes good care of herself.*

Bibi had thoughts of her own.. *This guy is handsome and smooth. Maybe he'll pick up the tab and I can come back next week. What the hell?* His smoothness hinted at experience she could only imagine "Thanks for the wine, but I don't allow myself to be picked up."

She's not someone who hides behind a face mask of makeup. She is gutsy.

He turned her words into a compliment. "I could tell you wouldn't; that's what makes you so attractive."

"I haven't heard that one before. Not bad." She masked her growing vulnerability.

Nicky pressed on. "Look, I'm alone. Here on business. Let's just have dinner together, instead of separately. Simple. No complications. I like having dinner with a pretty girl. Something wrong with that?"

"Not if you're paying." *He seems like the type who likes sassy girls, so let me give it a try.*

"Couldn't spend my money on a prettier girl." *She's gutsy. I love it.*

"You tell that to all the girls you try to make?"

Nicky raised his hands to his forehead. "Oh, oh, I guess I shoulda waited a while before passing out compliments. Irritated you?"

"Not really, I love compliments. Women live on compliments."

Nicky stared at her eyes. "I don't follow your logic."

"You're not supposed to. That's what makes us females."

"Oh...well...I guess so. Whatever you say."

Observing his frown, "Don't feel badly. Women can't figure out women either." *I'm getting to like this guy.*

"What is your name?"

"Bibi."

Leaning toward her and pointing his finger, "OK, Bibi, let me try again. Would you have dinner with me?"

"Yes, if your intentions stop there."

He finessed her remark. "No real man's intentions ever stop there, but you're in control, so there's no problem." A mischievous glint floated on the surface of his eyes.

She felt the palms of her hands moistening and her heart throbbing. A dreamy fog settled over her. She knew that a certain willingness to be compromised was seeping into her consciousness. Only two other men in her life had caused her to drop her defenses so quickly. *This guy has class. I wonder what he does for a living.*

She's got lavender eyes. Incredible! Nicky shook a cigarette loose from his pack and offered it to her. She accepted and bent close to his chest to catch the flame of his cigarette lighter. Her bosom grazed the buttons of his shirt. *Is she teasing me?*

Tipping her head back and lifting her shiny hair off her neck, she blew a small puff of smoke that glanced off his cheek. She was enjoying the mood engendered by candlelight, expensive linens and wine.

She asked, "What brings you to Los Angeles? I can spot out-of-towners. I work at a travel bureau."

"Family business."

Languidly, "And what kind of business is that?"

Nicky reached for an answer. "Ah, ah...we do security trading."

Wanting to flatter, "Wow, that sounds interesting, but I don't have the foggiest notion what it is!"

Nicky spoke solemnly. "My dear, neither do I."

They both giggled.

Nicky suggested, "Let's dance a bit to work up an appetite," to which she offered her hand. He led her onto the dance floor already crowded with hotel guests.

She cautioned, "I expect you want to dance, not wrestle." He only smiled softly. Gripping his fingertips, she took long, graceful strides as he moved her to the center of the crowd. She was unobtrusively sexy, and her blood was fired up like a furnace.

"You're a princess."

"That's a new one," she chided. "Who taught you to say that? An older brother? An experienced uncle?"

"I'm serious. I mean that's how I feel."

She smiled. "Well, even if it isn't true it's nice to hear."

Slowly and gently he pressed her slim waist to his, let her loose, pressed again, each press lasting longer than the previous one. As he swept her in a wide arc along the dance floor his tousled hair spread across his forehead. She reached out and swept it back. "Don't hurt me," said with a smile.

The warm and teasing tone of her voice excited him. "You like gentle men?"

She shook her head. "I wouldn't want to generalize."

His arched eyebrows preceded the question. "Just what does that mean?"

Her eyes sparkled. "I can imagine the kind of man I would not mind being a teeny bit roughed up by!"

Nicky pressed his forefinger into his cheekbone. "Do I fit that description?"

She smiled coyly. "I doubt it."

"You're not absolutely sure?"

"Ahh…no, just my gut feelings."

Electricity was now passing between them. Her head nestled onto his neck, her hand pressed mid-way between his shoulders. Her cheek was warm and silky, her aroma spicy. He murmured. He bracketed her slim waist with both hands. "You feel nice. Very feminine."

Bibi exhaled a soft, "Oooh" trying not to appear vulnerable, but her control was slipping away. His cologne filled her nostrils. Absorbing the sensual heat from his skin, she fingered his broad chest, feeling his heartbeat. Her nerve endings tingled, her legs weakened.

Cocking his head, he pulled her back." Will you spend the night with me?"

She drew back. "Depends."

"On what?"

"How I feel after dinner and dancing. Treat me nice."

He spoke with assurance. "Like a queen."

She was Cinderella, living a dream she feared would come to an abrupt end at the sound of midnight bells. Her breathing became uneven as he swept her from one fairy tale to another. *I'm at his mercy. I'll do anything for him. Crazy.*

Nicky buried his face along her blonde curls, moving until his brown eyes confronted hers of lavender, as a tiny silence overwhelmed them. A smile rippled along the curve of his lips. Her breathing aroused his masculinity. She was a rose unfolding to his warm and sensual touch.

Bibi assessed him for a few moments, then teased; "Do I bring out the man in you?"

Nicky smiled. "Mmm." He folded his arms tighter around her neck as she fit herself into his enclosure. He felt her longing and pressed firmer.

She gave in. "Please, take me to your room now!"

This would be another exciting night in the life of Nicky Albanese, a man on the rise, a man related to wealth and power, a man who could have anything he wanted.

At the moment of Nicky's triumph, Julio was calling his *consigliere*, Bruno Battaglia. "Bruno, I want you to track down Nicky for me. He's out in California. Get him here as soon as possible. I want to see him."

"I know where he is. I'll get him."

"Good. Make it tonight."

Bruno called the Los Angeles Hilton. It was near 10 p.m. in New York. With the time differential, it was late enough for Nicky to have arrived from the East Coast, but there was no answer. Bruno continued dialing, once on the half-hour until midnight when, finally, the phone rang only twice and Nicky answered.

"Hello."

"Nicky, this is Bruno. How are you?"

The call evoked surprise. "Hey, Bruno, how'd you know I just got in? I'm ready for the shower and bed. What's up?"

"Are you alone?"

Nicky replied solemnly. "Yes, of course. I'm a married man. What else would you expect?"

"Yeah, Yeah." *The kid's lying through his teeth.*

In as pleasant a voice as he could muster, Bruno gave him the message. "Nicky, Julio wants you to get on the next flight from L. A. to New York. In fact, I've already booked you. It's American Airlines, Flight 789, leaving at 2am. - a Red Eye flight - so, please be on it. I'll meet you at LaGuardia. Flight arrives at 10.15"

Nicky protested angrily. "Are you people crazy? Has my uncle lost his mind? I've got at least a week of work to do out here. I can't possibly come back now." He slapped the bed with a tight, white-knuckled fist.

"Listen Nicky, I don't like this anymore than you do. So, please, don't make it more difficult than it already is."

"I can't leave at the middle of the bloody night. I'm exhausted. I need some sleep."

Bruno lowered his voice to a whisper and said, deliberately, "Nicky, the Boss wants you to come home, and he wants you on that flight. There'll be trouble if you don't show up. I guarantee you that. I can't tell you anymore right now."

There was a long pause at the other end of the line, and then, in frightened stubbornness, "OK, Bruno, OK, but I think this is so stupid." He slammed the phone down like an enemy but, reluctantly, internalized the message.

Bibi was curious. "Who was that?"

Sulking, "The family lawyer, a real pain."

"Don't pout at me. I don't have anything to do with it." Her smiling face and sultry voice soothed his angry mood.

"You're even nicer than I thought, but I have to leave immediately. Our lawyer has already booked me on a flight and I just have time to make it. "If I miss the plane I'm in trouble. I promise I'll come back soon and we'll spend some quality time together. OK"

Pouting, "If I'm in the mood."

"Of course."

After Bibi left, he showered and shaved, applied Brut to his smooth face with a heavy hand, and dressed quickly.

The waiting lounge at American Airlines was crowded as passengers from Flight 789 poured out of the gate area. Nicky was one of the first to emerge.

Bruno called out, "Hey, Nicky, over here."

"Bruno, what the hell is this all about? The old man must be going off his rocker. He's the one who sent me out there. I barely get unpacked and I'm back on the damn plane. What kind of game is he playing?"

Bruno was soft, as he put his arms around the godfather's nephew. "Take it easy, kid. You know that Julio doesn't do dumb things. We're driving right out to his place. He's waiting for you. Do you want to use the men's room or get something to eat, first?"

"I'm not hungry. Who the hell could be hungry in this kind of nutty situation?"

Bruno's words had clearly disturbed him. He quickly reviewed in his mind the recent dealings in the Family business, but could not come up with anything that would call for this extraordinary meeting. There was a chill of fear and foreboding in his stomach. He knew that Julio typically never saw anyone in the middle of the night, except Tony or Victor, and only for emergencies. It would be useless to question Bruno further, so he leaned back in his seat and lit a cigarette.

The streets of Manhasset were quiet and empty. In the foggy atmosphere, the streetlights appeared as disembodied glowing balls. Here and there they highlighted the glitter of broken glass or discarded fast food containers lying in the gutters. At first, they drove through the populated working class area, where the night streets were crowded with shadows and objectionable smells. Some minutes later they met the open expanse of woods and lawns dotted with the homes of the rich and powerful. Bruno's Cadillac moved into Julio's flower-bedecked courtyard, where roses, azaleas and begonias competed with each other for "scent of the evening."

Julio could be seen in the frame of the open front door. Nothing about his demeanor suggested trouble. "Come in, come in, fellows. I've got some good wine for everyone."

Bruno disliked wine at that time of day. It often clouded his mind and made his note-taking much more difficult. (Julio insisted that Bruno take extensive notes) Gambi took up his usual position, near the front door. The other three moved into the den.

As he settled into his chair, Julio motioned the two men to sit down. He handed each of them a glass of wine. "Drink up. Relax."

Nicky tugged his blue silk tie loose from his collar and took a sip of wine. "Uncle, why did you bring me all the way back from California before I got any work done? Seems crazy."

Julio tossed him a stern, silencing frown. "Listen, Nicky, I've got some bad news for you, and I want you to take it like a man. I also want you to follow my instructions to the letter. I don't want to be explaining the same thing to you over and over again. I don't have time for that. I need to focus on the work of the Organization, not on your problems. You hear me?"

Nicky sweated in anticipation, and managed an almost inaudible, "Yes, Uncle."

Julio put down his wineglass. "Good. Now, I'm going to be brief, so listen carefully. Lisa has moved out of your apartment."

Nicky stiffened, the news giving color to his frightened, paled face. Julio continued, "I personally ordered her to do this. I've settled her in a good Manhattan neighborhood."

Nicky took a deep breath, dug his fingers into his thigh and leaned further back in his chair, but said nothing. He spread his hands and shrugged his shoulders in resignation, as his teeth nibbled at his lower lip. He experienced a rumble of the anxiety and anger that had been building in him since childhood.

Julio continued, fixing an icy gaze on his nephew. "Number one, I don't want you to look for her, or try to make any trouble in the family. Right now, she does not want to live with you because you have been a lousy husband. You hear me? Lousy!" Julio's voice, louder than usual, betrayed his exasperation.

Nicky murmured an almost inaudible, "Umm," as his shoulders slumped and his lips trembled. He could only stare into a void.

Julio was emphatic. "I think your wife is doing the right thing. The men in our family have rarely ever disgraced us in this way. America has been a mixed blessing to our people. Stop acting like a fool, Nicky."

Nicky was stung by the harshness. He was devastated. "Am I so terrible, Uncle Julio? Have I betrayed the family? Have I insulted anyone? Why me? Why am I the goat? Why is Carlo such a god? Damn my luck. None of you ever thought about me. I'm the black sheep of the family. Why do I have to spend my life apologizing for everything I do? Why am I treated so differently?"

"You're not listening, Nicky, you're not listening. You've disgraced the family by your actions. We don't do drugs." Pausing, he pointed his finger at Nicky. "And don't give me any nonsense that you haven't done anything. I know everything. Also, we don't abuse our women. Understand? That is not acceptable."

Julio's voice reverberated with a seething frustration, its tones echoing in the close confines of his study. He saw in Nicky's eyes blankness suggestive of non-comprehension.

Nicky felt absolutely powerless. His confidence shrunk like a rose hit by frost. The weight of his body in the chair seemed to triple. He balled his fingers into a fist; his stomach went nauseatingly watery. A flood of panic overwhelmed him. Perspiration lay on him like a mist. He could scarcely move. He knew that if he tried to stand at that moment, he would have fallen. "Am I the only one in the family who has struck a woman? Why am I suddenly an outsider. I'm confused." He braced himself for more.

Julio thrust his finger forward but softened his voice. "You talk too much. You ought to be listening. You don't do enough of that. Pay attention, Nicky, you are family. Just follow my instructions and I'll see that whatever can be done about fixing up this marriage will be done." He patted him gently on his cheek and smiled enigmatically. "So, be a good boy, OK?"

Nicky felt waves of shame and dropped his defenses. An apology began to form on his lips. The two men stood in a tableau of awkwardness. With a huge sigh he struggled to speak but the words came hard, as if some unknown force were strangling him, "Uncle Julio, I've really made a fool of myself. I'm sorry. You won't have to worry about me. I'll shape up. I'll be OK." He was outwardly submissive, but inside he festered with anger. His face returned to pasty white and his eyes blinked, unable to focus. His uncle's authority paralyzed him. He stilled, not trusting himself to speak. The silence signaled the end of the meeting.

Julio accompanied the three men to his driveway and waved goodbye as they drove off. As he prepared to turn over the reins of authority, Julio looked back with satisfaction on a life full of love, work, and loyalty and, he modestly acknowledged, a considerable degree of success. He was relieved that such scenes as this would soon be someone else's responsibility.

That night Nicky began to have, for the first time in his life, occasional feelings of intense dislike for his brother. *What is he up to? Does he want my wife? I can't believe what is happening to me.*

Chapter Nine
CARLO AND JULIO - THE PACT

Maria called from the kitchen, where she and a few of her friends were drinking coffee and chatting. "Carlo, the Bishop wants you to call him right away. He has an assignment for you! Come!" She read out the number she had written down as her son dialed.

Carlo spoke to the Bishop's secretary. "May I speak to Bishop Kramer, please?"

"Just a moment," she replied and, as he waited, his thoughts flip-flopped over possible assignments.

"Hello, Carlo," the Bishop's friendly voice bellowed out. "His Eminence has asked me to inform you of your first assignment. I suspect you'll be very happy to hear that you are to be Father Adolfo's assistant at St. Anthony's"

Carlo caught his breath.

"The letter of appointment will be mailed to you, but His Eminence asked me to read it to you over the phone. This makes the appointment official."

The Bishop paused as he reached for the letter. "The letter is addressed to you, Carlo, and it reads:

Dear Father Albanese,

In accordance with the recommendation of your Seminary Rector, Father Francis O'Reilly, and in consultation with Father Adolfo Cabrini, I am pleased to appoint you as Assistant Pastor of St. Anthony of Padua. You should consult with Father Adolfo as to the exact date on which you are to report for duty. With kind regards, etc."

Carlo was thrilled. "Great. When do I report?"

The Bishop continued. "I suggest you give Father Adolfo a call today, and work it out with him. He'll be happy to hear from you. I don't think I'm violating any secret by saying that he asked for you, personally. Good luck."

Carlo placed the phone back in its cradle, and then realized he had not thanked the Bishop. He snatched it up and shouted, "Thank you, thank you," but the line just hummed.

Maria hovered over him. "Well, don't just sit there, Carlo, come on, tell us!" they shouted.

Turning to his mother, he said, "Ma, I'm assigned to St. Anthony's! How about that! Let me call Father Adolfo."

As the room erupted in joyous cheers, Carlo got on the phone to his pastor and thanked him. "I just got the news. Thanks a million - no - two million!"

Adolfo was gracious. "The pleasure is all mine, fella. I'm the one who's going to benefit from a healthy young lad moving in here to share the load. Believe me."

"When do you want me to report, Father?"

Adolfo was casual. "Well, about ten days from now. Just let us know when you are arriving so we can give you a proper welcome." Jocularly, "I have to make a good impression on you so that you'll work hard."

Carlo ran his eyes along a kitchen calendar. "OK, Father, what about Friday, the 17th? That will get me there in time for the weekend Masses."

"That's fine, Carlo. See you on the 17th. In the meantime, enjoy yourself. There's a lot of work piling up for you here. I'll be long on advice but short on work," he said laughing, "I'm getting old you know."

Ten days remained in which to gear him for pastoral work. New offices had been established for counseling the divorced, and assistance to recent immigrants. The development of programs for the elderly and the handicapped required priests and nuns trained in these disciplines. He would sign up for seminars and lectures on these subjects as soon as he reported to the parish. In the meantime, he would check whatever resources might be available at the Seminary. The following day he spent several hours browsing through the Seminary's extensive library. He regretted he had not taken more advantage of it during his years of training.

The seminarians and most of the staff were on vacation. As he walked through the building the rooms revealed their emptiness through open doors, an emptiness that aroused in him a sense of alienation from what had been, for years, the substance of his life. Getting a sudden urge to visit his old room, he bounded up the stairs to the third floor and found a note pinned on the door for the cleaning woman. It read: "Please clean this room well and make ready for new occupant. Father Francis, Director."

Carlo experienced an out-of-body sensation, of floating in a weightless world. He felt uneasy and moved out into the corridor. He survived the antiseptic atmosphere of the seminary but knew he could never repeat those years. He experienced hot flashes of doubt and insecurity. Was the priesthood simply going to be an extension of the life he spent in this room closed off from the world? Like the others in his class, he imagined ordination to be a great and glorious day of liberation, but now he felt a noose tightening. What he had dreamed about, something larger, more expansive, and more spiritual than his family and the Organization had not happened. In addition, sexual stirrings for his sister-in-law haunted his nights. This, he was determined to control, but at what cost?

With this in mind, he headed for the library like a small boy afraid of his shadow. Three of the faculty priests sat at a long table discussing courses for the Fall semester. They were delighted to see him. "Well, look who's here? Isn't this one of the guys who couldn't wait to get out of this jail?" Father Dryden laughed as he got up to shake Carlo's hand. "Carlo, we're all delighted to hear of your assignment. We know how much you wanted to go to St. Anthony's. We also know how much Father Adolfo wanted you there. It should be a happy marriage."

The priests put their arms around Carlo's shoulders and offered their congratulations. He was now a full member of the clerical club. He joined his former professors in a cup of coffee. "I came here to do some of the studying I should have done while I was here."

Father Dryden said, "Glad you feel that way. Wish more of the guys would continue their studies once they leave here. It's an intellectual desert out there in the rectories. Plenty of golf balls, but few books."

"So I've heard."

The three priests shook his hand and returned to their work. "We'll let you get on with your studies. Good luck with everything. We're here if you need any help."

"Thanks."

Carlo walked over to the stacks and began taking notes on liturgical and administrative procedures, well researched studies on divorce, immigration policies, and programs for the elderly and the handicapped. After several hours of study and reminiscence, he took one last sentimental stroll around the seminary grounds and left for home.

Father Adolfo had just finished saying Mass. The liturgy that day celebrated the Feast of the Sacred Heart, so there was the usual large First Friday crowd. Several of the ladies were anxious to speak to him. It was the same old problem. "Father, there are no red vigil lights left, and we can only light red vigil lights at the Statue of the Sacred Heart. This happens almost every time we celebrate First Fridays. Can't you do something about it?"

Father Adolfo wanted to tell the ladies what they could do, but was afraid of burning in hell forever. He was tired of selling red candles, blue candles, and white candles. "I guess we've run out."

A shrill chorus. "How did that happen?"

Adolfo stared at the ceiling. "I don't know. Don't you ladies ever run out of salt or milk at home - or bread? It just happens, that's all. No great conspiracy." He was tired of well meaning but poorly educated senior citizens whose Christianity began with the Holy Water font and ended at the vigil light stand. He reverently cursed the Pope for writing "that damn *Humanae Vitae*," (the Encyclical on birth control.) It had driven a good percentage of the young married couples from his parish. To his sister, he said, "The only people left are the kids herded into Mass by their grandmothers and nuns, and every senior citizen on the local Medicare list. It's depressing." He had given up his practice of early morning meditation in the church, thus avoiding a good deal of problems. The arrival of the "Amazonians," as he called them privately would shatter any peace he hoped to get from sitting before the Blessed Sacrament.

"Why in the name of Heaven do you folks come to the seven o'clock mass at six in the morning?" he would ask, not expecting and not receiving a satisfactory answer.

He hoped Carlo would be appointed to share these frustrations with him. He waited for the Cardinal's call. When it finally came, he clumsily dropped the phone, sending a sharp banging noise into the Cardinal's ear. "Well, Adolfo, pick up the damn phone and answer me. Will you accept Carlo?"

"Yes, Your Eminence, I do accept him." That had not sounded grateful enough. "I mean, I'm damn glad to get him, sir, I mean, Your Eminence."

"Oh hell, Adolfo, we both know you want him and I'm glad to help you out. Simple as that. Enjoy."

Mrs. Cerrillo, the housekeeper, walked into Father Adolfo's office. "Father Albanese has arrived."

He rushed out to greet his new assistant, giving him an enthusiastic embrace. He needed to do something about Mrs. Cerrillo whom he overheard telling a parishioner, "I'm not sure about this Father Albanese. We don't need any more Mafia around here."

Adolfo had never taken to his housekeeper. She had the habit of standing close to any conversation. Her pinched face twitched as she memorized every word for later distribution to her friends. While the priests dined, she sat on a stiff-backed bench, crossed her spindly legs, and listened carefully for any morsel of news she could garner. Father Adolfo had been hinting for some years that Mrs. Cerrillo, now seventy-two, ought to retire. Her response to any such suggestion was, "No, I wouldn't think of abandoning the parish, after all these years. It needs me. I'm in fine physical condition."

Much to Father Adolfo's disappointment, she was.

The two priests sat at the dining room table, each with his second cup of coffee for the day. Mrs. Cerrillo approached. "Father Carlo, I'm so happy to see you," she gushed. "I've been telling all my friends how lucky we are to have you assigned here. If there's anything I can do for you, just let me know."

Adolfo cringed at the hypocrisy.

Carlo, sensing the dynamics, was polite. "Thank you, Mrs. Cerrillo. It's good to be here."

Adolfo raised his coffee cup in a toast. "Carlo, you were baptized here, confirmed here, and now you are assistant pastor. I want you to know I'm thrilled to have you. The house is yours." Turning to Mrs. Cerrillo, he said, "Isn't that right, Mrs. Cerrillo?"

Primly, "Oh yes, Father, of course."

Carlo put his hand on Father Adolfo's arm. "Thanks so much for your welcome, Father. I'll do the best job I can. I know I've got a lot to learn."

After coffee, the two priests went into Father Adolfo's office. Mrs. Cerrillo, in the adjacent room, stretched her neck to see what was going on. She didn't like the evident camaraderie between the two men. In the past she had been able to exploit the differences between the priests in the rectory. It might not be so easy this time.

Adolfo pointed to the large safe in the right-hand corner of his office. "This is where we keep parish records, baptism, confirmation, and so on. The safe looks impregnable but, in fact, we can't lock it. No one knows the combination."

"You mean we'd have to blow it open?"

" 'Fraid so."

Carlo joked. "Does that make us safecrackers?

They laughed at the absurdity.

Adolfo changed the subject. "I don't believe in the day-off system, Carlo. It's too constricting. You have an area of work to cover. As long as you get it done, you can regulate your time off as you please."

From the rumor mill, Carlo was aware that his classmates would not likely meet with similar generosity and equality. *I lucked out.*

Father Adolfo referred to his age and its consequences for ministry. "You've got a big job on your hands, Carlo. I'm a clock that's running down. If this parish is going to survive as anything more than a social club for retirees, someone like you is going to have to do it. I've no illusions about my ability, but I will give you all the support I can."

Then, motioning Carlo to go along with him, he said, "I think it's time for you to get acquainted with your bedroom. I put all the latest gadgets in there, TV, stereo, all that stuff. Just don't keep me awake at night with rock and roll!"

The two priests could feel a deepening friendship. Carlo followed Adolfo down the corridor. "See what I got for you." The door bore a sign, 'Father Carlo'. "That makes your appointment official! Come in."

Carlo gripped the old man's hand and smiled. "You really are one hell of a nice guy, Father."

They entered the room and Adolfo handed Carlo a large set of keys. "These fit everything from the front door to the boiler-room."

Carlo waved his head side to side, handling each key. "It'll take me a week to sort them out."

"It took me longer." Adolfo raised a finger to his lips. "By the way, there's a brown envelope stuffed with dollar bills in the drawer of the TV stand, in my bedroom. You can tap that anytime you want if there's something you need."

The generosity and humility of the older man touched Carlo. He was grateful. "Thanks for everything, Father. I'll move my stuff into my room now. My car looks like a junk yard."

"All right, fella, I'll leave you to yourself." He grazed one of Carlo's arms with his fist and said, "Supper's at six, see you then."

Adolfo rejoiced in the self-confidence devoid of arrogance that surrounded his new assistant. *He's just the medicine this ailing parish needs, and the Family's religious needs will receive a lot more attention now.*

Carlo set about fixing up his room. He hung a large painting of the Virgin above his desk that he had purchased from a young Jewish girl at a Greenwich Village street sale. He laughingly asked, "Why is a nice Jewish girl like you painting the Blessed Virgin?" She had replied, "Mary is a Jewish girl. Simple as that."

Carlo thought, "That's a good theology lesson." He was happy and feeling at home in this Italian parish, with the one priest of the archdiocese who could guide him as he served his people by changing the Mafia from within. There was one more thing he wanted to do before supper. He dialed Lisa's new number. She was at home. "I was thinking about you and thought I'd call. I'm now settled at St. Anthony's."

He gave her his private telephone number. "Call me here anytime."

"I've been thinking about you also. I'm beginning to miss you and I don't know if I should feel guilty about that or not."

Carlo felt no such guilt. "Nonsense. How about cooking me a meal some evening?" There was a momentary hesitation in her voice; then, with directness, "I'd really like that. I'll call you when I get myself organized."

That night Carlo slept the sleep of the contented.

Mrs. Cerrillo had been waiting in absolute dread for the day when the Godfather, the "*Capo di tutti capi*," would call his nephew at the rectory. She would actually hear the voice of "that murderer and gangster." She described him to her sister as "that evil of evils." She was certain that the evil person she had composed out of her many assorted images was not simply a fiction of her imagination.

The call finally came a few weeks after Father Carlo's arrival. Nervously, she buzzed Carlo in his room. "Father, your uncle Julio is on the line. Can you speak with him?"

"Yes, of course," he replied as he pressed the outside line button.

Julio's voice sounded less ebullient than usual. "Carlo, I've a very important matter to discuss with you. Do you have time to come and see me? Otherwise, I can come to see you."

"No, no, you stay right where you are, Uncle. I will come. Let me check with Father Adolfo, to make sure he has no plans to go out today."

Putting his uncle on hold, Carlo checked with the pastor. "No problem, Carlo. In fact, stay overnight if you wish. I'm not going anywhere."

He thanked Adolfo and returned to Julio. "I'll be out in a couple of hours; soon as I finish a bit of paperwork here."

In less than an hour, Carlo was ready to leave. The Buick purred as Carlo turned the ignition key and turned on the air-conditioning. The FDR drive was crowded, but after crossing the Triboro Bridge and entering Grand Central Parkway, Carlo was able to pick up speed. La Guardia Airport, Shea Stadium, Forest Hills and Kennedy Airport were colorful blurs along the way, monuments to the human spirit that continuously expressed itself in stone and steel.

Carlo pulled up along Julio's driveway and angle parked at the entrance. Julio stood by the opened door tending his flowers. He held a stubby glass of whiskey in his hands. As Carlo stepped out of the car, Julio plucked a tiny pink rose. "What do you think of this beauty?" he asked. "The one thing I like about God is the way he tosses beauty around all over the place. Did you ever think of that, Carlo?"

"Something like that - the mountains and the oceans sure make me think of Him." They embraced before entering the house. The smell of garlic and tomatoes teased their nostrils and quickened their appetites. "Uncle, I suspect you're getting ready to ask a favor, sort of fattening me up for the kill!"

Julio playfully pressed his fist against Carlo's stomach. "Yes, and more than a favor. But for now, let's eat. Go and kiss your aunt. Tell her there are two hungry men here waiting to be served."

Julio was not an extravagant man. Out of the public eye, he was very much the Sicilian peasant. He kept a good supply of his favorite provolone, regularly delivered by an importer on West 41st Street, where the best of things Italian could be purchased. "American provolone keeps you happy," he would say, "but Italian provolone keeps you both healthy and happy."

Carlo helped his aunt, carrying a large tray of pizza and thick slices of cheese to the dining room. A bowl of fruit and an Italian salad had already been placed on the table. The meal was punctuated with laughter, as Julio told stories of the local mayor, of the village where he was born. "He was so popular that, even after having been arrested for stealing village money, he was re-elected. He was everyone's friend and, after all, the stolen money went to buy gifts for everybody. So, the people thought 'what the heck'."

On finishing eating, Julio motioned Carlo to join him in the den. He quietly closed the double doors and sat down in one of the large burgundy leather chairs, inviting Carlo to sit in the other. "Carlo, I've something very important to tell you and I want you to keep it to yourself for the time being." He flexed his long fingers and bent them into the palms of his hands. "I've already confided in you that I'll be retiring. Well, the time has come. My health is bad. I'm not as alert as I used to be. I'm losing touch, and right now we've a backlog of legal cases. We need a very active man to deal with them. The future of the Family is at stake." Pausing, he squeezed his nostrils. "We need to have an election, Carlo, even if there's no doubt that your father will succeed me. Some say it's just a formality, but always remember, Carlo, formalities are very important. We make the pledge of allegiance even though we already know that most Americans are very loyal to their nation. Our life is marked by religious ceremonies, civil ceremonies; you name it. So, we need an important moment when we move from one leader to another. That moment is the election."

Julio paused to clear his throat. "Carlo, you should be my successor, but I know that now is not the time. You're not only one of us, you're the natural leader of this Family. But, your father will be chosen to succeed me. You promised me you would actively help him to make the right decisions. Some of them will be tough. Are you ready to take on the burden?"

Julio had, in one thrust, cut into the very core of who he was—an Albanese. His life and mind were being swept up like dust in a whirlwind, not of his own making. He rose to his feet, as in a trance. "Uncle Julio, I'll do whatever I can to see that our Family stays strong and secure. You have my pledge."

Julio's voice was soft. "Good. I knew I could count on you. I want you to call the meeting at the estate up in Hudson, count the votes, and announce the results. That will be a sign to everyone that you are in the family, with the family and destined to play an important part in the family. The meeting will be conducted with dignity. I don't want any jealousies and secret meetings. I won't have it. It's undignified and very disrespectful to our Family history."

Carlo felt himself being sucked into the heart of the Mafia. The attraction was too strong and too sweet to resist. "Uncle, how soon do you want all of this to take place?"

"Three weeks from now, but on a Sunday. OK?"

Carlo nodded. "Fine, three Sundays from now it is. I will check with Father Adolfo, of course, but I believe there will be no problem."

Carlo tore a sheet from a legal pad. "Let's start putting down names."

Julio had the list in front of him. "Well, first of all, of course, your dad, Victor, and Nicky. Our *consigliere*, Bruno; then our *Caporegime*, Corto, Leonard, Frankie, Annunzio and Speed. They'll choose two men each from their groups."

"That's an even twenty, Uncle Julio, including myself."

Julio joked. "That's enough. If we dip lower down we'll come up with a few monkeys. If we need monkeys, we'll go to the zoo." He said chuckling.

Carlo smiled. "You sound like a Darwinian."

"I am. Carlo, let' face it; let's be honest. We have to become more civilized. Today's Mafia is a black mark on the name of all Italians and Sicilians. We used to be public heroes. We've become criminals. It's time to get our honor back, our reputation as defender of the people. You need to help your dad accomplish that goal. I will talk to your dad and to Victor. I'll let them know you are arranging the meeting on my behalf." Julio paused to rub his face and hands. "Carlo, it'll be the most spiritual thing you'll ever do in your priesthood, believe me."

The priest and the godfather had just struck a deal. Neither of them was prepared for the tragedy that was about to befall them.

A few days later, at Julio's home, Tina prepared chicken cacciatore and macaroni with Italian sausages. Julio had invited his brothers to explain his decision. She set the table, and then cleaned up the den. Tony was the first to arrive. He and Julio had been chatting for a few minutes when Victor walked in. "What do you want to drink, Vic?" Julio asked.

"Bourbon with a little ginger ale."

Tony poured himself a glass of Chablis.

Julio approached the subject slowly. He asked Victor about his wife. "My God, Vic, Grace is getting too big. I know you don't want to hassle her, but you'd better get her on a diet."

"Like pulling teeth. But, you're right."

Tina called the men to the table. "I hope you men are hungry; there's a lot of food out there. *Mangiamo!*"

Julio was unusually quiet during the meal. His brothers carried the conversation with small talk. Tony explained how the neighbors asked him how they should now address Carlo. Father? Reverend Carlo? Father Albanese?

Julio leaned toward Tony. "What did you advise them, Tony?"

"Father Carlo."

"Good choice," Victor observed, and Julio agreed.

They took their coffee in the den. "Well boys, I've made my decision. I'm retiring."

Tony and Victor gasped.

Julio raised his arms and flattened his palms. "Now, let me finish. I want you fellows, together with the *Caporegime* to meet at my place in Hudson for an election. Three weeks from now, on a Sunday, is the day."

Tony gasped again. Victor stared at the ceiling. There was a long silence, and Victor said, "My God, Julio, so soon?"

Tony said simply, "Julio, I think you've done the right thing. You should retire and let someone else carry the burden."

The three men drew their chairs closer together and clasped hands for a brief familial moment of solidarity. Victor assured him, "Julio, you know that Tony and I will do exactly as you say. I don't like your retiring at this point, but if you insist on it we'll back you one hundred percent."

Tony nodded in agreement.

Julio was pleased at the way the conversation was going. "OK, then this is the way I am setting this thing up. I've asked Carlo to call a meeting of all those who have a voice in the selection."

His brothers were startled.

"Why Carlo, Julio?" Tony asked, "What does he have to do with this?"

Julio put his hand on Tony's arm. "That's precisely the point, Tony. Carlo has nothing to do with the matter - except that he's concerned for the good of the Family. It makes him the perfect man for the job."

Tony nodded and Julio continued. "Carlo's one of us and must share in the responsibilities of the Family. He agrees with me on this matter."

Julio pulled open the middle drawer of his desk and produced the list of those who would attend the meeting. "Carlo has a copy of this list and he will begin calling each one on the phone this week. Check the list. If either of you want anyone added or subtracted, let's talk about it."

They studied the list for a few moments. Victor handed it back to Julio. "This is OK with us, Julio. The other Dons can learn a lot from the way you're handling this matter."

The brothers stood up and embraced each other.

"My dear brothers," Julio added, "I'm officially retired." Tony's eyes were awash with tears and Julio's voice was unsteady. "You fellows get out of my house before we start crying like a basketful of babies."

Victor tugged at the cuffs of his Brooks Brothers shirt, a nervous gesture that was his signature. *I know what the hell Julio is doing. He's setting Carlo in position to wield power. Unbelievable. He's nuts.*

Julio accompanied his brothers to their cars and asked each to help make a success of the meeting. They assured him they would. As he returned to the house, Tina framed the doorway.

"Well, you really did it," she said. "I'm so happy and so proud of you." She hugged him and stroked his face.

Julio shuffled his feet and clumsily pirouetted. "Are there any strawberries left in the fridge? Let's celebrate!" Julio's body and mind felt airy and free. The responsibility for the Family's future no longer rested with him. He had finally retired, and it felt good. His dream of Carlo playing a major role in the evolution of the Family was becoming a reality.

Victor Albanese saw the handwriting on the wall. With Julio retiring, it was his brother, Tony, who had the votes. Everyone knows Tony's got no guts. He's good at books, period. Tony would become godfather unless something was done to stop him. He turned on the TV but his disjointed thoughts distracted him. Not only would Tony become godfather, it was clear that Julio was placing the real power in Carlo's hands. Tony would be the figurehead. My God, is he actually preparing Carlo to be godfather? What else could be the case? The Family won't realize what's happening until its too late. The old man's as clever as a snake.

Victor looked at his watch. It was 11:30 PM. Annunzio should be home. Victor had provided him with his first job, hustling in the garment district - later, bookmaker in the Park Slope section of Brooklyn. Annunzio was fond of Julio, but not devoted to him. His first loyalty was to Victor. "Yes, boss," was his response to any request from Victor, even in Julio's presence. They had become very close over the years and shared many secrets. Julio suspected behind-the-scenes dealings, but was resigned. What could he do? Nothing's perfect. These secrets, plus a healthy respect for each other's willingness to use any method that worked, were the bonds that held Victor and Annunzio together. Neither had been pleased to see the influence, power and wealth of the Family diminish. Annunzio could help Victor prevent this damn thing from happening. Julio must be getting senile. He phoned Annunzio. "Sorry to call you so late, Primo. Something important has come up. I want to see you tonight."

Annunzio returned from a day at the track where he had lost more than usual. He was in no mood for a midnight meeting with anyone. "Victor, you must be crazy! I'm dying on my feet. What about lunch tomorrow?"

"Primo, this is very important. It can't wait."

Annunzio caught the urgency in Victor's voice. "OK, where? Here?"

"No, drive to the diner underneath the West Side Highway, at l25th Street. It's usually empty around this time. See you there in a half an hour or so."

Victor was able to leave the house without awakening his wife. They had been sleeping in separate bedrooms for almost four years. He came and went as he pleased. He headed for 125th Street. The breeze flowing off the Hudson River carried the sour and fetid smells of the thick swill foam that covered the water like a blanket.

At Feline's diner he found Annunzio waiting for him. They ordered coffee. "Primo, we've got some tough decisions to make." He knew Annunzio felt as strongly as he did that, as Don, Tony would be a disaster. He also confided to Annunzio his suspicion that the real power behind the throne would be Carlo. "With a priest running the Family, up front or behind the scenes, the Organization will become the laughing stock of the nation, the butt of a thousand jokes."

Annunzio nodded his agreement. "It's just utterly ridiculous. We gotta do something to stop this."

"Exactly." Victor offered this as proof that Julio had gone quite mad. "We've got to save the family from this insanity." Neither wanted to see the influence, power and wealth of the Family diminish. This would, in their opinion, definitely happen if a priest ran the operation from behind the scenes. They plotted to prevent such an occurrence, discussing various options. Through a sleepless night they repeatedly went over the details of the plan which they had hatched.

Chapter Ten
THE ASSASSINATION

For Carlo, his work at St. Anthony of Padua Church had not been what he expected. Although he prepared himself as best he knew how, he learned that the reality of parish life was far different from what he had imagined. He had hoped to bring to the parish a vision of the world that transcended the boundaries of St. Anthony's, but he quickly got bogged-down in the quagmire of outmoded attitudes, structures and petty parish politics. He told Father Adolfo, "I now laugh at myself, at my great ambitions."

Father Adolfo rubbed his chin. "That's a sign you're beginning to understand parish work. The whole history of the kind of religion we bring to our parishes works against spirituality, if that makes any sense."

"It sure does, now."

Adolfo poured himself a beer. "The reality is that most of the time we worry about new gutters for the church to keep the walls from crumbling with dampness, and if we can afford new carpeting in the sanctuary. Guess how much talk about spirituality you will hear at these conferences?"

"Zero?"

"You get 100 per cent in the math test."

Sunday, Feast of the Triumph of the Holy Cross, was a turning point in the life of Carlo Albanese. This day the new godfather would be selected and Carlo was fully aware that this would bring about significant changes in his life. He awoke feeling ill at ease. He attributed this to the weather. From his window, he looked out at rain-swept streets. The heavy flow of rainwater along the gutters had piled loose garbage at water drains. After the Masses, Carlo and Adolfo counted the collection. On rainy days the collection plummeted. "I'm not as happy as the farmers today," commented Father Adolfo, glancing at the meager offering.

Carlo packed a bag and reminded Adolfo he would be away for two days, in Hudson. Adolfo's instincts told him that something important was about to happen. "No problem, Carlo. Enjoy yourself."

Carlo gave a short wave as he headed for the door. "I'm going home first for lunch. I'll say hello to Mom for you."

"Do that, please."

He stepped out beyond the shelter of the rectory porch and felt the cold rain on his hair. As he headed for the garage, he had mixed emotions about what lay ahead for him and his family this gray, wet day. Father Adolfo stared out the kitchen window, watching Carlo depart. His hour had come.

Maria was setting the table for the Sunday meal. "I hope you didn't eat at the rectory, Carlo. Call your father. You guys have to get on the road soon. The food is ready." Nicky had already arrived and was helping Maria set a plate of linguini, a bowl of salad and a bottle of wine on the table.

Carlo stretched out his arm, gave his brother "five," and then shouted for his dad to join them. "Come on down, Dad. We're all hungry!"

Tony appeared fit as he skipped down the stairs. His voice was placid and soft. "Carlo, Nicky, nice to be at the table with you guys. Like the good old days. Huh?" Nicky and Carlo agreed, hugging their dad.

As they ate, Carlo described some of his parish experiences. "Dad, a fellow has to have a lot of faith to work in these old parishes. I sometimes think that St. Anthony's is dead already. Someone forgot to bury it."

Tony laughed. "You can bring a horse to water but you can't make him drink," he observed. "Don't expect much progress and be grateful for what you get."

Carlo nodded. "Yes, I learn that more every day."

Nicky added. "I think religion is a waste of time. Somebody said it's opium for the masses, right?"

Carlo jumped in. "Right that someone said it; wrong that it's true for everyone."

Nicky was unconvinced. "Yeah."

The phone rang. Maria motioned to Tony. "It's for you."

He left the room to take the call, returning a few moments later. "Carlo, something has come up. I've got to go downtown in a couple of hours. I just got a tip that might help us with some of our litigation. You fellows go ahead. I'll take my car and meet you in Hudson. I should be there by the time you guys finish dinner. Entertain the boys with some of your parish stories till I get there."

Carlo was uneasy. "Are you sure you don't want us to wait for you, dad? It's no problem, you know."

"Nope, you go right ahead."

After lunch Tony walked his sons to Nicky's car. Carlo was suspicious. "Dad, are you sure you ought to go? Sounds fishy to me." Nicky agreed.

Tony brushed aside their concerns. "Maybe they want me to bring good news to the meeting." He waved them off, and returned to the house. Two hours later he kissed his wife with, "Be back after the meeting. Don't wait up; it's probably going to be very late tonight." Tony then drove off to a rendezvous with death.

To Nicky and Carlo, the drive to the town of Hudson along Route Nine from Manhattan is one of the most scenic routes in the Northeast. Nicky drove. The morning rain had dissipated but the horizon was slanted with ominous gray clouds that could pack another punch. The leaves had begun to change, with splashes of red and orange painting the countryside. Birch trees stood out like white highway markers. Along the route, roadside markets displayed colorful baskets of fruits, vegetables and jars of jams and jellies. The highway, a colorful ribbon of road, climbed and descended between thick walls of forest dotted with private homes trimmed with white doors and window frames. Here and there the Hudson River, threading its serpentine way, could be spotted. Every rise provided a panoramic view. Occasionally, nature's raw power could be seen in the form of jagged boulders that threatened to cascade down the hillsides. Nicky took the hairpin curves easily.

As they arrived on the town's outskirts they admired the planning. Nicky mused. "Carlo do you ever think of those pretty houses with the white picket fences; I mean, to actually live in one of those? Well, with Lisa out of my life, I guess I don't need one, do I?"

Carlo noted the edge of sarcasm.

Carlo simply said, "Neither of you is dead yet. Who knows?"

Nicky left it at that.

"Look at that, the way the streets follow the ups and downs of this hilly town. Never really noticed that before."

Carlo nodded in agreement, and added. "Maybe, one day, our Family members will able to live out in the countryside and enjoy all this."

Nicky was sarcastic, "Yeah, for about an hour…no poolrooms, no horse tracks, no skin bars. Well, maybe two hours."

Carlo reluctantly agreed. "We've got to change all that, over time of course. There are a lot of things I would do differently if I started life all over again. What about you, Nicky?"

Carlo and Nicky had spent many summers of their childhood in this idyllic surrounding. They revived memories as they drove along. Nicky recalled, "Remember how we used to run into apple orchards and grab a few, when dad would stop along the highway to take a pee?"

"Yeah," drawled Carlo, "and how he used to tell us to go to confession, but he always ate the apples."

Nicky laughed, "And, we'd tell him we were going to confession and we'd go down and shoot a game of pool. Then we'd tell him the reason we got home late was because there were so many people lined up outside the confessional." After a pause, "And remember the big fish I caught?" In one of his few triumphs, Nicky caught the largest fish, on a family fishing trip.

Carlo chuckled, as he slapped his brother's shoulder, "Of course I remember. You never let me forget!"

As fir trees whirred at their passing, Nicky tried to overcome the resentment at not having been consulted about the event taking place at the Estate. After all, I'm also Tony's son, he thought. Over the years he had managed not to blame Carlo for his popularity in the Family. But now, that discipline was beginning to evaporate. After all, Carlo could have mentioned that the meeting was going to take place. That would have been simple. It would have been family. Nicky learned of the event only the night before, in a brief phone call. "Nicky, they're electing a new don tomorrow. Uncle Julio has decided to retire. Care to drive up with me?"

Nicky took note of the language. "They're electing; care to drive with me?" he said in a way that seemed not to include him, as if he were a newsman invited to cover a breaking story. He had become an afterthought by his own brother. For the first time in months they were alone long enough to share thoughts, but there was a limit to their exchange. For his part, Nicky's preoccupation with drugs and women was drawing him more and more away from the family and its business. As for Carlo, his growing attraction for Lisa entangled his relations with Nicky.

Carlo suggested, "Let's pop in to see Carita."

Nicky agreed. "Great idea."

Carita Paterno, mother of Jonnie Paterno, Hudson's Mayor, owned the town's only Italian restaurant. The restaurant was crowded and noisy. The Sunday afternoon menu of Shrimp Scampi, Fettuccine Alfredo and Spaghetti with Clam Sauce attracted customers from many miles around.

Carita shouted as Carlo and Nicky walked through the door, "Oh my God, Carlo, you're a priest now. It was in all the papers." She dropped to her knees to receive his blessing. A group of startled diners did the same. Carita rose to her feet and asked, "What's brings you guys here? Somebody getting married? I know, none of my business, right? Oh my, Nicky, you look so good. Let me get you guys something to eat."

Carlo protested, "No, no, Carita, we just dropped in to say hello."

Ignoring his objections she quickly placed platters of steaming pasts in front of them. "I know you fellows drove all the way up here, without stopping to eat. That's not good for your health."

Carlo and Nicky ate quickly, while chatting with Carita. Washing down the last of his pasta with wine, Nicky put his arm around her shoulders, "We really got to go." They both kissed her on the cheek.

"OK, but promise you'll be back."

Carlo waved his goodbye. "We will, we promise!"

I *think they're up to something big,* she mused knowingly. She had watched their comings and goings since she was a teenager, and could read the signs.

Carlo and Nicky arrived at the estate house to find the driveway lined with cars. "Looks like we're the last to get here," Nicky said. On the verandah that encircled the house they could see Victor mixing with the men. Loud laughter and backslapping highlighted the locker room atmosphere of men gathered together. The large covered porch contained enough rattan and wicker furniture with comfortable pink cushions, for all. Potted plants were randomly placed on the floor and on the wide porch railing. The house, with its steeply canted roof, was built of rough-sawn cedar. Its six guestrooms framed the master bedroom, three on one side and three on the other, in the large second-story sleeping area. The house merged with, rather than stood out of, the surrounding grove of tall spruce trees.

Although he was not personally popular, Victor did function as an entertainer at Family gatherings. He spotted Carlo and Nicky, beckoning them to join the group. "Where's your father? Couldn't you get him away from the table? I don't blame him. Your mother is the best damn cook in the Family. Come fellows, have a drink; there's a variety of stuff. Even a priest should find something to his liking."

Carlo spoke. "Dad will be here in about an hour or so. Got some Miller beer? We both like it."

"At least a case." He gave his nephew a familial hug of the shoulders. It was at times like this that Carlo liked his uncle. His usual sobriety, even dourness, would temporarily evaporate during his storytelling sessions. Carlo and Nicky settled in wicker rockers, downed their beers and joined in the small talk.

102 Father Patrick Bascio

Frankie Montana, one of Julio's *Caporegime*, wearing a wrinkled sports shirt, blue jeans and tennis shoes, chatted with Carlo about the Yankees, as he ran his long fingers through his thick dark hair. "Looks like another great year for the Yanks." A light breeze played with strands of his hair as he spoke. "They're a New York institution, like motherhood and apple pie."

Carlo winked as he said, "Except that mothers and apple pie never lose, Frankie."

Frankie, nodding perfunctorily, held up his palms in acknowledgment. "That's true, Carlo."

Frankie was a friend of Yankee coach, Billy Martin. Like a schoolboy, he could recite the name and batting average of every important player in the League. He took particular pride in being a frequent Yankee locker-room guest and had dozens of autographed table napkins, match books and game programs glued to the walls of his basement bar.

Apart from the Albanese brothers, Frankie Montana and Primo Annunzio were the top men in the Family organization. Highly talented, they could have been successful in any number of professions. Both had been college students, and were naturally astute. Frankie, like Julio, his mentor, enjoyed great popularity in the Family; Primo, like Victor, his mentor, was admired for his cold efficiency. Every Family needed both types.

At about the time that Victor was hugging his nephew's shoulders at the family's Hudson estate, Tony walked into Luca's restaurant on 14th Street in Manhattan to meet with two men he did not know. Victor had called Tony earlier from Hudson. "These two guys from the West Coast tell me they have information that will help us with some of our legal problems. Maybe nothing to it, but I think we oughta check it out. If you want me to come down from Hudson, I will, but I thought you could run over to Luca's before you head up here."

Tony agreed. "Yeah, that makes sense. What about Julio? Did you tell him?"

"I figured no sense worrying him today. It's a big day for him. If there's anything, we can talk with him. Let's keep it between us for the time being. No sense raising hopes about something that may turn out to be just a puff of smoke."

"Makes sense, Victor. OK"

The waitress was familiar with all the leading New York Mafia figures. "Can I get you something, Mr. Albanese?"

"Cup of coffee, please. Thank you." Tony mused. *I hope these guys have information we can use. This Rico Statute is sure hurting some of our men.*

The waitress brought the coffee and the heel of a loaf of Italian bread. "Oh my, you remembered the bread. Thank you, my dear."

She had memorized how all the men who frequented the restaurant liked their coffee and what they ordered with it. As he was dunking the heel of bread, two men entered the restaurant and smiled at him. He returned the smile and waved them to join him. Over the rim of his glasses he saw them walk toward him with long strides. Sensing danger, he began to stand, but it was too late. Each gunman fired two shots into his chest. The horrified waitress stared in terror as blood and tiny pieces of flesh and bone splattered across the white of Tony's shirt.

The men fled in their car, which they had left running at the curb while they carried out their assignment. A taxi driver sitting in his cab across the street immediately contacted Emergency 911. Within minutes, paramedics were loading Tony's body into an ambulance. The restaurant owner, Doug Camas, overheard one of the paramedics. "I don't think he'll make it. God rest his soul, whoever he is."

Police immediately sealed off the area and began questioning the restaurant personnel, the taxi driver and several startled passers-by. As the ambulance drove off, Doug could see Tony laying still, an IV drip snaking down to his body. A local TV team had been notified. From a cross street they made visual contact and rode alongside the ambulance as it headed north along 14th Street, their cameras whirring. Supplied with their own generator, the van's crew was already editing and transmitting footage to their studio. Julio and Tina were horrified as the news program they were watching was interrupted with footage of the ambulance carrying Tony's body.

Carlo looked at his watch. It was long past suppertime and his father had not yet arrived, so he decided to go ahead and eat. "Anyone for supper? Let's go. It's roast beef today, no pasta. The regular cook is at a baptism. We got ourselves a very nice Korean guy to fill in."

The men let out a cacophony of groans and mock protests, and followed Carlo into the dining room. Carlo held up his arms, assuring them. "Just for today, just for today. Don't worry."

Victor noted the ease with which the men, Annunzio included, fell in behind Carlo. He felt completely justified in his decision to take action. A priest in charge of the Family? It would be a joke. Imagine how the other Families would react? One big laugh. The Family, he thought, should be grateful to him. He felt no animosity toward Carlo, who was not responsible for Julio's poor judgment.

During the meal some of the men taught the Korean cook a few lessons in colorful American profanity. Except for an occasional, "Scuza, Carlo," their ribald gaiety was not dampened by the presence of the Family priest. For his part, Carlo was comfortable being "one of the boys." Nicky felt more like an important member of the Family, having accompanied Carlo, and been treated warmly by Victor. Nonetheless, he did harbor some resentment. *After all, Carlo is a priest. Uncle Victor or Dad should have been the ones to call the meeting. If not them, then myself.*

Victor was telling one of his traveling-salesman jokes when Sarah, the housekeeper, came into the dining room and whispered in Carlo's ear, "Your Uncle Julio's on the phone - says it's urgent."

Carlo took the call in the kitchen. Julio's voice was soft and deliberate. "Carlo, it's my sad duty to inform you that your father, my beloved brother, was murdered this very afternoon."

"What? What?"

"I'm so sorry to bring you this news."

Carlo's body went limp. He tried to brace his arms against the doorjamb to keep from falling, but it was in vain, as he slid along the wall to his knees, slumped in misery. The telephone first dangled on his shoulder, then clunked loudly on the kitchen floor. The pain of it penetrated to the pit of his stomach. He managed to grip the dangling phone. "Oh God, Uncle Julio, Oh my God!"

Julio's voice became firm. "I want you and Nicky to drive home immediately. I haven't told your mother yet, but she may get it on the radio. Move quickly. I'll be with your mother when you reach home. Let me talk to Victor. He'll have to take charge of the meeting. He'll be Don now. We have no choice."

Sarah helped Carlo to his feet and wiped his brow with her apron. "Carlo, what's wrong with you? What's wrong?"

The tiles on the kitchen floor merged and separated as Carlo caught his balance. "I must leave right away." He pressed the palm of his right hand to his stomach. "I'm gonna be sick."

The others heard the commotion and ran into the kitchen. "What's wrong," Victor shouted.

Carlo was pale and shaking. "I must leave for home right away." He handed the phone to Victor. "Please talk to Uncle Julio." Then, "Nicky, come with me, come!"

Victor watched Carlo and Nicky as they sped away. He was elated. Annunzio's men must have done the job. He picked up the phone. "Julio, what's happening?"

"Victor, Tony's dead. I just got word. He was gunned down at Luca's on 14th Street."

"O Jesus, Maria," cried Victor, trying to match the deep sorrow in Julio's voice. "Who did it?"

"No idea. Tony was sitting in Luca's. He must have been waiting for someone. Two guys walked in and pumped four shots into his chest. The waitress saw it happen and she's still more or less in shock, but she gave the police a rough description. What the hell was he doing on 14th Street? He was supposed to be on his way north with Carlo."

"Beats me, Julio. What about the meeting? Shall we break up?"

"No, my health requires that I retire. The Family needs a leader, so take a quick vote. Take a quick vote. Then get going and find out who did this. Get the bastards."

Victor could feel power surging through his body and psyche. His head bubbled with exhilaration. He felt several inches taller as he walked into the room. These men were now under his command. His shrewd dark eyes surveyed them in a sweeping arch

"I want your attention, please. Tony was shot dead this afternoon at Luca's!"

Vibrations of shock and disbelief filled the room. Annunzio hid a smile as Victor continued. In the distance, on the Hudson, could be heard the faint bellow of a foghorn.

"I want each of you to have a Mass said for Tony at his own parish church. We must all pray for his soul. I can't believe it. We came here today to choose him as our new Don and now we're talking about the repose of his soul! May God help us all."

After three dramatic strides across the room he turned to the men and said, "I'm not going to rest until his murderer lies dead in the street."

Frankie noted that Victor was not wasting time with condolences. This cold, forbidding style, he knew, would characterize the new regime. Annunzio suggested a quick vote so that Victor could act with legitimacy. The men agreed. The votes were counted. It was unanimous. Frankie announced that Victor Albanese was the new Don. All were silent. It was clear that congratulations were not in order in this stunned atmosphere.

"Thank you for your confidence in me," said Victor. "I want to see the Caporegimes for a moment. Everyone else get moving. See your contacts and call me at my house by midnight. I want to find the bastards."

Victor and the Caporegimes sat at a table laden with food and drinks that had barely been touched. The new Don addressed his subordinates. "Let's check the dons and anyone else who might be able to help. Annunzio, you check Manhattan, Frankie, you check Bridgeport. I'll take Providence. Corto, you cover Boston. Something's got to turn up for us."

Annunzio asked about the promises of loyalty customarily made to the new Don. Victor replied with solemnity, "We haven't time now. We'll meet another day to take care of the matter."

You can be sure of that! Frankie thought. *This guy means to be crowned.*

Victor walked to his car alone. He did not want Frankie, at some later date, to recall that he and Annunzio had huddled at this sensitive time. *Frankie's a man I've got to get rid of eventually. In the meantime I'll make him my friend.*

Nicky drove toward Manhattan at a steady 80 miles per hour. His senses were heightened. Even the green of the trees took on an intensity he had never before experienced. The air was full of murmur, like frenetic beetles scurrying here and there aimlessly, anxious at having lost their way. For the first time in his life he felt in charge, as his brother sat beside him, mute and somber- faced, his eyes deadened by desolation. He knew this moment of superiority to be tenuous and uncertain, but it did hold out some hope for the future. He grasped at the proverbial straw.

Chapter Eleven
VICTOR

Victor realized that he would be expected to take the lead in consoling and helping the Family in the days ahead. *I am, after all, the godfather now, the consoler, the provider, the advisor.* He mused on many things as he drove back to Manhattan. Tony's wife would have to be assured of financial security. He would be "fatherly" to Carlo. As he topped a small rise he drove past a large grove of stately white birch trees, and remembered how Tony had enjoyed Robert Frost's poetry. He never understood his brother's romantic attachment to poetry, his frequent walks along the seashore, or driving all the way upstate just to pick apples. At a bend in the road the sun jeweled the surface of Lake Anapona. *Maybe some of that will rub off on me. The good Lord will reward Tony. It's a pity he had to go. There it is. Life and death. The cycle is as old as mankind.*

Tony, Victor was convinced, was a poet, a religious man, not a man cut out to make tough decisions. The real culprit in Tony's murder is Julio. It was Julio that forced his hand and made the assassination critical to the safety of the Albanese Family. He made the sign of the cross. It was time to pray for the dead.

Julio found his sister-in-law curled on the floor in a fetal position, wrapped in her own arms, convulsed in the sobs and moans of intense emotional suffering, afraid and desolate. The TV was tuned to Channel 4, where live coverage of the Westchester Classic golf tournament was in progress. She must have seen a news flash. He knelt down beside her and said, "I know, I know, Oh God, I know how you feel right now." And gently raising her arms, "Please darling, come and sit. Just cry. I understand."

Julio moved Maria to the large couch, his arms folded around her shoulders. She wept the tears of the emotionally devastated. Adjusting a pillow behind her head, he reached out for the phone and called his friend and family physician, Dr. Chick Brennan. "Chic, Tony's been shot. He's dead. Maria's very bad. Please come to her house."

"I heard the news on the radio. I've been calling your house. I'll be right over."

Julio sat silently as he held his sister-in-law in his arms, allowing her complete reign of her emotions. Tony had been her entire life, and he loved his wife with extraordinary thoughtfulness and tenderness. He assured Maria, "I swear to you, Maria, as long as there's life in my body, I will hunt down the men responsible for this terrible crime."

He would work with Captain Moynihan, and confide in Carlo alone. It was Moynihan who notified Julio of Tony's death, and personally took charge of the investigation. The official police record read:

Case No. 182, of the 35th Squad, New York Police Department. On or about four p.m., September 14, Anthony Albanese, also known as Tony the Accountant, of 200 Avenue C, Manhattan, while sitting in Luca's Restaurant, 358 14th Street, Manhattan, was shot several times in the chest by two unidentified gunmen who escaped in an automobile.

Moynihan promised Julio, "I will personally check on the progress of the investigation every day."

"I would appreciate that."

He owed Julio. As a young police officer he committed an indiscretion with a married woman that could have cost him his job. Through a friend of the Albanese family a private meeting had been arranged with Julio, resulting in the quashing of the case at the departmental level. Since that time he had worked closely with the godfather and had become one of his closest personal friends.

Dr. Brennan came in through the unlocked front door. Maria was sobbing as Julio wiped the tears from her cheek. "Chic, thanks for coming right over. I think Maria's going to be all right, but she should have a little sedation for a couple of days."

Brennan nodded. "Let's get her into her bedroom, Julio. I'll check her to make sure she's OK. Then I'll giver her something to help her rest." He got Maria settled, drew the curtains and closed the door softly, joining Julio. "Who in hell did this, Julio? Tony didn't have any enemies, did he? Could he have been in the wrong place at the wrong time?"

"Not a chance, Chic. Tony was about to be chosen the new head of the organization. It's got to be connected with that. He was lured into the restaurant by a phone call, but we have no idea who made the call."

Chic Brennan was startled. "A new head, what do you mean?"

"That's right. The specialist you sent me to was pretty straight with me. He says I don't have too much time left, maybe a year. I need time with the wife. She has been patient with me all these years, so I decided to move up the timetable. I've retired and a new Don was supposed to be elected this afternoon. It would have been Tony, but now Victor is Don, and you know that he's not popular, Chic, so that's our situation. Things are not so good right now."

Brennan offered sympathy. "I'm sorry."

"Yes, Chic, if I had known this was going to happen, I'd have hung in there a bit longer." Julio paused, reflectively. "Well, we've got Carlo, you know."

With surprise, "Meaning?"

"I don't know yet. Just a gut feeling." Julio checked the driveway at the sound of an arriving auto. It was Carlo and Nicky. He moved quickly to greet his nephews, embracing them. Dr. Brennan put one hand on Carlo's shoulder and pointed the other at Nicky. "Go and comfort your mother. I expect she's still awake."

Brennan got up to leave. "I'll stay in touch, Julio, just in case you need me. Physically she's OK but, emotionally, she's got a lot to go through yet. Carlo and Nicky look surprisingly strong to me, but if you think they need attention, give me a buzz."

Julio was grateful. "OK, Chic, thanks for everything. I'll keep you informed. Give my best to the wife."

Julio then discussed with Carlo the arrangements for the Requiem Mass and burial. Nicky joined in with the conversations, gave his opinions, was listened to. It made him feel good.

As the family gathered at Carlo's home, Victor was busy trying to console and reassure the family. He ordered round-the-clock protection for Maria. "Carlo, I called Frankie a few minutes ago and he's sending two of his best men over here right away. Uncle Julio is making arrangements with the funeral director. I want you to know that everyone in the organization is having a Mass said for your dad."

Carlo had been sitting with his head leaning listlessly on his left shoulder, his hands resting in his lap, fingers twitching. He sat erect and said to Victor. "Thank you, Uncle, for all your concern. We'll find out who did this and they must pay the price." His calm demeanor masked the hot blood roaring through his veins.

Victor felt the strength and coldness in Carlo's manner and words. It made him uneasy. *He's got ice water in his veins.* For a fleeting moment he wondered if Carlo knew something, sensed something. *I've got to keep control of my thoughts. I really shouldn't feel guilty. I did the family a favor.* He recalled the day Julio told him, "Look at Carlo, Victor, don't you see Enrico in him?" The reference startled Victor. Enrico Cardinale was the most prominent Don in Sicily. His name and reputation were so feared that the Sicilian Foreign Minister had been sacked after a casual remark made at a reception in the British Embassy. In response to the British Ambassador's observation that Enrico was a man to be reckoned with, the hapless Foreign Minister replied, "His bark is worse than his bite."

That bite was felt the very next morning when he was summoned at 8 a.m. from his residence in the suburbs to appear before a furious Prime Minister. "I am asking for your resignation. If I get it, nothing more drastic will happen to you."

The Foreign Minister got the message. "I'll have my resignation on your desk by noontime." His resignation enabled him to continue to live and die a natural death.

Father Adolfo heard the news of Tony Albanese's death in a phone call from his head usher. He immediately called the Vicar, Bishop Marty Allen "Just want to run this by you, Marty. You see any problem about giving Tony a Christian burial?"

"No, Dolphi, not at all. If you get any calls on this from the Press, refer them to the Chancery Office. We'll issue the usual statement about his loyalty to the Church, etc. OK?"

"Thanks, Marty."

Adolfo then phoned his Puerto Rican maintenance man, Manuel Ortiz. "Manuel, did you hear about the murder of Father Carlo's dad?"

"Yes, Father, my wife and I were just listening to the radio. They're talking about it."

"Well, we'd better get our grounds in good shape because the funeral is being held here. Get a couple of high school boys to give you a hand cleaning it up. The parking lot has more beer cans right now than Yankee stadium."

"OK, Father, I'll make this place as fancy as St. Patrick's. Don't worry about a thing."

Carlo's call came as Father Adolfo was making himself a meatball sandwich. "Carlo here. I'm sorry I didn't call sooner." His voice was sepulchral. "I guess you've heard about my dad already."

"Yes, Carlo, I 'm terribly sorry. You have my sympathy."

Carlo continued in a heavy, rasping monotone. "Can we have the funeral Wednesday?"

"Of course."

"The family would like to have it about 11 o'clock, in order to give all the members of the Organization and the other Families an opportunity to get here. Some dons will be coming from Providence and Boston, others from the Coast."

Father Adolfo was surprised at the ease with which Carlo spoke of his family's connection with the other Crime Families. "Eleven o'clock will be fine, Carlo, and don't worry about not being here to get things ready for the funeral. I need to do a bit of work once in awhile."

Carlo was appreciative. "Thanks." His voice still lacked inflection. The inner sadness was reflected in his monotone. "I must go now, Father. I'll see you Wednesday."

The funeral cortege made its way off the FDR Drive at the Houston Street exit in a long string of black limousines, close enough to each other that no stray vehicle could break into the line. From the vantage point of the WINS radio traffic helicopter, it was an enormous black, coiled belt, unwinding itself in a flow along the highway. The weather was in the low fifties, with a turquoise sky painted with fleecy clouds. Earlier that morning drops of rain had danced on rooftops and slid down the sides of Manhattan's lanky structures, finding their way along curbstones into the city's gulping sewers. Channel Five's helicopter crew prayed for sunshine; their prayers were answered.

Jack Wilson, pilot of the "True Blue" chatted with Bunny Allen, the first woman to have this airborne assignment. "I can never figure out why these Mafia guys are so attached to the Catholic Church. They aren't just putting on an act, Bunny. These fellows are for real. They really believe."

Bunny checked to make sure her microphone had been turned off. "Well, remember Jack; they all have Sicilian and Italian backgrounds. Did you ever hear of a Protestant Italian? They're as rare as gold nuggets on the Bowery. Besides, these Mafia Families have never considered themselves criminals - Robin Hoods perhaps, but not criminals. They see themselves as anti-establishment heroes. I'm not so sure the general public does not look at them the same way." Bunny said with a giggle, "Of course, they need the Church more than anyone else, don't you think?"

Jack Wilson concurred. "I think that would be a fair statement, Bunny. With their history, they need a priest blessing them as they come into the world and as they leave it. Go ahead, Bunny. Your time to shine."

She turned on her mike and reported, "If you can avoid using the FDR this morning, South of the UN building, I would advise you to do so. The funeral cortege of the popular Mafia lieutenant, Tony Albanese, has backed-up traffic to the UN Garage exit at 49th Street."

Carlo, Maria, Nicky, Tina and Julio rode together in Julio's limousine that had been polished to a glittery shine. The crowds that lined the street fixed their gaze on the limo's darkly tinted windows, hoping to penetrate its reflective glass for a glimpse of Julio Albanese. Photographers joined the crowd in the street and focused cameras on the occupants of the lead limos. Inside Julio's limo, only the humming of the air-conditioner and Maria's muted sobbing disturbed the silence. Each had his or her own thoughts. Carlo glanced at the long line of limousines. Somewhere in that black line sat his father's murderer. He was convinced of that. He also was aware that a signal had been sent from his emotions to his brain that determined the fate of these men once they were found.

Father Adolfo was waiting at the sacristy entrance when the funeral procession arrived. "Everything is ready, Carlo. I'll help you with the liturgy." Pointing to an envelope resting on the vestment cabinet he said, "There's a letter for you, hand-delivered, from the Cardinal. He also called and asked me to give you his condolences. Many priests have called."

Carlo embraced him. "Adolfo, thanks for everything. You've been so kind and understanding. The family is grateful."

The two priests vested and proceeded to the altar. The Requiem Mass for the repose of the soul of Tony Albanese was about to begin. The church was filled to overflowing. Carlo felt the incongruity of it all, as he raised his chalice in supplication before the principal leaders of organized crime in the United States. At the conclusion of the gospel reading, Carlo signaled his Uncle Victor to come to the pulpit to give the eulogy. Many thought it should have been Julio, but both Julio and Carlo deferred to the man who now bore the responsibility of leadership. Carlo introduced him. "It is fitting that my Uncle Victor, who now assumes a unique position of trust in our family, speaks for us on this sad occasion."

Victor felt a pleasurable rush of expanding benevolence. *I will be a father to all of our large family. They will grow to love me as they did Julio.* Waiting for his nephew to resume his seat at the altar, Victor made the sign of the Cross and began. "Every family experiences the joys and sorrows of life. Every family learns to cope with the misfortunes that come its way. But today, we mourn, not merely the death of a loved one, but the vicious, unprovoked murder of one of the most gentle of men who ever issued forth from the creative finger of God. Our family has not merely suffered sorrow. We have been struck with a great tragedy, an unspeakable and unforgivable crime." Victor intended to vow vengeance publicly for his brother's murder, but Carlo had prevailed on him not to do that in the church. "My family is grateful for your presence here today. We know how much you loved my brother and we're overwhelmed by the messages of support and condolence. It bears witness to the kind of man we had in Tony Albanese."

Then, in spite of his promise, Victor hinted at revenge. "We shall not rest until the day of justice." Glancing at the open casket, he said, "Tony, may the angels and our beloved ancestors welcome you into Paradise."

Carlo then continued the Requiem Mass. "The body of Christ," said Carlo, putting the host on the tongue of each communicant, among them several police who were on the Family payroll. As the Mass ended, Carlo moved, together with the three altar boys carrying incense and Holy Water, to the casket covered with a white pall symbolizing the baptismal garment. The altar boys moved to the head of the casket, one of them carrying a large crucifix. Carlo gave the final blessing.

"Eternal rest grant unto my father, Tony, O Lord, and let perpetual light shine upon him. May his soul and the souls of the faithful departed rest in peace. Amen." He then moved to embrace his mother and Nicky, as the procession started down the aisle and out of the church, to the waiting funeral car.

Carlo noted with appreciation that the press, while present in large numbers, chose to be discreet, taking photos from a distance, with none of the stampeding chaos that had characterized their actions at his ordination. Captain Nichols of the Mounted Police remarked to an aide, "Don't tell me these guys are actually acting like human beings!" The three major networks had settled for mini-cams, thus avoiding the use of the large vans that would have made the funeral look more like a political convention. Also, Victor had worked out a compromise with the news media. The networks had requested interviews with Victor and other dons around the country; they had been denied. Nicky would represent the family at an interview at Rockefeller Center. Nicky's insertion into the process was a calculation on Victor's part that his 'promotion' might help to gradually diminish Carlo's influence in the Family. Nicky was desperate enough to be used as a foil and easily manipulated.

Chapter Twelve
THE INVESTIGATION

More than two months elapsed before the first break came in the hunt for Tony's killers. Moynihan had put his best men on the case. One of these men was Detective Sean Flaherty. He sat in his precinct office and brushed his long blond hair aside as he read the latest reports on the Albanese murder case. Dressed in gray trousers, a charcoal-speckled white sport coat and loose fitting tie, Flaherty was the calm and casual personality his dress reflected. A former college athlete, he stood six feet tall, with wide shoulders that sloped down to big hands and narrow hips. He was confused about the circumstances of Tony Albanese's death, but of one thing there was no doubt. Tom Moynihan, his boss, in his most forceful language, with jaw squared off, had determinedly told him, "Sean, I want to crack this one. We'll use every resource at our disposal. Give it all you've got."

The pressure was on. The precinct was full of rumors that Moynihan had a special relationship with the Albanese family, but no one had ever been able to substantiate that allegation. As a protégé of Captain Moynihan, Flaherty had a special relationship of his own with him that transcended that of boss and underling. Moynihan trusted him with special projects that required secrecy and unorthodox investigative techniques. That very morning, Moynihan had said to him, "Sean, I want you to interview the waitress at Luca's, Millie Watson, at her home. She's expecting you about two." She had already been interviewed, but Moynihan, desperate for a clue, instructed Flaherty to interview her again. "Go over every damn detail ten times if you have to and get back to me before you make out your written report. We might have to sift something out. You know what I mean."

Flaherty knew very well what he meant. The last time something had to be "sifted out" of a report, it had contained an embarrassing reference to the son of one of the men in the next precinct. Flaherty respected his boss's judgment and the compassionate way in which he exercised his authority.

Millie Watson lived at 286 W. 18th Street, in the garment district, on Manhattan's Lower West Side. Sean Flaherty took the elevator to the 6th floor and pressed the doorbell at apartment E. He could hear water running and dishes being moved about.

"Who is it?" Millie sounded nervous.

"Detective Flaherty, from the 23rd Precinct, Miss Watson, I believe you're expecting me."

"Hold your badge up front of the peephole, so I can see it."

Flaherty held his badge against his chest, just below the knot of his tie. He heard the latch click. Millie Watson opened the door and let him in, locking her eyes on him with caution. She flicked water off her hands and grabbed a paper towel to dry them. A yellowed imitation pearl necklace dangled between two sagging breasts. She was dressed in a white cotton blouse and apricot-colored skirt. Hastily applied lipstick brushed the side of one cheek. She hand-brushed her bottle-blond hair, and said through thin lips, "Sorry Detective, but a gal living alone has to protect herself in this city." Her anxiety changed to friendliness.

Flaherty understood. "I would have given you hell if you had not asked to see the badge, ma'am. We have enough troubles in the City without citizens needlessly exposing themselves to danger." He paused to take a deep breath, and then said. "I'm here to ask you about the murder you witnessed at Luca's"

Scarcely illuminated by a flickering floor lamp, the apartment was depressing. It consisted of a kitchen/dining room and a bed visible beyond a beaded nylon drape circling-off a small corridor for sleeping. Its walls were painted a suffocating green, the monotony of which was broken only by two faded photographs of a young man and woman on what appeared to be the Coney Island boardwalk. Four unmatched chairs hugged a tiny dining table draped with an oilcloth. A frayed, overstuffed love seat was the only other furniture. "Have a seat," she said, offering him the love seat.

"Prefer hard chairs," he lied, sitting at the table and inviting her to take the love seat.

She shook her head. "I'm going to make some coffee for us, and I'll sit with you. Do you mind?"

"I'd love it."

Millie busied herself measuring ground coffee into the percolator basket, spoonful by spoonful, making a strong brew. She pointed toward the small kitchen table covered with a crocheted string tablecloth. A glass jar in the center of the table held sugar. "Do you take milk?"

"I sure do."

"Well, are you comfortable? I'll pour this coffee for you as soon as it's ready."

Flaherty, loosening his tie and crossing his long legs, smiled and said. "I am confortable."

"All I got is canned milk. OK?"

Flaherty nodded affirmatively. "Great, Miss Watson. You're a mind reader. Actually that's what I use. Makes the coffee creamy."

"What about a Fig Newton to go with it?."

"You really are a mind-reader! You know, that is the one sweet I can remember having since I was a kid."

She pulled a can of Evaporated Milk from the refrigerator, brushed dried milk drops from its edge and placed it on the table.

Flaherty sniffed the aroma, eagerly grasped the proffered cup, added the evaporated milk, and consumed half the coffee in one gulp. "OK, Miss Watson, let's get down to business. I'd like you to tell me absolutely everything you can remember about the killing." Flaherty readied his notebook. "I know you've already given a statement to the police, but sometimes it's good to do it twice, in case you missed something the first time."

Millie Watson recounted her remembrance of the events and Flaherty glanced over her original report, as she spoke. They tallied. He probed for something new. "Miss Watson, in your earlier statement you said the car was a Buick, but you could not remember the color. Any thoughts about that since?"

Millie was prepared. "Actually, after thinking about this -you know, I was nervous at the time - I did remember that the car was blue - yes, a blue Buick, definitely."

"Anything else you may have forgotten?"

Millie pinched her nostrils. "I've wracked my brain; that's it. Can't remember anything else."

Flaherty picked up his notebook and started to leave. "Thanks for the coffee, Miss Watson. You're remembering the color might prove to be a big help. You never really know in this business what little clue is going to crack a case; you just never know. Thanks."

As he started to leave, Millie accompanied him to the landing. "Whenever you're in the area, feel free to stop in for coffee."

"Might just do that ma'am, might just do that."

As he disappeared lower in the stairwell, Millie turned back to her apartment. She had been mesmerized by his voice, a voice that she mentally compared to a rich wine. *Let me crawl back into my hole. Imagine getting excited just sitting with a cop for a few minutes. I'm really hard up.* She bent over, reached up under her skirt, peeled off her pantyhose and sprawled onto her bed.

Flaherty was reporting to Captain Moynihan when Detective Dan Tobin walked into the office with his own report. "I interviewed a young couple who were strolling past Luca's when the gunmen exited and ran for their car. They were afraid to come forth until now, but felt it might be a civic duty. They asked that we keep their name secret. I told them, no problem. The couple confirmed Miss Watson's description of a blue Buick.'" There was more. "Sir, we have a potentially very important piece of information from their testimony." Moynihan, who had been listening intently from a slouch, quickly straightened up.

"What's that?"

"Sir, the couple noticed a sticker on the back fender of the car which read, 'Come and browse on Goat Island.' Neither of them had ever heard of Goat Island, sir, but the clever wording attracted their attention."

Moynihan struck his desk with his fist. "Dan, you've got something important here all right. Where the hell is Goat Island?"

Tobin consulted his notes. "Off the city of Newport, Rhode Island, sir."

Moynihan slapped the side of his head with the palm of his hand. "My God, Dan, you come in here, calm as hell, read me all that stuff like it's just another report! You've just earned your entire year's wages, fella."

Tobin's modesty never ceased to surprise his boss. "Does your parish priest know what a bloody saint you are?"

Tobin blushed. "Can I be excused for lunch, sir? Only had a cup of coffee and a roll for breakfast."

Moynihan raised his hands to his forehead, "Get outta here." Then, pointing to Flaherty, "You also. Go see your wife and kids. You guys did great today."

As soon as the detectives were out of earshot, Moynihan dialed Julio Albanese. "Julio, I may have something for you. If you're going to be home for the next couple of hours I'll drop by and fill you in."

"Come right out, Tom."

Moynihan went to the small closet in his office and exchanged his regulation shirt for a Munsingwear knit. Officer Davidson whistled her approval as he passed her desk.

"Who you trying to kid, Bernice? I'm old enough to be your dad. Listen, I'm out for the rest of the day. If anything comes in on the Albanese case, get me at home."

Officer Davidson let out another loud whistle as he left.

Moynihan's call lifted Julio's spirits. Until that moment, in spite of extensive phone calls, he had not gleaned a single clue to his brother's murder. It's *been frustrating. Just a break, that's all we need. Just something!*

As he swung his car along the curved drive banked with late blooming flowers, Moynihan could smell salty breezes coming off of the Sound's gleaming waters. He entered the front door and he called out, "Anybody home?"

From a distance, Julio's voice. "Come in."

He let himself in and walked straight to the paneled den, whose walls were covered with photographs of Julio standing or sitting with the rich and famous. Moynihan was surprised to see Carlo by Julio's side.

Again. "Come in, friend."

The room defined Julio in a way that little else did. His valuable library collection showed signs of use, with a Sicilian history volume and an atlas lying open on his desk. Beyond the room's large glass window, sailboats rocked back and forth in the Sound, their masts reaching for the sky. A squadron of herring gulls stood guard. In the den, a television set, its volume lowered, murmured from a niche in the wall. Julio stood in a wedge of shade so merged into the mottled light and dark as to be almost invisible. They shook hands, and Moynihan embraced Carlo. "It's so very good to see you. Sorry I couldn't make your ordination; the wife was sick."

Carlo was gracious. "I and my family appreciated your note about that. Thank you."

Moynihan noticed the lack of strength in Julio's handshake and movements. He was indeed aging. He thought: *How quickly the whole Mafia scene has changed from the certainty of this man's reign to the ambiguity of the present crisis.*

"What's your choice?" asked Julio, opening the liquor cabinet.

"You fix me something."

Julio poured Old Grandad onto a bed of ice. "Here's your favorite."

Carlo handed Tom a bowl of mixed nuts, as he asked, "What do you have for us, Tom?" Moynihan noted that it was Carlo who asked the question. Julio always held center stage in any discussions he ever had with him. That Carlo asked the question was significant. Julio had always told him that Carlo was a natural leader. And, he sure was involved in this matter. For a priest, this was heavy stuff.

Moynihan consulted his notes. "One promising lead. We questioned a young couple who saw these guys leaving Luca's and hopping into a blue

Buick with a sticker, 'Come Browse on Goat Island.' One of the waitresses confirmed that it was a blue Buick."

"That's off Newport, Tom." Julio lowered his voice. "But let's keep this to ourselves."

"Right, Julio."

The men discussed the lack of concrete information in the case. "It's got to be some sort of inside job, Tom. For the life of me I can't think of anyone who had it in for Tony. It puzzles the hell out of me."

As the conversation continued, Moynihan bent forward from his seat, both elbows propped on his knees. "There's an old saying or something, Julio, that one's enemies come from one's own household. We have to keep that in mind as we go along."

Julio shrugged, but he concurred. *How right he is; those were my own thoughts from the beginning.*

Carlo was somber. "That makes the crime all the more vicious and abominable. The revenge will be bitter sweet."

A long silence followed his remark. Moynihan glanced at Carlo and thought: *He never gets excited, no matter what. Just cold and factual.* Moynihan nervously glanced at his watch. "I've got to run. This is the night I take the wife to the movies. It's her only excitement, except for being married to me!"

As his friend drove off, Julio, with Carlo by his side, stood and watched the brilliant setting sun casting a long red shadow over Long Island Sound. He treasured these peaceful evenings by the sea. He viewed them as a preparation for eternal life. In his imagination he returned to his youth. He smelled once again the fields of his hometown, the taste of fruit ripe from the tree, and fish plucked out of the sea with primitive equipment. He reached deep into his soul's submerged memory, to that unconscious moment when he emerged from the hand of a living God. Turning to Carlo, "Does God understand what we need to do?"

"He does, Uncle Julio."

The solution to the Family's problems stood by his side, quiet, strong and determined. Carlo's strength made it possible for Julio to spend whatever time he had left refurbishing his soul, preparing to meet his maker. There were demons that needed expelling

That evening, at the movies, Moynihan whispered to his wife, "Whoever assassinated Tony is going to be assassinated."

Chapter Thirteen
THE SUSPECTS

During this time of investigating his Father's murder, Carlo made every attempt to be an effective priest and to enjoy the priesthood as he grappled with the realities of life in lower Manhattan. Denny Wilson was one of those realities. He stood before Carlo, his hands hooked in his pockets, eyes fixed in an unseeing stare. "I need some hard cash, Father, I really do. My back is bothering me. I can barely bend over, sometimes even sitting is painful."

Denny was about thirty years old, a former student at Long Island University where he had spent three years studying physics. The excessive and endless school partying led him down the road to alcoholism. Carlo had been trying to get him to do some manual labor in exchange for the food he was provided by St. Anthony's. But Denny always had an excuse. This time it was his back.

Carlo interlocked his fingers and spread them outward. "Denny, it's time you and I start calling it like it is. Your back is probably a lot stronger than mine. We're coming to the end of the line, Denny. You either start working a bit or we're going to close the door on you. Got the message?"

Carlo was already accustomed to listening to hard-luck stories, but Denny topped them all, forcing Carlo beyond the limits of his compassion. He had referred Denny to the alcoholic units of several hospitals in Manhattan and Brooklyn, and the VA hospitals on 23rd Street, and Fordham Road in the Bronx. As soon as he would say, "His name is Denny Wilson," there was, invariably a groan, "Father please don't send Denny to us. He's hopeless. We've tried everything."

Denny, it turned out, was the best known name in the world of alcoholic rehabilitation, a superstar.

The telephone rang. It was Julio. "Carlo, I'm at Beef 'n Burger near Bloomingdales, on 3rd Avenue. You know the place?"

"Yes, Uncle, I do."

"Good. If you can get away, I've got a few things to discuss with you. There's a parking lot just around the corner."

"Give me fifteen minutes."

"Good, I'll order a couple of hamburgers - should be ready by the time you get here."

Carlo returned his focus to Denny "I gotta go, fella. Try your art on another priest for awhile. Give me a break"

Denny reluctantly picked up his brown bag of cheap wine and left the rectory, muttering "Just my damn luck."

The Beef 'n Burger was not the sort of place to enhance Carlo's appetite. The lighting was poor; the walls streaked dirty brown from waterlogged foundations. He wondered why people left their comfortable apartments, especially on wintry or rainy days, to sit for an hour or more eating soggy hamburgers and drinking stale beer in a depressing atmosphere.

Julio had seated himself at the large plate glass front, and waved Carlo in. "Here's your hamburger, with lots of French Fries."

"Thanks, Uncle."

"Now, down to business." Julio pointed to a folder he held in his hands. "I've got a list of names and addresses of every guy who works for the Families in the New York area. Here it is. Study it and keep your fingers crossed. I've asked Frankie to invite every possible name on this list to Donna's birthday party. Hopefully, the bastards we're looking for will be on that list. If not, we got a problem."

Carlo agreed. "What did you tell Frankie about why you wanted to invite all these guys?"

"Oh, I just said we needed to cheer up after all our problems, so, invite the world."

"Fine, Uncle."

Julio explained. "It's our best hope. Pray for this one, Carlo. I figure that with so many people invited, the killers, if they are on this list, will come because they will think that if they are invited and they don't show, they will stick out like a sore thumb. Got it?"

"Got it!" Carlo never ceased to admire Julio's craftiness. He was a master of the art. ""I'll check all the cars to see if the Blue Buick with the Goat Island sticker is there."

"Exactly, my boy. It's our best shot right now."

When they finished eating, they walked arm in arm to Julio's car, joined by blood and the bonds of friendship, in a common project.

On First Fridays the attendance at morning Mass at St. Anthony's nearly tripled. Many people came for the Novena to the Sacred Heart, a custom that went as far back as anyone could remember. As Carlo read the Novena prayers, his mind was on the real business of the day. After the Mass and the Communion calls to the sick, he would continue the hunt for his father's killer.

Mrs. Orecchio, president of the Sacred Heart League, stopped him after Mass. "Please, Father, do you have a few minutes? I've got something very important to discuss with you."

Carlo was fond of the old ladies. They were the backbone of the parish, even if they did frighten away the young. It was a problem every parish priest had to face. "Sure, Mrs. Orecchio, come to the office."

Carlo pulled out a chair for her, and then sat down spreading his elbows wide on the desktop. "What can I do for you?"

Mrs. Orecchio was almost in tears. "Father, as you know, we've arranged a bus trip to St. Joseph's Shrine in Canada and now the bus company says we have to pay fifteen dollars more per person. They say the cost of fuel has gone up since we made our agreement. Our people, Father, they can't afford an extra fifteen dollars, and I don't want to call off the trip. They would all be so disappointed. What can we do?"

"Give me the telephone number of the Bus Company, Mrs. Orecchio, and the name of the person you spoke to."

Mrs. Orecchio gave him the information he needed. "Don't worry. Come, I'll let you out. I know you've got a lot of things to do at home. Have a good day. Everything will be fine." He could feel Julio's blood running through his veins.

She kissed his hand as she left the rectory. "God bless you, Father Carlo."

As soon as she left, he called Frankie. "Hey, Carlo, I'm still in bed. You think I'm a monk like you? What do you want?"

"Do you know the Belt Line Bus Company?"

"Yeah."

"Well, they just raised their price fifteen dollars a head for a parish excursion. You have any influence with them?"

"Sure, Carlo, I'll take care of it. Those guys rip off the public all the time with that 'extra cost' business. I'll just tell them we don't like them ripping off churches. That'll make them stop and think. Consider it done. I'm going back to sleep."

Carlo was relieved. "Thanks, Frankie. Have them call Mrs. Orecchio at 555-7931. She's the President of the Sacred Heart Society that's sponsoring the trip."

Frankie hung up and turned to his concerned wife, who associated early morning calls with trouble. "Know what, Norma? That was Carlo. Wants me to put some muscle on a bus company! What do you think of that! He's one of us, you know. If they ever find out who knocked off Tony, watch out! – the guys who pulled the trigger are gonna need police protection. That's for sure. This killing has us buffaloed, but when we find these guys there's gonna be some dead bodies in this town, and Carlo's gonna know how they got there. You can count on it."

Norma wondered if those responsible would ever be discovered. "Maybe it'll be like the Jimmy Hoffa thing. They never found out what happened to him, right?"

Frankie disagreed. "Not exactly, honey. The Jimmy Hoffa thing was different. There are probably twenty guys who know what happened to Hoffa. It's the Feds who don't know, and nobody's gonna tell the Feds. But with us, we'll find out and we'll take care of justice in our own way."

Frankie lay back as his mind wandered over a multitude of possibilities, each of which faded as he tried to grasp it. But, he did have a gut feeling that the killers would be discovered, and that Carlo would take care of business.

Frankie and Norma Montana were having a birthday party for their first-born child, Donna, a beautiful young girl who was to be four years old that Sunday. "The party has come at an ideal time," observed Norma.

Frankie agreed. "We gotta get out of the doldrums. Tony would approve of this. He was such a positive thinking guy. We gotta keep living."

In the months following Tony's death, the members of the Family had lived under a cloud of depression and indecision. It was time to do something joyful, to celebrate something, to break out in song. The Italian spirit yearned to explode again. Carlo himself had said to Victor, "Uncle, it's time to gather again as a family."

Victor agreed. He was a bit surprised at the large number of men invited to the party, but then, the party was a kind of coming out party for him. He would have an opportunity to meet men from the various Families. They would report back to others how he had solidified the Albanese Family, how everyone seemed so happy. This could only be a plus for him and his career.

Frankie and a couple of his men hauled beer and soft drinks all Saturday afternoon. Norma and Tracey festooned the living room and patio with balloons, paper lions, elephants and zebras. Sunday morning, all was ready.

There was another feeling in the air. Victor had tried hard to establish himself as the leader of the Family. He really had not succeeded. Not that anyone wanted him to fail. "He just doesn't have it," was the way Frankie put it to Carlo privately. "Besides, he has reptilian eyes. I don't like reptilian eyes. Makes me uneasy."

Carlo laughed. "Never heard of reptilian eyes, Frankie."

"They exist, Carlo, believe me, and Victor has them."

"They're something special?"

"Yeah, they belong to snakes. You know I don't like your uncle; no disrespect intended. He got the job by fluke; he's gonna have a long haul to be accepted by the guys." He was surprised at his own brashness.

The birthday party was also shaping up as a vehicle for the Family to look to Carlo for leadership, and Victor was not close enough to the members to pick that up. No one knew quite how to articulate this feeling, or how it could come about. They already had a Don, but he embarrassed them. Outside Families paid little attention to Victor and considered his ascension to power simply an accident. There was also the question of Nicky. How could one chat with Nicky and not say something like, "We look forward to the day when the responsibilities will be placed in your hands?" Poor Nicky, they said, he's just tagging alongside Carlo like a homeless puppy.

Similar thoughts were on Carlo's mind as he checked to make sure he had placed the vial of Holy Water and the liturgy book in the glove compartment of his car. The Mass at St. Anthony's would delay him. He called Norma. "I'm going to be a bit late, so please get started with the party."

The week had been disappointing. No information had turned up on the auto sticker. Inquiries had been made by Victor, Frankie, and Annunzio of every Don on the East Coast. Absolutely nothing. He prayed that Julio's plot would work. As he was about to leave the church the organist, Theresa Caldone, approached him. He was apologetic. "Sorry we could not get together for a practice today, Theresa. I'm rushing off to a little girl's birthday party."

She was gracious. "That's OK, Father, don't worry about it. We'll get together later."

Carlo felt a tinge of guilt driving off in a hurry. His loyalty to family and his creeping involvement in its internal affairs was drawing him away from his parish duties. The pastor said nothing about this and probably never would. There was an understanding between pastor and assistant that the pastor understood.

Carlo pulled into the driveway of Frankie's home. The party was in full swing. Many of the guests he had never seen before. Norma was the first to spot him as he walked toward the back lawn, where the Family was busy eating and drinking. She greeted him with a hug. "Carlo, come and say Happy Birthday to Donna. She's been asking, `Where is Carlo?`" And then, pointing to the crowd, "Isn't it wonderful? Everyone's having such a good time. It's good to hear laughter again."

At that moment, Donna noticed Carlo and rushed up to him, wrapping her arms around his legs, and looking up at him with the beguiling innocence of childhood. Her dark eyes and jet-black hair seemed to join her arms in one sweeping embrace. He looked down at her piquant face and lilting ponytail. Lifting her quickly, he swept her into the air like a drooping flag up a pole.

"Hey, look at the birthday girl! I've got a present for you. See what I brought you!"

Donna opened her gift, a small gold charm bracelet and matching brooch, a tiny butterfly made of bits of tinted glass "Oh, Carlo, put it on me."

Carlo obliged as the Family chanted, "Girlfriend, girlfriend."

Carlo lifted the girl in his arms, kissing her as the Family cheered. Julio approached Carlo. "I'm glad you could make it. I know you guys are busy on Sundays." Julio adjusted his trousers with a horizontal twist. "I tell you, Carlo, just seeing all these folks having a good time is like winning a million bucks. This is how your dad would want it."

Nicky made the rounds with a drink in his hand, demonstrating the false ebullience he had so assiduously perfected. Victor joined them, addressing Julio with an expansive gesture of hands, "Hey, you look fit enough to take back your old job. What right you got to retire? You don't have enough years in the pension fund."

Julio responded with an embrace. "The problems are in your hands now, my dear brother. We look to you for leadership."

Carlo thought that power had mellowed Victor. He was more relaxed and human. He confided to Julio, "Perhaps he will eventually get the Organization behind him. Certainly, everyone is giving him time to prove himself."

"Don't think he can do it," was Julio's bland reply.

Victor wanted and needed Carlo's approval. He assured him. "Carlo, I know this isn't the time to talk business. I'll fill you in later but, to be brief, we've come up with nothing so far. I'm really sorry. We're going to keep at it until we do. I promise you."

Carlo was appreciative. "Thanks, Uncle Victor; things will work out. In the meantime, life has to go on. Let's have a drink." The three men moved over to the liquor table.

"There you are." Norma draped an arm around Carlo's shoulder as he poured himself Chianti. She pulled at his waist, "Come and bless Donna and the house."

Carlo took a sip of wine. "Let me go out to the car and get the Holy Water. Be right back."

As Carlo moved along the long line of cars, he caught sight of an unusually large blue bird on a willow branch so low he could have touched it with his outstretched arm. As he redirected his eyes to the driveway he saw the sticker. "Come, Browse with Us on Goat Island," printed in blue letters on a white background. The car was a metallic-red Buick Skylark with New York State license plates. The palms of his hands oozed sweat as a host of conflicting emotions gripped him. Revenge flooded his psyche. He moved quickly to his car, gripping the Holy Water bottle and ritual book in a tight fist. Returning to the house, he paused to note the Buick's license plate number, PRW 117. His eyes swept the upper floor of Frankie's house as he targeted a room overlooking the driveway.

Norma met him at the door, Donna at her side. "We're ready for the blessing, Carlo."

"Oh, yes, of course."

Carlo placed his hands on the child's head and prayed, "May Almighty God, Father, Son and Holy Spirit descend upon you and bring you everlasting life. Amen."

He bent down, kissing Donna on her forehead and, addressing the family, he said, "Come, let's bless every room in the house."

The family and friends followed him as he passed through each room, spraying it with Holy Water and saying "May God bless this house and all that dwell in it, preserving them from every physical and moral evil. In the name of the Father, the Son and the Holy Spirit…"

All made the sign of the cross as he sprayed each room. When finished with his task, Carlo joined the others in eating and drinking. He kept an eye open to see when the first guests began leaving. Two women who had been talking to Julio made their farewells to Norma and left the house. He needed to get upstairs before others left, so he made his move. He got Norma aside and whispered, "Norma, do you mind if I rest upstairs for a while? I have a headache. It must be all the tension we've been under lately. Make an excuse for me."

"Of course, Carlo, take any bedroom and relax. There's aspirin in the bathroom cabinet. If you need anything else just call me." Norma pressed his hand with gratitude and moved to rejoin the Family. Julio noted the change in Carlo's demeanor, and his sudden departure from the crowd. He sensed something significant had happened, so he worked the crowd, especially Victor, to create a distraction.

Carlo moved quickly to the bedroom overlooking the driveway and positioned himself to observe the car. He pulled the blind closed, then opened it just enough to see without being seen. After some minutes, more guests began to leave. The owner of the Cadillac parked next to the Skylark pulled out, leaving it more exposed to Carlo's vision. Ten minutes more of waiting and two men approached the Skylark. Carlo got a good look at their faces as they stood by the car. Both appeared to be in their early thirties. He had never met them.

Sweat greased the palms of his hands. His right temple throbbed. He would soon have the headache he had pretended to have. One of the men lit a cigarette as they exchanged inaudible words punctuated by audible laughter before getting into their car. Carlo despised that laughter, wanting to cut it short, to eliminate it. He made a dash down the back stairs and out of the house. *I must follow them.*

He moved swiftly across the noisy driveway gravel that had trapped the sun's heat, got into his car, turned the ignition key and gunned the engine, leaving a shower of flying gravel and sand behind him. His left hand draped over the steering wheel as his right hand firmly gripped it, maneuvering the car at high speed. *I mustn't lose them.*

An anxious tightness gripped his chest. His head and arms made involuntary jerking motions as he trailed the Skylark to the entrance of the Long Island Expressway. The men moved quickly into the flow of traffic, so Carlo pressed the gas pedal until it hit the floorboard. The car lunged forward, entering the Expressway with a loud pneumatic wheeze, chewing up the Expressway's White Center lines. The traffic was heavy, so Carlo had no problem following at a discreet distance. *Oh my God, I hope I've got the right guys. Please Lord, let it be them so we can put this nightmare behind us.*

From the Expressway, the Skylark entered the Grand Central Parkway. Carlo followed in hot pursuit. Wind-blown puffs of seeds pummeled his car like tiny furry asteroids. The men headed towards the Triboro Bridge. From the bridge they entered the East Side Highway, heading south. The two men exited at 49th Street then headed West until they reached Broadway, then south to 45th Street where they pulled into an empty parking space. They walked a half block along the street and entered a bar. Carlo observed them through the bar's open door until they each placed a large stein of beer on a table and began to drink. Quickly, he rushed to the car and found the doors unlocked. In the glove compartment he spotted the car registration. Frederick Podanski, 6877th Street, Apt. 3C, New York, New York. On the passenger seat he spied a small clump of mail, including a telephone bill addressed to: Terrence Mahoney, 688 Riverside Drive, NY, NY. This had to be the passenger.

He waited for them to leave, and then followed them as they weaved in and out of busy Manhattan traffic, to 688 Riverside Drive. As Moroney slid out of the car, they both convulsed in laughter. Carlo was determined that they would soon laugh no longer.

Chapter Fourteen
REVENGE BEGINS

The Volkswagen drove along Harlem's 125th Street. At the Hudson River, the driver's long tapered fingers gripped the steering wheel and took the ramp onto the West Side Highway. He then headed south, exiting at 79th Street by the boat basin, then drove to 6877th Street. The driver pulled up in front of the building on the corner and spotted the Skylark parked further up the street. The bird was in his nest. He entered the building and took the elevator to the 3rd floor, quickly slipping on a stocking mask as he rang the apartment doorbell. Podanski opened the door and faced a Lugar thrust into this stomach. "Nice and quiet fella," said the voice behind the mask. After frisking him and finding no weapon, the intruder reached into his pocket and produced a piece of heavy twine. He tied Podanski's hands to the back of a kitchen chair, and then blindfolded him. Podanski knew all about guns but this was the first time he found himself at the wrong end of one. "What is it you want?" he asked.

"Where is your piece?" the intruder asked rhetorically.

"In the bathroom."

The intruder found it on a holster hung behind the bathroom door. Making sure the safety catch was on, he put it in a bag along with a few other items, including cash from a dresser next to Podanski's bed. On the way out he gently slapped Podanski on the left side of his face and whispered, "Maybe we'll meet again."

Podanski was able to position his hands at the table's edge and grasp a knife. Freeing himself, he called Annunzio. "Got robbed tonight. Answered the stupid doorbell, but I never had a reason to worry about anybody here in this building, so it was no big deal. I was expecting the landlord. He was going to fix a bathroom water faucet, so I just opened up without a thought. Imagine getting stiffed by a two-bit hood! It's embarrassing! "

"What did you lose?"

"About two hundred bucks, a camera, some gold cuff-links and my gun. You make anything of this, Primo?"

Annunzio was concerned. "Try to think, Freddie, was there anything about this guy that might give us a clue as to who the hell he is."

"No, nothing. He had on a stocking mask."

Annunzio paused a moment. "Could be just a fluke. I wouldn't worry about it. But you sure look stupid letting some punk rip you off like that. On the other hand, this guy will probably sell your gun and, who knows, maybe he'll be picked up and charged with you know what! Wouldn't that be sweet? I don't think there's anything to worry about. Just get yourself a new piece."

Podanski did not feel the same confidence. He poured himself a drink, reached for a copy of Playboy, and looked at the girls.

Annunzio thought he would alert Terry Moroney, but he did not answer his phone. *He's probably out celebrating with some of the cash I gave him.* Annunzio was wrong. Moroney was about to have a visitor of his own.

The driver of the Volkswagen kept a long vigil in front of 688 Riverside Drive. A supply of bread, sliced ham and several bottles of root beer lay on the front seat. It was almost four o'clock in the afternoon when he got his break. Podanski's partner entered his apartment building sportily dressed in a charcoal gray tweed jacket, and gray flannel slacks. The driver waited about an hour and then entered the building. As he pressed the apartment doorbell he donned the stocking mask and called out, "You left your car lights on, Mr. Moroney."

Terrance opened the door, and received a blow to his head that felled him instantly. He was carried to the kitchen, blindfolded, gagged and tied to a chair. The gun was on the counter next to a microwave oven. Taking some cash and a radio as well, the intruder quietly made his exit and drove straight to the home of Tom Moynihan.

Moroney reported the incident to Annunzio, as soon as he freed himself. Terror struck. "Oh my God, Terry, the same damn thing just happened to Podanski earlier today. This doesn't look too good. Could be a fluke, but we've gotta be very careful now."

Annunzio was clearly puzzled. "You and Podanski must have been taken by the same guy. He was clearly after the guns; the other stuff was smoke screen. What I can't figure out is, if the cops had anything on you guys, they would just pick you up. They wouldn't hire a hood to break in and take your guns. This has got to be some guy working on his own and, damn it, I can't figure it out. What the hell does he want with the guns?" Annunzio rubbed his left arm vigorously, as if the exercise would produce the answer to his questions.

"I tell you, Terry, this thing's got me worried. If you guys want to leave town, go to Manny's place in Jacksonville. Go separately and stay down there till you hear from me. Call Freddie and discuss this with him."

Annunzio got back to Victor who had called him earlier. "I just talked to Terry and advised him and Freddie to go to Manny's. The place is empty right now, so they can stay until we see if this lone ranger is going to drop the other shoe."

Victor's concern showed in his voice. "Primo, there's only one logical reason why someone would take the guns, and that's to make a ballistics' check. This was not a two-bit thief. Now, I've got a very important question to ask you. Give it to me straight. Are these guys safe? Would they talk? Remember, this is a murder rap, not gun possession."

Annunzio anticipated the question. "Look, Victor, these are just two guys who've done a job for us. If they're charged with murder-one they might plea-bargain. They don't really owe us anything."

Victor agreed. "Let me do some thinking about this, Primo. I'll get back to you. Don't panic or do anything out of the ordinary. The guy who took those guns is playing cat and mouse. We've got to figure out his moves."

Late that night Carlo received a call from Moynihan. "These were the guns used to kill your father."

Carlo awoke to the pleasant realization that some progress was being made in the hunt for his father's killer. *When this is over, I'm going to take a long spell in the sun somewhere.* He slid out of bed and made his way to the shower. After toweling himself, he dressed in the sunshine that poured in through the old-fashioned sash-windows. In the kitchen, he prepared breakfast. After eating two poached eggs and a cup of coffee, he said the eight-thirty Mass, visited the convent to chat with the nuns, wrote checks for the gas and electric bills, met with the organist for an hour, and then joined Father Adolfo for lunch. Carlo made some recommendations. "The organist would like some new hymn books for the children's choir. And you know, Father, I think it's time to elect a new parish council. I can't get the present Council to do anything except recite the same old litany of complaints."

Adolfo agreed, but asked, "Can we get some good people to take their place?"

"Absolutely. I've been talking to some of the young couples who have kids. They are the ones who should be on the Council because they are aware of what is going on out there in the streets and they have a vested interest in having a good parish…their kids."

"Good point, Carlo good point. I totally agree. Handle it the most delicate way you can. Some members of the Council think they're like the Pope - in power for life. I tell you what, why don't you begin the process. First thing you have to do is put a notice in the bulletin, and set a date for the election. It can be done right in church, at every Mass, by handing out and collecting ballots."

Father Adolfo paused, wrinkling his forehead as he tried to recall something. "Oh yes, it's OK on to order new hymn books, Carlo, so long as they're not carbon copies of the old ones put in a different order or with a prettier cover.

Adolfo then brought up the question of the clergy area conferences. "It's been six months since I've attended an area conference. I believe it's time for me to show my face. Otherwise, they'll think I'm dead. I'll do the best I can not to ruffle too many feathers." He shook his head and pursed his lips. "These meetings are not very productive Carlo. They're nothing more than gabfests. The Anglos are not really interested in the problems of the Italian community, so I get bored. All they talk about is idiot stuff, like baptism and confirmation." He shrugged his shoulders, "I'll go, but it'll be a year before I attend another one."

Carlo knew that regular attendance at clergy conferences often accompanied clerical ambitions. The entrance to the office of bishop was through the twin doors of clergy acceptance and assured orthodoxy. Clergy meetings were the place to establish one's credential on both issues. Adolfo had no interest in such things. He once described the meetings as, "The clerical equivalent of political caucuses."

Adolfo inquired, "What's the status of the books, Carlo? Are we solvent? Hate to burden you with this job but I'm hoping that one of these days they'll appoint you as administrator. You need to be ready. As you know, this parish is subsidized by the Archdiocese so we have to submit a financial report every month. We just get through handing in one and we've got to start another." They discussed parish business until noontime. Father Adolfo then went to his room for an hour of what he called "meditation in the prone position."

Carlo was passing through the office on his way to the church when the phone rang. It was Julio. "I looked up these guys. They were recruited in St. Louis and have done work for several of the Families. They are freelancers. Anybody could have hired them, so we must be careful not to draw any premature conclusions."

Carlo had a suggestion. "Uncle Julio, these guys are going to start putting two and two together. Could you place a twenty-four watch on both of them?"

"Good idea, Carlo. I'll get Moynihan to keep an eye on them also. I have a feeling we're all going to be very sick to our stomachs before this is over."

Carlo sensed the sadness in Julio's voice. That this murder might have originated in the Family was a thought devastating to a man who had worked for years to build mutual trust and loyalty in a large but close-knit organization.

Julio got on the phone to Moynihan and asked him to keep an eye on the two men. "OK, Julio, I'll get four men in unmarked cars over to their places right away."

For Carlo, the time for revenge had now arrived.

Victor was physically exhausted and emotionally tense. His wife, Annette, came in with the mail. He welcomed the distraction. There was a card from his cousin Johnny and his wife, vacationing in California, and a card from his wife's sister inquiring about his health. One envelope had no return address and bore the words, "Personal and Confidential" at the lower left-hand corner. Inside the envelope was a small white sheet of paper with a simple message, "I know who did it." Victor's pulse quickened, his head seemed to gain in mass and weight, as nausea permeated his stomach. He stared at the paper in his shaking hand. It was no bigger than a calling card. The note told the story. Someone out there knew everything. His life was surely in jeopardy. *I've got to take immediate and drastic measures to protect myself.*

Only one person could prove his involvement and that person was Primo Annunzio. Victor closed the door of his small den and worked on several possible courses of action.

Wanda Hutchinson was glad to find room 636 untouched. This happened occasionally, especially when a man had a date and the girl did not show up. It was an opportunity to close the door, open the window and enjoy a cigarette on company time. As she moved toward the window, she saw it was already slightly open. She pulled it up the rest of the way as she lit her cigarette. As she glanced at the alley below, she saw, to her horror, a man lying face-up in a pool of blood. "My God!" she gasped and, with trembling fingers, dialed the manager, Harry Hannigan, who notified the local precinct. Detective Steve Baines was rushed to the scene. He identified the body as Primo Annunzio, Caporegime of the Albanese Family. He got on the car radio to Captain Tom Moynihan. "It's your baby,

Captain. One of the Albanese gang. Figured you'd want to know about it pronto."

"You figured right, Steve. Stay at the hotel. I'll meet you there."

"Right."

Then, to the two young officers, "Get moving!" Maybe this case is beginning to unravel.

As they pulled up to the hotel entrance, Moynihan instructed the officers to secure the area. He checked with the manager. "Yes, Captain, Mr. Annunzio checked into Room 636 this morning. I remember him well because he winked at me and said he was meeting someone for a couple of hours. I presumed...well...you know..."

"Yes, I know."

Moynihan phoned Julio from the lobby. "I think I'd better pick up those two guys right away. They'll wanna split when they hear about Annunzio. I'll get back to you."

Officers Murphy and Abrams approached Podanski's apartment cautiously, taking off their shoes as they got off the elevator. They listened for sounds at the door and heard a radio playing. Officer Murphy inserted the manager's key in the lock and opened the door softly. They stood silently and fully alert, guns drawn, as they moved along a small corridor that led to the rest of the apartment. Murphy turned to Abrams and whispered, "Cover me."

"You're covered."

Pressing his back against the corridor partition, Murphy worked his way around the corner and found himself in a large living room. It was divided by a glass coffee table littered with the remains of a TV dinner. From where he stood, he could see the rest of the apartment. An open kitchen, the bathroom, and a small bedroom were all that remained to check. The two officers signaled each other and took up their positions on either side of the bedroom door. At another signal, they rushed into the room, their guns in firing position. They were too late. On the bed lay Freddie Podanski, a bullet hole prominent in the middle of his forehead, from which a large quantity of blood had flowed. The blood, now dry, had become red streaks across the white pillows and sheets. There was no sign of struggle. "Maybe he knew the murderer," Abrams observed.

Terrance Moroney gathered as much of his belongings as he could fit into the trunk and back seat of his Oldsmobile. Since he had no idea when he would be back, he threw some tapes into a plastic bag, pulled the refrigerator plug out of the wall socket, put out the lights and headed for his car. He drove along Riverside Drive in the direction of the George Washington Bridge. At that moment, Officers Stern and Hayes were asking the superintendent for a key to Moroney's apartment. "I believe that Mr. Moroney may have left on a trip. When he paid his bill he said he would not see me for a while. He had lots of luggage with him."

A quick inspection of the room showed this was indeed the case. It was almost bare. Stern went to the patrol car and notified Moynihan. Terrance Moroney was already across the George Washington Bridge, heading south on the New Jersey Turnpike. He had been on the Turnpike less than half an hour when the radio station interrupted its regular programming. "Frederick Podanski, a minor mob figure in New York City, was found shot through the head in his West Side apartment this evening. Officers Murphy and Abrams of the New York City police department discovered the body after arriving at the deceased's apartment to serve an arrest warrant in connection with the slaying of former Mafia lieutenant, Anthony Albanese, brother of Julio Albanese, reputed Mafia don."

"My God," he uttered, "I got out just in time." Suddenly a sticky warm wave flowed through his body and he became nauseous. Podanski pulled off the road onto a grassy knoll, braked the car to a halt and cut the engine just in time to vomit. As the heavens dripped large raindrops he cowered in the front seat, finger-combing his hair. The rain spattering against the windshield and the passing cars punctuated the stillness of the night. Stupefied with fear, Terrance put out the automobile lights and sat motionless, except for the nervous twitching of his fingers. He remained like this until the gaze of a curious State Policeman caused him to drive off once again. Primo alone knew of their involvement in the Tony Albanese affair, and now Primo and Freddie were dead. The house would be safe. Primo had said, "There's enough food there for two guys to hold out for a year." He would visit his girlfriend in Jacksonville, Florida, who lived only a few miles from Manny Rogers' place. He would not tell her where he was staying. He would simply say, "I'm at a local hotel."

By morning, the sky had cleared. The breeze from the vented window was refreshing and the radio music buoyed his spirits. As the day wore on, his confidence grew. By evening, he felt that danger was behind him. He had no idea that his every movement was being tracked.

Chapter Fifteen
MORONEY AND ANNETTE

As he pulled off the freeway onto the country road that led to Annette's Simpson's home, Terry began to relax for the first time in days. Annette was a bosomy blonde who once made a living at gyrating in sleazy nightclubs. In a world where he was rated no higher than "a common hood," Terrance was forever grateful to this twenty six-year old woman who adored him. Their earlier passionate lovemaking had developed into a close and deepening friendship, something that had not happened between him and any other woman. She did not expect more than an occasional visit from him, but her loyalty and faithfulness never faltered. Turning into Dixie Drive, he warmed at the inviting lights of her home. Quietly, he pulled into the driveway and took a moment to vent his growing confidence, stretching his arms toward the hills, which fanned out as far as he could see. Suddenly Annette appeared at the aluminum screen door. "Terry? Oh gosh, you didn't tell me you were coming. What a wonderful surprise." She ran to him, planting a kiss on his cheek and snuggling her face against his chest.

"Does that make a difference?" in mocked anger.

Pulling him by the arm, "Oh, of course not. Come in, come in."

"You look beautiful," he said, as he embraced her. He breathed in and exhaled noisily, "God, it feels good to be in the Florida. I'm glad you've got this nice rolling countryside, and yet you're not far from the beach. You've got the best of both worlds."

A city-dweller most of his life, Terry was impressed with the large farms that dotted the local countryside. White board fences wrapped with the clinging arms of field flowers surrounded most of the homes. The scene induced feelings of domesticity. He appreciated Annette more than ever before. She had become his refuge, his most loyal supporter, and his comforter. As Terry spoke, a pair of binoculars trained on him. A man who had rented a room that morning at the Golden Hills Motel overlooking the six homes that made up the small settlement where Annette Simpson lived, held them.

"Do you want a steak, Terrance? Got some strip steaks and can fix up a salad and a couple of baked potatoes. What do you say?"

Terrance was hungry. "Great. Got a nice wine to go along with that?"

"Sure have." As she bent over to take the wine from the refrigerator his eyes dropped down to her legs. Even without high heels, framed in the kitchen light, they glistened with shapeliness. "You look great "

She smiled. "Just for you."

With a hug, "Lucky me."

She placed two lit candles in the center of the table and lowered the lights. "A little candlelight would be nice. What do you think?"

"I don't really need it to warm up to you lady, but it won't do any harm, that's for sure."

She dressed in her one luxury, a shimmering blue silk dress that rippled with her every movement - a gift from Terry. Her naked throat was draped in strands of faux pearls.

"You finished the house repairs," he said, referring to the work he had funded. He glanced at the new ivory wallpaper, the new china cabinet made of shiny cherry wood, and a small but elegant table of black and green marble. He felt comfortable. *Being a husband may not be all that bad.*

She poured the wine as he lightly ran two fingers through her hair. "Stop it or there'll be no dinner!"

"I don't mind waiting for dinner."

With her hands on her hips, "Oh no you don't, not after all this trouble." Her nostrils tingled at his masculine scent as her ears delighted at the sound of his voice; her eyes feasted on his face and frame.

They studied one another in the candlelight as they ate. She savored the setting. "Isn't this romantic?" she said.

Terrance felt great affection for this disarmingly simple and generous woman. "You know, Annette, if a guy like me ever wanted to marry, you'd be the perfect wife."

"When?"

"We'll talk about that later."

"I've heard that before."

This was the moment Moroney had been waiting for. It was nice to give this patient and loyal woman some good news for a change. "Get ready for this, friend. I'm going to be eating with you and making love to you for a few months this time. How do you like that?"

She pushed aside her chair and rushed to him, wrapping her arms around him as tightly as she could. "Terry, you're not kidding me, are you? That would be cruel."

He pulled her down onto his lap, brought her face close to his and said, slowly, "I.. am.. not.. kidding. I ...am....very...serious."

Annette's eyes reflected her excitement as she clasped her face in her hands. "This is wonderful, Terry. Stay forever if you want. I just can't believe it."

Terrance often felt guilty that he had not done more for this woman who was so devoted to him. Enveloping her in his large arms he said, "Let's lie down."

Gripping her beneath her knees and arms, he carried her into the bedroom, controlling his excitement but kissing her open mouth. "It's been too long," he gasped.

"I agree!"

His impatience scattered her clothing on both sides of the bed.

"Oh, Terry," she said as she turned her face upward and locked his eyes into hers. "I've wanted you so much."

"I missed you Terry. It's been lonely."

"I missed you." His words muffled against her neck.

They made love until early morning. He was now ready to spring his surprise. "I've got a question to ask you?"

"Yes?"

"Would you marry me?"

Shock. It was as if a large stone had dropped through the ceiling, or the earth had opened. She gasped. "Oh, my God, Terry." She did not move, as she flattened her palms against her face. "Let's do it before you change your mind, or before we get too old."

He assured her it would be soon. "Go get yourself all outfitted and we'll get married as soon as you're ready." He handed her an envelope containing ten thousand dollars in cash. "Get yourself the best."

She had every intention of doing just that.

Annette pulled into the parking lot at La Manqua Bridal Boutique still in pleasant shock over the events of the previous evening. For the first time in my life I feel like a loved woman, like a real person. It's like completing a circle, like coming home.

The storefront glittered with its glass superstructure. The pink walls and soft rose carpeting were clearly visible from the street. She had never had so much money to spend, and even as she entered the boutique's doors she hesitated. Is this for real?

She began to check the prices.

These prices are outrageous. But for the first time in my life I can buy something really nice and it turns out to be my own wedding dress.

As she pushed open the large brass and glass doors she crossed her fingers and took a deep breath. The La Manque Bridal Boutique, which contained a hair salon, was a bi-level structure centered by a staircase with curved balconies.

"Good morning. Can I help you, or would you rather simply browse for awhile." The voice was soft and sophisticated.

"I'm getting married and need some help picking out a dress."

"My name is Sharon Whitby. I'm La Manqua's bridal consultant. I'd be happy to help you."

Sharon was of medium height and slim figure, twenty-five to thirty years old. Enhanced by a hint of makeup, her shimmering brown hair and dark blue eyes dominated her presence. Beneath a green gabardine mini-skirt her finely chiseled legs stood out like a neon sign. An open-necked silk blouse revealed a pearl necklace resting between her pillowy breasts.

"Would you like a cup of tea or coffee?"

"Tea, please." *I might as well play the part to the hilt. It's the cash I've got in the pocketbook that they're interested in.* Annette had never experienced this kind of social ambiance, but felt she could adjust to it easily. *Just a bit of training in etiquette and I'd be as good as any. She's dressed nice and speaks with an English accent, but she's just a laborer like me.*

In spite of her self-assurances, her stomach kept rising and falling as she tried to adjust to the luxury and strangeness of it all.

Ms. Whitby got down to business. "We need to make a decision on the following: a dress, the kind of veil, shoes, stockings, gloves and the bouquet. We want to make you a breathtaking bride" Looking at Annette's figure, "You have the body to make that happen."

Annette spread her arms, "It's great what money can do."

"You are quite right, my dear. Now, let's go to the bridal salon on the second floor."

For three hours Annette tried on gowns, veils, and shoes. She looked at gold and silver leafed handbags. When all had been chosen, Ms. Whitby assured her, "We'll prepare all of this for you and deliver them direct to your home by a young lady who will assist you in dressing for the wedding. There is no extra charge for that. We thank you for choosing to purchase your wedding gown from us. I know you'll be the lovely bride your boyfriend wants you to be."

"I hope so."

Terry was waiting when she returned from her shopping spree. "Got everything you need?"

She teased, "And, a whole lot more."

"Good."

They dined together and, as the night donned a black gown dotted with bright city lights, he thought it time to leave. But first, he gazed out at the overhanging hillock, its outline framed by the twinkling lights. The distant homes appeared as toy houses. As he left Annette's place, he felt secure in this world away from New York, a world in which he was just a figure in a crowd. Anonymity was the key to his survival. He made his way along the highway to an exit that led him in the direction of the small villa hidden from the road by a row of palm trees and the ebony darkness. The street was hushed. Only the distant sound of highway traffic rippled the silence. The man with the binoculars had reached the house before him, and was waiting. He trembled with the excitement of vengeance and retribution. His heart beat rapidly, his mouth was parched, his nerves as taut as a violin's strings. A tingling sensuality suffused his entire body as he carefully placed his finger on the trigger. The silencer reduced the sound to a tremulous whooossh. Terrance felt no more than a flash of pain as a bullet pierced his brain from a distance of less than three feet. The killer silently glided through the brush to his parked car two blocks away, and drove off into the darkness. There was only stillness and the bleeding, already dead body.

The next morning a passing motorist looking for water for his overheated radiator discovered a short trail of sticky blood running along the pathway to the front steps of Manny Dwyer's villa. He saw Terry, sprawled and bloodied on the porch, and notified the police.

Annette awoke early and mixed flour, milk, eggs and baking powder for waffles, Terrance's favorite breakfast food. Especially for Terry, she bought a bottle of expensive Vermont Pure Maple Syrup. She poured pineapple juice into two large wine goblets and placed them in the refrigerator to cool, and placed an unopened box of Shredded Wheat on the linen-covered kitchen table. She produced her finest silverware, a gift from Terry. *It seems like everything nice I have around here, Terry gave me.*

The phone rang. It was her friend, Elizabeth. "Liz, what you doing up so early in the morning?"

"Work, my dear, old-fashioned work. That's what gets me up. You called?"

"Yes. We need to discuss the wedding. I mean the dresses the bridesmaids wear, and all that. Right?"

"Of course. What colors do you like?"

Annette had her favorites. "Something pink and chiffon for you. I like cream for the bridesmaids. "Let's meet tomorrow afternoon, when you get back from work. Terry kinda wants me alone for the evenings."

A small giggle. "I know what you mean. OK, that's fine. What about five-thirty?"

"That'll be good. See you then."

Annette reached into the fridge for a carton of milk, popped open the spout and poured herself a glass of milk. She set the coffee - maker for six cups. She looked at her watch. It was already 7:15. Maybe he overslept. Oh well, I'll watch the news till he comes. The news commentator spoke of the tensions between Iraq and the United States. The Russians expressed their unhappiness as the United States worked at forming a coalition of States to reverse the Iraqi invasion of Kuwait. More meetings were taking place in Washington between the Israelis and Palestinians. Commercials for Coca Cola and Ford station wagons took up a few minutes. This was followed by the local news.

"A motorist who stopped at a local residence early this morning for water to fill his auto radiator reported to police that he discovered a murdered body; on the porch of the house. Police later identified him as Terrance Moroney of New York City. A Police spokesperson said he was wanted by the Manhattan Division of the New York City Police as a suspect in the murder of Tony Albanese, brother of the former powerful Mafia Don, Julio Albanese."

Annette slumped into semi-consciousness in her chair, the glass of milk tumbling onto her legs and dripping to the floor. "Oh God, no," she mumbled in shock. She tried to cry out but could not. She lay there in a pained silence, shattered by an occasional wailing and sobbing. *Sweet Jesus. Just when he fell in love with me! How cruel. How horrible*. She leaned over, her face almost touching the floor. After some moments in this position, she stood up and moved slowly to her bedroom. There she removed from the closet all of her wedding clothes, laying them neatly, in rows, on the bed. She undressed, took a shower, made up her face, perfumed her body and returned to dress for her wedding. After checking everything before the bedroom's full-length mirror, she reached into the closet once again. This time she removed a revolver Terry had placed there for her protection, put it in her mouth, and pulled the trigger.

Chapter Sixteen
DENOUEMENT

The television set resting on the liquor cabinet murmured in a low voice. It provided the only light in the room where Victor Albanese, sitting in the darkness, caught the eleven o'clock news. His troubled gaze fixed on Channel 7. The lead story told of the assassination of Freddie Podanski. A bilious fluid churned in his stomach souring his mouth. As the report unfolded, Victor took a bottle of Heinekens from a tiny fridge on the floor next to his chair. His lips curled loosely around the opening of the bottle, trying to assuage his deep-bellied fears. He felt scalded, his cheeks flushed, his heart pounding crazily. *Who is this guy? What does he want? I'll get the bastard if it's the last thing I do. I swear it.* He pressed his knuckles against his forehead and felt his blood rush to his extremities. Fear, shock and guilt coursed through his being. He switched off the television set, sat on the edge of the bed wrapped in a blue terry cloth towel, wishing he could sleep. It would be necessary to leave the city to protect himself. *I've got to get out of here and do it quickly. I'm a sitting duck. Let's see if this creep can get through my security net in the country. He's playing with fire when he plays with me.*

As a man weighted down with chains, Victor moved laboriously to the phone and dialed Zee, Annunzio's number-one man. Like Annunzio, he was completely dedicated to Victor Albanese. "Zee, I guess you heard about Annunzio?"

"Yes, I was about to call you."

"Zee, I want you to take Annunzio's place as Caporegime. It looks as though Tony's death was just the beginning of an attack on the Family. I want you to take personal charge of protecting me, as of now. Get over here with your men. I want to move out to Hudson and I want your entire crew out there with me. We'll set up operations there."

Zee was buoyed by the assignment. He was honored to be given the responsibility. He turned to his wife Linda, "Victor just gave me Annunzio's job. I have to move out to the Hudson estate tomorrow. Things are getting scary."

Linda clasped her head with both hands. "What else is new?" she replied with sarcasm.

Zee was irritated. "Aren't you happy I got a promotion?"

Linda remained sarcastic. "You call that a promotion? You know what that means don't you? It means you're next, my friend. Better to stay at the bottom of the heap, where your neck don't stick out so much."

Zee did not care to continue the conversation. He loved his wife but did not understand why she failed to support him in his work. *After all, she's got all she ever dreamed of.....furs, a convertible, a house in the country. She's never satisfied.* He sighed and shrugged it off. "Look, I gotta go. Lots to do. I'll be in touch."

Regretting her words, she lifted his face with the palms of her hands and looked directly into his eyes, saying, "You know my life would be empty without you. I just don't want you to die, that's all."

"Yeah," he said without further comment, as he pinched the bridge of his nose.

She watched him place a few belongings in a small suitcase, strap his gun around his shoulder, and walk out of the house without kissing her. She yearned to be back on her father's vegetable farm in Mystic, Connecticut, where life was slow and husbands came home at night to sit with their wives in front of fireplaces. She yearned for the small fundamentalist church where she worshipped in simplicity as a child. Life in the Mafia meant Cathedrals, Catholicism, elaborate baptisms, gifts to the hierarchy, guns and murder. Her father had not been enthusiastic about her marriage. "I want you to be happy, Linda, so I'd never get in your way. You have my permission to marry Zee, but I want to make it absolutely clear that, in my opinion, you're making a big mistake."

Victor had yet another sleepless night. The mystery of the note haunted him. Why was it that the person who knew all the facts had not confronted him? Had not turned him into the police?

"Come and eat." His wife had prepared breakfast. "Here's your pills. Don't forget to take them."

Her muted monologue was interrupted when Zee entered the kitchen and handed Victor a sealed envelope. "Mr. Albanese, one of the boys found this taped to the bumper of your car this morning. It's got your name on it."

Victor recognized the white envelope. It was similar to the first he had received. What, this time? Nervously, he tore it open, moving into the living room to avoid displaying his reactions. Typed in the center of an otherwise blank sheet was the message, "You are the only one left, but not for long."

Victor felt a cold chill creeping down his spine. He trembled and grew pale. He saw his wife, Grace, and Zee moving toward him as black figures rising, falling, moving their heads in large arcs surrounded by the shimmering morning air.

Zee observed the change in Victor's demeanor. "Are you OK boss?"

The voice seemed to come from the end of a long corridor. He collapsed into Zee's arms, squeezing the note into a ball in his fist. He held onto it tenaciously as his wife placed a cool damp cloth on his forehead. Zee put a glass of water to his lips.

Nervously fingering a gold chain draped around her neck, his wife shouted, "A doctor. I've got to call the family doctor. He might be dying. Oh God!"

As Grace phoned, Victor folded his body in a vain attempt to stop the shocks that caused him to shift several times in painful motions. He was aware he had suffered another heart attack and he prayed for survival, "Jesus, Mary and Joseph, save me. Jesus forgive me, Mary intercede for me."

The prayers of his childhood came to him, as the guilt of his brother's blood massively intruded into his consciousness. Images of his many hours as an altar boy at St.Gregorio's, in Sicily, flashed before him as his wife stroked his head, neck and shoulders. Zee was on the phone to Julio. "He's just had a very bad attack, a heart attack, we think. We've called the doctor. Thought you should know."

Julio asked to speak to Grace. "I'll be right over. Stay calm, darling. Everything is going to be all right."

Julio had compassion for his brother. He would say to his wife, "We're all part of the human race; we're all in the same boat, the rich and the poor, the weak and the strong. We all go to the bathroom in the same way, and we all get sick and die."

As he drove along Sunrise Highway to see his brother, he glanced out at the shimmering waters of Long Island Sound and imagined himself back in Sicily. He recalled the view from his mother's home, which sat on a rise above a bay. How pure the air was and how bright the days. *Blessed are the lives that feed on the ambrosia of sun-kissed grapes and figs.*

An ambulance sat at the curb in front of Victor's home. Its red and white lights rotated in blurred reflections. Victor lay on the living room couch. His physician, Dr. Wemberly, laid his hand on Victor and spoke words of assurance, as the ambulance crew prepared a stretcher. Julio bent over and spoke to him. "I'm here, Victor, just relax. Everything 's going to be fine, just fine."

Victor reached out involuntarily, and the crumpled note fell into Julio's open palm. Victor was unaware of the transfer.

Dr. Wemberly turned to Julio as Victor was carried to the waiting ambulance. "I'm keeping Victor at Mercy for a few days at least. I'll be in touch with you and Grace, and keep you well informed."

Julio asked, "Any idea how long he'll be in the hospital?"

"Assuming we do not run into anything unexpected, I would say about a week."

Julio made the sign of the cross. "Thanks, doctor." Then he turned to Grace. "Is there anything you want me to do for you?

She rose to a sitting position on the bed, one side of her face creased and reddened from the pillow. "No, thank you so much, Julio. I just want Victor to recover."

Julio picked up the phone and called St. Anthony's. Mrs. Cerrillo answered. "I'm sorry, Mr. Albanese, Father Carlo is away for the day. I'll have him return your call."

"Thank you, Mrs. Cerrillo. Please inform him that his Uncle Victor has had another heart attack. Ask him to pray for him."

"I'm so sorry, Mr. Albanese. I will tell him."

Julio got up to leave. "I'll be going now, darling. I'll stay in touch. Don't worry. Victor will be all right."

Grace loved her brother-in-law. He knew how to handle family problems. "Thank you, Julio, we all love you," she said, drying her tears, and waving goodbye.

Julio drove slowly toward the highway. Getting out of Manhattan was an obstacle course of orange-and-white drums, oil pots, reflectors, and flaggers all along the East River Drive. The Mayor, badly in need of a lift in the polls, had ordered all the potholes filled. As Julio merged his car into the Long Island Expressway, the solid bands of trees and elegant homes cheered him. He unfolded the white sheet of paper that had fallen from his brother's hand. Glancing at the message for a moment, he tore it up and scattered its pieces to the wind.

By the time Victor was released from the hospital he was feeling much better. He left home the following day for Julio's Hudson estate. He loved the house, with its large screened porch containing lounge chairs and card tables, which ran its length. It was a great place for privacy and watching sunsets. The heart attack provided him with the excuse he needed to avoid anyone except those he trusted completely. Zee heard a news flash about Terry Moroney but waited for the "right" moment to tell his boss. It came two days after they arrived at Hudson. "Boss, I hate to give you this news but Primo's old pal from the Chicago days, Terry Moroney, was killed a couple of days ago in Florida, shot through the head."

The words paralyzed Victor's movements. He tried to speak but no words came out. His eyes glazed. He leaned like a swaying reed and made his way slowly to the liquor cabinet. Reaching for a bottle of Crown Royal, he sank into the nearest armchair, and took a long drink. It helped. "Sit down, Zee. Have a drink with me. It will carry us through the day. I've got to keep calm or my ticker is going to give out. Between my health and this nut going around after our Family, I think I'd better restrict visitors to the family. Just tell everyone that the doctor has ordered me to take a complete rest for a month."

"Right."

Victor asked, "By the way, how many men do we have here?"

"Six, boss."

Victor shifted in his chair, nervously rubbing his shoulders. "I want you to get four more from Frankie. Keep this place as tight as possible. I'll use the upstairs bedroom and you guys sleep downstairs at the stair landing. Don't let anybody get by you."

Zee nodded. "Over my dead body, boss. Don't worry."

Victor walked to the large, black-and-white tiled bathroom for a shower. He scrubbed himself with vigor, as if to remove scales of guilt. He toweled, dressed and headed for Julio's well-stocked library shelves. He picked out an ornately tooled bible, returned to his armchair and started to read from the Book of Psalms. "The Lord is my shepherd. I have everything I need. He lets me rest in fields of green grass and leads me to quiet pools of fresh water." He laid the open bible down in his lap. His vision captured the sweeping vista of lawn rolling down to the placid water of the Hudson River. The river lazily moved its immense bulk as gracefully as a cumulus cloud on a hot summer afternoon.

Victor now realized that he was a prisoner of his own ambitions. He had woven the web in which he was now hopelessly entangled. Somewhere "out there" a hunter was tracking him down, a hunter who knew his prey and had the skills to do the job. *I've got at my command at least a hundred gunmen, all well armed and highly skilled. And yet, a lone killer bent on either revenge or profit has caused me to retreat to this goddam house - Julio's house - this friggin house on the Hudson. I don't dare move. It's ridiculous.*

As he sat in this meditative mood, he was suddenly inspired by an idea. *I'll invite Carlo to come and pray with me. This nut will stay away if Carlo's with me. Perhaps Carlo can get a couple of weeks off. He won't let me down. I'll ask him to bring a rosary, so we can pray together.*

The Mafia had great respect for priests and the Church, their only guarantee of salvation. No attack would be made on him while Carlo was present. That would give him space to figure out what to do. And, what if the attacker is not from one of the Families? *Well, I'll just have to take that chance. Nothing to lose.* It would be, he thought, a clever stroke of both strategy and piety. Nevertheless, that night he awakened with a scream, his body drenched in sweat. For a moment he did not know where he was. He reached for his bottle of Crown Royal and took another long gulp, drinking himself into a long sleep.

The next morning Victor invited Carlo to spend a few days with him. "You know, Carlo, your uncle needs you; I've been so sick and all that. Could use a spiritual uplift."

Carlo responded without hesitation. "I'd be happy to come out for a few days, Uncle Victor." *Now is the moment. I know what needs to be done. His heart is weak.*

Victor turned once more to religion to piece together all the events of the last several months. He saw himself in a new light. *I am the keeper of the Family tradition. I must see to it that we remain the most important and influential Family in America. This is my historic role.* Carlo's impending arrival lessened his fear considerably, but it would be necessary to keep a vigilant guard against what he perceived as a neurotic mind on the loose. Somewhere out there was a man who was too ignorant to understand the importance and significance of his contribution. He had no doubt that he would foil this mad man's plan. He now felt foolish and repentant for having worried about Carlo as a potential rival. That was all so silly. Carlo's strength and wisdom would add just the right mixture of legitimacy to his authority. Victor looked forward to praying with his nephew and discussing matters of eternal life. Perhaps he could take the lead in a religious revival that would give him a unique place in the history of the Albanese Family. He addressed his reflection in the large bedroom mirror. *To those who question my ability to rule and lead, a dramatic spiritual revival would be answer enough.*

Carlo was presiding over the monthly parish council meeting. Although the members, at his urging, had all agreed to a two-hour limit, the meeting had already been running for almost three hours. It had become very evident to Carlo that some Parish Council Meetings were an ideal forum for parishioners who led humdrum lives, to express themselves.

Mr. Alvino was holding forth. "I've asked the ushers not to allow people who come in during the sermon to walk down the aisles and take their seats. It is distracting to the priest and to the congregation. But on Sunday I noticed they kept right on with their bad habits. The ushers not only seated several young people who were giggling all the way down the aisle, but even Mrs. Gaglione. You know how much noise she makes shuffling down to the front pew. I suggest, Father Carlo, that you put a notice in the bulletin stating once and for all that no one will be seated during the sermon."

Every council head turned to Father Carlo, awaiting his decision. "Well, Mr. Alvino, I think your suggestion is a very good one," and every head nodded in approval, "but," and they all straightened up, "I do not believe that it's as practical as it first appears." Every Council head waved negatively. "We may end up discouraging certain members of the parish from attending Mass."

A quick vote was taken and the Council voted not to include such a notice in the bulletin. Then, Mrs. Navigato, representing the lay members of the Council, read a statement of official condolence to Father Carlo on the occasion of the anniversary of his father's death.

Mrs. Navigato emphasized that the Secretary (Mrs. Navigato herself) "had been on vacation and it was to her that the Council had assigned both the duty and the privilege of composing the statement." She looked at Carlo. "I'm sorry I was tardy in getting you this statement."

Carlo nodded that it was OK, and she received the thanks and understanding of all the members.

Mr. Russoni, who served as Chairperson of the Maintenance Committee, an offspring of the Parish Council and subject to its jurisdiction, read his report. "The members of the Maintenance Committee wish to express thanks for the expeditious manner in which Father Carlo has taken care of the janitor's complaints concerning the gym floor, namely the tendency of parishioners to walk on it without proper foot gear."

There was a polite clap of hands.

Father Carlo asked, "Is the Parish Service Committee willing to provide a soup kitchen for the many vagrants in the neighborhood? I believe that such a kitchen would reflect our Christian concern for our brothers and sisters."

Mrs. Navigato, raising her eyeglasses onto her hair, stood up. "Sorry Father, we've run out of time." Picking up a large spoon, she hit the table lightly and announced, "The time for the Parish Council meeting has elapsed and I ask that someone make a motion that the meeting be adjourned."

Mrs. Durso made the motion and Mr. Alvino seconded.

Carlo made one last attempt. "I look forward to bringing the question of a soup kitchen to the floor at the next meeting." His remark did not elicit a response.

There was plenty of coffee and cake at a side table. All the members helped themselves, even Mrs. Navigato, who was on a diet. The house intercom rang and Carlo, who was leaning against the wall near the phone, answered it. It was Father Adolfo. "Carlo, your Uncle Victor would very much appreciate your calling him in Hudson."

"Thank you, Father."

Father Adolfo asked how the Council Meeting had gone. "Well, for the second time in a row the meeting was adjourned when the subject of the soup kitchen came up."

Father Adolfo mumbled, "Typical. Well, at least now you know how to end Council Meetings when they drag on too long."

Tuesday morning began with the seven o'clock Mass, followed by Communion for the sick. After breakfast there was a meeting with the schoolteachers. Later, Carlo took the Sunday collection to Manufacturer Hanover Trust. That took him to lunchtime. The cook served Cape Cod scrod, with a healthy portion of rice and Italian stewed tomatoes.

The first part of the afternoon he spent making entries into the parish books. The problem of the Family's future was very much on his mind. A power vacuum would likely be filled by a series of internecine wars and there would be a turning back of the clock on the most significant advance in the history of the Mafia: Julio's visionary plan to transform the Albanese Family into a model for the legitimization of Mafia operations. Carlo was determined that Julio's vision must survive. He adjusted to the fact that the fulfillment of this vision would dramatically affect his personal life. He knew what he had to do.

It was late evening when Carlo arrived. Victor embraced him and showed him the Bible. "Look at me - reading the Bible. It has proven to be the most interesting book I've ever read. It's given me a whole new outlook, Carlo. Would you believe that?"

Carlo nodded. "The Bible is a powerful book. We are all moved by it," he said with a mechanical voice and a vinyl smile.

Victor noted the less-than-cordial sound in Carlo's voice but attributed it to tiredness. *The kid probably hasn't slept much lately, with all the trouble and a busy parish.*

"Well, Uncle, they say the things we learn as adults we learn best of all. They become part of us."

Zee called them to the supper table, where a large roast with potatoes, green beans and baked carrots awaited them. Carlo had some news. "Uncle Julio is coming this evening. He'll be able to stay a few days, and should get here late tonight. It's shaping-up to be a mini-reunion."

Victor was jubilant. Who, after all, would be able to question his authority and leadership when they observed that both Carlo and Julio had arrived to advise him and consult with him? It was more than he dreamed would happen. He was confident that his position was now completely secure. *I am the boss. No doubt about that.*

He instructed Zee, "Get Bruno on the phone. Tell him to come tomorrow for lunch and bring a few things, so he can stay a couple of days. Make sure we've got plenty of food and booze. Get a case of root beer for this nephew of mine."

Victor's mood was expansive. He felt that a new spirit of camaraderie was developing among the men. He reasoned that he was on the verge of stamping his own mark on the organization. After dinner he suggested to Carlo, "What about we say the rosary together later this evening?"

"Sure, Uncle Victor." Carlo suggested some Bible reading and the rosary combined. "That's my favorite way to pray."

Victor nodded his agreement. "What about ten o'clock, in my study?"

"Fine"

Victor retired to his room. Carlo chatted with Sarah, the estate's cook and housekeeper, a native of Trinidad. She had been surrogate mother to all the children in the family during the summers they spent with Julio. Carlo had a surprise for her. The following day was her birthday and, as a gift, he would give her a round-trip ticket to Trinidad. As they chatted, a white envelope containing the ticket prominently jutted out of his jacket pocket. He was amused that her gift was staring her in the face and she was unaware of it. Their conversation continued until shortly after ten o'clock, when Victor called down to his nephew, "Are you coming up?"

"Just one moment, Uncle Julio." And, grasping both her hands in his, "Sarah, I'll see you at breakfast tomorrow. And, Oh yes, Uncle Julio will be coming in late tonight. Please have his room ready."

He joined Victor, who signaled him to sit in the armchair next to his. Carlo opened the Douay Version of the Bible at a bookmark. "I see, Uncle, that you've been reading the Book of Genesis. I don't want to shock you but scripture scholars no longer believe that many of these stories are literally true."

"Yes, Carlo, the priests at Mass have said something like that, but I can't say I understand exactly what they're talking about."

Carlo explained. "These stories in the Bible are true in the sense that they present what man is like and what kind of relationship God has with him. It's like our cowboy movies. They're not exact accounts of what happened in Texas or Oklahoma, or wherever, but they do tell us what life was like in those days."

"There are a lot of Catholics who would not like to hear that."

"Right." Carlo removed two pairs of rosaries from his trouser pocket, giving one pair to Victor. "Anyway, let's start the rosary."

Carlo sat quietly in his chair as he recited the first half of the ten Hail Mary's. Victor recited the second half, piously and distinctly. "Holy Mary, Mother of God, pray for us sinners, now and at the hour of our death. Amen."

They concluded the first decade of the rosary with the customary prayer, "Glory be to the Father and to the Son and to the Holy Spirit, as it was in the beginning, is now, and ever shall be, world without end. Amen."

At this point, Carlo opened the Bible to the Book of Genesis and read, "Then the Lord God planted a garden in Eden, in the East, and there he put the man he had formed." Carlo put the Bible down. "Uncle, we can use this thought for meditation. Here we have the story of the creation of man. God said, 'At last, here is one of my own kind.' This is the earliest indication that man was made in the image and likeness of God and will lead an eternal life with him."

Victor was impressed with his nephew's grasp of Scripture. "I ought to take-in your sermons."

The two men then began the second decade of the rosary, "Our Father, who art in heaven, hallowed be thy name, thy kingdom come, thy will be done, on earth as it is in Heaven…"

At the completion of the second decade, Carlo presented the second meditation. "The snake was the most cunning creature that the Lord God had made. The snake asked the woman, 'Did God really tell you not to eat fruit from any tree in the garden?'"

Carlo expanded on that reading. "Here, Uncle, we have man's original sin about to be committed. The snake, who is Satan, tempts Eve, who then tempts Adam into believing that if they eat the fruit which God forbade them to eat they would become as powerful as God. So they went ahead and ate the forbidden fruit. The results were disastrous. This is a warning to man not to reach out for a power not destined for him."

As Carlo said these words, he looked straight into Victor's eyes causing him to feel uneasy and slightly faint. Was his nephew accusing him, or was he just imagining this? He stared at Carlo's austere face, listening to what sounded like a condemnatory tone. He felt two sharp pains in his chest and leaned back, resting his arms across his stomach. He wanted to get up but he could not move. Carlo grasped Victor's hands and felt a deathly chill flow out of them, chilling his own hands. "Do you want to stop praying, Uncle? Are you OK?"

Victor was not thinking clearly. Fear crept into his consciousness. He wasn't sure if his nephew's words were meant to be comforting or if they were said sarcastically. *Does he know something? These words seem full of meaning and knowledge. Am I just imagining?* His panic deepened, as his mouth dried and his nostrils quivered. He was determined to keep control of his emotions and reveal nothing by his facial expressions. He was silent, blinking, trying to focus. As calmly as he could he said, "Oh no, Carlo, by all means please continue. Just a gas pain. I'm fine." But the words were thick and shaky, his eyes watery.

Carlo recited the third decade of the rosary in the usual manner, Julio responding in a weakened voice. He then proceeded with the next meditation. His face hardened and he went on coldly, with a riveting stare. "Following the Genesis story, Uncle, we come to our next meditation. The Bible account shows how a man can betray and even kill his own brother. I think this meditation is very appropriate for us because there's always the temptation in our Family to resort to violence in settling disputes. As Don, it's something you must be ever vigilant about, but never guilty of. Do you agree?"

Victor tried to maintain his posture of confidence but inside he was melting away and sliding into a great abyss. The pains in his chest returned. A lamp across the room silhouetted Carlo, fitting him with a halo. He looked like an avenging angel, his eyes narrowing threateningly.

Carlo read, "The Lord was pleased with Abel and his offering, but he rejected Cain. Cain became furious and he scowled. Then the Lord said to Cain, Why are you angry? Why that scowl on your face? If you have done the right thing you would be smiling but because you have done evil, sin is crouching at your door."

Victor experienced an inner shriveling and wanted to crawl into some protective womb, but he sat there exposed to the cold glance of his nephew. He looked for meaning in Carlo's eyes, but they defied analysis. He never before noticed the dark intensity of Carlo's eyes and the aggressive jut of his chin. It was, at this moment, terrifying.

Carlo continued, no longer concealing the rage induced by Victor's duplicity. "Then Cain said to his brother, Abel, 'Let's go out in the fields.' When they were out in the fields, Cain turned on his brother and killed him. The Lord asked Cain, `where is your brother, Abel?' He answered, 'I don't know. Am I my brother's keeper?'"

At these words, spoken bitterly, the pain in Victor's chest sharpened and he fell sideways from his chair, dropping to the floor and rolling against a small table. The glass he had been drinking from tumbled, spilling whiskey over his face and shoulders. He was conscious of his predicament but the chest pains left him unable to control his body. He tried to ease himself up onto his elbows but fell back with a thud.

Carlo rushed to his side. "Uncle Victor, the avenging angel has come to bring justice to our family!"

As Carlo kneeled on the floor next to him, Victor caught sight of the white envelope in Carlo's shirt pocket. *O my God, it's another message, maybe the final message. My own nephew, O my God!* He stared at his nephew, seeing him only as in flickering light, a dark shape, menacing. The pain in his chest became unbearable, deeply etching itself into his flesh, his vision blurring further.

Victor reached out to grasp Carlo's shoulder but Carlo moved back causing Victor to slam his face onto the floor. Carlo lifted him to his feet and, as he was about to place him back in his chair, Victor crumpled in his arms, saliva dripping from his mouth. He managed one last sentence as he stared into Carlo's eyes, "You knew all along." His eyes bulged in their sockets, as he emitted one last trembling gasp. Carlo pulled at Victor's body, leaned it against a chair, and left the room. He had revenged his father's death. He felt cleansed and exuberant.

Dr. Wemberly, the ambulance, and two police cars had already arrived when Julio Albanese pulled into the driveway. A young police officer stopped him and asked for identification. "What's happening here, officer? This is my house."

"I'm sorry to have to tell you this, Mr. Albanese, but your brother died about an hour ago. A team was sent from the hospital immediately to try and revive him but they, sir, were unable to do so."

Julio entered the living room and found Carlo and Sarah sitting on a large couch facing the bay window, silently staring out into the dark night. Carlo rose to greet him. "What happened, Carlo?"

"A massive heart attack. He died in my arms. We were praying together upstairs."

As they spoke, Victor's body was carried out on a stretcher. Dr. Brennan was there. "Please accept my condolences, Julio. This last attack was just one too many."

It was very late and there were many people to notify. Julio asked to be excused, as he sat down at his desk and began to dial. Carlo suggested he ask Nicky to consult with Grace and take care of all the funeral arrangements. "He needs to be part of this." Julio agreed.

Julio was the first to stir in the morning. He felt rested and at peace. Sarah had already set the coffee maker up the night before. Its aroma beckoned him to the kitchen. Carlo soon joined him. Sarah served toast and the two men sang "Happy Birthday to you!" Carlo gave her the envelope with her round-trip ticket to Trinidad and noted that the return-trip date was open. "Come back after you've had a good long rest."

The three embraced. Sarah could not help but observe that there was a feeling of festivity rather than sadness in the mood of these men. She shared that mood; Victor had not been her favorite person. He appeared mean, selfish and arrogant, a small-minded man with big ideas. After coffee, Julio suggested to Carlo that they take a walk down to the river. "Let's go out and enjoy this lovely morning air."

The sun-filled morning was enhanced with slight breezes that rustled the leaves and sent whisperings of bird song throughout the trees that lined the field leading to the river. The sunrise praised the sky with golden streaks. Uncle and nephew were silent with their own thoughts for a few moments. Then, Carlo said, "I suppose I should say the funeral Mass at St. Anthony's. What do you think?"

"Yes, I believe your aunt would want that. She was too upset last night so say much. I told her Nicky will be helping her with the arrangements, and she was fine."

Julio swung his arms in a wide arch, exercising his neck and shoulders. "As you get older you have to keep the limbs moving or they'll stop altogether."

"Poor Uncle Victor," Carlo mused. "I guess it was his time to go. He never really got a chance to take over the job. Maybe that is how it was meant to be."

Julio nodded. "I suppose so."

Carlo changed the subject, suggesting that a small outdoor structure, without walls, could be built down by the river. The Family needed a gazebo in which to sit or picnic. He pointed out that the property needed some repairs if it were to continue as a gathering place for the Family. "The rain spouts are rusting and are leaking badly in several locations." Julio agreed. "Do something about it. After all, the responsibility for all of us is now on your shoulders."

Carlo nodded in agreement. A starling swept over their heads, and the two men raced each other down to the river like a couple of schoolboys.

Chapter Seventeen
CONFLICT WTH PRIESTHOOD

Victor Albanese's funeral service was held at the Dwight-Shapiro funeral Home on B Street in lower Manhattan. Ben Shapiro had been Victor's favorite bridge partner, a card game that Julio once described, in a moment of unusual candor, as "My brother's one concession to being human."

Shapiro was a tall middle-aged man, a non-sportsman with a weathered face and laugh-lines around his mouth. "My friends always ask me where I vacation. Palm Beach? Palm Springs? The fact is I use a sun lamp. Give me my den and a good game of draw poker. That's my sport"

Some members of the Family were not happy that a Jewish undertaker handled the funeral. Frankie complained. "I got nothing against Jews, believe me. But, they never use an Italian undertaker. Ever heard of them using one of us? Never, I tell you."

Carlo suggested that he might harbor prejudice. "I'll think about that," was Frankie's response.

Mourners were few in number. The Dons from Bridgeport, Providence and Boston were the only heads of Family present. There were, however, a large number of wreaths sent by many that declined to attend. One wreath bore a card enclosed in a white envelope. "My last note to you. May the good Lord give you what you deserve." No name accompanied the card.

Julio instructed that the body be "viewed for an extra half hour, in lieu of any special prayers."

Victor's widow quietly questioned Julio about the absence of prayers. "How can this be, Julio? This has never happened in the family before. Why?" she pleaded.

"There are reasons, my dear, there are reasons."

"Oh," was her quiet and unresisting response.

Julio had the feeling that she knew the "reasons."

Following the service, three limousines carrying the immediate family members took the lead in bearing Victor's body to Parkland Cemetery. As the limos crunched and crackled their way along the cemetery's gravel pathways there was, except for the widow, a mood of indifference. Father Adolfo, sitting next to Carlo in the second-place limousine, could feel it. *No one here really gives a damn. What a terrible commentary on his life and work.* As the casket was being lowered, an inebriated worker allowed the rope he held to slip. The casket bounced unceremoniously into a cold and uncaring earth. The mood was not lost on the local press. WINS-10 radio reporter, Joan McCormack, reflecting the funeral's atmosphere, droned into her microphone: "The funeral of Victor Albanese was solemn, but sparsely attended. Many of the Mafia leaders outside the New York-New England area pleaded busy schedules and did not appear. The crowds that attended the funeral of Tony Albanese did not materialize. It's rumored that Victor Albanese was disliked among the Families, and he was not leader long enough to make an impact on the Albanese organization."

At the funeral, Carlo spoke of the sorrow that had gripped the family and of the potential for leadership that did not have time to blossom. "A large void now needs to be filled, both in the bosom of the family and in the widespread enterprises controlled by our family."

After the Communion service, Julio approached the lectern and eulogized his brother. He spoke of their life together as children in Sicily. "Victor was the most dedicated altar boy in our small seaside parish. The parish priest always knew he could count on Victor when one of the other altar boys took sick."

There was a scattering of "Mms" in the congregation.

Julio's voice quivered as he described the recent decimation of the Family leadership. "God should have taken me instead of my brothers. I've been ill for some time now, and old age is catching up with me."

An elderly lady whom no one recognized cried out from the back of the church. "God bless you, Julio Albanese." A pigeon chirped as if in agreement.

Julio paused, then continued. "I want to emphasize that, in spite of the recent tragedies in the life of the Albanese family, the future will be bright and secure." He said this for the benefit of the other Dons, who, no doubt, were speculating how Victor's death could benefit them personally, and their Organizations.

Julio spoke of the strength and talent of Tony and Victor's sons and daughters. He turned to his nephew occupying the celebrant's chair in the church sanctuary, "We have with us, in these trying days, the strong moral and spiritual leadership of our nephew."

That statement evoked a sudden and thunderous applause that echoed throughout the vast expanse of the high-ceilinged church. The Dons present took it as a signal that Carlo would now be playing an important, if not dominant, role in the direction of the Family business. Rumors to that effect had already circulated, and Julio's crisply articulated references to his nephew appeared to confirm them.

The post-funeral reception was held in the church basement, another sign that Victor had achieved little status in the Family. The Dons present found their way to Carlo, offering sympathy and extending, in the words of Almato Quagliette, underboss of the Cleveland area, "our full cooperation in any future transactions."

The small area at the further end of the parish basement hall became the site where the power and dominance of Carlo Albanese took its first outward expression. None engaged Nicky in conversation beyond "condolences." He felt the humiliation of being ignored, shut out. *I need to get things straightened out with Carlo*. He saw an opening and moved quickly to his side. "Carlo, you know that if you need me for anything, just say the word."

"Thanks Nicky. There are many things I'll call on you to do, especially in the really private matters of the Family. I appreciate your loyalty."

Nicky felt patronized by the exchange. A sense of anger swept through him, and he immediately vented it. "What I really mean, Carlo," his tension betraying his anger, "is that I hope to be given the kind of responsibility that my position in the Family deserves."

Carlo's answer was devastating. "Nicky, there's no `position' in the Family. There's only service in the Family, based on ability and dedication. You'll get the kind of assignments you're capable of handling. Nicky, you know as well as I do that you've not been working as diligently as you should."

There was a taut silence. Nicky trembled at the violence of the words, accompanied by uncompromising eyes. He was angry. "Carlo, somebody's been feeding you a lot of nonsense."

Carlo leapt to his response. "Maybe it's been you." There was no hint of emotion, neither in the inflection of voice nor in the texture of Carlo's facial expression.

"Maybe it's been me?" Nicky asked, incredulously.

"Could be."

Nicky spat out the words. "You're crazy."

"I hope so. Tell me why."

Nicky vented his feelings. "You know, and I know that you've always been the big shot in the family. Did you ever think about how that affected me, your kid brother? I never heard you say to me, 'Sorry, Nicky, I know you are being treated unfairly.' Never did you say anything like that. You've been dumping on me all my life, pretending you are taking care of me, my protector." Nicky's voice echoed throughout the church basement. The gathered mourners smiled nervous smiles, glancing at walls and ceilings, initiating frenzied conversations about nothing, pretending not to hear or see. Carlo remained unmoved as he stared coldly and directly into his brother's eyes. Nicky continued, "I'm family. I've got my rights."

Carlo chose to be evasive as he moved close to his brother and whispered into his ear, "Only workers have rights." A chill hung like icicles on the edge of his words as he walked away without a glance, his footsteps echoing on the hardwood floors.

Nicky was transfixed, immobile as a fly caught in a web. He watched Carlo move across the hall. *I don't know him anymore. Maybe I never knew him.* Carlo's words jolted him like a dose of caffeine. "I don't believe what I'm hearing," he whispered to no one in particular. It was clear that Carlo was now the head of the Family. He had been bypassed. He felt he was observing the inexorable advance of his own destruction. *I've got no future. My relationship with my wife is nonexistent. My standing in the organization would be zero if I were not Julio's nephew and Carlo's brother.* At this informal reception his dreams were shattered. From that day onward, he began to dip more and more into the drug culture. Shame erupted like bile from deep inside him. "I feel as though I'm losing my grip on reality," was the way he later expressed his condition to friends in California.

St. Anthony's parish was reeling from the effects of two Mafia funerals in a relatively brief period of time. Some enjoyed the notoriety brought to the parish by front-page photographs of the Church and young Father Albanese. Manny, the parish handyman, kept every photograph pinned to his office wall in the school basement. "That's us," he would point out to every passing student. "We're famous now."

Mr. Durso, Father Adolfo's assistant at parish funerals volunteered. "Now, perhaps, the youth will return and we can have a future as a parish. Young people secretly admire the Mafia."

Others were not so sanguine. Mrs. Cerrillo hadn't stopped complaining to every ear she captured. In a flat voice, without timbre, she would say, "I knew we were in for big trouble when this Mafia priest came to our parish." And, "What has happened to peaceful St. Anthony's? Tell me."

Uncharacteristically brusque, Father Adolfo finally said to her, "Stop talking so much, woman."

She took this as a personal insult. Out of earshot she said. "My wonderful pastor has been unduly influenced by this young, inexperienced curate." She did, however, manage to be polite at all times to Carlo, seeing this as her duty, even in the face of distress and provocation. She fan-

cied herself both a woman of honor and a martyr. She spoke to parishioners, asking them to pray "that this scourge will pass, that never again
will the Mafia soil the reputation of our beloved parish." The head of the
Ladies Sodality, Mrs. Carmelo, distanced herself from Mrs. Cerrillo. At
the next meeting, she turned her head to stare at each member, explaining, "I want to make it very clear that we should not criticize Father
Carlo. After all, he's the nephew and the son of these men, and blood is
definitely thicker than water." The backhanded compliment did not
please Mrs. Cerrillo, who shouted "That's true."

Mrs. Carmelo was pleased with their response. She continued. "God
wants us to be kind to every man."

"Amen."

But she could not resist a small hook. "At the same time, He wants us
to preserve the sanctity of the church." These latter words were said with
such solemnity that everyone present fell silent. The meeting ended with
a prayer. "Lord keep all evil elements out of our parish. May Father
Carlo be able to resist the pressures from the devil. Amen."

As far as Father Adolfo could judge, the majority of the parishioners
enjoyed the momentary basking in bright media lights. He knew for certain that many of them had, with the help of friends or family members,
videotaped the television coverage in the hope of capturing their own
presence in the crowd that converged on the church.

Carlo asked Adolfo for time to deal with family affairs. "Father, I need
some time off." Adolfo understood. The old warrior was determined to be
as helpful as he could be to his young assistant in his hour of sadness.
"Carlo, I figured that already, so I called the Jesuit House at Fordham.
There are at least two Jesuits who'd be happy to fill-in while you're away.
So, please, make whatever arrangements are necessary."

"Actually, Father, I need a bit of extended time." He tried to find the right
words. "I should ask the Cardinal for a leave of absence. There's so much to
be done."

"Take whatever time you need " was Father Adolfo's unswerving, loyal
response.

Carlo fingered a rosary lying on Father Adolfo's desk. "I realize I've only
been ordained a short time and I'm so grateful for your kindness - can't
really express my feelings." With his arms outstretched and moving toward
his mentor, he asked, "Am I shirking my priestly duty?"

Adolfo was affirming. "Not at all. At the moment the care of your family
is your duty."

Adolfo moved from behind his desk and embraced him. "I have no
problem with your need to serve your family, Carlo." He paused in

hesitation, but decided to continue. "I'd be less than honest, however, if I didn't tell you I'm a bit worried. I'd sure hate to lose you, you know."

Carlo shook his head. "Thanks for saying that, Father, but I've hardly been a great boon to the parish."

"Don't sell yourself short, Carlo. You've done what no one has done before you. You've begun to attract the youth to the parish."

"Thanks."

Adolfo stared down at the carpet, his hands deep in his trouser pockets. He searched out Carlo's eyes, transfixing them with his own. "You may be starting out on a long road, from which any return may prove difficult, if not impossible." Placing a firm hand on Carlo's right shoulder, he said with quiet firmness, "Whatever you decide to do, my door is always open to you. Mia casa è sua casa. Always."

Carlo gripped the older man's hands in his. "Thank you, Father, I'll never forget your kindness."

Adolfo led the way to the kitchen where they shared a soft drink and discussed the ecclesiastical procedure. "My guess, Carlo, is that the Cardinal will go along with such a request. It's not unusual."

Ignoring an intercom call from Mrs. Cerrillo, he continued. "Write a formal letter to His Eminence. I'll support your request with a separate letter of my own."

"About?"

"I'll emphasize that I completely approve of your request."

"And that will..."

Adolfo interjected with an impish facial expression, "That's what you call, taking the old man off the hook. So long as he can later say - if things don't go the way he wants – 'I simply acceded to Adolfo's request,' he'll be satisfied."

Carlo admired the political deftness. "No wonder you've survived all these years, even though you've defended the family and never hesitated to associate with us. You'd be good at the UN."

They worked together on the details of Carlo's letter.

His Eminence
Cardinal John McManus
Chancery, Archdiocese of New York
1001 First Avenue
New York, New York. zip

Your Eminence:

Greetings to you from St. Anthony of Padua church. Before addressing myself to the principal reason for this communication, allow me to thank Your Eminence, on behalf of my family, for your words of comfort and sympathy addressed to my family on the dual occasions in which we have experienced great personal losses.

Your Eminence, as you are aware, my family is involved in various enterprises that require strong leadership. With the retirement of my Uncle Julio, the death of my dear father and the more recent death of my Uncle Victor, a large vacuum has developed. This vacuum places many members of my family and our extended family (our employees) in the most difficult of circumstances.

It is, therefore, with great reluctance that I request of Your Eminence a period of time away from my priestly ministry to assist my family in settling our affairs.

Awaiting your reply with full confidence in your compassion, I am,

     Sincerely Yours in Christ,
     Father Carlo Albanese

While Carlo typed the letter on parish stationary, Father Adolfo penned his own note. Dispensing with formality, he moved quickly to the matter at hand:

Your Eminence:
I wholeheartedly support Father Carlo's request for your permission to begin at the earliest possible moment, a leave of absence from his duties. It is difficult at this time to predict the length of this requested absence. In my humble opinion it should be determined by subsequent events.

Be assured, Your Eminence, of my continued loyalty and respect.

Sincerely in Christ
Adolfo

Father Adolfo hand-delivered the letters to the Chancery office. "Dolphi, what are you doing uptown?" Auxiliary Bishop, Thomas Flannagan, peeked out from his office with his hooded onyx eyes. He was effusive, "Can I do something for you?" He rushed out and swept Father Adolfo past his secretary, "Come into my office."

The office was bright, almost glowing. The sun had sliced its way through slatted blinds, lining the beige carpet. "Actually, Tom, I've got some bad news for the Cardinal. You know Carlo Albanese."

"Who the hell doesn't?"

"Well, with all that's gone on in the kid's family, he needs time off to help straighten things out. You know what I mean Tom?"

Bishop Flannagan leaned back in his chair and nodded. "Sure, Dolphi, but that's not going to set too well with the boss. There are already rumors in the press that Carlo is too much involved in whatever is going on backstage with these guys." Buzzing his secretary, he said, "Arlene, bring me that article about the Albanese family in yesterday's Daily News." Arlene Pressler walked in with the newspaper. "Open it up to the article and show it to Father Adolfo."

Ms. Pressler located the article and pointed, "This is it, Father."

A second-page story entitled, The Succession, read:

Rumors persist that Father Carlo Albanese, son of the slain Anthony Albanese and nephew of the deceased Victor Albanese, has been appointed interim head of the Albanese crime Family, and is playing a significant role in the discussions now underway to select a new 'Don.'

Adolfo heaved a heavy sigh. "I didn't see this, Tom, and I'd swear Carlo didn't see it either. I spent all morning with him and he didn't mention it." Placing the newspaper on the Bishop's desk and glancing at the Monet prominently displayed on the office wall to his left, he continued. "You know, Tom, these guys in the media are acting as though Carlo is different from any other son or nephew who gets involved in taking care of family affairs after a family death."

The Bishop nodded. "I realize that, Dolphi, but there's such a thing as public perception. You know what I mean."

"Yes, but we don't have to panic every time someone spreads a rumor. After all, the Cardinal did ordain the guy, knowing his name would always cause some gossip or rumor."

The Bishop agreed. "I guess you could say we are all in this together, for better, for worse. Well, Dolphi, let's not worry about this. The Boss is a reasonable man and we'll probably work out something."

Father Adolfo handed over the letters. "Tom, Carlo wrote this letter to the Cardinal, and I added a supporting petition." Give them to the Boss yourself? You know this is a sensitive case. It's better the secretaries don't see this stuff."

"Count on it, Dolphi. I'll catch him by five this afternoon. I'm sure you'll hear from him on this soon. "

Adolfo tilted his head and glanced at the Bishop. "Thanks, Tom. I'll let you get on with your business. My stomach's sounding the noon bell. Next time we meet, let's sit down and have an old chat."

"Yeah, yeah, Dolphi." Bishop Flannagan had a great fondness for Father Adolfo. As much as he would enjoy "an old chat," the busy priest was a difficult man to corner.

From his desk, the Cardinal looked up at Bishop Flannagan. "Tom, I'm caught between a rock and a hard place. If I don't give Carlo permission, the media will dig up the names of at least twenty guys now on leave and ask why the hell Carlo was refused. If I do give permission, some are going to say I've given him a year to mix with hoods."

Flannagan nodded. "Heads I win, tails you lose?"

"Yeah." The Cardinal explored his molars with a toothpick and stared out his office window. "It's the damnedest thing. Anyway, Tom, notify Dolphi that permission is granted. Tell him Carlo will be given a 'reasonable' amount of time to take care of family business. I want to play this by ear." Turning to his auxiliary, he asked, "What do you think, Tom?"

Bishop Flannagan hastened to agree. "Sure. Best way to go. If Carlo screws up we remain the good guys. We were compassionate. I think that's important. We always have to look like the good guys."

The Cardinal clapped his hands. "Precisely my view, Tom, precisely." Bishop Flannagan got on the phone to Father Adolfo. "The matter has been settled, Dolphi. Tell Carlo he's now officially on leave of absence. However we're not going to say anything about it publicly. This way members of the press will have to pick it up on their own. In the event they ask us, we'll simply say he's taken the normal leave of absence allowed after the death of a relative. Period."

The Cardinal nodded his approval of the phrasing and, as soon as Flannagan finished speaking to Adolfo, he said, "Let's have a drink, Tom. It's been a long day. No one knows how many burdens I have! People think that being Cardinal is one big joy ride. Well, let me tell you it is not. I would not wish this job on anyone."

Bishop Flannagan did not quite know how to take that remark. For his part, Flannagan would love to have been in the driver's seat, calling all the shots, instead of waiting around for a phone call informing him that he had a Confirmation is some small country parish upstate.

The two ecclesiastics relaxed with gin fizzes and a taste of kippered salmon sent over by Solomon Rubenstein, the Second Avenue supplier of the Chancery's office furniture. The Rubenstein family never missed Mass at St. Patrick's Cathedral Easter and Christmas, on which occasions they would place one thousand dollars in a parish envelop They always got a front-row seat and a discreet wave from the Cardinal. "Not," Father Moreno of the Cathedral staff pointed out, "a bad exchange for a yearly multimillion dollar business with the Archdiocese."

Chapter Eighteen
CARLO AND FAMILY BUSINESS

Carlo spent the first day of his leave of absence closeted with Bruno Battaglia, who had rented a suite at the Park Plaza with a spectacular view of Central Park. It was to be Family headquarters for a couple of days. Carlo instructed Bruno. "Call Uncle Julio and ask him if he could spare a couple of hours tonight - say about seven. Send a car to pick him up."

Bruno was a handsome, pleasant man who looked out at the world with a chiseled face, now etched with a net of fine age lines and set off with frank brown eyes that blended with the soft silkiness of his dark hair splashed with gray. "The first thing I want to make clear, Bruno, is that the Family operations must be resumed as quickly as possible. I don't want any of the other Families to take advantage of us during this time."

"I agree. We need to move on all fronts, as if nothing had happened." Bruno nibbled on chocolate-covered macadamia nuts

Carlo ran sweaty fingers through his hair. "Tomorrow morning let's start at nine. I'd like to see each of the caporegime. Tell them I want a detailed report from each. It should include plans they have for making their operations more efficient. Make it clear I don't want anyone coming in unprepared." Carlo set the tone for the following day's meeting. "Now is the time for new initiatives and new policies to be formulated." He paused to use the bathroom. Bruno noted his serious demeanor, and hoped that a lighter, softer side would emerge as time went by. He was confident the Family was in good hands. Respect for Carlo was high among the men, but they also needed from him a bit more camaraderie.

Wiping his fingers with the bathroom towel, Carlo continued. "Another piece of business that needs immediate attention is my brother's drug addiction. Get ahold of Nicky and tell him to get over here quickly. I must talk to him. He needs help. Let's get him that help right away."

Bruno moved to the telephone and dialed. "That you, Nicky?"

"Right."

Carlo wants to see you. We're at Suite 61, at the Plaza."

"Be right over."

After putting down the receiver, Bruno asked, "Want me to sit-in when he comes?"

"Bruno I want you to be in on every meeting. - just as you did with Julio. No secrets from you. If I hide things from you I may not get good advice when I need it."

Bruno had been wondering what his role would be in the new regime. This remark was a clear and unambiguous answer. During Victor's short regime he had been shut out of decision-making, being used more as a notary public than the family consigliere. He relaxed and popped more chocolate-covered macadamia nuts.

There was a soft knock. Bruno said, "Might be Nicky." It was.

"Hi." Nicky rushed to embrace his brother and Bruno. He was on time, an attention to punctuality he had rarely displayed. Bruno thought he looked like a man showing up for a job interview, trying to make a good impression but betraying some nervousness.

"Nice to see you guys."

Carlo walked behind the room's large mahogany desk and sank into an elegant beige leather chair, observing his brother closely. "Give Nicky a drink Bruno." Motioning to Nicky, "Come, sit down."

Nicky took the drink, removed his overcoat, ran his fingers through his thick dark hair and straightened his tie. He could feel Carlo's steely gaze boring in on him. His brother's low-pitched voice had the ring of authority. He gulped down his drink and handed the glass to Bruno for a re-fill.

"The same?"

Nicky waved a hand. "Yes, a little more ice." He lost his center. *Here I'm sitting with my own brother and I don't feel comfortable. What went wrong? I feel like I'm in the eye of a hurricane.*

In an attempt to appear relaxed he stretched his legs to full length, straightened the creases in his pants legs, and took the chair facing his brother. He realized that for many years he had mistaken Carlo's quiet demeanor for weakness. During seminary visits Nicky would display his macho personality to the brother he perceived as an effeminate personality. Now, in the Presidential Suite of the Plaza Hotel, he sat before him sensing his strength. It had all happened so fast. He tried to be convivial. "Carlo, what can we do to move the family forward? I'm right here by your side."

Carlo got up from his desk and walked around to the side of Nicky's chair, putting his hands on his shoulders, looking into his eyes with a hawk like focus. "Nicky, you're my brother and I love you. What the family needs right now from you is to see you well adjusted in your personal life. You can't serve the family unless you've got your act together. Right now everyone is concerned about you - the problems with your drinking - your playboy attitude toward your work. Worst of all, there's the problem of drugs. So, I've arranged for you to enter a clinic up in Hartford. It's called the Hartford Rehabilitation Clinic. I've talked with a Doctor Steiner there and he is making all the arrangements. You must enter for a checkup - expected there next Monday morning at 9am. Frankie will drive you there and get you registered. Think positive. If you don't, there's no place for you in the Organization."

Nicky rose from his chair, his face flushed with anger, and stared in disbelief as his brother talked. Carlo motioned for him to sit. He opened his mouth and emitted shattered vowels, as he swallowed the remains of a bourbon and water. He then rose again in a single, jerky motion, pacing the floor, feeling spat upon, and protesting the accusations. He returned to sit down and smacked the arms of the chair. His face froze as he sucked a deep breath. "Bunch 'a damn lies, all lies. Sure, I fool around a bit. Hell, why does everyone have to take work so seriously? We're not undertakers!" His face flushed and his body trembled with emotion.

Carlo pressed Nicky's shoulders, moving him back gently to the sitting position, and offering him his handkerchief to wipe the glistening face and forehead. "Don't get upset Nicky. You need to get some help and we're going to stand by you. You don't need to be embarrassed. We're family."

Nicky sobbed. His mind worked like a computer, but he could not come up with a response. His body slumped so low his head nearly touched the richly carpeted floor. The geometric patterns revolved, blurring perception. Pensively, he stared into a void trying to assimilate all that was happening around him. "What about Lisa? When do I see her?"

Carlo placed his hands together in an inverted V and stared at him vacantly. "That's not my business, Nicky, that's up to her. She's not like our mother and our aunts. She's a liberated American woman. You can't snap your fingers and expect her to run back after the way you treated her. Lisa won't do that."

Nicky's eyes flashed with irritation. He inhaled air noisily, exhaling as his shoulders trembled. His hands rummaged through his already-tousled hair. Sensing his brother's feelings, Carlo said, "I'm not patronizing you, Nicky. I'm talking to you man-to-man. It's not going to help if you start felling sorry for yourself." Then, gently, "Do what I'm asking you to do, and we'll see how it goes. If you feel we're all wrong, this is a great opportunity to prove it. Family is family, Nicky. We won't let you down."

Bruno sat quietly throughout the meeting, clipping his fingernails. *Not since Julio's earlier days has the Family been so fortunate.*

Nicky's voice became soft, almost a whisper. "I gotta think about this, Carlo. You guys got me all wrong."

"Take your time, but give it serious thought." Carlo motioned Nicky to follow him out of the room. "We'll be in touch."

The brothers embraced and Nicky left the hotel suite. Carlo turned to Bruno. "I hope that did some good. Let's look at all these other items."

Julio arrived shortly after five. He was hungry. "I can't talk business without food. This place has good pasta - they'll bring it up here. What about some linguine and clam sauce, huh?"

At a nod from Carlo, Bruno called food service and ordered three meals. "I'm getting in on this too. I'm starved."

Carlo turned to his uncle. "I need your advice." He outlined his agenda - the meeting with Nicky, the upcoming meeting with the Caporegime, the confirmation of Bruno as his consigliere, his plan to discuss finances with Anthony Fabrisco, the Family auditor.

Julio was delighted. "Carlo, my dreams have come true. You've got the brains and the right temperament for the job. I'll be able to sleep much better now." Pressing his fingers until they cracked, pointing to Bruno, he said, "Carlo, this man is our hidden treasure. Treat him well. He's the one man who'll give you advice even when you don't want to hear it."

The two men talked business until late into the night. Julio produced his box of secret files containing the names of informants, judges and police on the family payroll. He gave Carlo numbers of Swiss Bank accounts, profiles of every person in the organization and a host of interesting and useful trivia. A separate Accounts book listed the names of particular law-enforcement officials "owned" by the Family, vital links in its Family's success and security.

"Many thanks, Uncle Julio. I'm now ready for my meeting with the Caporegime tomorrow morning. One last thing. I need a place to live. I found an apartment in Riverdale with a nice view of the Hudson. What do you think?"

Julio did not hesitate. "Whatever appeals to you - get yourself a good housekeeper; someone who doesn't have telefonitis."

Julio got up and paced around the room. "How to handle this priesthood thing. I can't give you any advice on that subject. I only know that you're needed by the Family. It's a crucial time for us. If you ever need to talk about it, I'm always at home these days."

Julio embraced his nephew and Bruno accompanied him to his waiting car. "Take good care of Carlo, consigliere. Without him we'd have fallen apart. Without him we will not survive."

That night Julio fell asleep listening to his wife reciting the rosary for their nephew.

The following morning, Carlo was still in his bedroom when Bruno informed him that "Nicky called to say he has agreed to sign himself in at the Clinic today."

Carlo was relieved. "Great news, Bruno, we're making some progress."

Bruno changed the subject. "The Caporegime are all here. I picked up a few folding chairs, so we've got enough seating for everyone." The Caporegime, most of them annoyed, began to arrive at eight-thirty. They were not accustomed to early-morning meetings. Some complained openly to Bruno about this break with tradition. They preferred evening meetings held amidst the aroma of pasta, salami, fresh Italian loaves and noisy children. At the same time, they were conscious that a new and more efficient era in the Family operations was about to begin.

As Frankie put it to Bruno, "We know damn well that our survival depends on a new approach. We're just not ready for it yet, so there will be a bit of grumbling. Deep down they want it."

The unspoken but dominating super fact was that the new Don was a priest, a priest who had all the qualities needed at this juncture in the history of the Family. It was an exciting, if demanding, time. When they had assembled, Carlo stepped out of his bedroom and welcomed them. "Gentlemen, I appreciate your promptness. I've known most of you since I was a teenager, so we don't need any introductions. Let me get right down to business."

He invited Bruno to sit next to him. Symbolic gestures were very important to the Family organization, and Carlo knew how to use them. "You men are the key to the success of the organization. I'm going to demand the highest performance from each one of you. Bruno will deal with you directly on day-to-day operations. I'll be available any time if you need to see me directly." Carlo then fielded questions of a general nature. Most of them dealt with the kind of expenses routinely occurred. Julio had allowed a great deal of freedom. Carlo indicated this would no longer be the case. "I don't want to make any hard and fast rules about money, but you should consult with Bruno whenever expenditures are larger than normal." He was pressed for an example. OK, let us say that you think a police informant's salary should be raised. Talk it over first with Bruno. See what he thinks about it. If Bruno's not satisfied, come and talk to me and I'll make the decision. To be honest, I think it would be rare that I would disagree with Bruno because he's the guy whose been handling all these things for years. He's got the experience. But, I'm willing to listen to you if that happens." He glanced around at the men, "Make sense?"

There appeared to be unanimous agreement.

Carlo then informed them, "We now need to discuss something very important for the future of our organization, the RICO statute, the most serious threat to the safety of all of us. It all began with Robert Blakey, a dedicated member of the American Civil Liberties Union, who actually had a great influence protecting our rights. But, he wrote the damn Organized Crime Control Act of 1970. One section of the new law hits us hard and is very dangerous. It's the Racketeer Influenced and Corrupt Organizations Act, called RICO. We need to know all about this new law."

Frankie Montana wanted to know what was so different. "They've been coming up with all kinds of laws and Julio always found a way to get around them. No offense, Carlo, but Bruno would be able to handle all this new stuff."

Carlo was patient. Extending the palm of his hand toward Bruno, he said, "Bruno, why don't you explain this new law to the fellows. You know the legalese."

Bruno referred to his notes as he spoke. "Let me explain the difference between this new law and the old. Let's say one of you guys puts the muscle on someone in your district and some hot shot prosecutor decides to make himself a name by bringing you to court. In the old days that would have been your problem, but now it's our problem.

Willie Stanza still did not understand. "In what way?"

Bruno patiently explained. "So long as the prosecutor can prove that you're connected with the Albanese Organization he can put the heat on any of us, including Julio or Carlo. That's the difference and it's a hell of as big difference. Got it?"

Willie was impressed. "Wow, that is different."

Bruno continued. "And the guy who's taking this RICO statue and running with it is one of our own, a kid by the name of Rudolph Giuliani. He wanted to be a priest."

Carlo flexed his shoulders, clasped his hands behind his back and quipped, "I wish he had been. Let me tell you, he's one smart cookie. You don't want to mess with him."

Bruno held an article he clipped from the Daily News and read a portion of it. "A Justice Department official declared today that Rudolph Giuliani would make a very significant difference in the fight against organized crime. If anyone had ever suggested to me that a federal official would publicly state that he would scare the life out of the Mafia, I would have advised him to see a shrink, but this is exactly what Giuliani had done."

The meeting concluded with promises by all the men that they would begin a process of legitimizing their operations as best they could and would clear everything they did with Bruno, in the light of this new information. Before leaving the hotel room each man, in the ancient tradition, chatted with Carlo for a few minutes, offering an envelope stuffed with cash "in gratitude and respect."

Bruno learned from the informal discussions taking place among the men that they were pleased with their new Boss. He had, they said, "class." They left the hotel with a new sense of pride in their work and the confidence that if they followed the rules all would be safe.

Carlo decided to make a retreat before assuming even more duties of Don. Adolfo suggested the Dominican Retreat House, Our Lady of Solitude, in Tampa, Florida. "The Prior, Father Clarence Maxwell, is a noted psychologist and counselor, especially for the clergy. This is his telephone number. He rarely goes on vacation, so you'll catch him at the Retreat House.

Father Maxwell answered on the first ring. "Hello."

"My name is Father Carlo Albanese."

"From New York City?"

"Yes."

Father, I've read about you in the newspapers. What can I do for you?"

Carlo was brief. "I've asked for a leave of absence to assist my family in its affairs. I think I should pray and get counsel before I do that. Is it possible? Are you available?"

Of course, Father, when would you like to come?"

I'd like to fly down tomorrow, if that's OK with you."

Maxwell's voice was welcoming. "Yes, tomorrow is fine. Flying into Tampa I presume?"

"That's correct."

"We'll meet you."

Carlo did not want to impose on them. "That's very kind of you, Father, but I'll get there on my own. Should be there around noon."

Maxwell was very friendly. "Great. See you then. Let's say, for lunch? In any case, we'll save you a plate."

"Thanks."

Carlo packed a suitcase with clothes and spiritual reading. He took seriously his mission to save the Family from chaos. Julio's legacy had to be acted upon and developed.

Brother Walter led Carlo to Father Maxwell's office. "He stays in his room most of the day. He's got a small electric plate in there and a bathroom. For him, that's home."

"He's not strange, is he?"

The Brother was emphatic. "Not at all. He's just disciplined, ascetic and dedicated. His life consists in being available to others. It's the way he is."

Father Maxwell sat at his desk, looking the stereotypical unkempt, absent-minded professor with thick eyeglass lenses. He was thin but lean, with an air of asceticism. At age fifty he remained handsome with an aquiline nose, firm chin and broad shoulders. A thick swatch of gray, peppered hair fell down over his ears and down his neck. He looked up at Carlo over glasses perched low on the bridge of his nose, and ran his hand absently across his face. "Welcome. May I call you Carlo?"

"Of course."

Maxwell extended a handshake. "And please call me Clarence."

"I will."

The academic signs of a scholarly life were all about the office. On his bookshelf were rows of volumes written by the theological and philosophical giants of today and yesterday. Carlo counted four volumes of Thomas Aquinas, three volumes of Bellarmine and the complete works of Karl Rahner, Gustavo Guttierez, and St. John of the Cross. Augustine's Confessions lay open on his desk. "Sit down, Carlo."

"Thanks"

Father Maxwell chose a sheet of paper from a pile on his desk and handed it to Carlo. "Here's a list of the house rules, meal times and so on. The chapel is open twenty four hours a day. I'm also available twenty four hours a day." Chuckling, "I must admit I don't function too well after midnight."

Brother Walter, smiling broadly, reappeared at the office door.

"Can I help you find your room, Father?"

"Yes, thank you." To Father Maxwell, "Thanks, I'll get myself settled and look forward to talking with you during the next few days."

Maxwell's eyes radiated a controlled vitality. "I look forward to that."

Carlo gave a quick salute and headed out to the corridor, closing the office door behind him.

One of the books Carlo brought for meditation was a small volume, The Wit and Wisdom of Good Pope John (John XXIII). He read his words. "What did I feel upon hearing that I had been elected pope? The same sensation as a baby in swaddling clothes, because the cassock which they had slipped over me was very tight and I felt as though I were wrapped up as a mummy." It was this pope's humanity that would guide him in his meditations.

The Gothic chapel's dome covered the sanctuary, which was sheathed with marble. The statues and vigil lights produced an atmosphere of warmth and holiness. Several young monks entered the chapel garbed in long flowing Dominican robes. They gathered around the sanctuary organ and began rehearsing Gregorian Chant and the polyphonic music of Palestrina. Not since the seminary days had Carlo heard this music and it moved him. He sat back and meditated on his priesthood as the monks sang in soft, dulcet tones. His eye caught a red leather bound bible lying alongside him. He picked it up to read, fumbling through many pages, looking for something to inspire him, to lessen the pain of isolation he was beginning to feel within the priesthood. He found it in the Book of Jeremiah, 1, 48:

The word of the Lord came to me, saying, 'before I formed you in the womb I knew you, before you were born I set you apart.

The meeting with Father Maxwell took place the following day after breakfast. "Come to my office. Let's chat." The voice and demeanor oozed with friendliness and confidence. They sat around a low coffee table, a crucifix hovering over them from the table's center. Maxwell led. "Let us place ourselves in the presence of the crucified Lord." They sat silently for several moments of meditation before Maxwell said, "Tell me what is on your mind."

Carlo took a moment to frame his words. "Clarence, I love the priesthood. I love the concept of the priesthood. I have a problem because I see it so differently from my colleagues. I have come to change my mind about the value of celibacy, for example. I think it makes us selfish, out of touch with real life. What do you think?"

Maxwell's eyes lit up. "That, my friend, is the main problem with the priesthood. The more we are absorbed in ourselves, the more impoverished others become in our eyes. The highest form of development, really, is being in love. We are denied this in the priesthood. The tragic lives of so many priests are a testimony to the result of the rule of celibacy. The only way to restore the priesthood to a healthy condition is to allow us to have families, if we wish. There are some guys who are not interested in marrying. That's fine also, but, personally, I wouldn't accept them as candidates."

Carlo felt confirmed in his own views. He moved on to another subject. "My family business, as you know, Clarence, is 'Mafia' business. With our leadership decimated, the Family has turned to me for leadership. I have no choice but to accept, since if I don't there will be suffering and mayhem on a grand scale. The other Families are already looking at our weakened condition and are probably poised to strike. I need to move quickly and with all the vigor I have."

Maxwell knew Carlo was awaiting his response to this declaration. He drummed a forefinger on his desk as he reflected. "Special circumstances require special actions. Surely, your case is most unusual so there is no ready-made answer. You will have to ply your way through this maze with much prayer and a keen ear for the whisperings of the Holy Spirit."

Carlo nodded. "Yes."

"The easy answer would be to let someone else do the job."

Carlo shook his head. "There isn't anyone else."

Maxwell's words were measured. "In that case I can only say you will have to be especially vigilant. Surely, all that power and the many complicated and awful decisions you will have to make can bring a hell of a lot of mental and spiritual stress to your life."

Carlo quietly agreed. "Yes."

"You realize that you will be misunderstood, whatever caution and safeguards you employ. You may die in a war that has no heroes. I mean, you will struggle to change things in an organization that everyone presumes cannot be changed, and everyone despises."

"I know."

"There are those honest and thoughtful men who will feel ambiguity about a priest acting in your present role. History will exonerate you, of course, but in the meantime you may catch hell. Sooner rather than later the Cardinal will feel the heat from many sources. Then he will move from being pastor to being politician. It's the nature of the job, the nature of the Institution. You're going to need a great deal of courage. I will keep you in my prayers. God bless and keep you."

"Thank you, Clarence. I am very grateful for your guidance."

Maxwell produced a bottle of wine. "Let's celebrate. Another priest of God takes on a heavy task. Another cross to carry. I applaud you for your determination and your willingness to engage in a very tough ministry."

The next morning, Carlo flew back to New York feeling buoyed and confidant that he was doing the right thing.

Upon his return from Florida, Carlo moved directly into his new home in Riverdale. Viewed from the large mullioned window of his towering apartment overlooking the Hudson, October's colors splashed the tree foliage that ran from the apartment grounds down to the river with brilliant colors. He sprawled his body on the thick carpet facing the glass doors leading out to the balcony, folding his feet in an unconscious meditative pose. The bedroom was filled with a rainbow of light, filtered through the tinted glass doors and windows. The apartment suited him. The bed was large, with linen throw pillows resting against an ornate headboard carved with a hunting scene. Two thick-armed chairs covered in red leather sat, angled one to the other as antagonists, a glass table separating them. On the wall above the chairs two large abstracts dominated. The first time Lisa visited the apartment, she asked, "What do those paintings signify? They makes no sense to me."

Carlo teased. "They're not supposed to."

Lisa rolled her eyes and arched a brow. "Oh, well, that's good?"

Carlo's eyes danced devilishly. "Of course! Paintings are like women. The thrill would be gone if you had them figured out."

Lisa palmed her hair, tossing it to the left. "Well, since you put it that way, maybe I like abstracts after all. I'll check out the Museums and learn more about them."

Carlo slapped his thigh. "There you are. Good student."

"Have you figured me out?" she asked.

"Of course not."

"Nice."

As Carlo reflected on recent events he was grateful for Father Maxwell's advice and analysis. He phoned Bruno. "Just letting you know I'm back and ready for work, at least I think so. Florida can be very distracting, with palm trees and white, sandy beaches. I sometimes think how easy it would be to just slip into another world. But, maybe that's not possible. We can't be everyone and everywhere. We're limited by our destiny, I suppose."

Bruno agreed. "Yes, Carlo, I'm sure that's right. I fantasize sometime myself - you know - opening an offshore bank in the Caribbean somewhere and living on the seaside. I'd probably last about a month before I'd want to hear the sound of subways and screaming police cars. Crazy."

The next morning, Bruno filled him in on Family business. There was only one urgent message. "Frankie wants to see you. I told him I'd get in touch with you as soon as you got in. We can call him right now if you want?"

"Sure; do that."

Bruno made the phone call and said, "He'll be over this evening about seven. OK?"

"Fine. That gives me time to relax a bit."

After Bruno left, Carlo rested for a few hours before preparing himself a dish of Linguini with clam sauce. He listened to Pavarotti as he ate.

Frankie arrived promptly at seven. Carlo invited him to relax on the couch and joined him. "What's on your mind, Frankie?"

Frankie sprawled his legs and opened the beer. "Carlo, while you were away, something came up that I need to talk to you about."

"Shoot."

Frankie was Carlo's favorite Caporegime. He dropped out of Fordham Law School after three semesters because of the untimely death of his father from liver cancer. Julio quickly gave him more and more responsibility, happy to have an articulate and ambitious young man who understood the intricacies of the law. Bruno Battaglia adopted him as an apprentice. It was assumed in the Family that when Bruno either retired or expired, Frankie would become the Family consigliere.

"Frankie, help yourself to a drink. I'm not good at mixing them." Pointing to a cabinet that bore the weight of the television set, he said, "All the drinks are in there."

Frankie made his selection, plucked some ice from the refrigerator and mixed his drink. "Carlo, I've got a police informant in the 33rd precinct with whom I have a problem. He's having second thoughts about working with us - says he wants out. That already is bad news for us, but my contacts say he might do more than that; he might talk to a Grand Jury. I understand that his wife, a very pious Catholic lady, has been after him to do some plea-bargaining. She's laying some kind of religious trip on him and it's getting to him. That would mean lotsa troubles for us, Carlo, so we need to act quickly."

Carlo pointed finger at his chest. "Frankie, I'll handle this one myself."

"Sure, Carlo, whatever you say."

"What's his name?"

Frankie frowned. "You're not gonna like this, Carlo. It's Lt. Kennedy."

Carlo slapped his forehead. "What? You gotta be kidding. You gotta be kidding."

Jim Kennedy had been, for years, one of Julio's most reliable insiders. Their collaboration had turned to friendship, their friendship to a bonding Julio prized. He once told Carlo, "Jim Kennedy's not an informant in the usual sense. He understands what we do; he's simpatico."

"What do you suggest, Frankie?"

Frankie pursed his lip, then explained. "We gotta get him alone and talk to him and tell him he and his family could be in danger if the rumors we've heard about his talking to a grand jury are true. That's what we gotta do. If he comes to his senses, then that's it, no problem. If not, we gotta do more."

176 Father Patrick Bascio

Carlo stretched out his arms in frustration. "But he's always been straight with us. What happened?"

"It's the wife." Frankie paused. If Carlo was to be an effective leader, he had to understand the rules. "A deal is a deal, Carlo. Nobody forced this guy to make a deal with us in the first place. He's just a greedy, corrupt cop, that's all. Now he wants out, but he's a danger to us. That doesn't work. You know what I mean?"

Carlo nodded his assent and understanding. "Yeah. In an ideal world it would be different. This isn't an ideal world, is it?"

Frankie did not answer the obviously rhetorical question. "The Jebbies at Fordham used to tell us that original sin did a lot of damage."

Carlo agreed. "Yeah, Adam and Eve sure fouled us up."

Frankie rolled a drinking glass in his right palm. "Do you believe in the devil, Carlo?"

"Oh yes, absolutely. What else explains such terrible actions in history by people who are constructed so beautifully! There must be a devil."

"Carlo, what about the Family? What about us? Are we evil?" Carlo gazed at the carpet while shifting his feet in semi-circles. "That's a good question Frankie, a question we have to answer." Straightening up and enveloping Frankie's eyes with his own, he continued. "Sure we're evil. But, it's not quite that simple. A lot of evil is forced on us. For example, the used-car salesman. Do you think he'd be in business long if he tried to compete honestly? Impossible! And if he doesn't cheat, who puts bread on the table for his family? Do you think if he goes to City Hall and tells everyone, `Listen, I'm broke because I've been an honest used-car salesman.' Do you think anyone there's going to say, `Oh, you're such a nice guy, we'll help you out with your mortgage until you find other work.'?"

Frankie slapped the palms of his hands. "No way!"

Carlo put a finger to his cheekbone, and continued. "Let's say we made a public announcement that the Family will dissolve itself provided the police, the insurance companies, the loan sharks, and the narco people start acting honestly? What do you think? Are they going to do it?"

Frankie shook his head again.

"So you see, the problem is an enormous one. It defies solution, but we are in the unique historical position to try and change things." Carlo moved to the living room's large bay window and stared out over the Hudson River. "What we've got to do is continue to provide employment for our people and act as a force for justice where the law does not. We've got to go back to our roots. It's a big job, Frankie, and I need your help!"

"You got it."

Carlo concluded his instructions. "Call Kennedy. Tell him I'm going to meet with him. There are too many people's lives involved in his testimony. It's too late to convert. Tell him we'll let him off the hook, but he's got to stick to his agreement. No moralizing."

"When you gonna see him?"

"Tomorrow afternoon."

Frankie fingered his eyelids. "I'll tell him."

Carlo looked at his watch. Frankie took this as a sign he should leave. "Time for me to go. Thanks for the chat."

Carlo sat alone long into the night, reflecting. This was the moment he dreaded, a decision that might involve violence. He had come to terms with the inevitability, but that did not make it any easier. *I can't take on the responsibility of running the Family and, at the same time, plead piety when it comes to making the hard decisions.* That, he concluded, would have been more hypocritical than living with the contradictions he now faced. His priesthood hung like a heavy weight on him as he proceeded to handle Jim Kennedy. *I have to face the fact that my hands are going to get dirty. It also bothered Julio, but there is no other way. Life isn't simple.*

Jim Kennedy lived so close to Shea Stadium that he and his family could hear the public address announcements and the cheering. 1785 Roselawn Avenue was typical of the neighborhood homes, a modest size Cape Cod with red clapboard, white shutters, dormer windows, and a front porch set back from the street, fronted by a well-groomed lawn. *It all seems so domestic. Why should I have to come here and throw confusion into this scene?*

Carlo pressed the doorbell. It sent tremulous, uncertain rings throughout the house. Kathleen Kennedy came to the porch, cocked her head to one side and asked, "Who would you like to see?"

He recognized the young woman. Her voice rolled time backwards. The last time he had seen Kathleen was when she was twelve years of age. He recognized her by her high cheekbones and cleft chin. She was thin, almost breast less. Her hair was tied in a ballerina's knot. Her eyes were marbles of blue light glistening with interest.

"Good afternoon, Miss."

"Good afternoon." Suddenly, recognition mixed with fear. Her voice became wobbly and her cheeks reddened. "You're... Father... Carlo, yes?"

With a smile, "Yes, and you're Kathleen?"

A slight relaxation. "I guess you want to see my dad? I'll call him." Then fear again. She moved quickly into the house leaving Carlo on the porch.

He could hear the nervous voice of Jim's wife, Stella: "Tell him daddy's not home."

"He knows he's here."

"Oh God. Why did he come? Call your father."

Jim Kennedy appeared from the back of the house, sweating from lawn cutting. His greeting was both muted and awkward. He knew this encounter was going to take place sooner or later. "Hi, Carlo."

"James"

Kennedy pointed to two lawn chairs. "Come, sit down. You're well, Carlo?

"Yes, and you?"

He winced. "Fine, considering."

"Jim, would you be good enough to take a ride with me. You know, get something to eat. We need to talk."

Jim was diffident. "I don't think there's much to talk about, Carlo."

"Jim, I'm responsible for the welfare of the Family. We gotta talk about your contract."

Momentarily defiant, "I didn't make any contract with you. I made it with Julio."

Carlo's voice was soft but firm. "You made it with the Family, not Julio. You know that and I know that, Jim, so stop playing games and talk about the facts."

Jim made a gesture of deprecation. "You're wasting your time, Carlo, but I'll go with you. Just a minute." He ran onto the porch and shouted into the house, "Honey, I'll be out with Carlo for a couple of hours. Don't worry Everything's fine."

His wife knew that everything was not fine. He was not long on the force when he told his wife. "Hell, everybody's on the take." She sensed when he said that that he was already participating, but they rarely talked about it. It would just be something like, "Well, honey, I was able to pick up a little extra cash for the kids' education." His disillusionment with the NYPD, or at least his idealized version of it, led him to bitterness and cynicism. When New York's "finest" were not what they should be, he lost his belief in beauty and goodness and honesty, and found himself slowly descending and wallowing in negatives. The cynicism generated his creeping corruption, and his own corruption now began to feed his cynicism. It was a vicious circle. As an amateur hunter, he constantly saw himself mirrored in the wounded and dying animals he shot.

Carlo drove to Spanish Harlem. In the dashboard reflection Jim looked tired and frightened. Stopping at 92nd Street, they entered a small restaurant and ordered lunch. A waitress quickly arranged two place settings.

"What are you having?" Carlo asked.

Jim fingered through the menu. "Love broiled snapper."

"Get it." Glancing at the waitress, "Two broiled snappers, please."

The waitress jotted down their order, then inquired, "Would you gentlemen like something to drink while your order is being prepared?"

Carlo asked, "Coffee, Jim?"

"Yeah."

Carlo leaned toward the waitress. "Coffee, please."

Jim Kennedy opened up the conversation, "Carlo, you don't know what it is to be the father of a family. Please don't ask me to do anything that would put my family in any danger."

"Jim, from the moment that you decided to make money on the side you put yourself and your family in danger. I was not in the picture when all that took place. I'm dealing with now, with today."

Stubbornly, "I'm dealing with today also, the today of my wife's anger, her legitimate demands."

Shortly, the waitress set their orders before them. "Enjoy your meal, gentlemen."

Carlo wolfed down the hot and lemony snapper, while Jim nervously played with the peas and rice, taking small bits of fish at a time. The conversation resumed. "It won't do to suddenly turn your back on us Jim. Whatever you feel about your conscience, about your religion, about your family. If you want out, that's fine But, if you've some idealistic notion of being 'good' and, in the process, putting some of our men in jail, that's unacceptable."

Jim tried sarcasm, but could not allay the dread that filled his psyche. "Since when is doing or being good unacceptable to a priest."

"Maybe you don't understand what a priest is, Jim, even with your Irish Catholic background. The job of a priest is to act as a peacemaker."

Jim laughed nervously, as he stared out the diner's tinted windows. "You're putting pressure on me - that's what you call peacemaking?"

Carlo spoke deliberately. "Let me put this in context, Jim. You've been a corrupt cop for 20 years. If you want to convert, I applaud that; but if you think you can use 'conversion' as a cover for destroying people in our organization, that I won't tolerate. Frankie already made an offer to let you out, provided you don't talk to a Grand Jury. That's my offer. There's enough guilt to go around, Jim. You don't have a privileged position. We're all guilty."

Carlo's gaze was unrelenting. Jim Kennedy fell silent. Carlo's voice was stern. "I know your wife has appealed to you to come clean. I understand where she's coming from, but she doesn't understand where you're coming from. She says 'clean up your act,' go straight. Sounds good, but it's not so simple. None of this is simple."

Carlo's logic was not lost on his listener.

Kennedy made the "time out" sign. "Look, Carlo, I need time to think about what you're saying. I need time. I'm not pretending to be a saint. They've offered me immunity. I know that sounds bad, but I've got a wife and kids. My wife's looking at me now, Carlo, and what she sees she don't like. If I don't do this I lose her and the kids."

Carlo asked, "What does she want?"

"Stella's begging me to go to the Grand Jury. I know what you're saying. I understand. I'm in a hopeless position."

"Jim, the bottom line is that if the Prosecutor gives you a good deal at our expense, we've got to defend ourselves. It's like you defending a daughter from a rapist. No difference, Jim, no difference. Think about it." The lethal calmness in Carlo's eyes was not comforting.

The waitress, a young college student, picked up bits and pieces of the conversation and became nervous. She whispered to the manager, "Those two guys over there scare me, they're talking crazy stuff."

"Just be cool, sweetheart, it doesn't concern us."

A few minutes later Carlo paid for the meal. They left the building and walked aimlessly along the street. Carlo made an offer. "I'll give you immunity Jim, immunity from the penalty that goes with breaking your word with us." Jim caught the threatening spark that lit up Carlo's eyes. Carlo's quiet tone carried a message of death.

Kennedy rubbed the back of his neck and silently gestured his hands. *I can't believe a priest is saying this. Just as cold-blooded as any hood.*

Carlo calmly moved a finger across his eyelids and continued. "The District Attorney offers protection to witnesses - you know, new name, new address, maybe a job."

"Yeah, witness protection."

"Right. I'm making the same offer."

Kennedy placed a finger on his cheekbone. "How would that work? What do ya have in mind?"

Carlo was deliberative in speech and manner. "Jim, the Family will buy you a house wherever you want, get you a new job, new social security number. The money you make selling your assets here - and we can help with that if you like - can be used to help you get started in a new location."

Beads of sweat moistened Jim Kennedy's face. His hands nervously toyed with his belt buckle. They walked along in complete silence. Carlo placed his arms around Kennedy. "Jim, I only ask you to do one more thing. Talk with the wife. Explain my proposal. Don't presume that coming clean is of more importance to her than having you alive." This was Carlo's first direct reference to the nature of the penalty.

Jim Kennedy shook his head and screwed up his face into a frown. He was treading on very dangerous ground and he knew it. "I don't think I should put the burden on her. It's not fair."

"That's how you see it, Jim. She may not see it that way. Talk with her. What about your children? Do they want some kind of nebulous hero or a live dad to love them, and be a grandfather to their children? A hero? Come on, Jim, the story will come out. The media will look into the DA's files, you can be sure. The papers will carry banner headlines. Corrupt cop testifies to Grand Jury. A hero? What kind of hero is that?"

The logic of Carlo's argument was not lost on Jim Kennedy. Another period of silence followed as they were distracted by the pleas of a passing beggar. Each delved into his pocket for loose change.

Kennedy rubbed his hands together. "Let me discuss this with my wife, Carlo. Give me a few more days. I promise not to speak either with the DA or a Grand Jury until you've gotten your reply. Fair enough?"

"Fair enough, Jim." Carlo stared straight into Jim's eyes. "Let me add a personal note. I don't want an assassination ordered on my watch." Jim Kennedy shivered. *He's being straight. He's got the guts for the job.* "I know you don't, Carlo. We'll see what the wife says."

They returned to Carlo's car and drove to Jim Kennedy's home. Stella Kennedy stood on the porch as her husband alighted from the car. Carlo could see the pleading in her eyes as he made eye contact with her. He blew her a kiss.

Is that the kiss of death? She made the sign of the cross as her husband moved up the steps toward her. "In the name of the Father, and of the Son, and of the Holy Spirit. Amen."

Almost a week elapsed before Carlo received his reply. It came, not from Kennedy, but in the form of a telephone call from Moynihan. "He's gonna talk. They've got him heavily guarded in a safe house in the Bronx. The wife and kids are on their way to Hollywood, Florida, where a house has been leased for them."

A Daily News headline told the story. Police informant to testify against the Mob. The article explained that:

In the middle of the night, Police Lt. Jim Kennedy and his family were moved out of their home near Shea Stadium and resettled at an undisclosed location, under heavy police protection. It is rumored that Kennedy was on the payroll of Julio Albanese, former godfather who was forced into retirement recently by serious liver failure.

Commissioner of Police, Roger Doyle, had no comment on the newspaper headline other than, "There's an ongoing investigation of Mafia activities, but it is too early to predict what the investigation will uncover. I can say that Lt. Kennedy has been suspended from all duties in the NYPD, pending developments. It is too early to say what will be his position, if any, in the NYPD after this affair has been fully investigated."

Carlo and Moynihan planned Kenney's abduction. Carlo was emphatic. "It must be done immediately, before he begins to talk. I mean tonight. We don't know how soon they'll start grilling him. It will also take his keepers by surprise" Moynihan agreed. Carlo continued, "I'll get the men; you see to it that there's only three or four police watching over Jim. After all, you can make the argument that no one knows where he is, and he is on their side, so even one or two men would do."

Moynihan had already decided he would use that very argument. Chuckling, "Thought of that myself, Carlo, so if two very intelligent men come up with the same plan, it's got to be a winner? Right?"

Carlo nodded and immediately handed Moynihan the phone. "Let's get the ball rolling. Every minute is precious."

Moynihan called Lt. Norm Bevin, head of the special protection unit. Bevin agreed that since no one knew of Kennedy's whereabouts there was no need to assign more than 2 men. Of course, Bevin smelled a personal agenda at work here, but Moynihan was his boss and all the men loved Moynihan. Whatever he did, the rank and file assumed, was for the greater honor and glory of law enforcement. The smell got even stronger when Moynihan suggested that if, for reasons beyond their control, someone got to Kennedy, the officers should be instructed not to use a weapon, "for fear that Kennedy and our own men would be hurt." Moynihan knew that Bevin would know that something was up. Bevin knew that Moynihan knew that he knew. It was just the way the system worked. Hoods, whether the garden-variety form or law enforcement types were expendable.

Bevin assigned two detectives, Jack Warner and Silvio Gestino to stay with Kennedy until the following day. Then, Kennedy would be brought downtown to Police Plaza for a formal interrogation both by the NYPD's Bureau of Internal Affairs and by officials from the District Attorney's office. Each of them would have a different agenda. Given the fact that Kennedy was afforded immunity from prosecution, Internal Affairs simply wanted to know if there were any other guys on the Force who worked with him. Warner and Gestino were happy enough to be instructed not to fire should the unexpected happen, i.e., somehow someone in the mob knew of

Kennedy's whereabouts. A firefight under those circumstances would likely end in their deaths. The fiction of "to protect the witness" was a nice cover.

Carlo called Frankie. "Kennedy is going to talk. He's in a safe house at 60 Berring Avenue, in the Bronx. Only two officers are protecting him and they have instructions not to fire if anyone breaks in. So, get about five guys, you know, to scare the hell out of them. One of them should be someone who knows how to pick a lock. Go in quick, with lots of muscle. The officers should back off. Then, grab Kennedy. Got it?"

"No problem, Carlo, especially since no one is going to get hurt. Of course, if one of those officers pulls a gun, our guys gotta take care of themselves. Right?"

"Right, but only as a last resort. We don't want a dead cop. That's always been the policy and its good policy."

Frankie agreed. "Only as a last resort."

In the dead of night five heavily armed men of the Albanese organization dressed in police uniforms quietly picked the lock and let themselves into the Bronx apartment containing Jim Kennedy. Frankie's assistant, Mike Salerno, headed the operation. Officer Warner followed instructions not to fire. "Hit the deck," they shouted, "hit the deck," menacing Warner with semi-automatic weapons. Officer Gestino was asleep on the couch but awoke at the commotion. Warner lay on the floor as Salerno yanked the gun out of his holster. Gestino laid his pistol on the floor between his legs. "Don't shoot!"

"Get Kennedy," said Salerno, pointing to two of his men.

As they entered the bedroom they saw Kennedy sitting up. He knew in an instant what was happening, and what his fate would be. He had no choice, when told, "OK, Jim, come with us." Images of his wife and family flooded his consciousness. He knew he was a dead man. Carlo had been right. He had listened to his wife. Now, they and their children would suffer the consequences.

Kennedy was whisked away in a blue van with no license plates. Several months of an intensive manhunt failed to uncover a clue as to his whereabouts. Publicly, the Mayor proclaimed that the search would continue until the kidnappers were brought to justice. He did not believe his own words, nor did anyone else in New York City. Jimmy Breslin, referring to the Kennedy disappearance, remarked on a Sunday Talk Show, "The Mafia has taken care of its own business; at this, they are very efficient. It was house cleaning time."

Mrs. Kennedy always blamed herself for her husband's disappearance. She came to reflect on the rules under which he worked for the Albanese clan, and she never forgave herself for pressuring him into breaking those rules. In time, she also admitted that she looked the other way for many years as her husband accepted Mafia money. A few weeks after her husband's disappearance, she accepted a $50,000 donation from the Albanese family, who sent their sincere condolences. For Carlo it was the end of innocence. He grieved over it mightily. However, he set his face like flint and accepted his destiny.

Carlo was watching a football game on TV. The phone rang. It was the chief psychiatrist at the Hartford Clinic. "Your brother is resisting rehabilitation."

"What happened?"

Doctor Henry Steiner gave Carlo the bad news. "He's so depressed that we're unable to motivate him to make any progress."

"What should be done?"

"The staff has concluded that the best therapy for him now would be a limited amount of work in the atmosphere of home and family. Without his cooperation, we can't make any progress. Of course, the decision is yours Mr. Albanese, but that's our best judgment."

Carlo agreed. He already felt guilty for insisting his brother take treatment, and then leaving him on his own. He was ashamed of feeling a sense of elation that his brother was no longer able to dominate his wife's life and time. It was time for a heart-to-heart with Nicky. He would not tell him of his feelings for Lisa…Nicky knew that already, he was sure… but he would try to determine if there was any hope at all that Lisa and Nicky could live together. If not, then he would feel freer to imagine a life with her. "Doctor, I'll come to talk with my brother. After that, you and I can get together and decide what to do. How does that sound?"

"That's fine with me. When do you expect you can make it up here?"

"I'll be there about ten tomorrow morning. Tell my brother I'm coming."

Carlo watched the evening news, then called Lisa. "I'm going up to Hartford tomorrow morning to see Nicky. I thought you'd like to know. He's not cooperating with the staff, so I'll have a talk with him. I can understand his depression. I mean, his life is unraveling. But he's got to understand that it wasn't much of a life anyway. You know what I mean?"

"Of course. I saw that years ago. I feel sorry for him, but I don't want to get trapped by some sort of sympathy." Her voice quivered. "Do you think I'm right?"

"About?"

"About not getting involved?"

"Yes, I do. It would give him false hope and do a lot more damage in the long run. I'll keep you informed."

"Thanks, Carlo. I'll wait to hear from you."

Carlo wanted to see her, but was cautious. "You understand why I'm not just coming over and all that."

"Yes, I do, and I agree. You don't really know where you're going yet. Right?"

"Right. The only thing I'm certain of is that to the best of my ability I'm going to take care of the Family. A little selfishness on my part could cause a lot of harm. Glad you understand. I'll be in touch."

The nervous receptionist at the Hartford Center rang Dr. Steiner's extension. "Mr. Albanese has arrived," Sally Rogers belonged to St. Bridget's Church, a block away from the rehabilitation center, a daily communicant. Glancing at him, she tried to hide the excitement of chatting with "Mr. Albanese." Sally read in the Hartford Courier that he was now head of the Albanese Family. To her co-worker, Linda, she said, "He was absolutely sweet. You could see he was a priest. I could have knelt down and asked him for his blessing."

"But, isn't he Mafia?"

"I'm sure he's just trying to help his family get reorganized. This man wouldn't hurt a flea, believe me, Linda."

Carlo walked along the corridor to the doctor's office, box-like space containing a TV, a desk and a clothes rack. The smell of disinfectants, medications and body odors whirled around him like rotten eggs. Steiner was grim-faced, his hands nervously sliding along the edge of his desk. "Mr. Albanese, I deeply regret to inform you that your brother left the premises this morning, without permission. He told the nurse assigned to his room he was on his way downstairs to the gift shop to 'buy a little gift for my brother.' He's not been seen since. I tried to reach you at home but I guess you'd already left. I'm terribly sorry."

Carlo pushed his hands deeper into his coat, stared abstractedly and said, "We should've acted much sooner, but you know how it is with family. We sometimes kill each other with kindness."

Steiner was relieved that he was not being blamed for Nicky's disappearance. He had often been the object of a family's wrath when things did not turn out according to expectations. "I didn't notify the authorities. Thought I'd leave that to your discretion." "Thanks doctor. I appreciate it. You know how the press are."

Steiner accompanied Carlo to his car. "We're always prepared to resume treatment should your brother wish to return. I'll be mailing you a complete report of his stay here. God bless."

Chapter Nineteen
NICKY AND CARLO

Carlo received a call from Manhattan detective, Walter Piazzi, at midnight. He identified himself and said, "Mr. Albanese, about an hour ago we received a call from a Manhattan prostitute informing us that a man passed out in her apartment. After visiting the scene we determined that it was your brother, Nicky. We found him sprawled on the floor, stoned on wine and cocaine. EMS was called immediately and is on its way to Beth Israel. We don't have a reading on his condition."

Carlo drove at high speed to the Hospital. There was foreboding in the air as he drove along wind-swept streets that shook thunder and rain from the skies. Arriving shortly before Two a.m., he entered Ward A and saw a familiar face. Dr. Brennan had been notified by Bruno Battaglia, and had arrived a few minutes earlier. He was thoughtfully sipping a cup of hot coffee. "Carlo, I got a brief report from Dr. Epstein. He tells me Nicky appears to be dying from an overdose of cocaine. I'm so sorry."

They made their way to the hospital room. Nurses and physicians crowded around Nicky as Carlo made two attempts to elicit a sign of recognition from him. None were forthcoming. The nurses busied themselves straightening bed sheets and puffing up pillows, in an attempt to do something. Their patient was dying and they were helpless to prevent it. One nurse whispered to her partner, "Father Albanese is so nice. I feel sorry for him."

Nicky's head barely emerged, waxen, from the undersized hospital gown. His chest pulsated like a blacksmith's bellows; his heart beat like a hammer. On a table lay wrapped presents, guilt-tinged offerings from family members. Moving quietly so as not to disturb the medical personnel, Carlo, speaking softly, gave his brother the last rites of the Catholic Church.

"May the Lord forgive you by this holy anointing and his most loving mercy whatever sins you have committed by the use of your sight, the use of your ears, the use of your sense of smell, the use of your sense of taste and the power of speech, the use of your sense of touch, the use of your power to walk. Amen"

For one brief moment, Nicky stared at him, harshly, as if to say, "You never helped me." Closing his eyes, he heaved a heavy sigh and returned to oblivion. He had the last word. It was his moment of triumph over the brother who dominated him from birth. Carlo felt the sting of it, the righteousness of it. He could not escape the incessant longing for his brother's wife, even right there in the hospital as his brother lay dying. Time for righting the wrong was running out, as Nicky approached the valley of death. Tears found their way down Carlo's normally granite face. He lifted Nicky's hands and held them for a brief moment against his cheeks, then slumped noiselessly into grief.

Dr. Epstein was not encouraging. "Father, he may not last more than a few hours. His vital signs are all negative. I'm sorry." The doctor put his arms around him. "We've readied a room for you just down the hall. Why not rest there while we continue to do our best."

Dr. Brennan accompanied Carlo to the room. "The police kept out of this, Carlo, out of respect for the family. By getting EMS at the apartment right away, they were able to divert attention from the paraphernalia that was in this gal's room."

Carlo was grateful for the good will still residing in so many people whom he had never met. Julio's popularity and influence continued to benefit the family. For Carlo, it was just another example of the complicated nature of his family's activities. He paced the room with hesitant steps, his eyes becoming opaque and impenetrable as he reflected on the roots of his arrogance in dealing with his brother, and its tragic consequences. Somewhere in the fray of growing up, Carlo began to see himself as distinct. Having always been treated as exceptional and unique, he became in his own mind, unique. His designation for the Church was deeply ingrained and, at some point, he saw himself as more than a person He was a person with a mission, the Family messiah. The uniqueness, the messianic vocation, proved to be a two edged sword. He was now becoming conscious of his coldness and insensitivity. He admitted to himself that his determination "to do the reasonable thing," was beginning to make him unreasonable. He was beginning to see himself for what he had become and he was not happy with the image.

Brennan had been standing near the window, observing Carlo's deeply meditative silence, and respected that space. He moved across the room very quietly, tapped Carlo on the shoulder and advised, "You rest. If anything happens, I'll let you know." Brennan placed his hands on Carlo's

188 Father Patrick Bascio

shoulders. "Nobody's perfect, if that's any consolation. I'll join the medical team. See if I can help."

In less than an hour, Brennan, accompanied by Bruno Battaglia, came into the room. It was 3 a.m. "Nicky 's dead. He died just a few minutes ago."

Carlo shook off his sleep. For a moment, his matter-of-fact attendance to business swiftly came back into play. "Bruno, call Lisa and let her know. Tell her it's our wish that she attend the funeral for the sake of the family. I think she'll understand." But, almost immediately, he lost his bearings once again. He disliked himself for experiencing relief that Lisa had lost her husband. *I can't help the feeling. She's now free. That is the one good that comes out of this tragedy.*

Dr. Brennan left the room to take care of preparing the transfer of Nicky's body to the Funeral Home. Bruno sat quietly as he observed Carlo's body begin to tremble. He seemed oblivious of Bruno's presence. "How horrible," he shouted. "How evil I've been." Then, in a fit of self-rage, Carlo tore his shirt open at the chest and confessed the sin of coveting his brother's wife and rejoicing at his death.

Bruno got up to leave, but Carlo raised his arms. "Please stay a moment, Bruno.

"Sure."

"You know, Bruno, I left Nicky here all alone, left him to his own devices. I walked away from him. It was the last chance I had while he was still alive to ask for his forgiveness."

Bruno was sympathetic. "Carlo, I don't know why you had to ask Nicky's forgiveness but, listen, we all do stuff we're not proud of. Just the way life is. Accept your limitations. That might be the good that comes from all of this."

Carlo became very calm. "You know, Bruno, maybe you're right. When I was in college I learned a quote from Aeschylus – I think, Agamemnon - which says the same thing. "Even in our sleep pain that cannot forget falls drop by drop upon the heart, and in our own despair, against our will comes wisdom to us by the awful grace of God."

The sin and its consequences, along with the awful lesson learned, remained with Carlo for the rest of his life.

The Monday edition of the *New York Daily News* carried a black-bordered editorial.

Nicky Albanese, younger brother of Father Carlo Albanese, reputed acting Don of a New York-based Mafia Family, was admitted to Beth Israel hospital Saturday morning for cardiac complications and died in the early hours of Sunday morning. The family physician, "Chick" Brennan, at a hospital news briefing, said, `Nicky Albanese died this morning at three a.m. of cardiac complications induced by stress and hard work. The funeral will be held at St. Anthony of Padua Church in lower Manhattan."

Cardinal McManus fumed over the News' editorial. "Acting Don! What the hell is going on here, Francis? Do you know anything about this?" The Cardinal searched for words, unintentionally deflecting Francis' intention to discuss the need for a new water tank at the Seminary. "I'm getting damn impatient with Carlo." He moved his ashtray from one side of his desk to the other, in nervous frustration. "I gave him a leave of absence but certainly not to be a goddam `acting don'. What does that mean anyhow?"

Father Francis advised caution. "You know, Mick, the Daily News is not exactly the London Observer. They go for the flashy word, not worrying too much how it might be interpreted. They sell papers. They're good at it."

The Cardinal nodded a pouted acquiescence. "What do you suggest?"

"Mick, this could be a flash in the pan. Let it play out. If you still have some doubts about Carlo after this thing disappears from the front pages, you can talk to him yourself."

The Cardinal rubbed his ears and "harrumphed" a couple of times before responding. "OK Francis, I tell you what. I'll be patient, but if there's any more nonsense about `acting Don' I'll get you to talk to him first and find out what's going on. OK?" The words floated uncertainly, a sign that he looked for guidance while maintaining the facade of "boss".

"Sure, Mick, that sounds good; it makes sense." Francis often wondered why a man with so much power was in such need of a foil for his thoughts and actions. He saw his own role as shoring-up the Cardinal's vacillating convictions and theological positions. He tried to do this without appearing to be essential to the process.

The Cardinal, with relief, changed the subject. "Now, what was it you came to see me about? Oh yes, a new water tank. Of course you can have the tank. The seminary is the breeding ground for the future." On such subjects the Cardinal spoke with the greatest of confidence. "Go right ahead, get a few bids. I rely on your good judgment."

The Cardinal's ideal world was one in which he spent his time making non-controversial decisions. The complicated world of men, politics and social antagonisms was almost more than he could bear. After all, he would ask himself, was I not ordained Bishop and Cardinal to take care of the things that pertain to God? Could I not be left alone to meditate on the gospel?

Frustration left him exhausted, and the lack of loyalty on the part of former classmates hurt him deeply. Even his most trusted priest, Father

Francis, made a serious misjudgment when recommending Carlo for ordination. Francis' report called Carlo "one of the best in the seminary."

For his part, Francis often wondered what the ecclesiastical world would be like if Bishops were elected like other public officials. The nature of the selection process and the lifetime authority created an atmosphere in which bishops developed the illusion they were always correct. It all seemed very sad to him.

Mrs. Cerrillo was furious. "Another Mafia funeral in our poor parish. We're being asked to suffer so much because our Pastor has (God forgive me, but its true) a blind spot when it comes to this dirty Mafia thing. Blind, I tell you, he's blind. God help us."

Mrs. Biondi listened patiently to her friend of forty years. With a conscious effort she said, "We must accept this as our Cross. What else can we do?" Embracing and comforting Mrs. Cerrillo, Mrs. Biondi repeated previous advice. "Let's offer up this crucifixion for the pains of Jesus crucified."

Mrs. Cerrillo was not appeased. "I don't know how that will help Jesus now!"

Side by side they ambled to the kitchen, where they sat with their napes to the wall, like a still life. Mrs. Cerrillo would not be comforted, framing her anger with the loud tapping of her high-heeled shoes. "No, my dear, acceptance of evil is not what the gospel tells us to do." With emphasis, "We must fight this cancer that's destroying the life and the spirituality of our beautiful parish." Her anger would evaporate in the presence of Father Adolfo, who always calmed her troubled waters. Mrs. Biondi, however, did confide to her husband, "I am worried about the mood."

"What mood?" Mr. Biondi asked. He secretly felt proud of the parish's newfound notoriety.

"I'm upset the way the parishioners, especially the teenagers, are actually enjoying all this publicity. You would think that Mafia funerals were something to brag about. I just don't understand. Do you?"

Mr. Biondi thrust his hands into his jacket. "Well, in a way I do."

"Really? What do you mean?"

Mr. Biondi folded his arms and explained. "Honey, it's our heritage. That's what has the kids all excited. When you and I were young we were told to be American. The kids today don't think that way. They're interested in their backgrounds. They want to be Italian-Americans."

"Maybe you're right."

Mr. Biondi reflected the reality in Little Italy. Carlo had become a pop hero, with expressions like "our proud heritage" now being commonly used in the streets of lower Manhattan. One girl attended a parish youth meeting wearing a T-Shirt on which she crudely painted, "Mafia Moll." She was cheered as she entered the parish hall.

Mrs. Biondi was puzzled. "What bothers me most is the fact that many of the elderly who would be quick to criticize the wearing of lipstick or a mini skirt, aren't saying anything about what's going on."

Her husband offered an explanation. "The Irish condemn the IRA, but every time they carry out a successful attack against the British, the Irish people gather in their pubs and celebrate. Maybe that's the way it is with Italians and the Mafia."

Mr. Ortiz, the parish maintenance man, called the phenomenon "Carlomania." He covered the walls of his school basement office with photographs of the funerals. Some of the photos had been cut out from newspapers as far away as Pittsburgh. Its daily Gazette shouted in large headlines, "The Heat is on in Mafia Land."

Reporters from the Daily News roamed the streets in St. Anthony of Padua's neighborhood looking for newsworthy tidbits. Mr. Quaglietta, who sold Italian ices to the local school children, was featured on Channel Seven's evening news answering questions about the attitudes of primary school children toward Father Carlo. "One little girl told me she wanted to grow up and be just like him. When I asked her if that meant she wanted to be a nun, she said 'I just want to be a real Italian.'"

This interview caused alarm at City Hall, where a nervous Mayor studiously avoided any specific response to reporters' questions. He made the most of the situation. "The occasion of a death, especially after multiple deaths in one family, is certainly not a time to make sociological statements. I leave that to less sensitive politicians, some of whom, by the way, would like my job."

That evening, his wife glowed, "Darling, you were absolutely super. You handled those reporters so deftly." She pinched his glowing Irish cheeks. "I just love my bright sweetie pie! Besides, we don't want those presents to stop coming, do we?" The reference was to the fur coat Frankie had discreetly delivered to her in time for the City Hall New Year's party.

Other interviews took place with politicians, and scholars. Gabe Pressman invited two bankers to a TV seminar on The Economic Effects of Mafia Activities in the Greater New York Area. The bankers studiously avoided offending the mob, with such statements as, "Well, as regards economic activity, if you look at the concept in the abstract, whatever brings finance into the business sector is a plus." The other banker added,

"We are not in the business of ideology and politics. We leave that to others. Our job is to assist the community in economic development. That is what we do."

Jimmy Breslin wrote in his column, "We'll all be Italian on Columbus Day."

NBC reported that its coverage of Carlomania produced the highest viewer ratings since the ordination of Father Carlo at St. Patrick's Cathedral. Meet the Press brought the subject to its intellectual apex by interviewing the one Italian member of the President's Cabinet, Transportation Secretary John Castoni. He had been a former professor of Italian Studies at Columbia University. When asked if he could explain the sudden explosion of Italian "Nationalism" in lower Manhattan and the spectacle of young Italians at St. Anthony of Padua sporting "Mafia" T-Shirts, his profound answer startled a watching nation. "Tribal affinities can never be successsfully suppressed. We all belong to a tribe and the culture of that tribe will, eventually, given sufficient stimulus, erupt sociologically with conesquences that are both good and bad."

The President, when asked about the comments made by his Cabinet member, said, "I stand fully behind him. He has my full confidence."

The Washington Post reported, "The President has just won the battle for the Italian vote in the next election without firing a shot."

The erudite nature of the televised discussions prompted academic articles in prestigious national magazines from the *Atlantic Monthly* to *Foreign Affairs*. The latter magazine stated in an editorial: "We must never underestimate the effect ethnic nationalism has in the corridors of power in Washington. Ethnic unity can be harvested by a shrewd President into a sizable block of votes."

At the parish level, spaghetti dinners sold out. Some of the Irish clergy feared that St. Patrick's Day Dinners might be negatively impacted, as the sales of tickets moved slower than at any period since the Depression. The City was in a gentle and jovial uproar, as the rippling effects of Carlomania reached as far West as San Francisco, as far South as the Florida Keys and as far North as Michigan's Upper Peninsula. Italian ethnic newspapers around the country editorialized on the events taking place in New York.

Carlo observed this sudden ethnic, and sociological outpouring with amazement. Nicky's funeral also became a lightning rod for public expression. High school students assembled several floats with Italian motifs, and tried, unsuccessfully, to insert them into the funeral procession. Club 44, the Italian neighborhood's answer to the famous Club 66, uptown, advertised on radio and in the Daily News a special Mafia Night, a night of dancing to Italian music. They even promised to produce Carlo as their special guest.

The Club's owner, Joseph Gambino, a member of the Gambino Family, waxed eloquently. "It may seem strange that it took the death of two men to spark the long-smoldering ethnic fires of Little Italy. However, the wisdom of the ages has taught us that God writes straight with crooked lines." He made the claim that he had contacted Sophia Loren "for her take" on the situation. Her spokesperson in Milan issued a statement saying that she had never heard of Mr. Gambino.

He retorted by saying "I am offended by her callousness. Why doesn't she stand up and join our crusade? She cannot be a real Italian."

Before Nicky's funeral, police cordoned-off entire neighborhoods in the vicinity of St. Anthony's, for fear of crowds running rampant. The Press had themselves a field day. At the funeral, the majority of parishioners, dressed in their very best, made vigorous attempts to pass in front of TV cameras. The day of the funeral, the principal of the local public high school, whose majority of students was of Italian descent, declared: "The school's electrical system is experiencing some difficulties. Therefore, in the interest of child safety, this school will be closed for today." His popularity rose to an all-time high in the community, as hundreds of Italian–American students from his school poured out into the streets, joining the funeral procession, and carrying placards declaring their solidarity with Carlo Albanese. The cultural significance of this plunged deep into Carlo's consciousness. He internalized positively the contribution he was making toward the liberation of the Italo-American soul in his native New York and across the nation. He was very proud to be an Albanese, an Italian–American.

Chapter Twenty
THE DEFROCKING

The same events that so inspired and electrified a City had a different effect at the Archdiocesan offices at 1001 First Avenue. The Cardinal, buttressed by an army of clerical advisors, picked up the phone and called Father Francis. "Never mind what I agreed to last week. This farce, this scandal, this circus has gone on long enough. I'll talk to Carlo myself. Get in touch with him. Arrange to meet him and bring him to me. For God's sake, don't bring Dolphi. He'll try to argue a case already lost with me."

Father Francis agreed something had to be done. He became uneasy over the public phenomena that so energized the Italian-American community, and so fascinated the rest of America, from Maine to California. Carlo had become, due to events beyond his control, a symbol of Italian-American frustrations and secret admiration for the anti-establishment world of the Mafia. It was becoming increasingly clear to sociologists at leading New York Universities that the American ideal of financial security had neither captured the imagination of the young nor satisfied their souls. Ethnicity was the new god to be worshipped.

Such high-sounding theory did not satisfy the Cardinal. For him, Carlo's decision to assume responsibility for his family's affairs was an abandonment of his priestly office. It was in this context that Father Francis feared the manner in which the Cardinal would handle the case. He phoned. "Carlo, the Cardinal would like to see you." A meeting was arranged for that evening at 7pm. "The Cardinal prefers an after-hours meeting. Less likely anyone will notice."

Carlo reacted swiftly. "If the Cardinal is doing something honest, why the hell should he be afraid of someone seeing me in his office?

Francis simply said. "Oh, well, Carlo you know how it is."

Carlo was rough. "No, I don't know how it is," ending the conversation.

During the twenty-minute drive from Riverdale, Carlo remained silent. Francis made small talk in nervous response to the lack of dialogue. Both men felt relief when the ride terminated at the Chancery. Only two security guards greeted the priests as they entered 1001 First Avenue.

The Cardinal's welcome was less than enthusiastic. "Glad you're on time. I have another appointment."

Father Francis knew how to translate the remark: Code for "keep it short."

Carlo greeted the Cardinal with reserve and declined to take the proffered seat facing the enormous desk. He was self-assured. "Since Your Eminence appears to have little time to talk with me, I can stand, thank you."

The Cardinal, prepared to lay down the law, hesitated and retreated. "Well, Carlo, I'm not in that much of a hurry. We'll take whatever time we need." He once again offered Carlo a chair.

This time, Carlo accepted but moved the chair to the side of the desk, a playful toe away from the Cardinal's feet. "As you were saying, Your Eminence?"

The Cardinal sank his gouty bulk into an armchair behind a desk free of any personal memorabilia and untidy scraps of paper. Not even a bent paper clip was present to give at least a hint of humanity. He measured Carlo through squinting blue eyes, searching for a weak spot in the fortified wall that seemed to surround this young priest. He sensed he was dealing with more than a neophyte and became more cautious. He was fully aware of the money that went into Church coffers from the various Mafia Families, not only in the New York, Brooklyn and Queens areas, but around the nation. The American Church hierarchy would be unhappy with a Cardinal/Carlo confrontation. He felt a line of sweat making its way down his forehead to his eyebrows and smiled, to wish it away.

"Yes, well, Carlo, it's about all this nonsense I've been reading in the newspapers. The press, even Gabe Pressman, are saying that you're acting head of the Albanese Family." He looked into Carlo's almond eyes to gauge his reaction, but observed no ripple on that sea of glass - only a quiet, even respectful, non-response. "Now, of course, you do have permission to help tidy up your family's personal and financial affairs, but clearly," - at this point his self-confidence began to reassert itself - "any intimate involvement in your family's business would not be part of the permission you have received."

Carlo remained silent for awhile. He lowered his eyes. His face was devoid of expression. An unsettling tension pulled tightly at his emotions. Finally, softly, he spoke. "Your Eminence, I intend to be perfectly clear and open with you. It's true that I'm intimately involved in the family organization. I have no doubt about my responsibility to the organization and all who are dependent on it for their livelihood and safety."

The Cardinal winced at the words and pulled at his left ear. His visage hardened, his lips thinned, as he felt the initiative slipping away from him. "Carlo, your family is engaged, let's face it, in criminal activity. You could never possibly have a duty to engage in criminal activity."

Carlo replied with serenity. "Your Eminence, I'm not ashamed of my family and what it does for a living, anymore than the son of an international banker. In business there's plenty of corruption. That's the real world. If every young man in this country felt morally obliged to refrain from engaging in business because there is plenty of corruption in business, this nation would be shut down and misery would be widespread. No doubt there's corruption in our organization. I intend to devote myself to rooting it out. Purists don't exist anywhere except in the poetic imagination." He laid both hands on his knees, quietly awaiting a response.

The Cardinal's eyes tightened, almost closed. With a nervous twitch of his eyebrows, he decided to take the gloves off. "Carlo, I'm not prejudging either you or your personal family." He liked the reasonable tone to his own voice. "I must tell you however that the 'real world' you are talking about is moved by public perceptions. The public perception of your family is one of violence, fraud, murder, drug distribution, etc." He paused both to savor the taste of his own bold words and to give Carlo an opportunity to respond.

Carlo softly interjected. "I'm sure Your Eminence is aware of the long history of the organization my family represents. We were the only defenders of the common people at a time in Sicilian history when the local governments and the central government were oppressing us. You can understand that the power, which our Families acquired during this period of struggle, led to some abuses. These abuses continued as our Families immigrated to the United States."

The Cardinal was entirely comfortable with the pace and tone of the discussion. "Yes, yes, Carlo, I understand that."

Carlo continued. "My Uncle Julio dedicated his life to removing these very abuses but, as a leader yourself, you understand that in large organizations reform takes time, lots of time. I'm personally dedicated to continue these reforms in my Family. Such reform can contribute to reforms in similar Family organizations throughout the country. If others demanded that you step down as the Archbishop of New York because the occasional priest is convicted of stealing parish money, or accused of abusing an altar boy, then, my dear Cardinal, I'm sure you would consider that a very unreasonable demand."

A pregnant pause followed that remark, as the Cardinal's hands nervously twitched around a pencil. Carlo continued. "My intention is to create a model others may follow. It is, in my opinion, a cause as noble and spiritual as any other task I may undertake as a priest. It does little good, and it would even be hypocritical, for the Church to condemn these admitted abuses and then become an obstacle to an attempt to rectify them. This is how I feel, Your Eminence."

The Cardinal was impressed with the obvious sincerity of his young charge, but resented Carlo's making a comparison between their respective positions. *Carlo has been brainwashed with a misplaced idealism. Such a pity. I must be a clear and unequivocal voice in such murky waters.* "I appreciate your feelings, Carlo. After all, it's a question of flesh and blood. It's your family. On the other hand, you must understand and appreciate my point of view. The comparison you made with the business community is not a valid one."

"Why not?"

"The business community is engaged in honest labor, even though at times a bad apple slips in. The same, by the way is true of the priesthood."

"If you read the newspapers, Your Eminence, you'll see there are an awful lot of bad apples. That ought to tell you something."

With a huge sigh fortifying his own courage, and a flowing movement of the feathered age-lines at the corner of his eyes, the Cardinal explained. "The business of your family is directly crime-connected. It is therefore necessary for you to make a choice. My instructions, as your Bishop, are that you return to St. Anthony of Padua immediately, before events beyond our control force me to discipline you. If you refuse these instructions, then I shall refer your case to Rome, with my own recommendation that you be suspended from priestly duties. I must tell you that ordinarily I need not refer such a case to the Roman authorities but, given the extraordinary circumstances, I will do that, giving Rome the option of making the final decision."

The Cardinal moved out of his chair to Father Carlo's side, placed a hand on his shoulder and said, "The ball is in your court, Carlo. If you need some time, a day or two, to give me your response, I'll allow that, but not more. Events are moving too quickly to delay a resolution."

Carlo stood in military bearing and spoke. "I'm unable, Your Eminence, to agree either with your logic or your decision. The gospel message states categorically that the Shepherd must leave the ninety-nine sheep to look for the one that's lost. It's clear that your interpretation of that biblical text is not the same as mine or, as a matter of fact (and I say this respectfully) that of the theologians and scripture scholars."

The Cardinal's voice became testy. "The bishops are the official teachers, Carlo, remember that."

Carlo shot back firmly. "Your Eminence, you and I know that bishops are chosen, not for their wisdom, but for their loyalty to the Holy See. The theological consequences of that have been devastating."

"I won't dignify that remark with a reply."

"There isn't any dignified reply, Your Eminence."

The Cardinal was ruffled. "You're being quite rude, young man."

Carlo stretched out his arms. "If I am being rude, Your Eminence, I apologize, but I don't apologize for speaking the truth." Carlo stood silent and emotionless. "I must do my duty to my Family. This isn't said out of any disrespect to you, Your Eminence. I feel somewhat like Joan of Arc when she was warned by the Bishops interrogating her. They said, `How dare you use your own judgment', to which she replied, `What judgment can I use except my own'."

The Cardinal felt a mixture of anger and respect.

Carlo continued. "When I was ordained I made a commitment to the priesthood and I've not withdrawn that commitment." He reached out to shake the Cardinal's hand. "I'll await your final decision. Thank you."

The Cardinal was tightlipped. "You'll get it in due course."

The two antagonists faced each other in silence, weapons spent. The Cardinal turned to Father Francis, who remained silent throughout the proceedings. "I believe this meeting is over. You may drive Father home now." The tone was cold and business - like.

Francis nodded his head. "Yes, Your Eminence."

Carlo spoke to Father Francis. "Well, Father, I hope you're not disappointed in me. I'm trying to live by the gospel principles which you taught me in the Seminary." Then, turning to a perplexed Cardinal, he said, "Your Eminence, thank you for your time." His aloofness conveyed inner strength.

In the elevator, Frances said, "I don't know what to say about your approach, Carlo. Guess I'm old school at heart. I couldn't speak to a cardinal like that."

"Francis, that's because we're programmed that way. Let's face it. The system produces automatons."

They drove for a few minutes in a silence broken only by the soft swish of the windshield wipers dealing with a brief shower that had moved into the area. Francis concurred with the Cardinal. "I wish I could say I agree with you, Carlo, but I can't. You're struggling between you're family's interest and that of the priesthood. You've got to meditate on this."

Carlo felt utterly alone, as if floating in space. The feeling of alienation frightened him. He felt a growing anger at what he considered the institutional Church's coldness. "The Cardinal is too wrapped-up in the world. He uses the words of religion to cover up his lack of understanding of the Christian message."

Father Francis remained silent, concentrating on the heavy Manhattan traffic, as he made his way over to the West Side and north toward Riverdale. When they arrived at the apartment, Francis bid Carlo goodbye "God bless, Carlo. You know my number. If you ever want to chat, I'll always be there for you."

"I know that."

Carlo glanced out at the New Jersey cliffs beyond the river. Two couples were embracing at the Hudson River overlook, a favorite rendezvous for lovers. How wonderful and simple life is for them. The woman pulled a heavy scarf around her neck, snuggled close to her mate and embraced him.

In the building he pushed the elevator button. *Why the hell didn't I just opt to be an ordinary parish priest. I'd be happy and my life would be so uncomplicated.* Letting himself into the apartment, he headed straight for the bedroom where, fully dressed, he fell into a heavy sleep.

The Cardinal's letter arrived less than two weeks later, hand-delivered by a young seminarian doing duty in the Chancery. It read:

Dear Father Albanese,

It is my sad duty as Ordinary of the Archdiocese of New York, to inform you that, after long and prayerful reflection by the Secretariat for the Clergy, the Holy See has deemed it appropriate to suspend you of all priestly duties and privileges, in perpetuum. This decision is final and irrevocable. The usual process of appeal to the Holy See has been eliminated because of the urgency of the settlement of this most pernicious issue.

The Holy See has asked me to inform you that your intention to continue as de facto head of the Albanese Family organization is tantamount to overtly engaging in criminal activities.

I can only pray for your troubled soul, in the hope that you will, at some future date, convert.

Sincerely,
In the Risen Lord,
+John McManus
Cardinal Archbishop of New York

The coldness of the language profoundly disturbed him. He shook his head. *I've become the victim of an injustice perpetrated in the name of religion.* He felt he had been raped of his rights in order to satisfy a warped sense of religion on the part of the hierarchy. *This is terrible news, but I'll not let it destroy me. If I'm meant to be reinstated in the priesthood one day, it will happen, hierarchy or no hierarchy.*

That night, after showering, he watched television for several hours until he felt tired enough to fall asleep. Just before clicking the TV remote he glanced at his watch; it was 2 a.m. He was emotionally exhausted as he uttered a prayer for the night.

The following morning, Carlo awoke to a steely gray November day. The Hudson was bare of pleasure crafts. He roamed through the kitchen, opening and closing the white cabinets with mullioned glass panes that reflected pink countertops and hardwood floors. He had no appetite but looked for something that might entice him to eat breakfast. He glanced out and saw mounds of dead autumnal leaves littering the wooded descent to the river. Like the season and skeletal trees, his life had turned dismal. He moved closer to the window and observed a woodpecker hammering at a dead birch. *Lucky guy. Not a worry in the world.* He caught the beginning of the Today Show. After the international news, the anchorman made an announcement. "We have this breaking news. Father Carlo Albanese, reputed head of the powerful Albanese crime Family in New York, is rumored to have been suspended from all priestly duties. NBC News received this information just a few moments ago from an unofficial source. We will be contacting the Office for their comment later this morning and will update you on this breaking story during the course of the morning."

The anchorman, Daniel Almetta, then introduced Monsignor McDermott, professor of Sacred Scripture at Dunwoodie Seminary, in Yonkers. "Monsignor McDermott is an eminent scholar in the field of scripture and is also a member of the priest Personnel Board for the Archdiocese of New York. The function of the Personnel Board is to recommend to the Cardinal changes in priest assignments." Turning to the Monsignor, "Tell me Monsignor, is it true that Father Carlo Albanese has been suspended or defrocked or both?"

"Mr. Almetta, I'm not personally aware of any change in Fr. Albanese's status, nor have I ever met him. Even if I was aware (and I emphasize that I'm not) I wouldn't be at liberty to discuss such a change. That kind of information would be released by the Chancery office."

"I understand, Monsignor, but surely you read the papers and watch television and are aware that it's generally believed Father Albanese is either acting don of the Albanese crime Family or, at least, intimately involved in their operations. Isn't that true?"

"It's certainly true that I've read those reports, Mr. Almetta, but I'm not in a position to comment on them."

"Would it be a fair statement to say that because of your position on the Personnel Board you're not free to discuss the matter."

"Let me make my position clear, Mr. Almetta. Father Albanese is a family member of the Albanese organization. No doubt he is wrestling with the many problems that arise as a result of being in such a situation. For my part I wish him well, and I hope the media will allow whatever is happening in Father Albanese's life to be resolved in private, out of the spotlight. I'd ask this for any man in a similar situation."

"What do the priests in the Archdiocese say about all of this? How do they feel about the publicity?"

"Well, Mr. Almetta, there are about one thousand priests in the Archdiocese. I couldn't possibly know what each and every one of them thinks. Surely, however, many agree that simply because a man is a priest should not be a reason for the media to have a field day. Having said that, I do understand that public figures are subject to more than ordinary scrutiny."

"In your capacity as a member of the Personnel Board, has the question of Father Albanese's assignment ever come across your desk."

"If you mean across our collective desk, that is the Board, the answer is yes, of course. That's our job."

"Can you tell us about that?"

"About what?"

"About the nature of the Board's involvement."

"I can certainly describe that in simple terms, yes."

"Please do so."

"Well, after Father Albanese's ordination, the pastor of his Parish, Father Adolfo, requested he be assigned to his parish. We honored that request, and the Cardinal approved it. He has received no other assignment to date."

"But did he not receive a leave of absence?"

"Yes, I believe he did. I say `believe' because that is Chancery business; my knowledge in that regard comes from the media."

"Monsignor, I want to thank you for taking time out from your busy schedule to be with us this morning. I'm sure there'll be much more discussion about this affair in the future. I hope you'll be able to come back to talk with us again."

"Thank you Mr. Almetta."

The Monsignor left the studio working a toothpick in his mouth, as the anchorman began an interview with a famous New Orleans chef. Carlo felt a sudden and welcomed relief that he was no longer part of the "system."

Chapter Twenty One
THE LONELINESS

As Julio Albanese, dressed in corduroy trousers and a sweater that hung loosely on his thinning frame, danced to the music of a Sicilian love song, a blood vessel burst in his brain. He staggered and fell against the den's leather couch. Tina had been watching him through the large glass door, delighted to see him so alive, so happy in his retirement, even though he had become emaciated and fragile, a mere shadow of his former self. She ran to hold him in her arms as he slumped to the floor in a silent rendezvous with death. "Oh, my God. Julio, get up, get up! Julio, look at me, please." She tried to scream but, stunned into silence, the sounds would not tumble out. Her body reacted to the psychological shock, as she shrunk deep within herself like a frightened child. Her arms flailed, as if fighting off an enemy. From Long Island Sound, she could hear the faint bellow of a distant foghorn, lonely in its plaintive wail. She cradled as much of her husband's body as she could. Her gaze fell on his gaping mouth and transfixed eyes. It was clear that he was dead. She lay by his side and sobbed uncontrollably. He had been her dark, romantic hero, sober, patient and observant, a man of dry humor that fascinated her.

She later proudly related to relatives and friends, "There was no suffering, no artificial living on tubes, no experimental operations, just a sudden, blissful journey to the Lord's bosom. God loved him for all the good he did in his life." She was hurt that Carlo was unable to conduct the funeral of his beloved uncle, but remained silent, knowing it to be a subject of great delicacy. However, she did ask Carlo's advice about the burial services.

"Father Adolfo will conduct the funeral, Auntie. Uncle Julio would have wanted that."

As a former don, Julio's burial would take place out of the spotlight.

Late that night, after Family members left for home, she embarked on an extended search for all his clothing, reassembling them in his closet according to events and meanings that she alone understood. The New York Yankee cap Julio was wearing when he first met her on the beach, she placed on the TV in his den. The hammered gold ring she bought him while on a vacation in Italy she placed on the night table next to their bed. He loved the ring, and would raise his right fist to show it to friends and relatives, "Our love is as permanent as this gold," he would say, and kiss her on the cheeks. Without the presence of her husband in her bed, Tina never again slept right through an entire night. Her imagination would replay scenes from her life with Julio. So many things reminded her of him, and of their life together: The library where he spent many studious hours, the garden that Julio cultivated so assiduously. A thousand images of their life together danced in her imagination. She opened the doors of her husband's closet, revealing row upon row of tailored suits, jackets and shirts. The pungent smell of cedar tickled her nose, as she began the painful task of disposing of his personal things. *He would want me to do this. Life has to go on, he would say.*

She ran her fingers along the edges of coat sleeves, shirts and trousers before pulling them from the rack. She neatly folded everything and placed them in cardboard boxes. She reached into the cubbyhole storage places where his sweaters were folded. Beneath one pile she discovered letters she had written to him over the years. Three of them dated back to their pre-nuptial days. Their worn appearance led her to believe he had re-read them over and over again. She placed them in a separate box for keepsakes. It was more than material things she packed; it was the memories of a lifetime.

Carlo met with Julio's lawyers, taking care of the detritus left by Julio's death - the will, insurance accounts, bank accounts, and taxes. As for the residue of Family matters, he had custodial and executive powers. He notified Family heads across the country that the funeral would be private. All agreed it was the proper thing. At the funeral, Father Adolfo spoke eloquently of "the kindness, vision and love of family of this extraordinary personality."

The Cardinal expressed his condolences, indirectly, in a letter to Father Adolfo, in which he wrote: I want you to know that I am aware of the sorrow you must be experiencing at the death of your friend of many years. In a brief noto bene he requested: "For obvious reasons please do not share the contents of this letter with the press." Adolfo did show the letter to Carlo who simply said, "His words are of little meaning to me."

The day of the funeral, rain flooded the streets of Manhattan. As Carlo drove home from the cemetery his mood matched the weather. The rain drummed heavily on the soaked streets, raising tiny resounding bursts that formed running puddles draining into the city's sewer system. His breath condensed on the windows before the heater could wipe it away. The windshield wipers were of little help, as he peered intently into the early evening darkness. The tires emitted an abrasive hiss on the wet pavements. Approaching the apartment building, he touched the remote and the garage door lifted with an appropriate wailing scratch. The adjoining flowerbeds were soaked and flattened. Rain dropped in clusters through the downspout as the garage door rumbled to a close.

The Daily News, in spite of the private nature of the funeral, managed to photograph Carlo at the cemetery. Its front page was a large black border enclosing the headlines, "The Don of Dons is Dead." The back page carried a photograph of Carlo, at the funeral, head bowed, his forehead resting on the pew in front of him. Beneath the photo read, Father Carlo Albanese sits this one out.

The New York Times, in an unusual move, wrote of the caption, "We approve of all the news that's fit to print. We do not believe that this caption is deserving of being so classified." Its own editorial page speculated:

Rumor has it that Father Carlo Albanese has been disciplined, perhaps even dismissed from the priesthood. Inquiries of the Chancery office have produced a plethora of "no comments". A call to Mr. Bruno Battaglia, family attorney, was not returned. Whatever the facts are in this case, we do offer him our condolences. Julio Albanese was a blessed maverick among Mafia dons, a man who set the stage for legitimizing what is, to say the least, an illegitimate enterprise.

Julio's death increased Carlo's sense of isolation. "Who can I talk to now? Who else could understand the secret that burns deep within my soul, that only you, my dear Uncle, and I share? I'll never forget you. My life is dedicated to fulfilling your hopes and desires." Unable to express his emotions within the context of the community of church and priesthood, he turned to his developing relationship with Lisa. He rationalized that it was not his choice to live outside the context of priesthood. In his view he had been abandoned by a church which had unilaterally violated the compact made on the day of ordination, to serve and support each other for life. The Church no longer, therefore, could demand of him celibacy grounded on the ecclesiastical commitment of perpetual brotherhood. Lisa's friendship became his community, his only vehicle for self-expression.

As for Lisa, the need to love she felt when she first entered into marriage became incarnate in her deceased husband's brother. *It's simple. I love him and I know he loves me.* She could not predict whether or not this love would ever be expressed physically. She waited for a sign from Carlo. If it came she would respond without hesitation. A sign came shortly after Julio's funeral. Carlo called to say. "Why don't we go off together for a few days. There's a lovely island, Vieques, in Puerto Rico. What do you say?" He knew what her answer would be.

Chapter Twenty Two
VIEQUES

Lisa's bedroom was not designed for sleeping late in the mornings. Two large skylights flooded the room with light. It was modestly but pleasantly furnished, with red-checkered gingham draperies and heavy, highly polished maple furniture. On the north side of the room her dressing table, centered by a large oval hinged mirror, sat against a stretch of wall between two windows. On the East Side, under a large dormer window, sat a keepsake chest stuffed with photographs and memorabilia, including those of Carlo's early years. She discovered them among her husband's belongings. Carlo and Nicky swinging on ropes across the river that slanted through Julio's property. Carlo making his first communion, his hair slicked down with grease. Carlo and Nicky holding what might have been the first fish they ever caught.

Lisa awoke with the anticipation of happy hours ahead. The slanting sun played with her eyelids, awaiting her response. She lay there luminously wrapped in a rose-colored down comforter that billowed around her. *Carlo, I love you but I'd sure like to stay in bed another two hours.*

She brushed strands of hair away from her face with finger flicks, and began the physiological process of rising. Her legs dangled as she sat at the edge of her oversized bed, letting blood course through her veins. Her energy level slowly began to rise. Makeup! Flicking on the lights of the makeup mirror, she examined herself closely and flattened her eyebrows with a tiny brush. She chose a pair of diamond-studded earrings and continued carefully sculpturing the face she would present to Carlo. Raising her chin she ran two fingers up her throat, admiring her reflection. *Will he like this? I think so.* She got up, pulled the suitcase out of her walk-in closet, tossed it on the bed, and began packing. The phone rang. It was the front desk. "You mentioned last night, Miss, that you'd need a cab today. Is that still the case?"

"Yes, it is. Say, two hours from now. OK?"

"Fine, Miss. I'll call you when it arrives."

"Good."

"Do you need any help with your luggage?"

"No. Thank you."

She then turned back to her suitcase, her hands moving quickly as she chose the rest of her wardrobe. The phone rang a second time. It was Carlo. "Just checking to see if our trip is still on."

Lisa lay back on her bed, the receiver propped on her shoulder, as she played with its long, rubbery chord. His voice gave her instant relaxation. "Of course it's on, silly."

"Well, you know that old adage, 'A woman has a right to change her mind.'"

She leaned into the telephone as if reaching out for him, and laughed. "That's true, but I haven't."

"Anxious to see you."

"Me too."

"I'll see you soon."

Her mind imaged her presence on a sun-kissed stretch of beach, lying beside the man who now dominated her thoughts, her very life.

After her shower, she spent a half-hour covering her body with aromatic body cream, then gently worked the tortoiseshell hairbrush through her curls. *It's nice to dress again, wanting to be physically pleasing to a man, I've missed that. Must be part of being female.*

Dressed in her champagne-pink linen suit,she felt well groomed. Her earrings fluttered in the breeze from the East River. She studied her reflection in her bathroom door full-length mirror. The intercom buzzed. "Your cab is outside waiting for you."

"Coming." Lisa picked up her suitcase, closed the door behind her and headed for the elevator. Her adventure was about to begin. An incoming resident held the door open for her as she walked to the cab. A cold, blustery wind bit at her face. Lifting the collar of her coat, she moved her head into the wind, greeting the cabby who held the car's door. "In spite of the wind it's a very nice day."

The cabby did not agree but said, "Yes Ma'am."

On her way to La Guardia for the Eastern Airline flight to Puerto Rico, the one thing Lisa was certain of was the excitement of spending some time with Carlo. The flight to San Juan was scheduled to depart at ten a.m. She was annoyed at the slow pace of traffic on Grand Central Parkway, chiding herself for not having left earlier. Carlo was a stickler for detail.

As the driver took the La Guardia exit, Lisa took one last glance at herself in her pocket mirror, and removed a layer of lipstick. She was satisfied that her panty hose was properly aligned. *I hope these legs will never see a varicose vein.*

In the early days of her marriage she had wrapped herself in a warm blanket of sensuousness. It was all so playful and innocent this joy of intimacy. The same magic was once again invading her mind and body. She spotted Carlo waving to her at the entrance of the Eastern terminal. His eyes seemed blank, so she wondered what was going through his mind. She hoped it was her.

"Hi," he shouted, glancing down at her. "Thought you wouldn't make it. Was getting nervous."

"I'm here, look!" She splayed a hand on her body and moved toward him eagerly. In a trice she was by his side. "Happy now?"

"Very."

"I'm glad I make you happy."

He was close, setting her nerves jangling. She inhaled his after-shave odor and drank in his deep, charming voice. He was handsome in his gray flannel slacks and a white long-sleeved pullover, pinched at the waist.

He placed a proprietary hand on her shoulders as she emerged from the cab. "Don't worry, there's still plenty of time." Taking her bag from the taxi driver, he said, "Let's get ourselves checked in." The first call for boarding had already been made, so they moved directly to the aircraft.

Lisa's happiness flooded her consciousness. *We are just two nice people enjoying a trip together..* She felt desirable as he cupped her elbow with a firm, strong hand, leading her up the steps into the aircraft. This new and welcomed consciousness took up residence in a quiet nook of her soul until the day she died. It hummed a soft musical theme during her days and during her nights, like birds outside her window.

Eastern Airlines, Flight Fifteen, sat down at San Juan's Munoz Marin International Airport. Lisa and Carlo inhaled the jasmine-scented air, filtered by warm sunlight. A taxi took them to the smaller Isla Verde airport. En route, Lisa playfully pressed her left elbow into his thighs, and traced the back of her fingers down the side of his face and under his chin.

"You don't make it easy on a guy do you?"

"Didn't intend to," she laughed, as she brushed her fingertips across his cheeks. They talked and laughed, quietly, intimately, as the walls came tumbling down. As the aircraft began its descent, they took in the scene of clear blue waters and sparkling beaches.

At the airport they boarded the twelve-passenger Vieques Air Link plane. They joked as they were weighed before boarding. "Good," Lisa said, "we're just baggage. No one knows who we are. Isn't this fun?"

"Yes," Carlo agreed. No one would have suspected that the Don of the most powerful Mafia family in America would be staying at a tiny guesthouse called Trade Winds, in the obscure village of Esperanza, on the equally obscure island of Vieques. With a mere suitcase each, they attracted no attention whatsoever. The anonymity suited them.

"Carlo, anyone would think we are lovers, wouldn't they?"

He leaned close and said, "We are, in a way, aren't we? We are not only family but we like each very much. I suppose we can say we love each other in a variety of ways."

"Well, Carlo, it does mean more than that. I mean, lovers are people who make love!"

Carlo pointed out, "Yeah... well... lots of people who have sex, even married people, are not really in love."

"True."

Carlo tried to draw a history lesson. "Romeo and Juliet are the model 'lovers.' I don't think they ever had sex. Did they?"

She shrugged. "I don't know. Let's look it up."

"Lisa, I think lovers are people whose souls have come together in a special, star-crossed way.

"Sounds like what happened to us."

Speaking emphatically, "Yes. I'll tell you this. If I don't return to the priesthood, I'd sure want to marry you."

She was vaguely aware of the celibacy "rules" and felt threatened by the fact that Carlo would ask her to marry him only as a second choice. Nevertheless, she had come to trust his judgments and decisions. For her, the intimacy had already begun. Should the time come when Carlo wanted to take her, that decision would be his to make.

As the plane landed at the tiny Vieques airport, Carlo had never been so happy. As they taxied to the Trade Wind hotel, Lisa observed how the sun bounced off the small native homes in brilliant, shimmering waves that split the images of passing cars and beach strollers. Everywhere, tall coconut palm trees waved in the ocean breeze, gently tapping each other. It was Lisa's first trip to the Caribbean. As they approached the resort she marveled at the clear blue waters, topped with white foam as they smashed against the golden beaches. The hotel owners met them at the entrance. "Welcome to our humble hotel. We want you to be happy here. Please feel free to let us know of any need you have. We'll do our best to accommodate." Mr. and Mrs. Bierborn, owners of the Trade Wind, a couple from Philadelphia, could not have been nicer. Mrs. Bierborn's bushy hair was the prettiest peach color Lisa had ever seen, like maple leaf in the fall. A touch of mascara framed her eyes, a light pink lipstick highlighted the golden bronze of her Puerto Rican tan. Her white linen dress suited the tropical scene. Speaking to Lisa, "Come let me show you your room."

She guided Lisa to the room. "Voila," pointing to a small table bearing a bouquet of flowers. "I put them there just for you."

Lisa yanked off her tinted sunglasses with excitement, her elbows suspended in the air. "Thank you so much," she whispered to Mrs. Bierborn, "They're so beautiful."

"To be honest, we pick them up right off the roadside. That's one of the perks of living in Vieques."

Mrs. Bierborn was puzzled. *Why isn't this lovely couple staying with each other? Whatever it is, I hope the problem is solved while they're here.*

In Carlo's room a "Vieques" baseball cap sat atop a bed post. "On the house," laughed Mr. Bierborn. *Nice couple. His face is familiar.*

Meals were taken guesthouse style on a large veranda overlooking the Caribbean Sea. The newcomers were welcomed by the "seasoned" tourists of two to five days. Carlo was Charles Mantucci and Lisa was Phyllis McCann. The owners were discreet enough not to ask for IDs. Such a demand would have ruined their business.

There was always plenty of fish on the menu at the Trade Wind. Lisa and Carlo chose Shrimp Scampi. "Even better than at Red Lobster," was Carlo's comment. Both listened in to a discussion at the table about the US Naval presence on the island, a source of tension between Puerto Rico and the United States. Several defended the Navy's presence, while a few argued heatedly that the Puerto Ricans should decide on the desirability of the Navy's presence, not politicians in Washington.

Mrs. Bierborn gently interrupted the conversation. "Its dessert time and we've got pineapple chunks imbedded in vanilla ice cream. Care to have some?"

All agreed, and the discussion came to an abrupt end. The absorption in dessert produced a silence punctuated only by the tuneful chirping of birds. A milky-white mist off the sea blurred the sun in a muslin sky. The wind playfully ruffled the womens' hair. The verandah, an extension of the dining room, was railed in white with plenty of space for sea breezes to circulate. It was suffused with the scent of flowers. A vegetable garden ran along both sides of the steps that led to the beach. Carlo pressed his eyelids tightly together and floated on this calm sea of exotica.

"Let's walk by the sea," Lisa suggested.

They made their way across the short expanse of grass, where they sat on rocks and watched the sun drape itself across the water. A fleet of small craft, their colorful sails furled by the ocean breezes, entertained their eyes.

They took a walk on the beach and felt the sand slip beneath their feet as the ocean waves played their eternal theme of ebb and flow.

Carlo ventured, "I wonder why it is that we live our entire lives in Brooklyn and Manhattan, and never come to places like this to relax and enjoy nature, and each other. It's always some gambling town like Las Vegas."

"Good question, Carlo. We just don't know any better, I guess"

The afternoon sun was strong enough to burn through the nylon of his shirt, heating his back, forming small crystals of sweat. They watched the sunset, brushed off their clothing and returned to the hotel. At bedtime the guests were offered cordials of Amaretto and creme de cacao. It was not long before Carlo said, "I'm ready for bed."

Lisa agreed, "Me too." She clasped his hands to her lips, kissing them. "Sweet dreams."

A sign above the registration desk ensured a peaceful night's sleep: After ten p.m. please enjoy yourselves, but not in such a way as to disturb others. We fight noise pollution here for the benefit of all.

"A great sign," Carlo said to Mrs. Bierborn.

"What's even greater is, it's true."

He retired to his room. The only sound was that of the hum of insects exploring flowers that leaned against his open window. In a sudden urge he walked briskly to Lisa's room.

He knocked. "It's me."

"Door's unlocked."

Lisa was sitting cross-legged, hugging a soft throw pillow, her hair swept into a French twist, an open book at her side. Dressed in a pink satin teddy, her sensuous legs and thighs glowed in the bath of soft light and shadow. She reached into his eyes with her own.

"Nice surprise, Carlo. Spending the night?"

"No comment."

She laughed. "That is a comment."

As Carlo approached, she curled her feet beneath her on a pile of cushions, her knees tucked under her chin, her arms wrapped around her legs. She was relaxed. Their eyes met, commingling.

He stood, cross-legged, his arms folded on his chest. "I needed to say another good night," he said, as he bent to kiss her on the frorehead, his hands brushing lightly against her jutting knees. He frowned down at her with teasing eyes, then joked, "You could really become a habit very quickly, you know. I'm sure Doc Brennan would advise against having you as a permanent part of my diet."

She responded, inclining her head toward him. "Doctors know very little about nutrition." Lisa could hear his heart pounding against her ear as she ran her nails across his lips. She paused and stared at him intensely. Her eyes glittered with unshed tears. Her lips were tremulous. She could feel her heart tapping against her breast.

He spoke, quietly. "You mean the world to me." His words muffled against her lingerie, as silence enveloped them. He doubled his arms around her and buried his face in her shoulder.

"I love you, Carlo. No rules and regulations will ever change that." She stared into his eyes. For the first time he noticed she had a double row of eyelashes. A sudden breeze slapped strands of her hair across his cheeks, increasing the sensuousness of the moment. Tossing her head aside she covered his shoulders with her arms. They remained close enough to move from touch to exploration, but didn't. She laid a hand on his arm and felt his muscles tighten in response.

He tilted her chin so as to look directly into his eyes. "Goodnight," was his awkward retreat. See you in the morning."

She mumbled a barely audible, "See ya."

She watched the door slowly close and her eyes remained fixed on it for several minutes, listening as his footsteps faded in the distance. She remained immobile for several moments as she tried to unlock the secret of his personality. *He's probably trying to figure a way out of our dilemma. I simply must be patient.*

Back in his room, Carlo sat against a stretch of wall between two windows. He wondered if his hesitation to make love was a result of piety or lack of courage. He tried to look at himself through her eyes, her perspective. The soft night air reached out to touch him, as he switched off the light and watched the moonlight paint a shimmering sea and glowing seashore. He stretched out on the bed, studying the ceiling and cradling his head on his arms. The night held him spellbound and he became lost in a deep sleep.

For Lisa, the night's languid sleep was a sensuous immersion in luxury. Moonbeams cut across her bed in luminescent rows. Her underclothing lay like tiny islands spread across the parquet floor.

Carlo was already showering when the fading moonlight mixed with amber rays announced the sun's arrival. It poured through an open shutter, causing his eyes to narrow. He was hungry. After shaving, he headed directly for the verandah. The aroma of coffee, eggs, bacon and the ever-present flowers pleasingly assaulted his nostrils.

Lisa was there. He rejoiced at the sight of her. "Hi." His voice sounded deep and calm.

"Good morning," was her simple greeting, as she captured a few straying strands of hair, sweeping them behind her ears. She sat near the verandah railing, dressed in plaid shorts, white blouse, red socks and tennis shoes, her hair a pony tail trailed by red and blue ribbons that fluttered in the morning breeze. A shaft of sunlight played with her hair. In the dining room a guest-pianist was playing a medley of Johnny Mathis tunes. The mood was romantic in a beautiful morning sort of way.

Carlo ventured, "Good morning, pretty lady. Breakfast by the sea is sure a lot tastier than breakfast in Riverdale. Here I just want to stay put. At home it's one big gulp before running out the door."

She shook her head in agreement. "That's life in America. Rush, rush and nowhere to go."

"Yeah." He paused, looking out at the sea, then added, "You slept well?"

Whispering into his ear. "Yes, I felt loved."

He whispered in return. "You are."

One of the guests joked. "No secrets around this table"

Carlo. "It's a matter of national security."

"Oh," the guest said, "you can trust me.

His wife observed. "I wish someone were telling me national security secrets."

A wave smashed itself against the white sand that stretched out less than a hundred yards from the verandah. Carlo stood up and took Lisa by the hand. "So long as we have an ocean at our door step, let's get into our bathing suits and do something about it."

"Yes, sir. Give me a few minutes."

Carlo, dressed in blue and white trunks, stretched out on one of the verandah's two hammocks and waited for Lisa. He took in the scene. A border of blue sea and sky framed the billowing white sails of a passing sailboat. If Paradise was not located here, it should have been.

Lisa arrived wearing a white-laced black bikini and carried a beach bag and towels.

Carlo jerked himself into motion. "You look great."

"Thank you."

Lisa produced suntan lotion, which she held up. "Better safe than sorry."

"I agree."

As they stepped out of earshot, several guests discussed the oddity of this couple staying in separate rooms. "I sure feel sorry for the guy," said one.

"Something special's going on here," observed another.

They headed for the white sandy beach under blue skies laced with wispy clouds. An off shore breeze rustled palm fronds and rippled an otherwise calm and translucent sea. On the beach they rubbed each other's bodies with lotion. Lisa directed the operation. "No, don't rub up and down. Do it with a circular motion."

The hand movements drew them closer together. "What's going on inside me," Carlo said, "can only be described as controlled chaos."

"Make that two."

They moved hand in hand to surf that sprayed their faces with breaking waves. Lisa waited until a wave enveloped her legs and waist, broke loose from his grip and plunged into the surf, swimming out past the white caps. "Try and catch me," she shouted.

"You'll never get away."

She moved away from Carlo, pressing her body against the seawater. He watched as the surf licked her silky legs. She bent down to scoop up the milky froth, letting it fall from her fingertips. *This is so sensual.*

Carlo joined her and they swam together, alternately cutting strokes and floating on their backs as they moved effortlessly through the water. A swell raised and lowered their bodies, first in sensuous collision, then in forced separation. They laughed and played with childlike joy, floating in a mindless eternity in which their love uttered itself as articulately as it was voiceless.

I don't want to leave him. He makes me complete.

On shore, her hair cascaded about her neck, the sun changing its color patterns. His hands stroked the shining tresses as they walked arm in arm. Exhausted, they slumped down to the sand onto their backs, playfully rolling in the sand that stuck to their wet bodies in uneven patterns. Breathing hard, they spread their arms and legs to the molten sun, holding hands.

"May I," he whispered as he kissed her in her hair.

"Anytime."

"It reminds me of Rodin," he said.

Lisa thought he might be joking. "Of whom?"

"Rodin."

"Who's he?"

Carlo slapped his forehead. "You don't know who Rodin is? He's just about the most famous sculptor alive, that's who"

"Oh?"

"It reminds me of his greatest work."

She wanted to know. "What's that?"

'The Kiss. It sounds nicer in French. Le Baiser."

"Oh, I like that. Tell me about it."

He promised. "I'll get you a photograph. Two lovers are sitting on a bench."

"So...they are sitting on a bench, and?"

Carlo fingered his wet hair. "Well, what I like about the sculpture is not so much the kiss. It's the absorption that I like. A total togetherness."

"The absorption? What do you mean?"

Carlo explained. "It looks like, for them, nothing else exists in the world - like they're glued together, forever. The guy has his hand resting on the girl's thigh. It's like a circle that shuts out the rest of the world. It's not just a long kiss. It's a forever kiss, a kiss as long and silent as the night."

Lisa was moved. "That's so poetic."

Carlo confessed. "Yes, but not my poetry."

"Whose?"

"Elizabeth Barrett Browning's."

Lisa recalled. "I remember her from school. Is that how you feel about us?" she asked. "I want to see this sculpture. It must be in New York. Right?"

"Wrong, it's in the Tate Museum in London."

"Oh damn, I want to see it."

"First thing. But as soon as we get home I'll get you a copy of it...you know...a small sculpture, for your bedroom."

She pulled him closer. "You are wonderful. Race you to the verandah," she shouted. He let her win.

The night before leaving Vieques for New York was a sleepless one for both. The night air was warm, punctured by the sounds of tropical insects and cascading waves. That the exigencies of life demanded a return to "reality" seemed so unfair.

For Lisa, it was more romantic than fulfilling. *We've made love already, no matter what he thinks.*

They remained sexually apart, linked by their eyes and body language. "Let's take care of each other." She nodded in agreement. For the time being at least, they would have a meeting of minds rather than bodies.

Their departure coincided with an overcast sky accompanied by a morning shower. The four-hour flight from San Juan to New York was taken up with a Woody Allen film and a meal. The flight attendants had scarcely collected the meal remnants when a stewardess announced that they would soon be landing at Kennedy Airport. Carlo looked down on a Manhattan glittering with early evening lights. It was back to business as usual. It was depressing.

Upon their return from Vieques, Carlo and Lisa agreed to meet regularly for a trip to the countryside or a show on Broadway. They teamed up to fight ennui and loneliness. On several occasions they sat up half the night doing crossword puzzles in his apartment, had an early breakfast, and strolled along the wooded pathway leading to the Hudson River. A favorite trip was a ride to Darien, Conn., whose Main Street was lined with turn-of-the-century buildings and a collection of quaint shops and restaurants that served the affluent visitors from New York City. There, they discovered the "best pizza" either had ever consumed, in a shop run by Greeks. "I hate to admit it," Carlo observed, "but these guys cook Italian better than the Italians."

During countryside walks they agreed to talk about Nicky, a subject the entire family had collectively avoided, and no one knew exactly why. They admitted to each other guilt for having flirted while he was still alive. They both cried for the thought of it. They talked about the common interests they shared, acknowledging the complexity of life, the difficulty of living without love, the unreality of many church doctrines. Carlo vented his grief for not having been a loving brother, for not having extended himself more, for accepting the role of the superior, older brother, fostered by his own parents and the rest of the family. "We are all guilty," was his final judgment. Together they visited Nicky's grave and begged forgiveness, later encouraging other family members to do the same. They agreed to fast one day a week in reparation for their sins, but never did they feel guilty about being in love.

They strolled under canopies of large, oak trees interspersed with red Japanese maples, alongside majestic homes flanked with stone planters bearing a wide variety of flowers. For Lisa, every leaf was more colorful, every drop of rain a friend, every cloud a vehicle to transport her to a city of joy. As she confided to her friend, Angela, "It's a totally new experience for me. I was 'wifely' with Nicky. You know, trying to please; it was an effort. Now, it comes natural. I don't say, 'Well, let me see what I can do for Carlo today? We just meld together."

Angela understood. "I know. I had that experience once, with my first boyfriend. He wanted to marry me. But I was looking for 'bigger' things. I blew it. Takes a lot of living to understand the simple basics. My husband's a nice guy, but the magic I had then will never be there."

Lisa's frustration peeked. "Here I'm so lucky - we're so lucky - and he's not sure what he should do. Damn it."

Angela envied Lisa's dilemma.

For Carlo, this was a time for reassessment. He gazed into his essence. People, even friends, said he was cold or indifferent, even as they loved and admired him. He asked himself the question, *Is this indifference completely natural to my personality and, therefore, wholesome?* He realized that he could only assess his own personality in reference to Nicky, for its formation took place in the interplay with his brother. What about Nicky? Perhaps, in reflection, he was more attuned to his real self, whether that self was behaving well or not. He was connected, and his life was a true reflection of the heart that beat within his body. For better or worse, Nicky was fully alive and participated in a life as he saw it, free of any artificial restraints or assumed moral values. *Have I been celibate simply because the system tells me I must be? What about all the broken personalities in the priesthood? Shouldn't somebody study that?*

He prayed to Nicky asking for forgiveness, telling him how much, looking back, he admired his honesty. *When I grow up, I need to be more like he was.*

Chapter Twenty Three
MAFIA INTERVENES

Nicco Laces was indebted to the deceased Julio Albanese. When a federal prosecutor had gathered indictable evidence against him in New York City, Julio managed to have it deep-sixed before it got to a Grand Jury. It had been the very cautious Nicco's one major misstep, and it could have been very costly indeed. Julio's intervention saved him from a long prison term. He assured Julio, "If ever there is something I can do for you, please don't hesitate. It would make me very happy."

Julio did have a request. It came shortly before he died. Hearing that Nicco was in Long Island visiting a young woman friend, he called him. "Nicco, I need a favor, a big favor."

"You got it, Julio. You want John the Baptist's head? Huh? Whatever you want, my friend."

Julio, sagely suspecting Carlo's ultimate dismissal, explained the events leading up to Carlo's running the operations of the Family. "Carlo's made his sacrifice for the Family and he's in the process of putting it back on its feet. So, far the Cardinal has not zapped him, but the day is going to come when this could happen. Then, my friend, he might need you, and I may not be around to give you a call. When that day comes, the family will need you and your Church connection."

Nicco was emphatic. "Julio, if Carlo ever needs me, I'm there for him. You know that. But, don't be talking about not being around. I've already left instructions with my attorney that you are to speak at my funeral."

The "church connection" was a reference to Nicco's friendship with a Vatican ecclesiastic, a native of Chicago. Out of instinct he befriended a young Chicago priest who had been assigned to Rome. The young priest, Father Pulaski, became an archbishop and the head of the Vatican Bank. After a long period of calculated wooing, he managed to receive the cleric's cooperation in moving Mafia money through the Bank. "There's nothing wrong, Your Excellency. We have to move our money and we will move our money. Difference is, instead of the bankers getting rich, the Vatican will make the money - more than it ever dreamed - for its charitable work."

The Archbishop showed interest. "I'll think it over, Nicco." He did. About a month later he called and said, "We need to talk."

The Mafia /Vatican connection was a tightly kept secret. Except for Julio, no Mafia don in America was aware of the deal that had been struck. They only knew that Nicco had found the perfect bank and that he knew how to launder their money. No questions were asked. Nicco's dealings with the archbishop had been very profitable to both parties. As the Archbishop explained, "Banking is the art of moving money to make money, and the Vatican needs money. The work of God is sometimes very expensive."

Archbishop Pulaski was no ordinary cleric. The Vatican needed a tough man to represent it in the financial circles of the world, where no quarter was asked and none given. Nicco's admiration turned to fondness, and a strong bond of friendship developed between the two men. He and his family enjoyed a private audience with the Pope. The Archbishop introduced him as "a prominent Catholic" businessman in Chicago; a pillar of the church. "Except for my wedding ring, it's my most precious gift." Mrs. Laces often referred to the silver-plated rosary she received from His Holiness.

During the tragic series of events that befell the Albanese family, Nicco discreetly remained in the background. The mystery surrounding Tony Albanese's death was one that puzzled Mafia dons throughout the country, and Nicco deemed it prudent not to get involved. At the time he received Bruno Battaglia's phone call, the Albanese problems, he assumed, had been resolved with Victor's death. Nicco's relationship with Bruno Battaglia was very close. On many occasions he called on him for legal advice. His own consiglieri, Matteo Ricci, was competent but limited. "I really should let Matteo go," Nicco would tell Bruno, "but he's family and he's done his best over the years. I just go around him. You understand?"

"Of course."

Thus, Nicco occasionally borrowed Bruno from Julio, benefiting from his expertise. He made frequent attempts to compensate both Julio and Bruno for the services rendered, but without success. Julio would insist. "This is a question of friendship, nothing more, nothing less. Never a cent from you." So, when Bruno called saying he needed a favor, Nicco promptly assented to a meeting.

Bruno informed him. "I'd like to bring Carlo with me."

Nicco was delighted. "Wonderful, I've not seen him since he was a kid."

Bruno and Carlo left the following afternoon for Chicago.

"Well, what brings you gentlemen to our lovely city? What can I do for you? Just tell me, and it's yours!"

Nicco's youngest daughter, Gillian, served the men wine and cheese. Nicco raised his glass to meet Bruno's, "Salut, my friend, salut!"

Carlo commented on the wine. "Mm, this is good wine Nicco, real good!"

"The brand is Salamandre, from a winery in Aptos, California. It's a precious secret to most of America. I'll put a few bottles in your luggage."

"Thanks.

Bruno said, "We've come about a problem Carlo has with the Church."

"Tell me."

"Julio told me that you and he had a discussion about Carlo. He said that if Carlo ever had a problem with the Church authorities, and he was not around, I should contact you. You might be able to help."

"Correct. We did have a discussion. Bring me up to date."

Bruno explained. "Carlo has done the job he set out to do - taking care of the Family business. Now he wants to return to the priesthood, but the New York Cardinal convinced Rome to ban him for life. On top of that he has openly taken his deceased brother's wife, Lisa, out to dinners and movies, etc. They even went to Puerto Rico together. Naturally, some self-righteous creep has been reporting that to the Cardinal."

"Probably for some self-serving reason."

Carlo entered the conversation. "Actually, Nicco, there's nothing sexual about the thing, although I admit I'd like that. But, I've been sticking to my vows. It's as simple as that. It's no big deal, but someone in Rome might make a big deal out of it. You know what I mean?

"Yeah, I do."

Carlo continued. "I took time out to get the Family back on track after all the troubles we had, and now I'd like to get back to the priesthood, but Cardinal McManus has had me defrocked, with no chance of returning. Don't know if you can help me."

Nicco tossed a small piece of cheese into his mouth. "Not easy, but. I'll check with my archbishop friend in Rome; he's an understanding guy. Leave the problem with me. I'll do my best."

Carlo was appreciative. "I know you will. Thanks in advance, Nicco."

Bruno added. "Carlo's a great guy. We'll miss him if this works out, but whatever makes him happy. That's what we want."

Nicco smiled and raised his glass. "If we succeed, we'll celebrate in New York. I need to get away. I'm beginning to think I can't live anywhere else except Chicago, even for a day. That's bad."

Bruno was expansive. "We'll lay out the red carpet for you, Nicco."

"Don't rush out to buy that carpet yet." Laughing, "Carlo, say your prayers."

Nicco explained his plan to call Archbishop Pulaski, head of the Vatican Bank, and ask him to travel to Chicago. He suggested that Carlo remain on with him after Bruno returned to New York, to speak with the Cardinal personally.

Chapter Twenty Four
ARCHBISHOP PULASKI

Archbishop Pulaski ordered a Bloody Mary in the first-class cabin of Alitalia Airlines flight 1270. His briefcase, bulging with papers and documents of the Vatican Bank, lay opened on the adjoining unoccupied seat. He pulled out a document entitled "Cash Flows" and glanced through a file marked "Nicco Laces." The previous day he received a call from Nicco who asked, "Your Grace, can you please come to Chicago for a visit? I've a very important matter to discuss with you. It's about Carlo Albanese. As you know, Cardinal McManus has defrocked him. We think this is a great injustice and want to meet with you to see if anything can be done to help him. Carlo is here with me and he can explain all of this to you himself."

The Archbishop did not hesitate. "I'll be there tomorrow, my friend."

"You're Grace, are you sure? That quickly? Don't put aside all your work. Carlo can remain here until you come."

"That's what friends are for, Nicco. I'll be there tomorrow."

As a street-smart kid on Chicago's Polish East Side, the Archbishop never imagined that one-day he would be president of a large financial institution, the Vatican Bank. It operated in utmost secrecy, giving him wide scope to use his imagination and talent. The Archbishop enjoyed creating large surpluses of money the pope could use for the Church's worldwide charities. He saw himself as a latter-day Robin Hood, rationalizing, as Nicco had convinced him, that the financial transactions in which he was engaged were going to be done anyway by someone. Why not let the money made be put to good use, not for wild philandering.

Not all ecclesiastics agreed. For the Jesuit Father General, Pulaski was nothing more than a financial manipulator. "Every time we try to make a contribution toward progress in the Church, the conservatives slap us down. This guy launders Mafia money and these pious Cardinals, even His Holiness, cheers him on."

The State Department advised the Alitalia flight crew that a prominent Vatican official would be on board. Pulaski charmed them as he distributed rosaries blessed by the Holy Father. "He's not a bit stuffy," remarked one stewardess. Another said, "I love his soft gray eyes. If he were younger he'd make me melt."

Her partner replied, "I've melted already."

Nicco sent a prominent local Polish Catholic businessman to meet Pulaski at the airport. Alitalia airline officials had notified the Press of his arrival. Upon landing, he faced a battery of reporters representing local newspapers and television stations. He paused before the microphones and read a prepared statement. "I wish to greet all the people of my beloved Chicago. I bring to you the blessings and warm greetings of His Holiness." With a flourish, he made a wide arching sign of the cross as he finished his statement. Much of the press awkwardly knelt on the tarmac, bobbing up and down in disorganized reverence. The Archbishop loved the theater of it all and relished his notoriety. He realized that even the return of a traveling Mayor Daly would not have produced such a large press contingent. There was one discordant note. In its editorial, the *Chicago Daily Tribune* asked the question:

With all due respect to Chicago's noted Vatican ecclesiastic, why is it that every time he comes home the city must expend thousands of dollars just to greet him at the airport? We have asked this question of the mayor on several occasions, but, as of this edition, have not been favored with a reply.

Nicco Laces's home did not stand out in any particular way on the street where he lived amidst stately brownstones. It was a large, old-fashioned three-story house surrounded by a plot of manicured lawn. The front entrance was unpretentious, but it did contain camera monitors discreetly hidden above the lights that ringed the large porch. The ground floor entryway led to a large living room with built in bookshelves. A small end table holding an ebony piece of African sculpture sat in the center of the room surrounded by white leather, deeply cushioned furniture. A fireplace warmed the room. The Archbishop arrived in time to have a few drinks before dinner. The meal was the Archbishop's favorite, baked stuffed cabbage covered with steaming tomato sauce. "A nice combination of Polish and Italian," he would say.

After embracing Nicco, the Archbishop turned to Carlo. "You must be Father Carlo Albanese. I am so happy to meet you. The family loves you so much. That's a very good sign." Dinner was passed in small talk about Italian politics and why the Italians changed governments so often. "Pick what you like," said the Archbishop. "Italian politics is chaotic, or the Italians know something the rest of the world has yet to learn, namely, no government is good government!"

The men reserved their private conversation until Nicco's wife and daughter had retired for the night. They then began their chat. Nicco brought up the subject of Carlo's defrocking. "Carlo has done a wonderful job guiding the Albanese family through very difficult times. You know, Your Grace, he always maintained - and it is true - that he never wanted to leave the priesthood. Cardinal McManus forced him to do so. As far has Carlo is concerned, he's still a priest. That's also our opinion. The Family business can now be left to others, so Carlo wants to return to his life's work. We - all of the Families - are asking your help in this matter."

The Archbishop rubbed his chin. "Mm, that's a tough one, a real tough one. Let me tell you something. The archdiocese of New York is one of the richest in the world. Lots of cash flows between Manhattan and the Vatican. Not only that, but all Americans have a certain respect for the Cardinal Archbishop of New York. When the Pope wants to sell an idea in America, he gets the support of New York. You see what I mean? It's big bucks and big politics. The Vatican would not want to ruffle any New York feathers."

Nicco refilled the wineglasses as the Archbishop continued. "Cardinal McManus is very determined about this kid never getting back to the priesthood. I learned just before leaving Rome that the FBI has been keeping tabs on you, Carlo, and they shared this information with the Cardinal. They calculate that since you took over there have been two contracts carried out by your men. Now that is down from previous years, it's true, but a priest ordering two hits is no easy thing to deal with. Capice?"

Carlo rubbed his hands. "Capice."

"Besides, Carlo, you are not making things any easier for yourself. There are strong rumors that you're having a relationship with your dead brother's widow!"

Nicco interrupted, "Former sister-in-law."

"Oh, hell, Nicco, what's the difference."

Carlo interjected. "Well, on that score I can tell you quite honestly that although I have a great affection for Lisa there has been absolutely no sex in the relationship."

The Archbishop settled back in his chair. "Well, Carlo, just between the two of us, if every cleric who's seen a woman were taken off the rolls, we'd have few left. So, whatever the reality is, it's not such a big deal in itself. But, you're a public figure and that makes it a big deal. You know what I mean?"

"Yes, I understand."

The Archbishop paused as Nicco refilled his wineglass. "Look, fellow, from the time I got your call I had a feeling this subject was going to come up, so I did a bit of thinking about it. There's one possible way out, if we can pull it off."

Nicco and Carlo pulled their chairs closer, in excited anticipation.

"What? Tell me"

"Well, the Cardinal is only three years away from retirement."

Nicco interrupted. "But, Your Grace, three years would be a lifetime for Carlo!"

"Yes, yes, I know" the archbishop said soothingly. "Let me finish."

Nicco apologized. "OK, OK, sorry."

"It's just possible that we could work out a deal. If His Holiness would agree, Carlo could be given another name and assigned to some Bishop in the States who would give him a parish out in the boondocks."

Nicco exclaimed, "Madonna. Brilliant!"

"There's always the risk that someone would find out who Carlo really is. That would hit the press like a bombshell, and the Vatican's relations with the New York Archdiocese would become very bad. And 'bad' means potential loss of millions every year. You understand?"

"Uh ha."

"And you know whose rear end would be in the proverbial sling?"

"Yeah, yours!" said Nicco, pointing at the Archbishop's derriere.

"On the other hand, if this could be kept under wraps until the Cardinal retires, then it won't make any difference. His Holiness would appoint someone to New York who will leave it alone. Got it?"

Nicco appreciated the tactic. "I got it, Your Grace, fantastic! You're willing to take a run on it?"

"For all of you and your dear families who are so close to me, I give you my word I'll do whatever I can. No promises; just the best I can do." Nicco and Carlo reached out to shake the Archbishop's hand. Carlo offered. "Can't ask for more, my friend. We love you. Thank you."

"I might need that love one day, Nicco. Lots of people are out to skin me alive." He said this without being aware that he would soon be viciously attacked in Rome. "The department of the clergy is Cardinal Morretti's, and I can tell you that Morretti is no friend of mine. So we've got a few hurdles to jump over. Say your prayers. One more thing, Carlo. Be prepared to come to Rome at a moment's notice. I think it would be a good thing for you to make your case in person."

The Archbishop glanced at his watch. "It's been a long day, Nicco. I'm ready for the sack. It was great seeing you again."

Nicco pressed a small brown envelope into the Archbishop's hand as he entered his car. "Get yourself a drink on the plane. Bon voyage!"

The envelope contained a check for twenty five thousand dollars. The Archbishop admired people who knew how to grease the wheels of industry. He arrived at the Cardinal's residence just after two in the morning and slept for nine hours, awaking just in time to rush out to the airport. The following day he was back at his office in Rome. There he met with three Italian bankers who needed money moved. Their quid pro quo for the archbishop was juicy insider information on industrial stocks in Geneva. Another day in the business life of Archbishop Pulaski, the Most Reverend President of the Vatican Bank, had begun.

American Airlines Flight 980 was due to arrive at Rome's Fiumicino Airport at 5pm. Father Joseph Casey, of the archdiocese of Chicago waited patiently as the flight, already delayed for half an hour, was reported circling above because of heavy air traffic. Chosen by Boston's Cardinal to fill a post at the Congregation of the Clergy, Father Casey handled clerical cases involving Americans. He was aware that the Cardinal Archbishop of New York had stripped Carlo of all clerical privileges. Nevertheless, Cardinal Morretti, head of the Congregation had sent him a memo with instructions.

"For your eyes only."

"Father Carlo Albanese, formerly of the Archdiocese of New York, has requested a meeting with this Congregation to review the circumstances of his dismissal from the priesthood. Father Albanese will be arriving in Rome next Saturday, the fourteenth of July. Please meet him at the airport in civilian clothes and discreetly bring him to your office. Discretion here is due to the fact that he is known as a priest who is also a Mafia Don. You will tape-record your discussions with Father Albanese and the tape will be handed to me, personally. No other record of the meeting is to be kept."

Shortly after the landing of the American Flight, Carlo identified himself to Casey, who wore, as pre-arranged, a blue denim jacket and a pair of jeans. "I'm Carlo. Nice to meet you Father."

"Call me Joe," he responded in a spirit of clerical camaraderie. The ride to the Vatican lasted a half-hour. The two men chatted as Carlo took in the passing scene. His eyes feasted on the beautiful buildings and broad avenues. "What a city!"

Father Casey was dour. "I don't really like being in Rome. The people are nice. The city is beautiful. But I'm sitting at a desk shuffling papers while my buddies are out golfing, or boating at Cape Cod. I get letters from some of these guys and they say `Well, you'll be a bishop one day,' as if that's a big deal. Even if that did happen it would only mean more paper shuffling."

"Mm, I see what you mean."

They drove slowly along the Via del Belvedere The two men warmed to each other as they drove past the office of Osservatore Romano, and on to the Ethiopian College and Father Casey's office. Once inside, Carlo came right to the point. "I want to get back to the priesthood. I didn't leave it voluntarily. I understand how the Cardinal felt and all of that but, in fact, I contend he acted unjustly. Whatever anyone in the Church thinks about my family's operations, the fact is that, number one, I had no choice but to step into the vacuum."

"There's some understanding of your position, here in Rome."

Carlo continued. "Secondly, I'm working hard to legitimize operations that are illegal. My hope is that Rome will look at that side of the picture and permit me to return."

Father Casey was sympathetic but he recalled the wording of the document sent to Rome from New York. He was not optimistic. "I'd sure like to be able to encourage you, Carlo, and I certainly will pass on your request to the Sacred Congregation, but I must tell you the prospects are not very good."

"I appreciate anything you can do for me."

From a file marked "Secret," Cardinal Morretti removed a letter from Bishop Andavoro of Brooklyn. It read:

Your Eminence:

It is with a great sense of delicacy that I write to you concerning the case of Father Carlo Albanese. His case is, of course, not within the province of my jurisdiction. I write only because I feel that perhaps Cardinal McManus, in spite of his good will, does not understand the cultural dimension of this complicated case. I must confess that a considerable amount of advocacy on his behalf has been represented to me by leading members of Mafia Families in the New York-Brooklyn area. Their argument, in brief, is that Father Carlo was under extraordinary pressure to assume family leadership in a moment of crisis. They maintain that he desired to remain in the priesthood, and that his temporary assumption of leadership has considerably lessened the amount of violence associated with Mafia activities in the Metropolitan area.

Hoping that you will be able to find a way to restore this young man to priestly activity, I remain,

Fraternally and Cordially Yours
+Anthony Andavoro
Bishop of Brooklyn

The Cardinal had already heard from Archbishop Pulaski, who made a personal and confidential visit. He recalled the Archbishop's parting words. "Such an opportunity for this young priest to present his case would be welcomed at the highest level of the Church."

The Cardinal knew as well as anyone else that the flamboyant Archbishop had the ear of the Roman Pontiff. He also knew of his ties to Mafia figures both in Sicily and the United States. But Morretti had to play his cards right. A strong rumor was circulating in the Vatican that Pulaski was in deep trouble, that his banking practices had attracted the Attorney General's Office. Also, his rival, Tardolini, might not appreciate a favor to Pulaski. If the rumors were true, Pulaski was on his way down. That would leave Tardolini on top. It was Tardolini, therefore, whom it would be necessary to please. He and he alone, now, could get him the post he wanted, Vatican Secretary of State. Even more complicated however was the power the Mafia exercised in Rome and in the churches of Brooklyn and New York, a subtle but real power. To be on the safe side he had to do something to give the impression that he was giving Carlo Albanese a fair hearing. Giving the appearance of being fair; that was the thing to do.

Father Casey called on Carlo at the Roman Jesuit House, where he was staying. "I don't want you to get over optimistic, but Cardinal Morretti wants you to make your case to him personally. It's a great opportunity. Want to go?"

"Of course! When?"

"Now! We have an hour to get there, so shave and shower first. We're only about 15 minutes away from his office."

Carlo could not contain his excitement as he lathered his face. The Cardinal would not be inviting us to his office to say 'no'. It's got to be a 'yes'. They drove to the Vatican with great enthusiasm and heightened hopes.

Cardinal Morretti was gracious. "Please, sit down Father Albanese." Looking at Casey he says to Carlo, "Do you have any problem with Father Casey being present?" Morretti shrewdly assessed that Carlo would have no objection and that Casey would be a witness to the scenario he was manipulating.

Carlo was unsuspecting. "No objection whatsoever."

The Cardinal began his script. "Father Carlo, you have been accused of having a relationship with your sister-in-law. I must ask you if there is truth to this rumor."

Carlo took the bait. "Your Eminence, it is not true that I have had a sexual relationship with Lisa, but we have grown close to each other and have affection for each other." His honesty was grist for the Cardinal's mill.

The Cardinal spoke as a father to his son. "Of course, Father Carlo, you know that the essence of priesthood is to devote oneself solely to the Church. Affections for a female, while commendable, have no place in the life of a priest." Then he proffered more bait. "Do you agree with this? How do you see celibacy in the priesthood?" He glanced over at Father Casey to be sure the cassette tape was running.

Feeling secure in the Cardinal's presence, Carlo responded, "Well, to be honest, the priesthood has a lot of alcoholics and pedophiles. I can't say to what extent the lack of female companionship contributes to these problems, but certainly there is a connection. Perhaps in the future there will be a different discipline in the Church. The present discipline is discouraging heterosexuals from entering the seminary. When one looks at the damage done, one wonders about the wisdom of retaining this discipline."

Casey, much more sophisticated in the ways of the Vatican, began to feel uneasy, but he kept his silence.

The Cardinal, smiling, continued questioning Carlo. "I admire your openness. Now, let us get to a more serious problem. It is my understanding that since you have been dismissed from the priesthood, and under your direction, your Organization has committed two assassinations. Is that true?" Raising his hands and cocking his head to the right, he emphasized. "Now, Carlo, we are speaking in secret. What you say will remain right here."

Carlo was still comfortable. "Your Eminence, it is true that during the time I have been presiding over the Family two murders took place. I know it will be difficult for you to understand the morality here, but perhaps I can put it this way." Carlo paused to drink the orange juice placed at his elbow. "Since my Uncle Julio became the head of the Family, murder contracts have dramatically decreased by more than fifty percent. That was great progress in his goal of legitimizing all the Family's activities. In this past year, under my direction, we have practically eliminated such violence. I believe that this, for me and for the society in which I live, is an important ministry. I have furthered my uncle's dream and can now hand it on to the men whose mentality I have trained and influenced to continue toward those goals. The alternative would have been for me to wash my hands of it, like Pilate, and God only knows what might have happened. For one thing, the vacuum would have been filled with the ambitions of other Families, causing death and mayhem as they jockeyed for dominance. This is my defense, Your Eminence."

The Cardinal could not have been more cordial. "Let us have a drink of good Italian wine and then I have a few more things to ask about."

Carlo trusted this easygoing and seemingly compassionate ecclesiastic. Casey was not entertaining the same feelings. He wanted to say something but was trapped in Morretti's presence.

The Cardinal continued. "The recommendation made to me, Carlo, is that you take on a new identity and work in an obscure town in Colorado. I see some problems with that. First of all, can you be comfortable living as if you were someone else?"

Carlo was straightforward. "Well, of course, it would be difficult, but if it were the only way for me to live my priesthood, I would certainly try."

"And your family, Carlo, would they not miss you?"

"Yes, of course."

"Mm. Well, Carlo, let me think on these things. I'm sure the Holy Spirit will guide us to the right answer." Morretti stood and put his hands on Carlo's shoulders. "There are many ways of serving the Church. I'm sure that whatever the response that comes from the Sacred Congregation will be one in which you will find spiritual strength."

Casey noted that Morretti had shifted responsibility to his office and its officials. That, he thought, does not bode well. That evening he and Carlo dined together prior to Carlo's flight to New York. Carlo's upbeat mood during and right after the meeting with Morretti appeared to have dimmed as the evening wore on. Casey offered no personal opinion of the meeting. After all, he thought, I have to live in this town long after Carlo flies away

The decision of the Congregation of the Clergy came in a letter to Pulaski from Morretti.

Your Grace:

I have considered your request that the case of Father Carlo Albanese be reviewed. I have studied the case very closely and have come to the conclusion that, given the agreement with the Cardinal Archbishop of New York for permanent disbarment from the priesthood, I cannot, in good conscience, permit his return. It must be remembered by all of us that this priest may have ordered the assassination of two men. Imagine, will you, the impact on the Catholic populations of the world if the Holy See should agree to reinstate him.

Yours In Christ,
+Cardinal Archbishop Pasquale Morretti

Pulaski was stunned by Morretti's lack of cooperation. *What has happened that would lead him to expose himself to my displeasure?* He was soon to find out exactly why.

Early the following Sunday morning, Pulaski received a phone call from the Pontiff from his summer residence at Castle Gondolpho. "Please come out here immediately, Gregory. Come alone." Pulaski received many such calls from the Pope and, once again, felt the pride of intimacy with the highest official of the Catholic Church, arguably the most powerful personage in the entire world. As he drove from his Vatican apartment, he glanced at Giovanni Lorenzo Bernini's magnificent colonnades, standing guard at St. Peter's Basilica. The Vatican flag on his car, made of two vertical bands of yellow and white, with the keys of St. Peter and the Papal tiara in the center got immediate attention from the local police. For his immediate relatives and banking friends the Pope would graciously set aside a few minutes for handshakes and conviviality. *Who would believe it? Gregory Pulaski, son of the janitor of St. Catherine's Church in Chicago's dilapidated East Side, is driving out to see his personal friend, the Holy Father, in a Mercedes Benz. Unbelievable.*

The Pope sat at one end of a long, oak table and invited Pulaski to sit next to him. "Thank you, Your Holiness. What can I do for you today?"

Frowning, "Let me get right to the point, Gregory. I've some bad news for you. The Public Prosecutor requested a private audience with me yesterday. He said it was a matter of great urgency. I wondered what could possibly be the problem. It was a very painful meeting."

"What did he say?"

The Pope fidgeted with his pectoral cross for a few seconds, then looked Pulaski directly in the eyes, saying, "He informs me that it's quite possible that you will soon be indicted by an Italian grand jury."

"A what?"

"Yes, a grand jury."

Pulaski took a deep breath. "Oh, my God! For what?"

"He said the indictment will concern laundering money for the Mafiosi."

"What else did he say?"

"That's not enough?"

"Yes, of course, but I mean did he elaborate?"

The pope continued. "Well, he said that wire taps on Anthony Carpucello contain many conversations with your good self. In those conversations, he said, it's evident you've been using the Vatican Bank to launder a great deal of money - millions - hundreds of millions - for the Mafia, here, in Sicily, and in the United States. Your friend, Nicco Laces, is deeply involved in this matter. The Banco Ambrosiano may collapse as a result of your dealings with Laces. The charges are very serious."

"Oh, God!" Pulaski pressed his hands so hard against the table his knuckles turned white. *Now I understand why Carlo didn't get permission. Morretti knows something about my problem!*

"He said that he'll be presenting this information to a grand jury next month. The evidence is so compelling as to convince him you will be indicted."

"But your secretary knew about these transactions."

"That's not the point is it? The point, my dear Gregory, is that you're in deep trouble with the authorities. You certainly cannot implicate Monsignor Tardolini. He understood you to say that you were engaged in unorthodox transactions, and that you were doing this for the good of the Church. Unorthodox, my dear Gregory, is not the same thing as criminal."

This is such nonsense. He knew everything Tardolini knew. "My recollection is that he didn't want to know more. He wanted deniability, didn't he?"

The accusation was met with a cold silence. The Pontiff moved toward the door. "I've informed you of this, Gregory, to give you some advance warning. Since this is a criminal investigation, I cannot become involved in any manner. You do understand that?"

He didn't mind spending all the money we made on these operations. "I understand, Your Holiness."

"I've promised the Attorney General that you'll not leave the Vatican grounds. This saves you the embarrassment of a public decree to that effect. Castel Gondolfo also enjoys extra-territorial jurisdiction, as does the Basilica of St. John Lateran, but, obviously, it would be embarrassing for us if you were to visit these locations. You understand?"

I'm being tossed to the dogs. "Yes, Your Holiness."

"I expect you to drive directly to the Vatican and not leave its boundaries until matters are sorted out. Let's pray that the grand jury will decide not to indict you. If it does, you are in God's hands."

Such hypocrisy. How much like Pilate that sounds.

Pulaski's world of power and prestige was crumbling, suddenly, unexpectedly. *It never occurred to me that the civil authorities could intervene in Vatican matters.*

He tossed a question to the pope. "As a citizen of the Vatican, do I not have immunity from any legal actions contemplated by the Italian Government?"

"This is not a question you should ask of the Pope? That is for the legal counsel you retain. I suggest you do that as quickly as possible."

Pulaski pleaded. "Will you not use your enormous influence to help me in this matter? I only did that which would bring money to your treasury for dispersal to the poor, worldwide."

The Pontiff's fingers drummed noisily on the desk. "This conversation is not proper. Calm yourself. Seek counsel." The Pontiff glanced at his watch. "I've another appointment momentarily. Go in peace and God be with you." With that, the Pontiff pressed a button on the lip of his desk. Several papal officials appeared and escorted the Pope out of the room. Monsignor Samani remained behind. "Come with me, Your Excellency. I shall accompany you to your car."

How rapidly fortunes change. Sic transit gloria. These same sycophants would be vying with each other to invite me to their apartments for dinner, looking for favors, promotions. Look at them. Ambition now requires that they avoid me. Not a true friend among them.

"Monsignor, things can change rapidly, can't they?"

"I agree, Your Excellency." The Monsignor's face remained expressionless, but he felt the sadness that blanketed the Vatican's popular, ebullient Ecclesiastic. The conversation came to an end. They walked silently to the VIP parking lot. *From now on I'll have to park in the streets.*

Sister Rosalita had been Monsignor Tardolini's secretary for seven years, and hated every minute. What she found in Tardolini's office shocked her to the core. This "man of God" was brutal, devious, a person who plotted against bishops and cardinals. Anyone who crossed his path or did not display the kind of subservience he deemed proper "to the Pope's secretary" was doomed to acts of revenge. An Indian bishop who called twice to change the hour for an appointment was dismissed as "arrogant and crude." Tardolini dictated a letter to the Congregation for Bishops stating the Holy Father wished a cautionary note be placed in the Bishop's file. He was never to be considered for a larger diocese or any promotion "for reasons kept secret in the Pontiff's heart." The last straw came when she discovered that Tardolini was skimming money off Vatican finances. Sister Rosalita was fully aware that Pulaski had dealings with the Mafia, that he laundered money. Documents in her files were clear evidence of this. She also knew, however, that he personally sought out for assistance the neediest missions on the African and Asian continents. As his secretary, Rosalita was aware that Tardolini had already laid the foundation for destroying Pulaski's reputation. She decided to act. Late into the night she formulated and reformulated a letter to Archbishop Pulaski that would lead to far-reaching changes in Vatican personnel, policies and politics:

December 8, 1975
Archbishop Gregory Pulaski
President, Vatican Bank
St. Peter's Apartments
Vatican City

Your Grace:
After much reflection and prayer, I have decided to write this letter. I am aware that His Holiness has recently informed you that you are the subject of a very serious investigation by the Office of the Public Prosecutor. Monsignor Tardolini supplied the information acquired by the Prosecutor, Mr. Guilliermo Martini, secretly. A portion of Mr. Martini's reply to the Monsignor is also enclosed.

The Monsignor has a partner in stealing money from the Vatican, a man you have met many times, Mr. Frederico Fellici, the principal supplier of Vatican church linens, wine and altar supplies. My prayer is that this information will not have arrived too late to save you from a public, humiliating dismissal. I know you will handle this letter with the greatest confidentiality. God bless you.

In the Name of our Savior
Sister Maria Rosalita

The next morning, proud of her courage, by means of a member of the Swiss Guard, she secretly delivered the letter to Carolina De Medici, Archbishop Pulaski's secretary "Please darling, give this important letter to the Archbishop as soon as he arrives at the office this morning. If, for any reason, he does not come in today, see that he gets it."

Chapter Twenty Five
VATICAN INTRIGUE

Carolina opened the letter Sister Rosalita left for Pulaski. I hope they haven't moved up the date for the Grand Jury. Her hands trembled as she used the letter opener to slash open the envelope. She was stunned as she read the contents, which included copy of a letter from the Public Prosecutor to Tardolini, thanking him for providing incriminating evidence against Pulaski. *Oh, my God. Oh that terrible man. I would never have dreamt that even he could be so contemptuous.* She paced to-and-fro across the office, shaking her head and loosely throwing her arms into the air without direction. She grabbed the phone and dialed Pulaski's private phone number. "Get here quickly. I'm going to cancel all your appointments."

Pulaski shaved and showered in record time. He drove his Mercedes faster than usual. The carbinieri looked the other way as he darted in and out of morning traffic. *What could this be all about? Maybe the Grand Jury has already been called. The backstabbing has probably begun.* His shirt dripping with sweat, his ruddy face contorted, his hands shaking, he tried to stabilize the center of his being. "I'm losing it!" he shouted to himself. Gripping the rear view mirror and turning it on to himself, he shouted at his image," How could you have been so stupid all these years?"

The Swiss Guard on duty at the Vatican auto garage watched with concern as Pulaski stumbled out of his car, his hair and clothing disheveled, his face reflecting a palette of pain. "Are you OK Your Excellency? Can I help you?"

Waving him off, "I'm fine, fine, thanks" as he darted to his office.

Carolina greeted him at the door. "Come, come, "I've got the most incredible evidence here for you."

"Evidence?"

"Well, I guess a court of law would call it evidence."

"What are you talking about?"

She handed him Rosalita's letter and an enclosure, a letter from Martini to Tardolini,

Please accept my sincere thanks, and that of the Italian people, for the information confirming long-held suspicions that Archbishop Pulaski has been money-laundering Mafiosi funds for many years. I realize that it was, as you stated in your letter, very painful for you to inform on a fellow-cleric, especially one so highly placed in the very center of Catholicism. I only thank God that he is an American rather than an Italian.

Pulaski read with startled incredulity. "Carolina, the damage Tardolini could inflict on the Church by a public disclosure of the Vatican Bank's dealings with the Mafiosi is incalculable. He must be stopped for the good of the Church. His cold-blooded ambition is chilling in its indifference. We need to act immediately, but how?"

They reflected on what should be done. After considering and discarding some options, Pulaski decided on a course of action. "Listen, Carolina. I've an idea. You call Nicco, read him this letter and tell him I said to use his best judgment, whatever it is."

"Brilliant. After all, he is involved in this. His name would come out in any investigation, and he could be indicted by an American court."

Getting another idea. "Oh, tell him it's possible that when the Pope told me about Martini's upcoming investigation he did so simply to give me time to prepare my defense. But, there could be an additional reason. What if he wants Tardolini stopped? After all, the scandal to the Church would be enormous. Surely the Holy Father would not want this to happen. At the same time, as Pontiff, he couldn't afford the risk of asking me to do anything about it. He may just be hoping that I will."

Carolina touched his shoulders. "Right!"

Pulaski heaved a sigh. "This is just a guess on my part, but it makes sense."

"Of course. It's a real possibility. You know better than anyone else how his mind works."

Carolina De Medici felt the blood of her famous ancestors as she dialed Nicco Laces, in Chicago. "Well my dear Carolina, how are you" It's so nice to hear from you. It's not Christmas Day; it's not my birthday. What's up? How's the Archbishop?"

"He's fine. You know him. No matter what happens he's always in a good mood. But, right now he's in deep trouble."

"What kind of trouble?"

"I'm going to read you a letter the Archbishop got from Monsignor Tardolini's secretary, Sister Rosalita. The letter will explain everything."

"Shoot."

Nicco slumped into his chair and stared at the ceiling as he listened. Not only was his friend under fire, but the entire money laundering operation was in danger. *I could be jailed!*

Quietly, "Carolina, I don't believe this. Tardolini must be out of his friggin mind. This is dynamite. We gotta stop this arrogant cleric."

"There's not much time."

"There's no time."

"The Archbishop said do whatever you feel is appropriate. Since it's too dangerous to communicate right now, all is in your hands. He approves in advance whatever you want to do."

"I will handle this with great delicacy, but we need to act quickly."

"Thank you so much, Nicco. A lot rides on what you decide to do."

Nicco spent several hours formulating an approach to the problem.

Telephone service in rural Sicily had its ups and downs, but Don Cosimo Germana, Capo di tutti capi in Sicily, didn't mind. The sight of his olive, orange and mandarin trees made up for whatever inconveniences country living brought in its wake. That particular morning, during his sleep, the phone had quickly beeped several times, only to go dead by the time he picked up the receiver. Now, it was ringing again. He moved quickly to the phone. This time he heard a voice. "Don Cosimo, my dear friend, this is Nicco. I'm sorry to bother you so early in the morning, but I have a situation that requires urgent action."

"Nicco, you know you can call me any time. At my age, I'm up half the night peeing anyway, so it makes no difference. Damn prostate stuff. You'll get it soon."

"Already have."

"A young Turk like you?"

"Yeah."

Cosimo was curious. "Anyway, what's up? What's so urgent?"

Nicco's voice rose. "Pulaski's in trouble. That means we're in trouble."

Don Cosimo is puzzled. "How come?"

"Tardolini wrote a secret letter to the Prosecutor General telling him about the money-laundering. He wants to get Pulaski out of the way in time for the next papal election. The jackass wants to be Pope."

Unbelieving, "What? That guy's nuts! Does Pulaski know about this?"

Nicco added, "Yeah. Carolina just called and read me a letter written to Pulaski from Tardolini's secretary, Sister Rosalita."

"And?"

"The letter explains that Tardolini gave Martini sufficient information for him to initiate an investigation."

Cosimo, who prided himself on having inside information, was surprised. "Mama mia! I didn't hear anything about Pulaski being investigated."

"Exactly."

Cosimo asked, "Meaning?"

"Listen to this."

"Tell me."

Nicco explains. "The Pope's at Castle Gondolpho. He sends for Pulaski and tells him Martini's got enough information to hang him. He wants Pulaski to know well in advance of a Grand Jury convening. That's the key?"

"The key to what?"

"The key to our problem."

Cosimo, still not understanding. "Whadaya mean?"

Nicco is excited. "I mean, my dear friend, the Pontiff's playing his own game."

"What's his game?"

Nicco explained. "Look, the Pope's job is to guard the Church. Right?"

"Yeah. What's the connection?"

Nicco speaks deliberately. "The connection, my friend, is that the Pope doesn't want a big scandal on his hands. He doesn't need this. The Grand Jury isn't called for another month. That gives Pulaski time to do something about Tardolini. Translation: Pulaski will contact us and we will take care of the problem.

Cosimo is stunned. "You mean the Pope is putting out a contract on Tardolini?"

"Of course - through us!"

Cosimo knew his Vatican history. "Won't be the first time."

"Yeah, the Borgias and the de Medici."

Nicco agreed. "Exactly. Brilliant, isn't it?

"Yeah. What a way to send us a message. No trace. Right?"

"Exactly."

"Any suggestions?"

Nicco did have a suggestion. "One. The rest I leave up to you."

"And that is?"

"Tardolini has a co-conspirator in ripping off the Vatican treasury."

Cosimo was caught by surprise. "You gotta be kidding."

"Dead serious."

"Kill them both?"

Nicco suggested, "I've got a better idea."

"Tell me."

"Blackmail. We can convince Tardolini that he should write a letter to the Public Prosecutor stating it was all a big mistake. He apologizes for the misinformation and recommends that he go no further. For the prosecutor, a false accusation against a powerful cleric would be the end of his career."

Cosimo liked the plan. "Incredible, Nicco, absolutely incredible. I'll take care of it."

"Speed is important."

"I understand. And co-conspirator? Who is he?"

"Federico Fellici."

"You mean the Vatican's supplier?"

"No other."

Cosimo warmed to the chase. "Damn! I never did like that bastard. Don't worry, Nicco. I'll take care of everything."

"Thanks Cosimo. God bless."

Laughing, "Well, God should bless me. We're responding to the request of the Holy Father himself!"

"You're a saint Cosimo. Give my love to your wife and children - and your grandchildren."

"I will, and you know we should visit each other now and then. We're not getting any younger?"

" Yes, but you know what they say about aged wine?"

Cosimo chuckled. "Right. Ad multos annos. Goodbye for now."

"Ciao."

Cosimo issued instructions to his Caporegimes that Monsignor Tardolini and Frederico Fellici be put under twenty-four hour surveillance. Their movements, in detail, were to be reported to him. He then made a phone call to Stefano Lazaro, a former seminarian, to whom he was entrusting this mission. After a dinner of fried clams and vegetables, Don Cosimo retired to formulate the details of his plan. He was doing the Pope's work. It's a question of loyalty to the Holy Father. On that note, Cosimo went to bed and slept soundly until daybreak. That same evening, since Carlo's future was intertwined with the resolution of the problem, Nicco called him and explained "what is going down." Carlo was in full agreement.

Chapter Twenty Six
MORE VATICAN INTRIGUE

Monsignor Giuseppi Tardolini was planning an evening with his co-conspirator, Frederico Fellici. There would be dinner at La Dolce Notte restaurant, Verdi's Aida at the Opera House, followed by a night of drinking and chatting. His life was reaching its apex. *How sweet life is. Pulaski is about to drop from the political scene. My opposition will just fade away. I could be elected on the first ballot.*

"Your seats have been reserved at the Opera House, Monsignor. Your table has been reserved at La Dolce Notte." Sister Rosalita was trying to be her normal self. *I've got to control my emotions, not allow him to suspect anything.*

"Thank you Sister. I don't know what I'd do without you."

She felt a pang of hypocrisy as she smiled. "Thank you, Monsignor."

Tardolini's private wish seeped out. "One day you may be the personal secretary of the Roman Pontiff."

"Could that be you, Monsignor?"

"Oh heavens, no. I'm not worthy of such high office."

That's true you bastard. One of the few truths you've told all week.
"You're too humble, Monsignor."

"Humility is the chief characteristic required in the priesthood."

"Would that more of the clergy had your attitude, Monsignor." *Surely the Archbishop's friends will act quickly. His punishment will come like a thief in the night.*

"Sister, you may come in late tomorrow morning. I'm sure you have some personal matters to take care of - say, ten o'clock."

"Thank you, Monsignor." *Oh yes, a night on the town with his fellow-thief. He'll drag in around noon tomorrow.*

"Thank you, Monsignor. Enjoy your night at the Opera."

"I always do, my dear. Music refreshes my soul."

She felt a tinge of compassion for this empty personality.

As Monsignor Tardolini and Frederico Fellici drove from the Opera House to the Vatican apartments, a black Porshce followed them. "The Birds are going to their nest," said Peter Sorello, Stefano's assistant for the evening.

Stefano was satisfied. "Good, we can get our job done." Earlier in the evening he had received a master key to the Vatican apartments from Eugeno Manto, maintenance man for the Vatican condo complex. "Let's give them time to get settled down before we break in on them."

"Yeah."

They listened to music from a local Roman station for about an hour. Stefano thought that was ample time. Turning to Peter, he said, It's show time."

Using the master key, Stefano and Peter, moved quickly into the apartment lobby, entered the elevator, and pressed for the 4th floor. The elevator moved slowly so Peter drummed his palms on the wall to a beat inside his head. When it arrived, the doors hissed open instantly. They made their way to Tardolini's apartment. Peter quickly slid the apartment key into the door lock and, noiselessly, they entered. A dim light sprayed from the bottom of the bedroom door. Peter pressed his ear against it and could hear the faint voices from inside the apartment. His toe accidentally bumped against the bedroom door.

An excited "Who's there? Is anyone there?"

Peter and Stefano, guns in hand, moved quickly, flinging open the door.

"Oh my God!" Tardolini shouted.

Peter used the authority of his gun to issue orders. "OK, each of you, don't move."

Tardolini trembled and asked, "What are you doing?"

Stefano stared at the cowering men. "These guys are disgusting. And Tardolini wants to be pope?"

Tardolini grimaced. "What is it you want?"

O.K., let's get down to business, Mr. Tardolini." He did not use the clerical title. "I'm going to read you a copy of a letter you received from the Public Prosecutor, Mr. Martini." Stefano read: "Please accept my sincere thanks and that of the Italian people..."

Tardolini sat erect, listening with studied attention.

"Do you acknowledge receiving this letter."

After a pause, "Yes, I do."

"Good. What I want you to do is write a letter to Mr. Martini explaining that your information on Archbishop Pulaski was wrong. Explain that someone was trying to destroy the Archbishop's reputation and that you were terribly misled. You'll apologize for having inadvertently passed on scurrilous and false information."

"And if I do?"

Stefano explained. "When you do, you will have nothing to fear. I will destroy the letter. But, if you ever rip off one cent from the Vatican treasury again, I will come after you. What really bothers me is not the money you get from teaming up with this creep. What bothers me is that you are trying to destroy a decent man. You're prepared to write the letter?"

"Obviously."

"We need your letter into Martini's hands in the morning. I suggest you hand-deliver it. That will give you an opportunity to set up a meeting with the Pontiff."

Pleading, "But that hardly gives me any time. It's not that simple."

"Make it that simple. Your life depends on it."

Tardolini summoned anger. "I'll do the best I can. I really can't do more even if you humiliate me, beat me or whatever it is you do for a living."

"Shut up."

Tardolini went silent, but the anger showed in his face. After a moment, he ventured, "You are a very strange young man."

"How is that?"

"Well, perhaps strange is not the right word."

"What is the right word then?"

Feeling a bit more courageous, "You're on a crusade for the good of the Church and you are probably Mafiosi. Isn't that strange?"

Stefano was sarcastic. "Politics and religion make strange bedfellows, Tardolini. We've taken care of business, so we're leaving now. Obviously it would not be in your best interest to sound an alarm." At that, Stefano motioned to Peter and they left the apartment.

Tardolini and his friend and co-conspirator, Fellici, were devastated. They knew the cash cow would no longer produce milk.

Chapter Twenty Seven
THE RETURN

At an early 7 a.m. emergency meeting in the office of the Public Prosecutor, Guilliermo Martini talked with his staff of prosecuting attorneys. They were interrupted by his secretary. "A call from Monsignor Tardolini, sir."

"Tell the Monsignor I'm in the midst of a very important meeting. I'll return his call as soon as I can. In fact, tell him our business concerns the matter which he brought to my attention."

Ms. Bettina Callaxi left the room but returned almost immediately. "The Monsignor says the call is extremely urgent. He must talk with you before you continue your meeting."

What the hell could this be about? "Excuse me, gentlemen." At his secretary's desk he picked up the phone. "Yes, Monsignor, what's this urgent matter?"

Tardolini spoke in an almost breathless voice. "Guillermo, there has been a terrible, almost criminal mistake. Much to my great sorrow and embarrassment, the information I passed on to you about Archbishop Pulaski is incorrect."

Shocked. "What!"

"I don't quite know how to apologize to you, sir. This is terrible. A person who had, God forgive him, clerical ambitions, gave the information to me. He meant to destroy Pulaski's reputation, removing him from the list of the papabili. It's horrible. I can't describe how terrible I feel. So, please, good sir, do not pursue this matter."

Martini was confused. "But, Monsignor, this is incredible. How could this have happened? You told me you had proof positive, which you would submit to me. Bank records, and so on." Wiping his brow with a handkerchief, "I can understand a person giving you information, but bank records, that's another matter. Is it not?"

"Please trust me, Guilliermo. I will explain in greater detail later. For the moment, please accept my word and call off the investigation. It will end up embarrassing you - and me - and the Holy Father, whom I know you revere."

"I will try."

Tardolini was nervous. "What do you mean, try?"

"I have already requested subpoena power for the Vatican Bank records from the Chief Criminal Court Judge."

"Can that order be reversed?"

Martini begins to cave in. "Theoretically, yes, but it would greatly diminish the reputation of this office if I were to make such a request. These requests are never made unless we have sufficient evidence to warrant them."

"But you do not have such evidence, do you?"

Martini almost whispers. "Yes, I do. I have the word of the Secretary to the Holy Father."

Tardolini caught the sarcasm in his voice. He was desperate. "And if the request came, not from you but from the Holy Father? Then what?"

"Yes, that would certainly do it. But there would be the suspicion that the Pope was obstructing a criminal investigation."

"You mean if it became public knowledge?"

"Well, that's true, of course, but it's my duty to prevent any such activities."

"You mean, you would not believe the Pope?"

Martini was cautious. "Oh, yes, I suppose I would, but such a move on the part of His Holiness would, under ordinary circumstances, be highly suspicious."

"Since the charges are false, appearances aside, there's no reason to believe that anything inappropriate is going on. Isn't that correct?"

Martini's voice lacked conviction. "I guess so. But there's one thing."

"Yes?"

Martini vented his inner feelings. "The person who made the charges has committed a criminal offense."

"But no one is bound to confess such a crime."

Martini would not let him off the hook. "That's true. Do you know the identity of the person?"

Tardolini sidestepped. "I'm not bound to reveal the person's name because the Archbishop has not been charged with anything. It's not yet in the public forum."

"You'd make a good lawyer, Monsignor."

"It was my second choice."

"I see."

Tardolini had no illusions. *He knows damn well that I'm involved in this somehow.* "Good, Guillermo. I'll request a meeting with the Holy Father for both of us. I will try for lunch time if that's OK for you?"

Martini returned to his conference room and announced to his staff, "The investigation is dead. Long live the Vatican." The young prosecutors were startled, but kept silent. One of them whispered to a colleague, "You don't mess with the Vatican."

His Holiness, Pope John XX, awaited the arrival of Monsignor Tardolini. He noted that in a morning call Tardolini's voice was nervous and surprisingly muted, "Your Holiness, I request a private audience at 11:30 this morning," adding, "and I'd appreciate it if the Public Prosecutor can join us at 12:30, perhaps for lunch.

The pope reflected: *Pulaski's friends have done well it seems. Tardolini needed humbling.*

Tardolini arrived promptly at 11:30 am, just one hour before the anticipated arrival of the Public Prosecutor. He moved into the Papal presence timidly and with downcast eyes, kneeling at the Pontiff's feet, asking for his blessing. "I ask your fatherly blessing. I've come to confess the most grievous of sins. I'm the unhappiest of men.

The Pope marveled at Tardolini's transformation. *He appears genuinely contrite. His soul has been saved. Thanks be to God.*

For almost an hour Tardolini confessed his sins, even the most humiliating of all, his desire to succeed the Holy Father. Lifting Tardolin up from his knees and sitting next to him on a spacious couch, "You're the prodigal son, returning to your Father's house. He forgives you all your sins and wipes them away in your copious tears. Be still and enjoy the quiet that comes with a clean conscience."

Tardolini had more. "I've one request, Your Holiness, a request based not on selfishness but on the good of the Holy See. The men who visited me insist that Father Carlo Albanese...you remember the case?"

"Yes."

"They insist that he be permitted to return to the active ministry. If that does not happen, they will make my foolish and reprehensible actions known to the media."

"Who has been handling this case?"

"Cardinal Morretti."

"Fine. You inform him to take care of this in a speedy fashion, respecting my right to deniability. Morretti has been desirous of being appointed Secretary of State. I believe such an appointment would serve two purposes. First, he is perhaps the best man available for this position.

Second, he will insure that this delicate matter of Carlo Albanese, and your role in it, will be kept secret. The good of the Church demands this."

Tardolini knelt on the floor and kissed the Fisherman's Ring. "I cannot tell you how grateful I am. No words could express such heartfelt sentiments."

The Pope pressed a button that summoned a servant. "Bring my brother some fruit and some of our most precious wines."

Moments later a cart overflowing with grapes, peaches and melons was wheeled in. Its edges were wooden frames containing spaces for a selection of wine bottles and tall, elegant glasses rimmed in gold leaf. Folding tables of ebony were also brought in and set up in front of the couch.

There was sound at the door. A Papal Chamberlain entered the chamber and announced the arrival of Guilliermo Martini. "Your Holiness, the Prosecutor General."

The Pope moved toward the Reception Room entrance with open arms and a broad smile. "Good day, my dear Guilliermo. Welcome to our home again." Pointing to the fruit and wine, "Come, sit with us and enjoy nature's bounty." They embraced.

Guilliermo, comfortable with Presidents and Prime Ministers, froze in the presence of the Pontiff. His bushy eyebrows oscillated up and down almost touching his hairline.

Looking at Tardolini, Martini commented. "I did not know you had a visitor. Good day Monsignor."

"Good day."

The pope said: "You may discuss anything in front of my secretary."

"Fine. I've come to Your Holiness to apologize for having been misled in the case of Archbishop Pulaski. A conscientious person of great integrity supplied the information. However, as it turned out, it was incorrect. That happens many times in the course of an investigation. Human error."

"Yes, of course, my son. I understand."

"This information came to me only this morning, as I was meeting with my staff. So, I immediately terminated the investigation. There will be no calling of a Grand Jury. I'm sure this will be of great relief to Your Holiness."

"And to the Universal Church."

Martini was expansive. "Of which you are the true representative."

The Pope played with his pectoral cross. "Yes, this humble servant is entrusted with great responsibilities."

"I'd like to ensure Your Holiness that any and all files involved in this investigation will be destroyed by the end of this working day. My staff is under solemn obligation not to leak any details. Their responsibility is much graver in a case such as this, which was built on false reports."

The Pope blessed Martini as he spoke. "I thank you for your care and consideration, an attitude toward your work which I've always admired. I shall see to it that the President is made aware of the delicate and professional manner in which you conduct yourself."

"Thank you, Your Holiness."

The Pope continued to be cordial. "If all men acted in such a manner the world would be a much sweeter place in which to live. Don't you agree, Guilliermo?"

Raising his glass, "Absolutely, Your Holiness."

Tardolini chimed in. "It's the essence of a civilized society."

A papal Chamberlain entered without knocking and whispered in the ear of the Pope, who then turned to Martini, "The President of France is waiting for me in the next chamber. I want to thank you for bringing me news of such importance to the Vatican and the Church. I shall soon invite you and your family to enjoy a visit to the Vatican gardens."

Martini bowed and knelt to kiss the papal ring. "My family would be honored, Your Holiness."

The Pope then turned to Tardolini. "You know what you must do, Monsignor."

"Yes, Your Holiness." *This is the last time I shall see the Pope face to face. My life at the heart of the Church has ended with this meeting.* "And I thank you for everything."

The Pope, accompanied by a Papal Chamberlain, swept past the men. As he passed through the door, a Papal aide appeared through a side door of the reception room. "This way, gentlemen," as he led them into the passageway from which he had emerged.

As they walked into the sunshine and moved toward their respective cars, Tardolini reached for Martini's hand. "Goodbye my good friend of many years. God bless you and your family. I'll follow your career with great interest. Perhaps you'll one day honor our nation by accepting the nomination of the Party as President." The silence that enveloped them was pregnant with Tardolini's potential departure from the clerical scene, a scene he had dominated for fifteen years. Martini reflected, *How sad to see a giant fall. How tiny he seems, in retrospect.*

Tardolini reached his office just as Sister Rosalita was preparing to leave. "Can you stay a bit with me, Sister. I need to prepare some documents."

"Of course."

"Let's prepare a letter for Archbishop Pulaski. Please date it yesterday."

"Yesterday?"

Tardolini tried to sound casual. "Yes, I'm overdue sending it out."

"Go ahead." Rosalita prepared herself to take dictation.

August 22, 1947
Archbishop Gregory Pulaski
President
Vatican Bank
Vatican City
My dear Archbishop Pulaski:
I regret my tardiness in answering your letter of August 1, 1947. I am, on my own authority, dispatching today a letter to Cardinal Morretti. The letter will instruct the Cardinal to open negotiations with the Bishop of Denver, Colorado relative to the Carlo Albanese case.

Since I intend to take a leave of absence soon, may I take this occasion to wish you the very best in your work in the Lord's vineyard.

> Fraternally in the Lord's Service
> Monsignor Marcello Tardolini

Rosalita did not feign surprise, a fact noted by the Monsignor. *No shock, my dear? You've played a part in all this, have you not? Oh well, we are all damned, aren't we?*

"Now, a letter to His Holiness. Today's date."

August 24, 1947
His Holiness
Pope John XX
Papal Apartments
Vatican City

It is with great regret that I inform Your Holiness that I feel obliged to render my resignation as your Secretary. The years I have spent with you have been wonderful. The honor of standing with and assisting the Vicar of Christ on earth is a privilege that neither any other man nor I deserves.

> With deepest affection,
> Monsignor Marcello Tardolini

Rosalita continued her attitude of non-surprise. *This is her way of telling me that she shafted me. The Witch.*

"Sister, please call Cardinal Morretti and ask him if he can come to my office tomorrow morning at nine. Tell him it is a matter of great importance."

Tardolini handed Morretti a file. "I have for you a rather complete file on the matter of Carlo Albanese. I understand that you have already made a decision, but His Holiness asks if you might reconsider your decision in the light of new facts that have come to His attention."

Morretti was a Vatican insider. *The facts have nothing to do with this file. Tardolini is in trouble.*

"I'd be happy to look over the file, Monsignor. Flexibility in charity is a gospel virtue."

Tardolini was uncharacteristically gracious. "Permit me to accompany you to your car, Your Eminence."

Morretti was confident that this meeting was the first step in his appointment as Secretary of State. *One hand washes the other. I get the job, Tardolini is preserved from whatever trouble he has gotten himself into, and the pope gets his deniability. We're all happy.*

Morretti called Tardolini the next morning. "Monsignor, I've looked over the file. After considerable thought on the subject, I do believe that the priest in question could be, under prudent circumstances, permitted to exercise his ministry. He could, for example, assume a new name. The Bishop of Denver is a compassionate man, and, I believe, will cooperate with His Holiness."

"I'm grateful for your own understanding and compassion, Your Eminence."

Morretti put on his pious hat. "It is the essence of Christianity and the Gospel message."

Putting down the phone, Morretti remarked to his secretary. "Pulaski's fingerprints are all over this. You got to hand it to him; he gets thing done. All these pious guys who want his scalp, together, can't produce as much as this man. Carlo gets back to the priesthood. The Mafia is happy and continues their generosity to the church. The pope knows nothing about it. Tardolini gets booted out of the Vatican. I move over to the office of Secretary of State. Brilliant! My hat 's off to Pulaski."

"And his friends," referring to his Mafia connections.

"Correct. And his friends."

The Cardinal paused for a few moments to work out a strategy. "Call the Bishop of Denver and feel him out. I imagine he'll be glad to cooperate. He studied at the American College and is a good team player. He's being considered as Archbishop of San Francisco. That would mean a Cardinal's hat. His cooperation on this matter could ice it for him."

The telephone call to Bishop Sauer of Denver resulted in an agreement that Carlo would be invited to join the Diocese under an assumed name. The Bishop asked if the request could be put in writing, for his secret files. After consulting with Cardinal Morretti, the secretary said, "That's fine with His Eminence."

"Now that's real class," said the Cardinal. "He's willing to, but doesn't want any skeletons in his closet. He'll go far, that one."

The Cardinal's secretary soon had the letter ready. "Ah yes, that's just right. That should do it." The letter read:

August 23, 1974
Bishop Peter Sauer
Bishop's House
300 Adelaide Avenue
Denver, Colorado

Your Excellency,

Fraternal greetings from Rome. I write to you in the case of Father Carlo Albanese, a member of the clergy of the Archdiocese of New York. A series of family circumstances has put him in an untenable position vis-a-vis New York's Ordinary, Cardinal McManus.

Feeling the compassion of our Lord and Savior, I have decided, sub secreto, without consulting the members of this Sacred Congregation, to permit his return to the priestly ministry.

Father Carlo's notoriety in the media does not permit his return to the ministry under normal circumstances. I ask your Excellency, therefore, if you would permit him to work in your diocese under an assumed name.

Of course there is always the possibility that at some future date his presence in your diocese may be discovered. I want to assure you that should such an event occur, your position would be defended vigorously at the highest levels of the Vatican.

Your cooperation in this matter would be greatly appreciated and, at some future date, properly rewarded.

Yours in our Blessed Savior,
+ Pasquale Morretti
Cardinal Archbishop
Congregation of the Clergy

Nicco Laces cursed the bitter cold Chicago winter as he prepared to visit the Caruso nightclub that housed his office. As he was adjusting his wool-lined boots, the phone rang. It was Sister Rosalita. "Nicco, it's all over. Tardolini has resigned and the Public Prosecutor has agreed not to convene a Grand Jury. Our friend is saved."

"Thank God and the Blessed Virgin."

"And, Father Albanese is being restored to the priesthood."

Nicco was ecstatic. "Great news. Thank you so much for the role you played in all of this. The Archbishop must be happy."

"Oh yes!"

"The good guys won this time."

"They did."

Bruno Battaglia got the news from Nicco Laces. "Bruno, the matter has been taken care of. Carlo will be hearing from somebody soon. Give him my best."

Bruno tingled with excitement. "Hey, Nicco. You did it! You did it! Gratia! Carlo will be very grateful."

"Tell him I kept my word to Julio, and that makes me happy. As for you, my dear friend, it was payback time for all the things you've done for me."

"Why don't you get yourself made a Cardinal? Then, when we have a problem, we can call you direct, in the Vatican."

"Cardinal? I'm not even a priest!"

"You don't have to be a priest to be a Cardinal."

"You gotta be joking, Bruno. Right?"

"No, it's a fact. Any Catholic can be made a Cardinal."

"How is that?"

"Well, the way Julio explained it to me, being a Cardinal has nothing to do with ordination. It's an honor the Church gives to a guy for some great thing he did, or for some important job he does. It's got nothing to do with the priesthood."

"Well, I'll be damned."

Laughing, "That's not likely, with all the friends you have in the Vatican. Anyway, Nicco, stay in touch."

Once again the Mafia delivered justice where an institution failed.

Chapter Twenty Eight
COLORADO

Carlo was having breakfast in his apartment, while surveying the sloping land that made its way down to the Hudson River. It had snowed during the night. The hilly embankment was a smooth surface of white, uninterrupted by footfalls. Tree trunks reflected the patterns of fresh sprinkling snow. Early morning sun poured in through a large kitchen window, falling across the mosaic of black/white kitchen floor tiles, heightening the colors. The windowpanes ran in rivulets with condensed moisture, tiny islands of sparkling ice collecting at the bottom edges. The phone rang, breaking his concentration. He rocked to his feet from the swivel chair and picked up the receiver. The call was from Monsignor Louis Dolan, secretary to Peter Sauer, Bishop of Denver. "At your convenience, Father, I'd like to meet with you privately, in New York."

"Sure. I can see you any time. What would be a good day for you?"

"What about Monday? I've checked the flight schedules and can get into LaGuardia about 3 p.m.- United Airlines."

"Fine."

"Good. The Flight number is 303. Oh, Carlo, please keep all of this to yourself."

"No problem."

"I won't be dressed in clericals. Just look for a little bald guy with a Denver Bronco sweater."

"OK, see you."

Wet snowflakes fell outside his windows, splattering the maple branches with white streaks, and dissolving instantly as they touched the Hudson River's waters. Carlo slipped on a heavy sweater and headed for the path leading down to the river, admiring the snow-covered evergreens. The increasingly heavy snowfall, churned by a breeze, made him momentarily dizzy, as the swirling snowflakes moved in motion all around him. Flakes cooled his lips and he flicked his tongue to playfully absorb them, as the tree-swaying wind whipped around his face. He had succeeded in returning to the priesthood, but he had lost the love of his life. The price was almost unbearably heavy.

The flight from Denver arrived on time. Carlo spotted Monsignor Dolan as he emerged from gate seven. "Welcome to New York, Monsignor. Hope you had a nice flight."

The Monsignor tossed his copy of the Denver Times on the seat of an airport lounge chair. "Someone else can now enjoy this."

"Any luggage?"

"No. I return on a six o'clock flight. That gives us plenty of time to grab something to eat and take care of business."

"Do you like Chinese food?"

"Love it."

"Good, there's a restaurant not far from here with great food. I'll take you there."

The Monsignor was impressed that a young man with so much power, was willing to return to the priesthood, especially under the harsh conditions set by Rome. The Bishop himself remarked, "My guess is he'll turn out to be one of the best priests in the diocese. Let's face it Dolan, what he's doing takes courage and lots of faith. They say he's got a girlfriend now. That won't make it any easier for him. He's got guts."

At the Taipei restaurant the two men ordered and began their discussion.

"Carlo...can I call you Carlo?"

"Of course."

"Call me Louis"

"Right"

"Bishop Sauer got a call a couple of weeks ago from Cardinal Morretti of the Sacred Congregation of the Clergy. The Cardinal asked if he'd be willing to accept you into the Diocese. He explained all the circumstances. The Bishop responded affirmatively"

Carlo remained expressionless as the Monsignor continued. "The Cardinal laid down some conditions. You'd have to come into the Diocese under an assumed name. You'd have to agree not to contact anyone who might possibly reveal your identity to the general public."

The Monsignor paused, looking directly into Carlo's eyes. "Can I be straight with you, Carlo?"

"That's the way I want it."

"The word in Rome is that while you were running the Family business you ordered one or two assassinations. They don't want to have to deal that kind of publicity if it can be avoided. You know what I mean."

With emotion, Carlo said, "Listen Louis, I understand all this. I've always understood the problem the authorities had. I don't like living anonymously, but even if Rome had not made that a condition, I would want it anyway. It would be tough on parishioners who had to live with my real identity."

"Maybe impossible."

Carlo nodded. "Maybe impossible. Agreed."

"OK let me move into another subject. I'm not fishing for information here, so let me say what I have to say."

Carlo sipped his rice wine. "Of course, shoot."

"Cardinal Morretti says you've been seeing your deceased brother's wife." The Monsignor raised his hands, palms facing Carlo. "Don't want you to say anything. It's just that we'll assume at our end that you'll be coming to Denver with that business taken care of. Fair enough?"

"Fair enough."

The Monsignor ordered green tea. "We've got a nice little mountain parish picked out for you. The pastor there has been begging to retire, so he'll welcome you with open arms. The majority of the parishioners are military types; some of them are from the Air Force Academy, others from military installations in the area. The parish has a high percentage of young couples with small children, so a young pastor will delight them. I believe it's made to order for you."

Carlo had a question. "What if one day the people find out about me, then what?"

"A two-part answer to that, Carlo. First of all, the Diocese will not abandon you. Secondly, what happens at the parish depends on how the parishioners would react. Beyond that, Carlo, I'd be speculating. We'd have to play it by ear."

"That's fine."

Putting his right hand on Carlo's shoulder, he said, "Just remember, we will welcome you as a brother and we will stick by you. The Bishop is a man of his word. Solid gold. You'll like him."

Carlo felt comfortable. "How much time can I have to wind up my affairs?"

"How about a month - an extension if needed?"

"Fine."

The Monsignor wrote on his napkin. "This is my unlisted number. Call me any time, day or night. I'll chat with the present pastor and tell him we're expecting a replacement. He'll be delighted."

"Thanks."

" By the way, your new name will be listed in the Catholic Directory as coming from another Diocese. I've come up with a plan. Do you speak Italian fluently?"

"I do."

"Great. We're going to say that you're an American ordained for the Diocese of Naples. The Bishop there has released you to come to us because of our shortage. I think we'll get away with that. What do you say?"

"You ought to write mystery novels, Monsignor," Carlo said, laughing, and glancing at his watch.

"Time for us to go, Louis."

At the airport, Carlo expressed his appreciation. "Thanks a million. I won't let you down. I think I'm going to like Denver, I've got a friend there" he said, playfully bouncing his fist off The Monsignor's shoulder.

"You've got three! Myself, the Bishop and the pastor you're replacing!"

They waved goodbye as the Monsignor walked down the ramp that led to Gate Seven.

Chapter Twenty Nine
THE DEPARTURE

Lisa was angry with herself for having gulped three cups of coffee. It was not yet eight a.m. She had read warnings in the Ladies Home Journal about excessive coffee drinking but, as she complained to Carlo, "I just can't seem to kick the coffee habit." She was living in limbo, not knowing what direction Carlo's life would take. The previous night she dreamt about him. He appeared at her bedroom door, moved to the bed and swept her into his arms. She felt his strong hands spread wide against her back and shoulders. *I just want him. Why is he so hung up on the priesthood? Anglican priests marry; Methodist priests marry. No one criticizes them. It's that stupid celibacy thing.*

She was ready to be his mistress or his wife. *It's the uncertainty that bothers me.* Her apartment reflected her state of mind. Dishes piled in the sink. Two dresses draped on a kitchen chair. Shoes and slippers were scattered throughout every room.

"I'm a mess," she shouted at her mirrored reflection. "No husband, no lover, no goals!" She tossed a hand towel across the room, frightening her cat. The phone rang.

"Hi."

It was Carlo. "Hi. Glad you called. I was just feeling sorry for myself. What's up."

"Well, I've got a month left before I return to the priesthood. They worked it out somehow or other in Rome."

Lisa's nightmares took flesh. "Oh God! I kept hoping things might turn out differently. You know what I mean."

Carlo needed to soften the blow. "I can't say it's what I want. It's what I feel obliged to do. There is a difference."

"Is it a difference without a distinction?"

"No."

"I'll take your word for it." She thrust her jaw deep in the feather pillow. *Why can't life be simpler?*

"I wonder if we could take a ride to Greenwich and kinda talk about this - like how we will handle it - and all that."

Lisa clutched her dressing gown close about her neck, as an uncontrolled tear slid down her cheek. She pressed her fist hard against her lips.

"Are you there?"

Lisa composed herself. "Yes, yes, sorry. You took me by surprise, I guess. Yes, I can go to Greenwich. What time will you come by?"

"If we leave your place at eleven that gives us time to get to Greenwich for lunch. So, what about eleven?"

"That's fine. See you."

Lisa rose and paced the room, digging her fingertips into her temples. More tears trickled from her eyelids, hung for a moment on her eyelashes, then slowly made their way down her cheeks. The vibrations, which began as Carlo talked, lingered. Her eyes ran misty and her fingers trembled as she tried to remove her dressing gown. She felt she was hanging on the edge of life. *I promised myself that when the time came I was not going to make him feel guilty for leaving me. He made it all clear from the start. I'm behaving like a child.*

In frantic motions she moved a brush through her hair, gathering it in her hands and sliding it through a rubber band. In a last furtive look in her mirror, she drew a line of lipstick on her pursed lips, dressed in a daze, and left her apartment.

Carlo drove along Grand Central Parkway. He clutched his nape, tipped his head back, and inhaled deeply. The sense of impending loss buried itself deep within his psyche. He tingled to his nerves' ends with memories of those enchanted moments they had spent together. He crossed the Triboro Bridge and headed south to the 76th Street exit. A few moments later he reached Lisa's apartment. She was waiting for him by the curb, looking lost and lonely. As she entered the car he stole a glance, admiring the curve of her shoulder, the slim neck, the calm profile.

"It's hard to talk isn't it," he offered.

Lisa hesitated for a long moment, then brushed her open lips against his, and looked searchingly into his eyes. She felt like a bewildered child. "Yes, awful!"

The foreboding, anxiety and perplexity had been simmering for months; it was now boiling over. She wrapped it all up in, "It's so hard."

Her arms circled his neck.

Their eyes linked. Their time together was coming to a close. Lisa asked: "Have you thought about how it would be if we were married?"

Carlo nodded. "Yes. I've got to admit though that a lot of the thinking is sexual."

"That's OK That's men - the one track mind."

Pointing his finger at her, "True, but I'm on your track, nowhere else."

"I'm glad." She brushed his face with the tips of her fingers and pursed her lips. As he turned over the engine, he tugged himself loose from her eyes. The reality of parting was now pressing on them. "I guess we'd better go."

"It's hard."

He agreed. "More difficult than I've ever imagined - which was already bad enough."

"Oh God," Lisa cried, and then quickly controlled her voice.

They embraced, exchanging heart-rending emotions. "I'll miss you terribly, Carlo."

"And I ...well...I can't express how difficult and lonely it will be. I can't say what I'm doing is right. I can only say I'm driven. I..."

She put a soft finger to his lips. "It's OK. I'll always be here for you. Always!" She leaned towed him and pressed her thin lips on his cheek.

Silence enveloped them. He had so many things he wanted to say, but the ride to Greenwich passed with very little conversation. He knew she belonged to him and him alone. He stared straight ahead. *My mind is trying to catch up with my emotions, but I don't think it ever will.*" He did not look at her. "I will do my duty, but I will never be happy again."

"Even though you know I love you?"

He paused. "Perhaps I should have said I'll never be completely happy again. Never."

"Me too. Never...unless..."

"Unless we get together one day?"

"Yes."

"It may become impossible to live apart. Time will tell."

She wanted him to say that he already knew it would be impossible. She felt that way and believed he also did. But she remained silent. *Is he afraid to be who he is? Was the seminary such an insulated existence that he became an image not of himself but of some abstract "priest?"* In Vieques they had looked deeply into each other's souls, making it no longer possible that a veil could now fall between them.

The Showboat restaurant hugged Greenwich's shoreline. The blue Atlantic waters softly lapped the dining room's glass-enclosed East wing. Moored motor boats lay in undisturbed in the silky water. Two sailboats, gently swaying in the breeze, were being prepared for a trip. Inside the dining room sparkles of ocean-reflected sunshine tantalizingly played around the edges of glass and dinnerware. The owner, Michael Doyle, an Irish-American of charm and hospitality, took great pride in the various species of orchids that decorated and perfumed his establishment. Here, the rich and famous came to pamper themselves with the unrivaled cuisine. He was at the bar as Carlo and Lisa entered, and rushed to greet them at the slate-floored foyer. "Welcome, Carlo. I'm sorry I could not attend your brother's funeral. I didn't even know about it. I was in the Bahamas looking into investing in of those time-share things."

Carlo dipped his head in Doyle's direction. "I know, Michael. We got your letter. Appreciate your sentiments - you know Lisa?"

"Yes, of course. I never forget a pretty face! I met her at some baptism or other. Don't remember exactly."

Carlo did not reply to that, so Michael extended his hands. "How are you my dear?"

Lisa did not remember him but was diplomatic. "I'm well. Good to see you again."

Michael leaned forward. "This one's on me, Carlo. I suggest you order the shrimp scampi we've cooked up today." With a flourish of arms, "Drop by anytime. The staff knows you. They'll take care of you. I've got to visit the dentist. Getting old. Enjoy the meal."

"Thanks, Michael."

After several pregnant moments of silence, during which they studied each other's expressions looking for clues, Lisa sliced through the somber mood. Her arms created tiny eddies of swirling air. "Let's be happy. We haven't died. The one naughty thing I'm asking you to do is to keep in touch somehow, even if they tell you otherwise. Agreed?" She gripped his hand for anchoring.

"Agreed."

They ordered the shrimp scampi and steamed crab claws.

Lisa's stomach churned as she kept the tensions she felt inside, not wishing to spoil his day. She was tempted to shout out he was abandoning her. She knew it wasn't true, but the frustration overwhelmed her. *I must control myself. He feels as badly as I do. Don't make it worse for him!* She took a deep breath, released it slowly, and smiled.

Carlo related the details of his meeting with Monsignor Dolan, the help given by Nicco and the maverick Archbishop in the Vatican. The waiters rolled their cart to the table. The shrimp scampi smothering mounds of linguine absorbed their attention immediately. The waiters poured a red Chilean wine into their glasses, and withdrew. Lisa half turned away, glancing at a passing yacht, her perfect profile outlined against the sparkling waters. "I don't want you to worry about me, Carlo. Love and pain go together, I guess. We can't isolate them. But I'm strong. Don't worry about me."

"That's a sweet lie." Carlo leaned over and touched her cheek. The relationship with Lisa had been such a revelatory experience - his first-ever encounter with love, with the psychology of a woman. He put his hand over his heart. "You're right here."

She ventured. "Carlo, I want to ask you about God. I mean, it kinda seems that God, for you, is located in this institution, the Catholic Church. Your loyalty, forgive me, seems wrong somehow." She paused, and then, "Do you mind my saying that?"

Carlo shook his head. "Not at all, and maybe you are right. What is your idea of God?"

Lisa was happy for the opportunity. "I think I've seen God, felt him, and followed him many times, but he never looks the same. He's the bird I picked up after he was wounded in a rainstorm, then died in my hand. He's the beaten mother with breast cancer who walked two miles in the winter rain carrying her asthmatic boy to see a doctor, jolting me out of my whining as I sit in a warm room griping about some stupid thing or circumstance. He's Bob Dylan's brain."

Carlo leaned back, spread his fingers over his shock of hair and said, "I think you have a lot to teach me about God. I think women know all about God, and we preach about Him."

"Carlo, there are two of you; perhaps there are two of all of us. You got me thinking about things, like philosophical things."

Carlo smiled, "Who are the two?"

"Well, there is the Carlo Albanese who is almost passionately devoted to his vocation, even if it interferes with his real life. I mean, for example, that although the family needs you, the priest thing is more important on a kind of philosophical level."

Carlo was curious. "The other me?"

"The other you is the man who bases his actions on principles rather than some of that doggerel you hear from the pulpit. There is a clash at some point, but that's the gut feeling I have. I really can't explain it at all."

Carlo expelled an audible breath and made a suggestion. "You know what? You just said some very important things. You are speaking the female view of the world. It's in contrast to the male view, but you sure get to me with it. I need time to absorb it. In the meantime, let's finish this delightful meal, enjoy the wine and keep our fingers crossed that everything will sort itself out." He looked at her with a broad smile, his white teeth standing out against his tan.

His voice and smile raised the gooseflesh on her skin. "You're on!" she said, her eyes filled with things she had not yet mentioned.

During the ride back to Manhattan they sang along with the radio music. The disc jockey played an old Frank Sinatra love song. "I only have eyes for you." Darkness had already fallen. The headlights splashed a cone of light against the darkness. They were sealed off from the rest of the world, aware of each other's thoughts. How could they not? Here they were, driving into the lonely land of separation.

Lisa rested her head against the seat. Her lips were moist, her head leaned to one side; her half-closed eyes rested on Carlo. She tried to say something, but only her lips moved. The soft hissing sound of the tires hummed in the background.

"I like your perfume."

"It's Joy. I wear it only for you. I threw out all my old stuff."

"Thanks."

Lisa felt that a door had been closed behind her. The shared confidences, the being-there-for-each-other, the love expressed - all of this was about to come to an end. She was devastated. She stared out the window, vacantly, thinking about things she had lost.

He pulled up to the curb in front of her apartment building, shut off the engine and stared through the windshield. More silence. Then he propped his chin on the palm of his hand and stared at her. She stared back. A few moments went by as they caught the pain reflected in each other's eyes.

"Let me walk you up the steps," he said.

"Please."

They moved along the sidewalk and up the steps, hip to hip, heads bowed and leaning on each other's shoulders. He suddenly backed up to the edge of the step, pulled her to him and held her tightly. In this wrenching moment their eyes spoke volumes of their need for each other. At the apartment door, she suddenly burst into tears, broke loose from his grip, and ran into the apartment foyer without looking back. He stood alone, watching her nervously punching the elevator button, then disappearing into its moving enclosure. *Goodbye sweet love.*

Carlo moved the car from the curb slowly, not wanting to leave. He pulled into a gas station two blocks from the apartment and, in a sudden impulse, sped away, back to Lisa's. He rushed into the building, startling the doorman. "I'd like to visit Ms. Jackson (the pseudonym she chose to avoid being discovered by Nicky), please. I'm Mr. Albanese."

The doorman made the call, then turned and said. "You may go right up, Mr. Albanese."

When Carlo reached the apartment, the door was slightly ajar. "Come in, Carlo."

They rushed into each other's arms. "I couldn't leave without holding you," he said.

"I had given up hope."

"It's irresponsible."

"Love can't be irresponsible. Besides, I want you."

He reached out to her, pulled her to his chest, and kissed her full on the mouth. "You'll have to teach me."

She felt his anxiety. "Just hold me. It'll come naturally." Her mouth went dry as she froze in anticipation.

"This is the real world," she said. "The rest is imaginary."

With a nod he agreed, and added, "Our world is right here, in this embrace. Why is it we have to do other things, go other places? Be apart!"

"Is it necessary?"

His organized and competent personality had run up against the barrier of ambiguity and he did not know how to respond. "I think so, but I honestly don't know why. What purpose does my leaving serve?"

"None, as far as I'm concerned."

Carlo offered his own thinking. "I wish I could feel that way. I mean, with conviction. I don't"

"I know."

"Am I cursed to do my duty?"

Lisa lowered her head. "You have to find that out."

"Yes."

It was his first experience. She put her arms around his neck and held him to her bosom, kissed his face and hands. Tears streaked down her cheeks, the reflection of awareness that in the midst of this dream-come-true she was kissing him goodbye.

"Don't cry," he whispered into her ear. "Somehow, everything will be OK." He felt inadequate in expressing his feelings. Covering her forehead with his lips, he said, "I don't know what I should say. This is so new to me. I can only say that I love you."

She simply responded with a purring "Mmm."

In the depths of their eyes each could see the joy and the pain the other was experiencing. They were locked into a space of exquisite harmony. Silence hovered overf the room as they held each other and fell asleep. He awoke in the early hours, leaned on his elbow and watched her calmness. She was at peace with the world.

Chapter Thirty
THE PAIN OF LOSS

Carlo made his way along thick-trunked cedars, down the trail that led to the small stream bordering the lower part of the church property that sat astride Colorado's U.S. Route Six. Meter was a small town, with low-roofed buildings and friendly shops that sold expensive clothing, coffee and apple pie. The terrain nestled in the rugged and hilly Colorado Mountains. Mulled cider and draft beer were the town's favorite drinks. Located south of Denver, where the mountains meet the plains, Meter had the distinction of being the smallest and most remote town in the Diocese. The parish of St. Agatha's was small but affluent. Just beyond the outskirts of town quail strutted like pullets. Carlo's newly-acquired dog, Possum, rolled onto his back like a June bug waiting to be turned over. "You just want to be hugged, don't you, you spoiled brat."

Carlo's thoughts, provoked by the pine tree perfumed air and the sparkling sunshine, were of Lisa and the love they had shared together. Her face floated in and out of his memory bank. Since his arrival he continued to prepare himself for life without her, but he made no real progress. There were days when he became so obsessed with images of her that his fist tightened, as he struggled to remain at his post rather than abandon the parish and rush to New York. The almost physical presence was unsettling, even painful. Her body, in every detail remained etched in his imagination.

As he drove and walked along the countryside, he thought of what life would be like with a married priesthood. He imagined a little stone house in the hills, among aromatic pines. There, he would visit his loved one every day, enriching his soul and absorbing her love. *Today makes eight months since we made love.* His love had not diminished; it had deepened. He received an occasional phone call and inevitably asked the same question, "Have you met anyone yet?"

"Still waiting for you," she would say. Once she added. "I consider myself your faithful spouse, and you mine. We love each other. You know, I used to have women friends. Going out with them helped to absorb the pain of living with Nicky. With you it's the pain of loss. I don't need girl friends for that; I need mostly to be by myself. Maybe it's not good for me, I don't know, but without you I need to be alone."

He muttered a brief, "Yes, I'm the same way."

Movingly, she said, "I miss you so much."

He was quick to respond, "Missing each other is part of what love is all about. No love, no real missing. It's the price we pay for the joy of it."

This particular evening, he prepared himself a small dinner to celebrate their relationship. He immersed himself in thoughts of holding her against his chest, burying his face in her loosely falling hair. Locked in an attaché case in his bedroom were more than twenty photos of Lisa. They constituted a chronicle of their time together. Lisa, with her luggage at the Vieques airport. Lisa standing on tip toes, peering into Macy's windows. Lisa bending over, her head appearing between her legs. Lisa dancing on a Connecticut stone wall, in the wooded outskirts of Darien. Lisa, Lisa and more Lisa. He was experiencing intense loneliness for the first time in his life. As he strolled aside the stream he read a letter from her he had received that morning.

Dearest Carlo

The night is falling into blackness and the new dawn will approach before these eyes open. I sleep to sail yet another day in your sea of love. I remain completely enchanted with your essence. I know all is on hold for what you assume are practical reasons. For me, the circumstances mean little except for the closeness. You remain essential to every breath I take. God's peace to us this night of stars

Love to you as ever.

His parishioners knew him as Father Anthony Marino. The Diocesan files identified him as a priest ordained for the archdiocese of Naples "who generously responded to the needs of the Diocese of Denver." The file had been prepared in Rome, in a small office overlooking St. Peter's Square. It was handed personally to the Bishop of Denver, in the office of the Vatican Secretariat. The Bishop was instructed never to reveal, even to a close confidant, the background of the latest addition to his clergy. As the bishop was leaving his office, Cardinal Morretti said, "I understand the Holy Father has seriously considered you as Ordinary for the great archdiocese of San Francisco. You will be hearing from us on that matter as soon as the diocese becomes vacant."

That was the payoff.

When first assigned to the remote parish, Carlo frequently failed to respond to his new name. His flock at first believed he had a hearing problem. Occasionally he would accept an invitation to dinner, but added little to the conversation. "Nice but remote" summed up the parish's evaluation of their quiet pastor. They did not complain. For years they had been saddled with an old and sickly pastor who preached anti-communism every Sunday. Captain Johnson, Chairman of the parish council, observed, "That's hardly a problem in a military parish."

Carlo wanted to focus his energies on the parish, but wondered if it would ever happen. He felt alienated from his heritage, the Italian cultural life of New York City. This had been the wellspring of his energy, the milieu in which he lived and breathed naturally. The previous six months he had heard only from one friend from the past. (Other than Lisa and his mother). Bruno Battaglia called to speak in general terms about several initiatives the Family had taken since his departure, the favorable settling of three court cases against men in the Family, and two that had gone badly. Three of the men convicted of tax violations. This drew a comment from Carlo.

"Bruno, when will the guys learn that ever since Al Capone, the Feds have used tax evasion as a means of getting inside the various Families. The one thing they should not do is fool around with tax returns!"

"I tell them all the time, Carlo, and most of the men go along, but, you know, there are always exceptions."

Carlo agreed. "Yes, I know, but maybe you have to keep reminding them. It's very important."

Less than a month after that phone call, Bruno called again. "Gotta talk to you, Carlo. Can I come out?"

"Of course. When?"

"Tomorrow. I've already checked on flights. I can get to Denver about two in the afternoon. I'll rent a car and be out at your place about three thirty."

"Sounds good." *For nearly a year this guy's been looking after my mother as if she were his own. I owe him a big debt of thanks.*

Bruno's face was one big smile. "Carlo, you look great, but we sure as hell miss you."

"Me too, friend. I often think of you and wonder if you still eat too much." Glancing at his stomach, "I see you do."

"I'm on a new diet, Carlo. I skip the main meals and eat only desserts. It's great!"

"I don't give a damn what you eat. It's just nice seeing you." He tapped him lightly on his cheeks. "Your flight?"

"Boring."

Carlo found himself appraising Bruno - black shoes shining with a high gloss, his expensive Brook Brothers coat, and his miniature horse cufflinks. "Tell me, how's the Family?" Then, after a pause and focusing better, "Bruno, you haven't told anyone where I am, have you?"

Bruno shook his head. "No. People are pulling their hair out wondering where the hell you are. The Daily News is going bananas. One wise-guy reporter called me up and said the newspaper would offer me a bundle if I told them where you are."

Laughing, "That coulda taken care of you for life."

"I wouldn't give those guys the time of day. That goes for the Vatican also."

"How so?"

Bruno moved his chair closer. "Personally, Carlo, I don't like the way the Vatican handled this case. Sure, they let you back into the priesthood. Big deal! They shoulda never have thrown you out in the first place. These Vatican guys always get their pound of flesh, don't they? And they talk about usury!"

"I agree, but all of us do things like that sometime."

Bruno stretched the palms of his hands. "Yeah, but we don't pretend to be pious monks."

"Got a point there." Carlo changed the subject. "The kids?"

"Well, the three kids are doing well in college. They keep me busy writing checks, especially Gene. He's got a girlfriend with expensive tastes." Bruno reached into a plastic bag he was carrying. "I brought you some canoli. Not easy to get in Denver. How do people out here survive on this lousy food?"

Carlo held his forehead in his hands. "We just suffer, that's all, suffer!"

Bruno laughed. "Imagine big-sinning Italians getting to heaven because they live in the boondocks where they can't get Italian pastry?" Carlo turned serious, expressing his inner turmoil. "Bruno, I've missed New York terribly, and the family even more. Sometimes I wonder if I did the right thing, you know."

The words trailed off abstractedly, so Bruno did not comment, but it was sweet music to his ears. *Maybe he'll come back.*

Carlo poured the coffee and took the initiative. "Well, Bruno, you said you wanted to come out here to talk. Fill me in. How's Frankie doing? Lisa? The Family? I want an honest answer, not something sugar-coated."

Bruno nodded. "Glad you said that, Carlo, because I had two answers ready for you. One was sugar-coated, the other, bare bones." For twelve months he had faithfully adhered to the agreement made almost a year before: "Bruno, once I leave for Colorado I don't want to know anything about the Family except baptisms, birthdays and funerals. I want you to promise." Now he could speak out. It was report-card time. He reached into his pocket. ""Here's a note for you from Lisa."

Carlo placed it in his shirt pocket. "Thanks. I'll read it later. Now, give me a summary."

Bruno pressed his knuckles and thinned his lips. "Carlo, not all the news is good."

Carlo sat still, not wishing to interrupt the thoughtful pause that followed.

"Carlo, Frankie's loved by the fellas, but they don't respect the way he runs the organization. That's the heart of the problem. He just doesn't have it, Carlo. He just doesn't have it." Touching Carlo on his right sleeve, "You and I both thought he was an excellent choice. Frankly, Carlo, he was the best we had, but not good enough."

"Don't be shy about giving it to me straight, Bruno. Between you and me, never a problem. Right?"

"Right."

"Continue."

"Well, that damn DA Guilliani is picking us off one at a time since he started applying the RICO statute to the Families. Not just us, Carlo, members of Families all over the Tri-State area are doing time. But we're doing the worst because Frankie doesn't know how to handle things. Sometimes he panics; other times you can't get him to move. He's over his head."

"Doesn't he listen to your advice, or what? I don't understand."

"Oh God, yes, he does, hours and hours of it, but it's the application, the application, Carlo. He just doesn't know how to put things together. I can lead him to water but I can't make him drink. Know what I mean?"

"Yeah, I do."

Bruno twisted his face and took a deep breath. "And the damn thing, what makes it so hard, is that he's got the brains, the devotion. He's a good underboss, Carlo, not a take-charge person. You can't get blood out of a stone. Now you see why Julio needed you. Not because he didn't respect your wishes, or the priesthood. Nothing like that. He saw you're the only one for the job. Simple as that, Carlo. Call it ironic, call it crazy, call it God's will but that's the way it was. It's like you want to remain faithful to your calling, but something much larger than yourself keeps intervening."

"Guess I was being selfish."

Bruno stabbed his cheek. "No. You've wanted to be a priest since you were a kid. But, the Family's in bad shape. You're needed. Get it? Simple."

"How're the other Families reacting to our situation?"

Bruno sipped at his coffee before answering. "Good question. In matters like this, Carlo, there's a respectable mourning time. Nobody wants to offend either Julio or you. But, about a year has gone by and we're quietly losing our clout. Some of our guys have gone over to other Families. It's kinda like death-by-slow-motion. The mourning period is just about over, Carlo. Things may start heating up any time now. I mean one or two of the Families could start moving in on our territory and, even worse, attracting some of our guys. Carlo, let's face it. It's tough to be on a dull and going nowhere team."

"You have any ideas, Bruno?"

"Just one, I'm afraid."

"Oh, oh, I'd better get myself ready for this one."

"Carlo, come back and pull this thing together. Make it work."

"That's hard."

Shifting his body in the chair and wiping a sweating forehead, Bruno spoke softly. "Carlo, you asked for the facts. I've given them to you. As consiglieri, I'd have to say you gotta get back in the ring. That's it."

Carlo's response was brief. "Thanks, Bruno. I appreciate your honesty."

The gravity of what Bruno said meant a whole new round of soul searching. "Bruno, I need time to think. I need to visit with my mother. When I do, we'll talk some more."

Bruno looked at his watch. "Gotta get out to the airport." He embraced Carlo. "What can I say? I'm so happy to have spent a few hours with you."

"Mm. Yeah". *I'd like to shout, don't go. Stay with me. You're my only touch with the real me.*

"I got lots to think about, Bruno. Give my love to the family. I'll see you - and them - soon."

"God bless, Carlo. I'm no prayer-wheel, but I'll light a couple of candles to the Madonna for you."

Before retiring, Carlo tore open Lisa's letter:

Carlo,

I just returned from a quick trip to Italy. I think we young ones in the family can better understand our parents if we see where they came from. I have been to Firenze, meandered in Milano, voyaged in Venice, and toured the seven "wolved" hills of Rome.

I have prayed in cathedrals and basilicas. Knelt at roadside shrines and traveled along rivers, canals, and vineyards. I have watched pheasants strut, walked under umbrella pines, and watched the halting steps of newborn goats. I have witnessed the remains of ancient civilizations and seen stolen New World gold gild countless vaulted ceilings. I have walked among the dead in catacombs, drank wine in Pontesieve, listened at La Scala and seen frescoes and mosaics, paintings, and sculpture by the thousands. It was beyond description and utterly incredible. The history provoked, the buildings inspired, and the people lent their warmth and graceful charm. This is where we come from. This is who we are, and we've somehow spoiled it all. So, my dear Carlo, I understand your mission. It's just how it affects selfish me that's the problem.

Love,

Your returned traveler

With a heaving sigh, he laid the letter aside and unlocked his attaché case. He chose a photo of Lisa and placed it on the bed-stand. He could hear a deep-throated howl of a coyote in the distance. It framed his mood. He lay on the bed and switched on the bed-stand light. It provided just enough glow to highlight Lisa's face and shoulders. Vivid images of the past forced themselves into view. He spoke to her, "Let me take you to bed as I always do - wrapped in my thoughts and heart if not my arms. God watch over us both and keep all devils away." He missed her intensely, feeling the loss in the pit of his stomach. He recalled her unswerving devotion, the physical and emotional attention she lavished on him, the time spent in Vieques, in Darien, Connecticut, the visits to each other's apartments. He felt sharp pangs of guilt for having abandoned her. Once again he was not sure of himself. He had difficulty drawing a self-portrait because he lacked a model for his situation. He would have to continue reaching down into his psyche, discovering his real self, his hidden nature. *What is the right thing to do? I haven't found the answer in textbooks or in the Ten Commandments. The answer is inside me, I know, and I haven't found it yet. It's all too murky; I'll keep praying for light, for clarity. At times, he felt like a child looking at his own belly button.* He only knew that he must be true to himself, even if cast him into the role of 'outcast.' He fell asleep glancing at Lisa's image.

When Bruno returned; to New York, his wife asked, "Did you tell him?"

"Yeah, I did."

"How'd he take it?"

"Honestly, Nancy, he's got the instinct. He wasn't surprised. He suspected things were bad. He's feeling guilty for leaving us. I'd swear to it. He's sad. There is a part of the guy that always wanted to be a priest and will always want to be a priest. The stars have dealt him a lousy hand. What can I say?"

"It was your duty. You had to do it."

"Yeah, big consolation; it's like winning the dummy prize."

That night Bruno slept very little. He wondered how it would all turn out.

Chapter Thirty One
LOVE CHILD

Two months after Carlo's departure, Lisa suspected she was pregnant. She stopped menstruating, but her periods were so irregular she waited for more signs. They came. Her breasts enlarged and were tender to the touch. A woman of energy, she now experienced long periods of fatigue. *Could it be I've carrying Carlo's child? Is it possible? Oh God, I pray it's true.*

She visited Chick Brennan at his clinic. Chick was not her family doctor, but she felt comfortable with him. She explained. "Sometimes I have a period once in three months and, at other times, two periods in one month. Some are heavy and some are light. I've been told this is because I don't ovulate every month. My breasts are sore. I feel nauseated quite often. I'm tired and I feel bloated."

"Obviously, Lisa, you must have had sex recently or you wouldn't be asking if you are pregnant."

"Right."

"How long ago?"

"Two months ago."

Brennan decided, "I think I'd better do a pelvic examination on you. OK?

"Yes, of course."

Chick sent for a nurse. "Ms. Carlyle will take you to the GYN room. I'll join you shortly."

In the GYN room Ms. Carlyle pointed to the examining table. "Miss, lay down." She helped her place her feet in stirrups and draped her legs with a white sheet.

Chick Brennan entered the room. "I'm going to examine you now. Just relax." After a few moments into the pelvic examination, he asked. "Does this hurt you right here?"

"A little."

Chick examined her. "What about this spot?"

"No."

"You can get dressed. I'll see you in the office."

Lisa was hopeful. *Please God, let me be pregnant. Part of Carlo will always be with me. Please God!*

Chick offered her a seat next to his desk. "Lisa, you have a cyst on your left ovary. This could be due to a number of reasons. What we need is a urine test. That will give us more information. If the test is positive, we'll know you're pregnant."

"I understand."

Chick sent for the nurse. "Ms. Carlyle, please run a pregnancy test on Lisa's urine. Do the Icon II type."

"And if you are pregnant, Lisa, will that make you happy?"

"Oh my, yes."

"Glad to hear that."

"You haven't asked me who the father might be."

Brennan felt he knew the answer, but left her an opening not to discuss that. "Should I?"

"Well, I'm family, you know."

"True, but let's wait for the results. OK?"

Lisa smiled and winked. "You're so cautious."

Laughing. "That's what I get paid for, my dear. Medicine's not a game of checkers, you know."

The nurse returned with the results. Chick glanced at the lab report. "The test is positive."

"I'm pregnant!" Lisa shouted.

"Not so quick, my dear."

"Yes, but there's more to it than that."

"What?"

"I need to know if it's an ectopic pregnancy. We need one more test."

"Which?"

Brennan explained. "A sonogram, on your abdomen. That will locate the exact position of the baby."

The nurse prepared Lisa. "Miss Carlyle, I didn't know getting pregnant was so complicated."

Joking. "Oh, getting pregnant is not complicated; it's what happens after."

Once again, Lisa stretched out on an examining table. "Lisa, I'm putting some ultrasonic jelly on your stomach. Then I'll place this probe on the stomach and slide it up and down. If you watch the monitor over there, you'll see what I'm seeing."

"Help me if you see anything, Chick. It all looks kinda fuzzy to me."

"That's your uterus. Oh, there it is."

"What?"

"You see this little pea-sized mass? It's pulsating. See it?"

Lisa, excitedly, "Yes."

"That's the baby's heart."

"Is the baby in the right place?"

"It's right where it belongs...in your uterus. Congratulations."

Lisa rushed her words. "In other words I'm going to have a normal pregnancy - a normal child?"

Brennan spoke firmly, and with a chuckle. "Yes."

Lisa clasped her hands in prayer. "Thank you, Jesus. Thank you." She paused and glanced out the office window. "It's Carlo's child, you know. I am so very happy!"

Brennan feigned a surprise look. "Well, if you're happy, that makes everybody happy. Are you going to tell him?"

Lisa shook her head and glanced down. "No. He's just returned to the priesthood. We made love once. We didn't really think about it. It just happened. I don't want to put any pressure on him. I'm happy to have his child. I'm not insisting on anything. I'll tell him when the time is right."

"When will that be?"

"I don't know, but it'll happen."

Chick mused. *She's got a lot of wisdom for her age. I wonder how he's going to react to this.* "Now let's get down to business. There are a few things you need to know."

Lisa cupped her ears and said. "I'm all ears."

"You're gonna start feeling different."

"I already do."

"Right. The baby's has to be nourished, so you're going to have more blood in your system. This is going to increase your heart beats. Your nipples are going to get dark around the edges. Your kidneys are going to start pumping faster. That means more trips to the bathroom. The baby's going to get territorial. It'll start pushing things around, including your colon, so there's going to be constipation."

Lisa winced. "Ouch, got any good news?"

"Yeah."

Lisa spread her arms. "Tell me, please."

Pointing his finger at her, "You're going to be exquisitely happy."

"I am, already. Anything else?"

Brennan cupped his chin in his fist. "There's going be some stretch marks on your tummy and your breasts. You may even get a few dark spots on your face. It's all normal stuff. Part of being pregnant."

"I hate dark spots. I'm going to hate them."

"What about weight? Can you handle up to thirty more pounds?"

Lisa sounded a slightly sarcastic note. "I don't have anyone to look pretty for. I can handle it."

"There's one more thing."

"Yes?"

"There's gonna be a lot of hormone activity going on. This can affect your mood."

"I'm already moody."

"All women are. It just gets worse during pregnancy."

"That's a sexist statement."

"That's a fact."

"OK I need you, Chick, so I won't argue. I've hardly been nauseous. Is that normal?"

"You're lucky to be in the fifty percent who don't have a problem with that. Congratulations."

"Anything else?"

"Yes, I'd like to see you in two weeks. At that time we can take a blood sample and send it to the lab for a pre-natal screen. This will tell me about the condition of your blood. For now, I'm going to write you a prescription for pre-natal vitamins and folic acid. The nurse will give you a container so you can bring me a urine sample every time you come for a check-up. Now, you're free to go home."

"Thanks, Chick. I appreciate everything."

"See you in two weeks."

"In two weeks."

Lisa had never been happier. *Today is the first day of the rest of my life. I'm going to have a baby! I'm going to have Carlo's baby. I'll never be unhappy again. Never!*

From that time onward, Lisa made frequent visits to Chick Brennan's office to have herself weighed, her blood pressure taken and occasional blood and urine tests.

It had been almost nine months since Carlo moved to Colorado. He was oppressed by what was, for him, a foreign culture, almost a foreign nation. He never imagined that it would be so difficult. He had returned to the priesthood, isolating himself from a large part of his real life. He now realized that this had been a big mistake. Idealism, yes, but not a reflection of his persistent reality as a member of the Albanese family. He had, perhaps mistakenly, identified his priesthood with what he saw as "the right thing to do." In spite of all the conventional wisdom to the contrary, perhaps it was not the right thing to do. As he reviewed Father Maxwell's words he began to feel that Maxwell would have advised him not to return to clerical living. Maxwell had dug deeper. Perhaps what he was saying was, "Yes, remain in the priesthood, but not in the clerical life!"

Father Francis had no doubt about Carlo's vocation as priest. Father Adolfo had once cautioned him. "Do not identify 'priesthood' with 'clerical life.' He now saw more clearly that they had to be separated. He had, unconsciously, accepted the institutional definition of "priest," i.e., one who lives the clerical life style. *The apostles were very definitely priests, but not one of them lived a clerical lifestyle. That lifestyle, in fact, was severely criticized in Jesus' attack on the Pharisees and Sadducees.* Seeping into his consciousness was a clear realization that he needed to return to New York. He needed to be in touch with his entire self. He was more than his clerical identity. He needed to resolve, once and for all, where his duty lay. *My work here is totally joyless. Do I continue with this kind of work simply so I don't disappoint all those who helped me return to the priesthood?* Bruno's visit brought out clearly that the Family had been suffering from honest but poor leadership. Was he able to simply wipe his hands clean of this because he wanted to a "priest"? He was beginning to have serious doubts. He would return home for a visit and make his decision in the bosom of his family. He was unaware that events taking place in New York at that moment would soon sweep him up once again into the mainstream of Family activity.

Lisa was nearing term. Her stomach was round and firm. She had been experiencing mild contractions for more than a month. Chick Brennan called frequently to check on her. He insisted she take vitamins and skim milk regularly and encouraged her to engage in muscle-relaxing exercises. On the day her water broke, she called Bruno. "I have to go to the hospital. I'm ready."

"I'll be right there, with my wife."

"Don't speed. I'm OK"

"I'll speed anyway."

He called Chick Brennan, who said: "She's about two weeks early, but the baby's fine. Strong heartbeat. Another healthy Albanese. I'll see you at the hospital. She'll probably have the baby in about fourteen hours."

Bruno waited in the lobby for Chick's arrival. They rode up the elevator together. Bruno was concerned. "Chick, shouldn't we call Carlo? Doesn't he have a right to know his child is being born? What do you think?"

"Sure, but in this case it's not so easy. I think the best thing is to talk it over with Lisa. Let her decide."

Chick entered the room first. "You even look pretty in hospital clothes."

"Thanks, Chick."

He held her hand and tousled her hair. "I'm so happy for you, Lisa. I know this child means a lot to you."

"It's a real love child, Chick."

"I know." He took her pulse. "Just breathe normally, nice and steady. Don't let the excitement throw you off your rhythm. Stay cool"

"You kidding? You mean like nothing's happening to me?"

"Do your best, darling. The nurse tells me that the fetal heart tones are fine. I'll put a fetal monitor on you so we can keep track of the baby's condition while you're in labor."

"Thanks, Chic, I hope I'm not being too much trouble."

He ran his hand over through her hair. "You're a princess. By the way, Bruno wants to see you. I'll get him."

An obstetric stethoscope dangled just above Lisa's forehead, as the labor-room nurse gave her instructions. Sweat covered her forehead and neck. She could feel the beads of sweat sliding down her face and shoulders.

"You're more than three centimeters dilated. Doing fine."

"Good." She didn't understand, but it sounded reassuring.

Bruno came in. After giving Lisa a hug, he put his large hands on her shoulders and said, "Please, Lisa, let me call Carlo. It's his baby. He should know about this. Please."

"Not now, Bruno. If he sees me like this he'll feel sorry for me and want to leave the priesthood to take care of me. You understand? Don't you think I want him standing right here beside me? Of course I do. Every woman wants that. But, I want to tell him when we're comfortable, at home, in a calm atmosphere. Not under pressure."

Hesitantly, "Well, maybe you're right. I don't know." Laughing, "Anyway, this isn't the moment for a long, philosophical discussion."

Later that day Chick whispered to Bruno. "Time for you to leave, fella. She's just about ready to deliver. Why don't you go home and stay by the phone. I'll get you here in a hurry if we need you."

Bruno commented, "I can use a shower. See you later."

Brennan returned to Lisa's bedside and checked on her progress. The dilation was now more than six centimeters. "Blow out as much air as you can, honey. You're getting near."

Lisa's dilation was now eight centimeters, with contractions coming every minute. "How do you feel, Lisa?"

"I was feeling uncomfortable, but now it's kinda painful."

"You'll soon be ready, honey. You're nearly completely dilated. I'm running off to complete another patient's records. Be back soon." He turned to the nurse. "I'm heading for the Medical Library for a few minutes. Call me when Lisa's completely dilated. Then call the anesthesiologist and the pediatric specialist I have been consulting with. The delivery is progressing just fine but I want the best back up just for my own comfort level. It has been a long time since I delivered a baby, let alone such an important baby!"

Lisa made a motion for the nurse to approach her and said, "Please, nurse, can you take a moment to give me two small pieces of paper. I want to write a very brief note to Dr. Brennan."

The nurse complied, handing her a pen, her notepad, and an envelope. Lisa scribbled her thoughts, enclosed the notes in the envelope and handed it back to the nurse. "Thank you so much."

The nurse thought it odd that Lisa would be writing a note to a doctor that was working on the floor, helping her. Maybe just a thank you.

Miss Carlyle prepared the delivery room and reported to Chick. "I checked Lisa and she's completely dilated. The baby's head is at a plus-two station."

"Have you called the other doctors?"

"No, not yet. I'll call them now. We'll be ready for you in about twenty minutes." Then, as an afterthought, "Oh yes, Lisa wrote a note for you. Here it is."

Chick Brennan was preoccupied and slipped the envelope in his jacket pocket.

Lisa was on the delivery table when Chick arrived. His old friend Dr. Peterson, a highly regarded pediatric specialist, was there to assist if necessary. Miss Carlyle handed Chick a gown and gloves. He dressed and joined the already gowned and gloved Dr. Peterson at the end of the delivery table. The nurse was recording her blood pressure. She reported, "Lisa is on the perineum and just beginning to crown."

"Good. I'll scrub up." Miss Carlyle handed Chick a gown and gloves. He dressed and moved to the end of the delivery table. "Lisa, your baby's head is at the opening below. You now have to push hard with your contractions. I'll guide you."

"It's hurting more."

"That's normal. You're fine." Chick then placed sterile drapes over her legs, below her buttocks and over her abdomen. "When your pains come and you have an urge to push down, hold your breath and push hard."

"I'm trying, Chick."

"Bear down. That's it. The baby's head is bulging out. Very good. Keep pushing."

"It hurts."

"Lisa, the baby is coming. Push hard and long. That's it. Push, push hard; don't stop. Here it comes. Take a breath and push again. It's a beautiful boy. Congratulations!"

Chick showed the child to Lisa, and handed it over to the nurse, who placed it in the infant bed. He spoke to Miss Carlyle, "The placenta hasn't separated yet. She's not bleeding much. I'll go ahead and repair the episiotomy." Turning to Lisa. "Just relax darling. You just listen to the lovely cries of that baby of yours while I put some stitches here below, where I cut you."

The episiotomy was repaired in thirty minutes. Chick said to Lisa, "We're waiting for the placenta to separate. Everything is fine."

After consulting with Chick Brennan, Peterson turned to the nurse and directed, "Start an IV drip with five percent dextrose and water. Put an ampule of pitocin in the IV. Start the drip at thirty drops per minute."

Lisa was anxious. "Is there anything wrong, Chick? If anything doesn't look good please call Carlo. He would want to be here, I'm sure."

"That's a promise."

"We're having a little problem because the placenta has not yet separated. You're not bleeding very much, but I am going to order the lab to get some blood ready, just in case." Chick turned to Miss Carlyle, to send for the anesthesiologist. "Get Dr. Lubac."

Walter Lubac had been waiting in case he was needed and appeared quickly. "Chick, you want me to put her down?"

"Yes."

"Miss Albanese, I'm going to give you some medicine to relax you and put you to sleep so that we can remove the placenta from your uterus. Don't be afraid. Everything is going to be all right. I'll give you a little oxygen with this mask."

"OK"

"Now, breathe deeply. Fine."

Chick, once again, consulted with Peterson, who said, "Chick, "let me know when you're ready, and I'll remove the placenta."

"She's down. Go ahead. She won't feel anything."

"This shouldn't take long." Peterson inserted his hand into the vagina and began pulling at the placenta. "This placenta is a tough one. I can't find any cleavage plane. She's beginning to bleed pretty heavily." To Miss Carlyle, "Is the blood ready?"

"Yes."

"Bring two units, and order six more."

"Right."

Chick's voice grew somber. "I think she's got a placenta accreta. She's beginning to bleed heavily. Start a unit right way."

Two more units were immediately available. Chick ordered. "Miss Carlyle, give them to Lubac and he'll start one. Get ready for a possible hysterectomy. Set up the operating room and call in the nurses."

"Right."

"And get a senior resident physician to scrub up and wait for me in the operating room." To Lubac: "Start the second unit and tell the lab to speed up the type and cross matching of the blood. She continues to bleed heavily and I can't control it. How's her blood pressure?"

"Well, it's fluctuating, but not bad. Her pulse is accelerating. I'll get her stabilized."

Chick consulted with Peterson, then made a decision. "We're going to have to perform a hysterectomy. This placenta can't be removed. Let's get her to the operating room immediately."

Chick Brennan, Peterson, Walter Lubac and the resident physician, Kwame Kiusu, readied themselves at the Operating table. Lubac placed an anesthesia mask over Lisa's face.

Chick called for a scalpel, made an abdominal incision and performed a hysterectomy. "I'm closing up, Walter. Give me ten minutes more."

"Right. She's receiving her sixth blood unit and is stable. I'll stay with her and transfer her to the Recovery room."

Chick rejoined Lisa in the Recovery room. "Walter, how's she doing?"

"I'm not satisfied. Her vital signs are stable, but there's something wrong. She's not bouncing out of this the way she should. The recovery room nurse will take care of her. If we need to call you we will."

"OK I'll go to the staff room to rest up a bit."

Chick then called Bruno. "Think you'd better get over here. Lisa is touch and go."

After getting Chick's report, Bruno decided it was time to act. "Chick, I gotta call Carlo."

Chick emphatically agreed. "Yes, absolutely. I'm sure that's her wish now."

Bruno had a plan. "We can get Canto, in Denver, to charter a plane for Carlo." Antonio Canto, the local Don, ran a relatively small organization in the Denver area. "When I visited Carlo recently I found that the town of Meter has a small Executive airport. But, I decided to drive from Denver, to take in the beautiful scenery in that area."

Chick was excited. "Get him here as soon as you can, Bruno. She needs him."

As soon as Brennan hung up, Bruno checked his telephone book, Here it is. He reached for the phone next to Lisa's bed and dialed. Antonio Canto's wife answered. "Hello?"

"Mrs. Canto, this is Bruno Battaglia, consiglieri for the Albanese Family. We met at Julio's funeral."

She recalled. "Oh yes, Mr. Battaglia. I remember. What can I do for you?"

"Is Antonio there? It's an emergency."

"Yes, he is. Just a minute. He's downstairs. I'll call him."

The two minutes it took for Antonio to come to the phone felt like an age. "Antonio, this is Bruno Battaglia."

"Oh, yes. Bruno. What can I do for you?"

"Antonio, remember I told you that Carlo Albanese was going to be in your area?"

"Yes, out at Meter."

Bruno spoke rapidly. "Exactly. Well, we need to get him back here as soon as possible. Can you charter a flight and get him out to La Guadia? We'll pick him up."

"Sure, of course. He's out at St. Agatha's. Right?"

"Right."

"I'll pick him up myself."

"I'm calling Carlo. I'll tell him to expect you."

Antonio made a call to Mountain Aviation and arranged for the flight.

Carlo was watching a late night movie when Bruno called. "Carlo, Lisa is very ill at New York Hospital. Antonio's gonna pick you up late tonight and put you on a charter flight to La Guadia."

Carlo was startled. "What's wrong?"

"I'll explain it all when you get here. I'll meet you at the airport."

Carlo was not satisfied. "How ill? What illness? Tell me for God's sake."

Bruno paused. "Carlo, she delivered a baby. Your baby. Something went wrong. The next few hours are crucial. She's in intensive care."

"Oh, my God. Why didn't somebody tell me she was pregnant?"

"Carlo, please, let's talk about this when you get here. Too complicated to discuss over the phone. Please."

Reluctantly, "OK Bruno, OK" He hung up and waited for his visitor. My God, what happened? Why didn't she tell me? He wrapped his arms around his head, as if to block out the bad news. He leaned his head against the kitchen wall and slapped it with his open palms. *I let my profession take priority over my feelings. It was contagious. She did the same. I trained her. She probably didn't want to disturb me Imagine! How institutions and ideologies dehumanize us. Damn!*

280 **Father Patrick Bascio**

Antonio arrived two hours later. "I don't know what the hell's going on, but they want you in New York. I got a charter jet waiting for you at Meter airport. Ready to roll."

Carlo gripped Antonio's hands. "Thanks, Antonio. You needn't have bothered to do this yourself. You could have sent one of your men."

"I know. I wanted to."

"Let me throw a few things together."

Carlo was very pale. "Carlo, you OK? Anything I can do?"

"To be honest, Antonio, I'm shook up. The gal I'm in love with is very sick."

Respectfully, "I'm sorry. Anything I can do?"

"Pray for her, Antonio."

Antonio didn't pray much anymore. "I'll get my wife to say the rosary."

Antonio gazed about the bedroom. A small photo of Julio sat on the bed stand. *That's probably the gal.*

Carlo felt pangs of fear, guilt and uncertainty. *If anything happens to her, how can I carry on?* To Antonio, "I'm ready. Let's go."

As Carlo was leaving Meter for LaGuardia Airport, Chick Brennan was heading for the intensive care unit where Lisa was sleeping. The resident, Dr. Kiusu was present. The various monitoring instruments were attached and an IV drip was going. "Good morning, Doctor. How's our patient doing?"

"She complained of pain last night, so we gave her Demerol. Since then she's slept well."

"What about her urinary output?"

"She had very little."

Kwame Kiusu ordered a hemotocrit. When the results came back he ordered one liter of normal saline IV, and gave her forty mg. of Lasix.

"How is her output now?"

Kiusu consulted his chart. "She's put out four hundred fifty ml. of urine during the past three and one half hours."

Chick greeted Lisa. "Good morning, lady."

"What happened, Chick? Is my baby all right?"

"The baby's just fine."

"Thank God you're here." Bruno greeted Carlo as he stepped off the plane. "She's fighting for her life. She doesn't want to die. She did not expect any difficulty, nor did anyone else at the hospital. So, she was going to have the baby and then notify you herself. When she realized things were going badly she asked us to notify you. Until then she had adamantly refused to let us do it. Sorry we caved in to her, Carlo, but it looked like it was going to be an easy delivery. You know she made us promise not to tell you. She didn't want you to feel guilty about having returned to the priesthood. She wanted to tell you herself, after the hospital, in her own apartment; just the two of you."

"Bruno, why didn't you just call me anyway?"

"I wanted to respect her wishes. Simple as that."

Abstractedly, "Yes. I should have respected her and stayed with her. I hope it's not too late."

"What are her chances, Bruno?"

"Slim."

They arrived at the hospital and Carlo moved quickly through the foyer. Bruno tried to keep up. They waited nervously for an elevator. "Bruno, does she have the best medical care?"

"Of course, Carlo."

An elevator opened its cavernous doors for them.

"Sixth floor, Carlo."

Carlo continued to press his fist into his hand until they entered Lisa's room. A curtain surrounded the bed. Carlo pulled it aside and found her strapped to the bed, her body sprouting tubes linked to suspended bottles. A machine blipped unrecognizable messages about her physical condition. "Bruno, I hate seeing her like this. She doesn't deserve this." He reached over and touched her hand, then ran his fingers down along her face.

"We're all praying she'll make it, Carlo. The whole family."

A young doctor brought in an extra chair. Bruno thanked him.

"Mr. Albanese can stay as long as he wishes."

"Bruno, I really appreciate everything. I'm here for the night."

"I'll stay with you."

Softly, "Bruno, you understand, I'd rather be alone with her."

"Yeah, sure. But you call if you need me, OK?"

Carlo leaned his head toward Bruno. "I sure will. Thanks."

Bruno left the hospital, regretting he had not informed Carlo sooner.

There was no sign of recognition as Carlo bent over Lisa. He held her hand. "Lisa, it's me. It's Carlo." He thought he felt a reaction in her fingers. As he looked at her, he was helpless, had guilt feelings.

He felt a hand on his shoulder. It was a hospital administrator. "Do you want to see the baby?" She could sense the pain. *It might help him.* She took his hand. "I'm sorry, I'm so sorry. We've done the best we could. She's in God's hands now."

"Thank you." His voice was sadness.

The woman led him to the nursery where he saw his son for the first time. *I haven't had time to absorb this. I wish I had known for months, so I could feel like a father.* He glanced at the child and said, "Nurse, I need to go back to Lisa."

"Of course."

He sat by her side until dawn, and prayed for her life, oblivious to the "sorrys" of nurses and doctors who passed in and out of the room. Several times her eyes opened. He thought she recognized him, but wasn't sure. Twice more her eyes opened and he prayed for recognition, but they fixed on the ceiling. He sat on the bed next to her and took her in his arms. His eyes closed and, for a few moments, he slept. Two nurses standing next to a moaning Lisa awakened him. They nervously connected the oxygen mask to her face. "She's become diaphoretic," one nurse shouted.

The other called out: "Code Blue! Code Blue!"

"Ms. Albanese's room."

Other nurses in the corridor shouted "Code Blue? Where?"

"One informed them, "Ms. Albanese's room."

Carlo glanced at Lisa and held her tightly to his chest. She appeared to be dead. He shook her violently twice. "Lisa, Lisa," he cried, until a nurse pulled her body away. Another nurse phoned in to the hospital operator, who immediately paged Code Blue. Two resident physicians came rushing down the hallway pushing a "crash cart." All the nurses on the floor rushed to Lisa's room. The Chief Resident physician barked out an order. "Call her doctor." They then begin working furiously on resuscitation.

"Please Sir," a nurse asked politely, "can you move away from the bed. We need the room."

Carlo watched helpless, pacing the floor, weaving in and out of attending physicians, nurses and technicians. His head swiveled from one to another, looking for a last-minute sign of hope. None came. His eyes were puffy and red, his hair unruly, as he moaned and mumbled unintelligible words. He felt a tautness in his stomach, as if a tightly wound spring had been placed there. He sucked in his breath as he feared his rubbery legs would collapse from under him. He caught himself against a wall and teetered unsteadily to a corner chair and slumped into it.

Chick arrived in the midst of all this activity, asking, "What happened?"

The Chief Resident was perplexed. "We're not sure. The Aide called a Code Blue. When we arrived Lisa had no pulse and was not breathing. We've been trying to resuscitate her ever since."

Chick queried, "What did the cardiac monitor show when you arrived?"

"She was in a systole."

Has she had any signs of response to treatment?"

"None at all."

"Well, we might as well stop. I don't think we can accomplish anything more."

Chick dismissed all staff excepting the Nurse Aid who called the Code Blue and the Head Nurse. To them he said, "Come to the conference room with me." And, to Carlo, "If you care to come, please."

"I'll stay with Lisa," Carlo said, as he held her in his arms and pressed his lips against her right cheek.

Chick spoke softly. "I know how you feel, Carlo, but they'll be right in to take her away. I'm so sorry."

"I understand."

Chick spoke to the nurses. "I want to review what happened to Lisa. Let me see her chart." He fingered his chin. "According to the Nurse's notes, she was checked at 10:30PM. She had just gone to the bathroom and wanted some help in returning to bed. Who helped her?"

"We saw Mr. Albanese helping her so we left the room."

"Did she make any remark to you?"

"No, but she did appear weak."

"Did she have a problem with her leg?"

"She did, actually, but she said she had bumped it."

"Thank you, nurse."

Chic made a note on a report. "Lisa Albanese died, most likely from a massive pulmonary embolism. I recommend an autopsy. I will call the pathologist." He then issued instructions for the baby to be cared for until the father returned for it.

Carlo's reunion with his mother was poignant, but overshadowed by Lisa's death. He knew he was brooding, that he was listless, but had difficulty shaking it off. Observing his mother's concerned gaze he assured her. "Don't worry, Mom. Everything's going to be OK"

He kissed her softly on her forehead. "I'm going to visit Uncle Julio's and Nicky's graves."

"I'll go with you, Carlo."

"Thanks, Mom, but I need to go alone. Need to think about lots of things. Later, maybe tomorrow if you're feeling better, we'll visit the graves together. O.K."

Maria was sad. *Not a very nice homecoming after a year of self-exile. The poor boy. It's not easy for him - for any of us.* "All right, darling, whatever you think best."

Maria watched Carlo as he pulled out of the driveway. Silence pervaded the home. Carlo would see no visitors. He did not mention Lisa. She joined him in his silence, not knowing what else to do. She had never seen him so joyless. She shivered as to what all of this might mean.

A gray, overcast day increased the sacred solemnity of the cemetery grounds. Carlo left his car at the entrance and strolled through the archway, along winding paths lined with gravesides. The headstones stood as grim sentinels, reminding all who passed of the brevity, almost inanity of life. This is how it all ends, the bottom line.

Suddenly, at a right turn of path, he came upon Julio's graveside, a large marble monument. He leaned forward and read the inscription:

Roberto Albanese
b. Sept 1, 1915. d. June 6, 1982
Devoted father to his family and the extended Family
God bless his brilliant and generous soul

Newly placed lilies stood firm against the blustering wind. Attached to their stems with a rubber band an anonymous message read:

I should have loved you more while you were still alive. I will pray for you, Julio, all the days of my life. I ask you to pray for me.

He wondered. *An old friend? A former enemy? Perhaps a tearful mistress? It could be any one of the many whose lives he touched.*

Looking down at the grave, he recalled Julio's words, "I need you, Carlo. The Family needs you." A pang of regret invaded his psyche.

It now appears I did what I wanted to do, not what was in the best interest of the family. I thought I was holy, and I was selfish. I thought myself the righteous priest returning to his calling, and I was a hypocrite. I entertained visions of solitude and peace, when I should have immersed myself, gotten my hands dirty, carried out my duty. I should have loved Lisa. I loved myself. Oh what a foolish self-centered egotist I've been. How could I've been so blind?

Carlo had searched the scriptures the night before, this time not for solace. He was looking for a particular passage, and he found it In the Gospel of St. John. I am the good shepherd. The good shepherd lays down his life for the sheep. The hired hand is not the shepherd who owns the sheep. So when he sees the wolf coming he abandons the sheep and runs away. Then the wolf attacks the flock and scatters it. The man runs away because he is a hired hand and cares nothing for the sheep.

One hundred years of Albanese culture and duty invaded his psyche. Julio, Tony, and even Victor, in his own way, paid the price of leadership. Only he had run away, hiding himself behind his priestly garments, pretending to be someone he was not.

I'm ashamed. I beg forgiveness from all of you - Julio, father, Nicky, and Lisa. If I'd taken on my responsibility Lisa and I would now be caring for our son and living a life of love together. I didn't have the courage to be with the woman I loved....all this in the name of religion. I need to cleanse my soul.

Julio's words continued to resonate in the chambers of his mind. "Without you, those we are responsible for will be lost, will lose their means of livelihood, their history, their very culture. I need you."

Carlo stood, circling the grave as if expecting to find something, or see someone. He stooped and plucked two lilies from their paper wrappings, laying them against the tombstone. Their scent filled his nostrils. His blood ran hot through his body. He had returned. He had come to do his duty He vowed, "I'm back, dear Uncle. Rest peacefully." At Nicky's grave, tears welled up in his eyes. He was too overcome, even for thoughts. He collapsed to his knees and sobbed for a long time. "God forgive me," he shouted. Carlo felt imprisoned by his guilt and regrets. He had not loved Nicky as he was, but loved the illusionary what-he-wanted-him-to-be. He finally realized that being perfect is not the point - that learning and growing is. He had castrated himself with the narrowness of his heart and mind. In addition he had also lost the love of his life. It was not the teeth and claws of religious faith that had caused this cataclysm. It was, he concluded, his selfish arrogance. He felt the greater fool for having all the pieces and none of the puzzle together. He was caught between wishes and regrets.

The following day, Carlo drove with Maria to Woodlawn Cemetery to visit both gravesides. They stopped along the way to purchase flowers. In contrast to the pervious day, the sun was bright, the cemetery grounds appealing. His mood had also changed. *I know now what I'm going to do.*

They knelt on the damp sod in front of Tony's headstone, where they placed the spray of red roses, and prayed. A pair of bluebirds dancing the dance of lovemaking distracted them. Then both walked over to Nicky's grave and stood silent. Maria sensed this was not a good time for conversation about her dead son, but was pleased when Carlo placed the spray of white roses at the grave, audibly praying, "Pray for us, dear brother, for we have much left to do.

Maria could not resist. "Will you say a Mass for your father and brother while you're home?"

Carlo felt a sting of depression as the question reminded him of the consequences of returning as Family head. *Already she's had little benefit from having a priest son. Soon she'll be totally deprived of that consolation. Both of us are caught up in the vortex of our family history.* "Mom, there's something I gotta talk to you about. Come" He led her to the car, where they sat. *She knows something's coming and she's scared.*

Maria fidgeted. Her eyes stared vacantly at rows of headstones, waiting for her son to speak.

Carlo spoke gently. "Mom, I don't know an easy way to say this, so let me just come right out with it."

Maria sobbed, raising her arms and placing her head between them, hiding her face. "Don't Carlo, don't tell me anything. I can't bear to hear anything. I can't take any more sadness. Please."

Carlo took his sobbing mother into his arms, and wiped tears from her face with his fingers. He recalled Hamlet. This above all: to thine own self be true. "Mom, just bear with me for a minute. I don't want you to hear this from anyone else."

"I know what it is. Do you think I don't know what you're going to do? You're going to come back and run the Family, aren't you?" Maria's sobbing intensified, as her body convulsed.

No explanation will help. She and I simply have to live through this ordeal together. We've got to go on.

For several minutes they sat without exchanging a word. Finally, Maria stood up, with courage she acquired during thirty years as the wife of a Family man. She looked at her son and uttered the words she had spoken countless times to her husband. "Do what you feel is right. I'll always support you." Straightening her dress, "Let's go home." *Virgin Mary, please don't be angry with him.*

Carlo let his mother's hands slip out of his as she moved away from him. *She deserves better. I wish it could be different.*

She glanced at the tombstone. "Your father is pleased you are here. I know that. He loved you so much." Her eyes watered and she daubed her face with a lace handkerchief. She then remembered the envelope Chick Brennan had asked her to give to Carlo. It had already been opened but resealed with a bit of tape. "Carlo, Dr. Brennan asked me to give you this. I only just remembered." He pocketed the envelope and, as planned, they left the cemetery and drove to the hospital.

A nurse recognized Carlo. "Have you come to take the baby?"

"Yes, I have."

"He's good and healthy. He'll be happy to go home. He needs his family."

"Thank you, nurse. What do I do?"

"You just fill out a couple of forms at the desk. I'll help you."

"Thanks."

With the nurse's help the forms were quickly prepared.

"Come with me, Mr. Albanese."

"Nurse, can you give me a moment to be alone?" His voice was hushed, his eyes vacant.

"Of course, I'll be at the Nurse Station. I'll meet you there when you're ready."

Carlo sat facing the large window overlooking the playground across the street. He lost himself in conjuring up an in the flesh Lisa floating in his ambiance. His mind flailed its wings in a Herculean effort.

A few moments later Carlo carried his son out to the car and handed him to Maria. "I'd like to stay with you, Mom, until I get myself together. I don't know anything about taking care of a baby. You can teach me."

"Of course, Carlo, of course."

After supper, Maria queried, "Carlo, did you read the note Dr. Brennan gave you?"

He had not. "Sorry, Mom, everything is so confusing right now." At that, he opened the envelope and found two notes inside, in Lisa's handwriting. One was to Chick Brennan, and read, "Dear Dr. Brennan, if something should happen to me please give the enclosed note to Carlo. Thank you for all you do for me and the family."

The second note was for Carlo. "My dearest love. If anything should happen to me in this hospital, go to my apartment. Next to my bed you will find a book of poetry. Read number 82.

With a "Gotta go, Mom," Carlo rushed out to his car. The key to Lisa's apartment was on his key ring. The doorman waved him in without comment. Once inside the apartment he nervously handled the book of Poetry until he found poem 82. The author was cited, as "Anonymous" The apartment was quiet except for minor noises filtering in from the traffic below. He read:

Do Not Stand at my Grave and Weep
Do not stand at my grave and weep
I am not there. I do not sleep
I am a thousand winds that blow
I am the diamond glints on snow
I am the sunlight on ripened grain
I am the gentle autumn rain
When you awaken in the morning hush
I am the swift uplifting rush

Of quiet birds in circled flight
I am the soft stars that shine at night
Do not stand at my grave and cry
I am not there. I did not die

As he drove home, he placed one hand on his chest. In his breast pocket he carried a photo of Lisa. *There will never be anyone else.* Arriving home, he rushed to take the baby in his arms and glanced lovingly at the tiny form. *You are part of her. Lisa and I shall love each other through you. Thank God you're here, and so is she. She has not died.*

Carlo picked up the phone and called Bruno. "We need to meet with Frankie and the men soon. I need to get back to work."